I0643624

Also by K. Aten:

THE MYSTERY OF THE MAKERS SERIES
The Sovereign of Psiere

THE ARROW OF ARTEMIS SERIES
The Fletcher
The Archer
The Sagittarius

THE BLOOD RESONANCE SERIES
Running From Forever
Embracing Forever

OTHER TITLES
Rules of the Road
Waking the Dreamer
Burn It Down
Children of the Stars
Remember Me, Synthetica

The Lost Temple of Psiere

Book Two in The
Mystery of the Makers series

K. Aten

Silver Dragon Books
by Regal Crest

Copyright © 2020 by K. Aten

All rights reserved. No part of this publication may be reproduced, transmitted in any form or by any means, electronic or mechanical, including photocopy, recording, or any information storage and retrieval system, without permission in writing from the publisher. The characters, incidents and dialogue herein are fictional and any resemblance to actual events or persons, living or dead, is purely coincidental.

ISBN 978-1-61929-448-6

First Edition 2020

9 8 7 6 5 4 3 2 1

Cover design by AcornGraphics

Published by:

Regal Crest Enterprises

Find us on the World Wide Web at
http://www.regalcrest.biz

Published in the United States of America

Acknowledgments

I've always had a great team while publishing with Regal Crest Enterprises. They are dedicated and knowledgeable folks that make the magic happen. And the last three years have been a whirlwind of learning, improvement, and new friendships. But everything changes with enough time and I find it a little bittersweet that this will be my last novel under the RCE label before we all move to Flashpoint Publications. I know most of the same people will be in place, my editors, Micheala and Mary, and my author liaison, Patty. I'm also very excited for the future of Flashpoint. But there will be a hole in my heart going forward that only Cathy Bryerose could fill. I'll miss you, Cathy, but I wish you all the luck in this next phase of life. Enjoy your retirement.

Dedication

This book is dedicated to Ted. You've been a rock and mainstay to so many authors in the community and I know that without you we would all be just a little less. The talent, knowledge, and dedication to the women's romantic fiction make you an excellent alpha or beta reader. And the sensitivity and experience with the genre mean that you are true treasure to so many people. Thank you, brother.

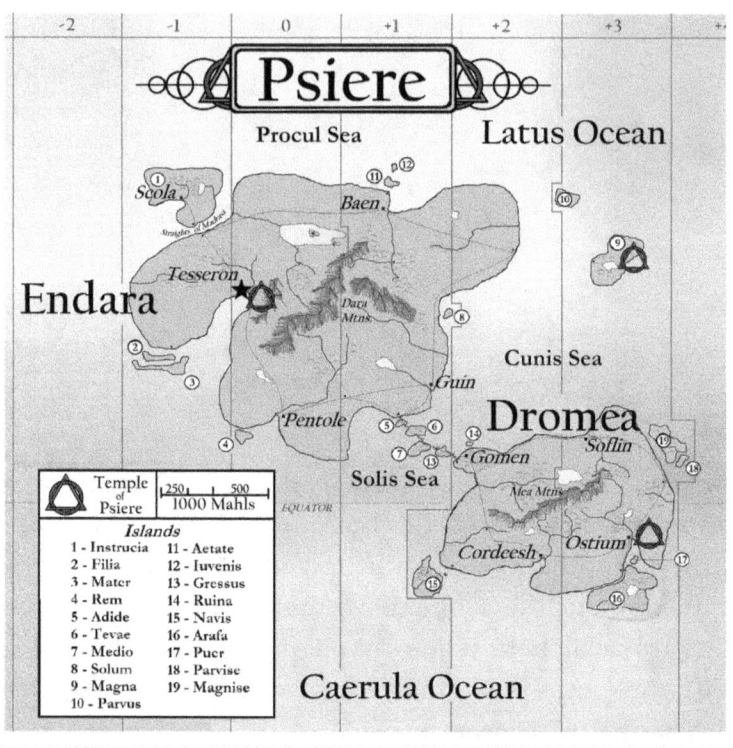

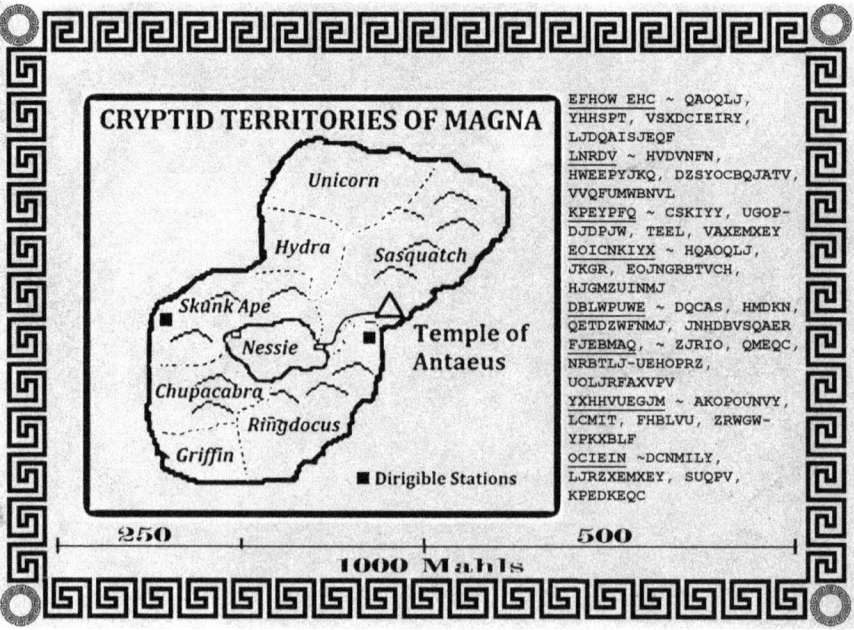

CRYPTID TERRITORIES OF MAGNA

Unicorn

Hydra   Sasquatch

Skunk Ape

Nessie   Temple of
                    Antaeus
Chupacabra

Ringdocus

Griffin

■ Dirigible Stations

EFHOW EHC ~ QAOQLJ,
YHHSPT, VSXDCIEIRY,
LJDQAISJEQF
LNRDV ~ HVDVNFN,
HWEEPYJKQ, DZSYOCBQJATV,
VVQFUMWBNVL
KPEYPFQ ~ CSKIYY, UGOP-
DJDPJW, TEEL, VAXEMXEY
EOICNKIYX ~ HQAOQLJ,
JKGR, EOJNGRBTVCH,
HJGMZUINMJ
DBLWPUWE ~ DQCAS, HMDKN,
QETDZWFNMJ, JNHDBVSQAER
FJEBMAQ, ~ ZJRIO, QMEQC,
NRBTLJ-UEHOPRZ,
UOLJRFAXVPV
YXHHVUEGJM ~ AKOPOUNVY,
LCMIT, FHBLVU, ZRWGW-
YPKXBLF
OCIEIN ~DCNMILY,
LJRZXEMXEY, SUQPV,
KPEDKEQC

250   500

1000 Mahls

Chapter One

"STOP FIDGETING!"

"It's not my fault this process is so poxing slow! I think I should die of boredom long before our oathing ceremony."

The royal clothier gave another long-suffering sigh and attempted to measure and re-pin Castellan Tosh's left trouser leg, yet again. "Please, ser. I really must get this right or you'll be walking with a noticeable hitch to your step."

Commander Tosh raised a pale brow. "All because I've moved an ince or two? I highly doubt that would give me a physical hitch—"

"He's politely telling you that you're about to have a needle stuck into your foot." The Connate, Olivienne Dracore, rolled her eyes at her future par. "What's gotten into you? You're like a twitchy child."

"Savon and Madlin are putting together duty rosters for the ceremony right now. I should be wi—"

"Straighten."

"—th them to make sure you are well cov—"

"Ser, please straighten."

"—ered with the sovereign threat level still on high alert." She finally straightened exactly as the clothier directed.

Olivienne sighed. "The lieutenants have everything well in hand. Meanwhile, we have the first of three dinners tonight and your outfits have to be ready for all three plus the oathing ceremony." She paused to move her gaze from her lover's clenched hands to Castellan's tightly closed eyes. Concerned, Olivienne reached out to touch one of her fists. "Castellan, is this really what you want?" Castellan immediately froze while standing on the pedestal and the clothier worked even faster, sensing that the stillness wouldn't last. "I understand that oathing to the heir of Psiere can be a highly stressful event. And once we consor, you will become the future King to my Queen. Nothing has been publicly announced yet. Official proclamations won't be made until after the three oathing dinners. If you don't want—"

The fist under Olivienne's hand opened immediately as did the commander's expression. "No! That's not it at all." When

Olivienne looked up, she was awash in the brilliant pale blue of Castellan's eyes. "I adore you and I will do whatever I need to do in order to stand by your side for the rest of our daes. Oathing is merely the first step to our eventual consorage. My concern isn't about the oathing." The clothier gave a great sigh of relief as the last pin was placed and he stepped back from the intense woman. He wasn't even noticed as the Connate and her Shield Commander stared at one another, as if trying to read the map of emotions and motivations contained within the lines of each face. All he could do was wait for a break in the tension to request that Commander Tosh slip out of the pinned suit of clothing.

"Well what is it then? Because, by the Makers, I can tell that something has you in fits." Castellan scowled and ran a hand through her hair, mussing it ever so slightly. While Olivienne loved seeing her so deliciously rumpled, she also knew it was telling to the level of Castellan's nervousness. A soldier's soldier, the commander was notorious for being brave, dashing, and put together even under the most trying of circumstances. Her uniform was always pristine, her hair neat, and her bearing of the utmost professionalism.

"It's my family. Specifically, my maman."

Seeing that the clothier was finished, Olivienne urged Tosh from the pedestal and helped her out of the suit. She watched her handsome commander dress once again in the official uniform of a Shield Corp Guardian as the clothier packed all his gear along with Olivienne and Castellan's modified oathing outfits and scurried out the door. She made a discrete motion toward Spc. Devin and Spc. Yazzie, and they stepped out of the room as well, shutting the door behind them. They were safe enough in Castellan's suite within Olivienne's residence. "You don't speak of them much but I never got the impression that you were on the outs. What did your maman say when you told her of the oathing?" Tosh's face grimaced as if she were in pain and she mumbled something beneath her breath. "I'm sorry, what was that?"

"I said I haven't informed her yet."

Olivienne stepped back abruptly. "You *what*? Tosh, the official dinner with *your* parens is tomorrow evening!"

Castellan sighed with defeat and strode to her lounger before collapsing to the cushions. "I know, I know! It's just—"

"Hey, it's okay. You know you can tell me anything." Olivienne sat next to her and took Castellan's hand into her own.

"It's just that my entire life, my maman has been begging me to switch corps. There hasn't been a conversation gone by where she doesn't express her wish for me to settle down and consor. She has never approved of my chosen career or the way it takes me all over the two continents. Both my sibs have pars *and* children and I got sick of her nagging so I'll admit that I rarely speak with them. Of course avoiding my family was made fairly easy by my schedule in the Defense Corp, and now the Shield Corp."

A dark brow rose with a mix of astonishment and chastisement. "Do they even know you switched to Shield Corp? What about the fact that you saved my life in Pentole? They must have heard about that. You didn't speak with her then?"

"Erm, I sent a long missive?"

"Oh, Tosh." She sighed. "As much as you hate it, you became even more of a hero to the people when you saved my life in that plaza. Your actions all but guaranteed that your moniker, 'The Hero of Temple Beach,' has now spread beyond the southern continent." Castellan Tosh grimaced at the hated name. "Not to mention that it's an honor to be invited to the Shield Corp. The sheer notoriety that you've garnered coupled with a promotion...you don't think she would have wanted to hear it in person?"

Castellan looked away. "You don't know my maman. Despite all that, she'd still give me a mindful for risking my life, just as she has found fault for every other decision I've made over the past ten rotos. She thinks I am wasting my talents in the militia corps and always had dreams that I'd become an instrae up in Scola, or even a judex."

Olivienne laughed. "Even I can see that between your channels and your personality, you are most definitely best suited to action. You would go mad if you had to sit in a classroom or on a bench!" She ignored Tosh's smirk. "She only loves you, she's your maman."

"She is stubborn!"

The words were on the tip of Olivienne's tongue, but she wouldn't say them. The Connate knew for a fact that Castellan's maman wasn't the only one who was stubborn in the Tosh family. Despite Olivienne's frustration with her lover, she couldn't help feeling endeared to the staid and upright woman. Commander Tosh was someone everyone counted on to get the job done. The woman was dauntless, tireless, and a hero to many. But Castellan had fears and failures just like everyone else. And Olivienne had fallen in love with Castellan just as much as she had with the commander. "This will never do. You need to speak with her right now. We have no more time to waste and your family will want to have outfits ready in time for the dinner tomorrow."

Olivienne stood and grabbed Castellan's hand to pull her up as well. She gave the recalcitrant woman a quick kiss and a shove toward the door. "As a matter of fact, you can tell her that I can make a few inquiries to get a clothier on short notice if she needs help securing an outfit for the oathi—"

Both were startled when Spc. Yazzie pushed into the room ahead of a helpless Spc. Devin. He was busy trying to hold back a tall middle-age woman with long pale hair pulled into a thick braid. "My apologies Connate, Commander, but Psera Tosh—"

"Oathing? Shield Corp? Have we fallen so far from your graces that you don't share news with your family anymore, Castellan? Instead I am forced to hear the details of such things from a gossiping interpretist walking by the charging chamber rather than my own daughter!"

Castellan paled. "Maman! What are you doing here?"

"It's funny, but I would expect the brightest psi in three generations of Academy training to have better communication skills. First, you tell us in a letter that you've switched from one gadabout Corp to another. A velum, Castellan! And then you don't tell us at all about the most important change in your life. Just what kind of woman has agreed to consor with you, that you're ashamed to even speak her name to us?"

Olivienne smirked from where she stood behind Castellan. The commander took a short step forward and her hands came up in a pleading manner. "Maman, you must not say such things! My future par is the most amazing person on all of Psiere, save the Queen of course." Castellan hoped that Olivienne could forgive her, considering the Queen was the one person in all the land who sat upon the Divine Cathedra.

Cassiene Tosh snorted at her daughter's exaggeration. "As great as that? Oh please. Everyone across both continents insists their beloved is as fair as Archeos and Illeos combined. But I highly doubt that you'd come across a woman worthy of all that in your wanderlust career. I know I've pressured you a bit to find a par but don't just rush into it with the first person of interest that you spend an evening tupping."

"Pressured? A *bit*?" Castellan's voice rose with each word then she sputtered and turned red as she realized the rest of what was said. The next words came out as an uncharacteristic hoarse yell. "By the Makers, she is more than someone I've been tupping—" Castellan's words cut off with the touch of Olivienne's fingers to her forearm as the Connate stepped around her within sight of Cassiene.

"Psera Tosh, I may not be on level with the Queen of Psiere, but I certainly hope she passed some of her good traits on to me."

"Connate Dracore!" Shock registered on the stern woman's face then it morphed to one of calculation as she noticed the familiar hand on her daughter's arm and realized with whom she faced and why. She bowed deeply, as custom dictated. "My apologies, Connate, I had no idea it was you that my daughter was oathing to." She turned to Castellan with her lips drawn into a thin line. "And you! Letting me go on like that in front of a royal sovereign!"

"But, Maman—" Olivienne hid a smile behind her free hand while Castellan squirmed like a child instead of the Shield Commander that she was. All roar and rage disappeared as Olivienne's hand slid down Castellan's arm to entangle their fingers together. Castellan sighed and her shoulders slumped for a sec before straightening once again. It was a familiar motion, as she mentally reset herself for the conversation to come. "Maman, I'd like for you to meet my future par, Her Royal Sovereign, Connate Olivienne Dracore. 'Vienne, this is my maman, Cassiene Tosh." She glanced to the woman who would be her future in all ways. "Maman is as brilliant as she is infuriating."

Olivienne held out her hand to clasp with Cassiene's and gave the older woman a mirthful smile. "I'm sure we will get on famously then since Castellan says much the same about me." She paused as she considered the dae ahead and the woman in front of her. "Would you care for a tour of the house? I'd like to get to know you a bit better before the second oathing dinner tomorrow evening." She rushed to waylay any worries the older woman could have at hearing the news of the imminent official dinner. "Have no fear, I'll make sure you have a top-notch clothier at your service to be ready in time." Cassiene sighed with relief and Olivienne jaunted out an elbow toward her. "Shall we?"

Cassiene was torn. On one hand, a person simply did not turn down a sovereign's request. She also really did want to get to know the woman that everyone had heard rumors about, but Cassiene suspected no one really knew. On the other hand, Cassiene was a little intimidated to be in such high company. "But what of Castellan?"

Olivienne waved her free hand carelessly through the air

while Castellan wore a look that was a cross between worry and pain. "Oh, she'll be fine. Won't you, Tosh? She was just lamenting that she hasn't been able to check in with her lieutenants and we know how Castellan loves to be in control of everything around her."

Castellan opened her mouth to protest but recognized the look on Olivienne's face. Her lover wanted time alone with the Tosh matriarch and the commander could do naught but oblige. "She's right, I do need to check in with Savon and Madlin. You're in fine hands with Olivienne, Maman. I'll be back in a short while and you can yell at me then." She said the last with an apologetic smile and both Olivienne and Cassiene laughed.

Cassiene straightened smartly and gave a nod, recovering her composure. "Well enough, Lanny." She turned to Olivienne and threaded their arms together at the elbows. "I'm ready when you are, Connate Dracore."

"Psera Tosh, none of that! You are my future mamanar, so call me Olivienne. I insist."

Cassiene smiled and it transformed her rather plain face to one full of character and mature beauty. "Then please, it is Cassiene for you. Or maman Tosh if you like."

"Now, tell me more about this nickname, 'Lanny.' Is there a story behind it?"

Castellan sighed as the two women wandered through the doorway into the main house, chatting or collaborating on her future, it was hard to say. She shook her head in consternation and quickly followed them in search of Lt. Savon and Lt. Madlin. She put her worries about her maman into a box and resigned herself to regular duty for the next few oors.

CASSIENE TOSH WAS tall and strong from her rotos of managing the illeostone charging room of the Endara Temple. She was older now and the system had long been automated, but Psera Tosh was still fit as she was thirty rotos before. She kept up with Olivienne easily as they toured the house and eventually the grounds outside, speaking about a variety of subjects. Olivienne was curious about Castellan's entire family since the commander rarely spoke of them. Even though Castellan's maman came across as severe and serious, Olivienne had a feeling there was romance beneath the older woman's front. In an effort to get to know that part of her better, Olivienne steered the conversation into a more personal arena.

"Tell me how you met Castellan's papan. She mentioned that you worked in the charging room of the temple and that he was an illeostone miner's son but hasn't said much else."

Cassiene chuckled at the thought of her eldest child. While Castellan had certainly inherited her papan's good looks, she most definitely got her penchant for seriousness and duty from Cassiene herself. It didn't surprise her that Castellan had not spoken at length about her past and family because the woman very much lived in the present. She always had, even as a child. Cassiene thought of Olivienne's request and the corners of her mouth turned up at the memories it provoked.

"I was young and newly placed in my Resource Corp service job at the temple when I met this ridiculously handsome young man. Tello was the son of an illeostone miner, there to drop off a load of stones that needed charging. I'd like to pretend that I kept my wits about me and didn't have my head turned by such a pretty face but alas I cannot. I don't know how to explain it but there was this...immediate chemistrae between Tello and me."

As they strolled between the royal residence and side buildings each woman stopped to look up at the marvel of architecture around them. Olivienne had grown up with the awe-inspiring grandeur of the palace but never took the sight for granted. She considered it the most beautiful building she'd ever seen, outside the great temples of course. Those held a beauty of a different sort for her. "How did your romance progress from there? What was he like?"

"Oh, he was painfully shy at first but he had a smile so bright it could practically melt a room. Even now as a mature man, his smile holds a special radiance that I have a hard time saying no to. And back then in the prime of his youth he had half of Psiere sniffing after him like canids after a meal. But he never saw his contemporaries' interest, for his focus was firmly on the ground and the mineral it contained." Cassiene shook her head with a wry smile. "Perhaps I got lucky in that Tello was born and bred to be in the Resource Corp if anyone was. He was sheltered and delivering illeostones was his papan's way of getting him out into the world."

Olivienne cocked her head curiously. "What about Academy? Did he not get exposed to the world there?"

Cassiene snorted. "Oh, what I haven't told you was that we are the same age. But while I had graduated a roto early, Tello was still in Academy. But I knew of him there, certainly. We were in the same Corp, after all." She shook her head. "He was practically the talk of Scola with his good looks, sweet smile, and well known family, but Tello remained clueless. If he wasn't in the classroom or libre, then he was out hiking the rocky shore nearest to the city. I'm telling you, the lad had rocks on the brain and he never noticed the attention. Especially not from some plain girl with more brains than beauty." She sighed. "So I absolutely knew of Tello but I never once imagined that the most beautiful man of my generation would look at me twice, let alone strike up a conversation with me that fateful dae in the Temple."

Cassiene gave a little laugh as they rounded the royal stable and turned back toward Olivienne's residence. "He was such a miner's son. My Tello even kept illeostones in his pocket, for good luck he said. He still does it now."

"Castellan keeps one in her pocket at all times but refused to tell me why. Now I know." Olivienne could easily see the love and affection that Cassiene carried for her par. "You really love him."

"Oh yes. Now and forever, until the great Makers come back to us and spill the rest of their secrets. Beyond even. Tello Tosh is my one." She gave Olivienne a sly look. "The pseros and pseras of the Tosh family are incredibly hard to resist."

Warmth gathered in Olivienne's chest and a blush worked its way up her neck to stain her cheeks. The way Olivienne felt about Castellan was written plainly across her face for Cassiene to see. "They certainly are. What of your other two children? Castellan has two younger sibs, right?"

"Oh yes, Tellesen and Tessior are both good men. Neither has been as adventurous as my daughter. But truth be told, neither was as powerful or smart as her either. I'll admit, we struggled a bit with Castellan when she was younger. Her penchant for action coupled with a too-intelligent mind meant many clashes with her, both at home and in school. We finally had to advance her a few levels in primary to assuage that natural drive she has. By that and her stubbornness you'd think she was my child alone."

She laughed because it was easy enough to laugh about a difficult time after so many rotos had gone by. "As for all my children, we did our best to space them out properly. With the help of the Makers, of course." She winked at Olivienne. "Castellan is the eldest at thirty-two, which I'm sure you already know. Her sibs are thirty and twenty-eight respectively. Tellesen, is a member of the Politia Corp and is the Representative of Portorium, two oors outside Tesseron. His par, Aeryn, is in the Medi Corp and works as a doctore's assistant. They have two children, Aelysen and Tellen. They are ten and eight rotos in age."

Olivienne cocked her head to the side. "Portorium, ah yes. That's the next largest city northeast of Tesseron, where Mir Tessere meets with Mir Altum. He's doing well with himself as their elected official since it is a major hub of river trade in Endara."

"That's the one. Now my youngest, Tessior, seemed to crave action nearly as much as Castellan. But alas, he satisfied his maman's wishes and stayed close to home. We actually have dinner with him and Temera once a lune. And of course it is my privilege as avia to spoil little Temiora. She is a delightful babe."

"How old?"

"Two rotos next lune."

"If you forgive me for saying so, but you certainly don't look as though you are an avia three times over. I'd say I'm a good judge of youthfulness since my own maman has always looked nearly half her age. But then, neither I nor my younger sib have had children of our own yet."

Cassiene tightened her grip on Olivienne's arm and patted affectionately as she laughed. "Oh, that is no offense at all and I thank you for saying it. I'm quite honored since the Queen is known the world over for her beauty and seemingly eternal youth. Such great company you've placed me!" While she played it off with humor, Olivienne could see the light blush that dusted the older woman's cheeks as she continued speaking. "Tessior is actually a sergeant in the local Security Corp here in Tesseron. I worry for him, of course. Even though society is safe as a whole, there are always those who could and would do harm. No psi is perfect after all." She sighed and met Olivienne's eyes. "But I don't worry for him nearly as much as I do for Castellan. I suspect that half the time she doesn't visit or teleo is because of my nagging, but the other half of the time I always fear something has happened to her and I simply haven't received the dark news. At least now she is closer to us."

The sudden image of Castellan bleeding on the cobblestones of the Pentole plaza caused Olivienne to shudder and suck in a breath. Guilt washed through her. "I'm not going to lie to you, Mamanar, she is no less safe within the Shield Corp, especially with all the unrest brewing throughout the two continents. I suspect she has left many close calls out of her missives to you and her papan."

"I see the pain in your eyes, and Tello and I have both heard the stories of Castellan's exploits on the southern continent. She is still in danger with the Shields, true, but there is a big difference between here and there."

Olivienne looked at her curiously. "How so?"

"When she was a lieutenant commander, her duty was to the Defense Corp, spending her daes fighting a senseless war against creatures of the deep. But at least with Shield Corp her sole duty is to defend the woman she loves. I'd like to think that is the more noble profession of the two."

Olivienne blushed at the implication and praise. "Thank you." Since it was a nice dae, Olivienne led them around to her outside lounging area and motioned for Cassiene to have a seat. "Drink?"

Cassiene had just settled onto a padded cushion when Olivienne's words registered. She stood abruptly with an appalled look on her face. "Oh, I can get that! You shouldn't have to wait on me, Connate Dracore." Specialists Yazzie and Devin both smiled from where they stood near the entrance.

Not to be dissuaded, Olivienne continued to the outdoor sideboard where drinks were kept stocked for guests. "Nonsense! You don't seriously think I have servants waiting on my every whim do you? My own maman would surely take me to task if she thought I let my position go to my head."

"But, Connate, I'm merely a manager of the charging room at the temple. While my par and I co-own the Tosh illeostone mines, neither of us come close to royalty. You must not serve me!"

"I most certainly will. As my future mamanar, you are going to sit there and let me fetch you a drink. So what will it be, scotch or perhaps something stronger?"

Seeing the stubborn glint to the younger woman's eyes, Cassiene sighed and resigned herself to her fate, settling back onto her seat. "No thank you, I'll just have water. Spirits make me flush."

Olivienne grinned. "I see Tosh didn't inherit her love of the drink from you then."

"On the contrary, I do love it. Unfortunately it doesn't love me and I suffer a skin reaction. It's a shame really."

Olivienne carried a tray loaded with glasses and a pitcher of some pale liquid. "I've brought you a glass of water but I thought perhaps you might enjoy some juice as well. We actually grow the vineo fruit on a tract of land south of Tesseron. There is an area of rolling hills that does well to hold the heat and bears the sweetest fruit each season. It's quite refreshing."

"I would be delighted to try some." Rather than wait to be served, which she was loath to do, Cassiene poured them each a glass of the juice and raised it to her mouth for a first taste. She smacked her lips in delight and savored the crisp flavor on her tongue. "Wonderful!" She cupped the glass in both hands and met Olivienne's gaze. "I do enjoy a good vineo from time to time. It doesn't seem to affect me quite as much as the scotch."

"I can imagine it doesn't. Do you know the origins of scotch?"

Cassiene shook her head but leaned forward slightly, eager for a tale. Olivienne spoke with her hands when she was excited about a subject, betraying that she was a woman of action as much as Castellan. Cassiene took special note of the Connate's mannerisms and facial expressions, looking for anything that would indicate she was at all like the rumors insinuated. So far the Tosh matriarch had found Olivienne to be a delightful young psera and her curiosity got the better of her. Historical adventurists were full of knowledge about the various implements and items of society and they were known for their tales as much as their missions.

"It was recorded that the recipe for scotch was one of the first ever translated from the Temple of Archeos scrolls. As you know, generations ago when the temples were first opened, hundreds upon hundreds of agricultural samples were found. Not only that, we also discovered schematics for building a variety of illeo-stone-driven processing and cultivating equipment. And recipes, by the Makers did they find recipes!" She shook her head in wonder. "To be alive at that time...divine." Her gaze went unfocused when she thought of the past and the deep purple of her eyes sparkled with her energy. Olivienne blushed and met Cassiene's indulgent gaze. "My apologies, I got off track. Anyway—"

"I can see why Castellan loves you."

"Excuse me?"

Cassiene gently touched the back of Olivienne's hand with two fingers. "Please don't think me too forward, but you are so full of life and your entire countenance speaks of wonder for the history of this world as well as its welfare and future. You are nothing like the rumors of some spoilt Connate who is as unserious about her job as she is about bed partners."

Connate Olivienne Dracore suffered an uncharacteristic loss for words. "Um, I—" She paused and looked into Cassiene's light lavender eyes.

"You don't have to say anything. I can imagine that you don't hear such things often enough simply based on what the gossip-mongers have to say at the temple, and that seems quite the shame. As for me, I believe you bring honor to the Dracore name and I think you will sit quite well upon the Divine Cathedra when the time comes."

Suddenly serious, Olivienne tilted her head forward slightly and brought the first two fingers of her right hand up to touch her forehead, then down to lightly tap the center of her chest. "On the contrary, you honor me with your words, Psera Cassiene Tosh. I see now that many of Castellan's finest traits came straight from you."

Cassiene flushed at the praise but their serious mood dissipated with her response. "I suppose...if you consider stubbornness a fine trait." Both women broke into a fit of laughter. Cassiene waved for Olivienne to continue. "You were saying?"

"Oh yes, the recipes..." And their conversation moved on as if the time-honored acceptance from a maman to her daughter's future par had never occurred. The two specialists selected to guard Olivienne while in the official residence smiled to each other at how well the first meeting was going. Commander Tosh was sure to be pleased.

Chapter Two

COMMANDER CASTELLAN TOSH was not at all pleased. Her voice was low and rough as she held the tarpaulin covering the burnt-out moto shell, examining the wreck beneath. "What do you mean you were going to tell me at the next briefing? You didn't think it worth mentioning that someone planted an explosive device in one of the Connate's private transports? Tell me, Lieutenants, do either of you belong in this job?"

Tosh was livid and Savon had the good grace to look away. Madlin though continued to meet her commander's eyes. She knew they had erred when it came to informing their senior Shield officer about the attack but they also knew how much stress she was under with the coming ceremony and were hoping to save her some trouble. "Please, ser, we were still gathering all the details and would have made a full report at the fifteen hundred oor meeting."

"Pray tell me what you would have done if Spc. Calderon had been killed when that thing went off? This lack of communication is unacceptable, especially when the Connate's life is directly in danger! I've half a mind to—" She stopped speaking and dropped the edge of the tarpaulin as she caught sight of Olivienne approaching from the distance with four of her Shield guards. "Bollux!" The one-word response was whispered under her breath but the lieutenants heard it quite clear. Savon and Madlin both turned to see the Connate. Castellan refocused her attention on the two officers. "I want that report ready at fifteen hundred oors." She then strode away toward the woman she feared for with all her heart, desperate to not let her emotions interfere with her duty.

"Olivienne! Have you finished visiting with my maman so soon?"

"Oh yes, she is a most delightful woman. We waited a bit for you to return but in the end opted for a light lunch without you. I made sure she was well set up with a clothier before she left and she told me to tell you that you better stop ignoring her teleo calls or she'd give me even more stories from your childhood."

Castellan wrapped an arm around Olivienne's shoulders and

attempted to steer her away from the covered moto. "Well enough then. Perhaps I'll even contact her first. What are you up to now?"

Olivienne stopped and turned to look toward the street outside the palace grounds, at whatever was under the nondescript tarpaulin. "Tosh. What is that?"

"That? Oh, it's nothing. Just a damaged transport that needs to be replaced. Do not worry yourself about it, 'Vienne. The lieutenants will have it remanded back to the Shield Corp yard straightaway."

Castellan tried to gently pull Olivienne away again but the Connate was having none of it. Olivienne's face turned serious. "What's under the tarp, Tosh?" She saw it in Tosh's blue eyes before words even left the commander's mouth. Worry and denial. "Never mind, I'll simply see for myself." Olivienne flexed her four rating apportation power and the tarp disappeared from the wreck and appeared on the ground next to it. She gasped. "By the Makers! Is that one of ours?"

The commander glanced around as a large hauler pulled up on the roadway near the destroyed moto. Conscious of more than just her Shield team in attendance, she was careful with her words. "Yes, Connate Dracore. Earlier this morning Specialist Calderon picked up one of the team's assigned transports from its routine maintenance appointment. It wasn't until he was underway that he noticed the strange package on the floor of the passenger side. From there he pulled over and immediately exited the moto but was caught in the blast." Olivienne gasped and Castellan held up her hand. "He suffered minor injuries. A sprained wrist and a few abrasions but overall he was lucky. As you can see the moto never made it back onto the Sovereign estate but it was near enough to give me pause."

Seeing that Lt. Savon had things in hand as he directed the newly arrived soldiers in loading the burnt wreck, Castellan motioned for her and Olivienne to begin walking back toward the gates that Olivienne had come through meens before. "Let's talk back at residence where it's more secure. I'd feel significantly better if you're out of sight for the interim."

Olivienne hated having her freedom curtailed but gave in when she looked closely at her lover and took in the tense stance and constantly roving gaze. Tosh was looking for danger and Olivienne knew her commander wouldn't relax until the sovereign was safely out of the public eye. "Fine, let's go. But I want to know everything. That's our deal, remember? I give you full compliance where my safety is concerned and in return you give me full disclosure."

Castellan followed the motion of the winches on the hauler and sighed. "So I did."

Olivienne gave a gentle mental push and Tosh answered.

"Yes?"

"It will be all right, my love. Whatever happened and whatever is to come, we will not let them win. After all, I have the world's most dashing and capable commander at my side."

That earned her a small smile but Castellan's eyes remained troubled for the entire walk back to residence.

EVENING HAD FALLEN and Commander Tosh found more to be worried about than a destroyed moto from the newest assassination attempt. Oathing tradition meant that the first of three dinners would always be with the immediate family of the initiator of the oathing request. Since Olivienne had been the one to ask Castellan on the back of a dirigible high above northern Endara, they took their first dinner at the palace. It was a quiet meal with only five in attendance. Perhaps what surprised Castellan most was that the family dined at a smallish round table. It seemed strangely intimate in such a grand room, and certainly less formal.

Castellan was seated between Olivienne and her sib, Sub-Connate Kesharan Dracore. On the other side of Kesharan was King Keshien, and the Queen sat between Olivienne and the King. The Queen watched Castellan with those disconcerting purple eyes that were so like her daughter's. Even though everyone in attendance had met each other before, it was strangely awkward. Olivienne couldn't stand the tension but her words were tightly directed to one person.

"Maman! Quit staring at her like that. I know you like Tosh, be nice and stop trying to intimidate her."

Olivara turned her gaze on her daughter. *"Who says I'm intimidating her? I think you know your commander better than that. But fine, I'll do my official duty and welcome her to the family."*

The Queen casually swallowed a spoonful of soup before turning her regard back to Castellan. While she was fairly positive about Castellan Tosh's feelings for her daughter, as the ruler of the nation she felt it was her job to be one hundred percent sure. The upright commander was much too powerful to simply slide inside her thoughts without her knowing but Olivara was not so easily deterred. The only way to get the information she sought was to make Tosh momentarily slip the tight reigns of her control. But her daughter was wrong about Olivara's technique. She knew that something as crude and simple as intimidation would never work on the noble commander. The Queen had been ruling for many rotos and was a consummate schemer. Olivara had other more subtle ways of getting the information she needed.

"So Commander Tosh, you are certainly unceasingly handsome. Have you had many lovers?" The King snorted and Kesharan clapped a hand over his eyes and prayed to the Makers that his maman wouldn't do such things when he finally brought home someone to oath to. Tosh had just taken a swallow of her vineo and began choking on the liquid as the Queen's words registered.

"Maman!"

"I'm only asking with a paren's concern, after all. I need to be sure that my daughter isn't just another dalliance with you."

Castellan turned red at the implication that she was less sure of her love for Olivienne simply based on her lack of past serious relationships. She abruptly stood from her chair and the entire table held its breath. The King sighed first, recognizing what his par was trying to do but he too waited with bated breath to see the commander's response. The Queen smiled as Castellan's tight focus momentarily slipped, not that she learned anything more than what the commander's own words iterated in the meen that followed.

"Does Archeos dally in the sky with Illeos? Olivienne is my sun and I am hers, and together we burn more fiercely than any I have met before or will meet after. By the Makers I pledge you this, there are no words you can utter that would cause me to doubt or turn me away from her!"

Castellan glanced at her lover and was surprised to see tears in her eyes. *"'Vienne?"*

"I love you."

Castellan took the offered hand and let Olivienne pull her back into her seat. When she once again met the Queen's eyes, she saw affection warring with pride. "My apologies for the outburst, my Queen."

Rather than Queen Olivara answering, it was the King. He

knocked upon the table twice and gave Castellan a smile. "Well-answered and welcome to the family, Commander Tosh."

Queen Olivara smiled at Castellan and the commander knew then that her future mamanar was only trying to provoke a reaction with her off-color remarks. And based on her past interactions with the sovereign, she had a feeling she knew why. But unlike past incidences, Castellan didn't get angry at the flagrant breach of privacy. When she met the purple eyes of Olivara Dracore she addressed her suspicions in a silent exchange. *"Did you get what you were looking for when my shield dropped?"*

The Queen didn't respond to the accusation directly, but Castellan was mollified nonetheless. *"Olivienne is very lucky and I gladly welcome you as a consoral daughter."*

With that response Tosh gave a slight nod and let the subject die. It wasn't as if she hadn't spoken with the Queen on many occasions. And she knew for certain that the woman approved since Olivara had all but forced Castellan and Olivienne together initially. She sighed at having conquered the most difficult hurdle when entering into a consorage with a royal sovereign, the Queen's official approval. However, the commander's reprieve didn't last long since the Queen turned the conversation to another more serious matter. She was straight to the point as usual. "Tell me about the moto incident todae."

The King looked up from his dish of seared greens and roots. "Moto incident?"

Castellan sighed. "Yes, ser. Specialist Calderon was sent to retrieve one of our team's transports from a routine maintenance visit. Just before reaching the front gates, he noticed a suspicious package on the floor the next seat over. He quickly pulled over and exited the moto as the explosive device ignited. The blast flung him away from the transport with some force. Luckily he was able to slow himself with levitation but still received some scrapes and a sprained wrist from the ordeal. The doctore said he should be fighting fit in five daes time."

"By the Makers! I spend an entire dae stuck in meetings with the Imperium and this is what I miss?"

Olivienne put down her eating utensil. "It's all fine, Papan. The moto didn't even breach the palace walls. Whomever was responsible did a shoddy job."

The Queen spoke up with a clipped tone that betrayed her fear and frustration. "That's beside the point, 'Vienne!" She turned her purple gaze toward Tosh. "What is being done about this, Commander?"

"Lieutenants Savon and Madlin were on the scene first as I was in the middle of our clothier appointment. They contacted Shield headquarters and requested quarantine for the transport and a team of investigators. I spoke with General Renou and she informed me she'd flag the incident for high clearance only, per my request."

The Queen narrowed her eyes. "What are you thinking, Tosh."

Castellan sighed and rubbed the space just above her nose. "I'm thinking that the moto is already a high security item by nature since its part of the sovereign's fleet. The maintenance yard is within the joint Defense and Shield storage area with limited personnel having access."

The King grunted and sat back as his dark brows drew together. "An inside job then."

"I'm afraid so, ser. But too many people have access and unfortunately the maintenance area has no record of comings and goings so we have no guesses as to whom could be the culprit. In an effort to glean any clues, the general loaned me one of their top Shield psychometrists. Unfortunately the blast rendered most physical items, including the explosive device, naught much more than slag. So it looks like a dead end where that is concerned." Shoulders slumped around the table as the initial course grew cold in their dishes.

"I hate this!" The outburst came from the youngest member of the Dracore family. Seventeen rotos in age and a new Academy attendee, Kesharan still had the youthful timbre to his voice and no facial hair to speak of. And while he remained tall and slender like his maman, his bone structure and deep blue eyes were all that of the King.

Both the Queen and King looked confused at his outburst but Olivienne knew. She was his sib after all. "It's fine, Kesh. I have many protectors and this one didn't even come close."

He turned to look at Olivienne in full. "But it *could* have. You have a target on your back at all times while I sit safe, twelve hundred mahls away at the Academy in Scola. It's not fair to you!"

"Kesh..." Olivienne trailed off and glanced toward their maman. He was more than a decaroto her junior and there were things she knew their parens kept from him. Things they kept from her until she came into full maturity. And it wasn't her place to tell her sib what those things were. Castellan watched, understanding that someone had been keeping the Sub-Connate in the dark about certain details. Their oathing dinner had turned quite serious, but then they were residing in serious times.

The Queen shifted and moved her napkin to dab at the corners of her mouth. A server came in with the third course and she waived the man back out. "Kesharan, there are truths that come with being a Dracore that most of us don't learn about until we reach a certain age. Your papan and I were hoping to wait a bit longer to tell you but the security threats against our family dictate otherwise." She paused to order her thoughts. The words were difficult because no paren wanted to have to tell their child that their life was in danger, that it would always be in danger for as long as they lived. The ruler of Psiere turned strangely hesitant and she cast her dark gaze toward her par, hoping for some help.

King Keshien grasped her hand tightly in his and gave a nod before turning to Kesharan. "My son, what your maman is trying to say is that you and your sib were born with targets on your back. There have been assassination attempts on every member of the Dracore family for as long as Dracores have been ruling Psiere. Even you. To date, your Shield team has been able to handle any incidents that crop up, but the guardians maintain a diligent vigil over our persons at all times. So if you think that you sit on Instrucia Island safer than the rest, perhaps there is some merit to your thought due to the distance alone. However, I assure you that you are no less a target."

"Kesh, I have a dangerous job compared to the rest of my family. We all know that. And my duty as an adventurist takes me all over the two continents, which exposes me to peril significantly more than you at Academy, or Maman and Papan here in Tesseron. The attempts on me tend to be more public, more dramatic, because I am in the public eye quite a bit. That is why you see me targeted more than yourself or our parens. I'm sorry that you're worried for me, truly. I'm sorrier that any of us have to worry but we all have excellent teams to guide us and guard us from danger. Trust your team, and trust ours.

The young psi looked stricken, his pale face standing out dramatically against the nearly purple black of his hair, a hair color that was a signature of the Dracore line. His voice was quiet. "I had no idea. My whole life I just assumed we were always safe, that attacks were rare."

"Big attacks like todae, or in the plaza down in Pentole are

rare. What is different now, the reason such things have acceler-
ated, is that your sib is working on a secret mission for me and
your papan. Very few know the truth of what she searches for or
the treasures that success could yield."

Kesharan looked at his maman, then turned his gaze toward
Olivienne. "The lost temple! You've found it then?"

Olivienne nodded and grinned back. "We did."

"And you're only just telling me now? You used to tell me
about all your great finds."

His dark brows furrowed and lips turned down into a frown.
Kesharan's hurt feelings were written all over his expressive face
and Olivienne couldn't have that. She loved her sib immensely as
they'd grown up quite close despite the thirteen roto age gap
between them. "We've only had the final key for a lune or so. We
retrieved it on my last adventure to Dir Nubila. You were away at
Academy until a dae ago and the mission is so restricted that I
could not send you a missive for fear of interception. But with
Maman and Papan's permission, perhaps you could come to my
residence after dinner and Tosh and I can fill you in on what
we've discovered."

Kesharan's face lit with excitement as he turned to his
parens. "May I?"

Olivara looked to her par and everyone could tell a wordless
exchange occurred between the Queen and King. Then Olivara
turned toward her only son. "I think that should be fine. You are
a Dracore and a trusted member of this family. As long as you
know that what we say is to be kept under the highest security.
Savvy?"

"Yes, Maman."

Olivara didn't look toward them but she directed her
thoughts to Olivienne and Castellan. *"You can tell him about everything but the skeleton and the antoraestones. I'd rather no one have that
knowledge but the few of us, for now."*

"Yes, Maman."

"Yes, my Queen."

The King clapped, startling all of them. "Good, now that the
heavy discussion is complete, let's turn our conversation to
lighter things. For instance, who wants to lay odds with me that
the good commander here," he winked at Castellan, "suffers a
faint when she stands for the official oathing?"

Olivienne laughed delightedly, much to Castellan's chagrin.
"You better hope not, Papan. Otherwise the actual consoral cere-

mony may just kill her!"

Castellan cleared her throat. "I think I will manage just fine, my King."

"Oh, none of that!" he exclaimed. "I'm to be your future papanar. No need to be so formal."

"Yes, ser."

Keshien made a face and Olivara patted his arm. "Sorry, love. But our dear commander is vexing like that. So very formal."

Seeing an opportunity to give as good as she had gotten throughout the dinner, Castellan called out with a smirk. "And dashing, my Queen. Don't forget that you once called me dashing and said that I would have turned your head to oathing in your youth."

The Queen winked back at her and raised her glass in salute. "So I did."

Olivienne looked scandalized. "Maman!"

"Oh, stuff your aether, sib! You know Maman only ever looks at Papan. They are nauseating like that."

"Stuff your aether?" Olivara's right eyebrow rose, so very similar to her daughter's familiar reaction.

"I think it means to hold tongue, my Queen."

Before Olivara could respond, both the King and Olivienne burst out in laughter. "Oh, Makers save us, Kesh, but you're totally right. Maman and Papan are completely gone on each other." She turned to her lover. "I suppose I have no worries then since...what did you tell your own maman? I believe you said that I was the most amazing person on all of Psiere, save the Queen." Castellan made a slight noise of protest as an uncharacteristic flush moved from the commander's neck up to the top of her forehead.

The rest of the table responded with laughter as the staff brought out the next course. The Queen had telepathically contacted the head of the kitchen when she sensed that the conversation was steering into safer waters. Castellan wished the next night's dinner suffered from a lot less drama, though knowing her maman as she did, she wasn't holding out hope.

Olivienne knew that only half of Castellan's worry was due to the upcoming ceremony and dinners with their parens. The other half was owned solely by her duty as Shield Commander. Occasionally when Castellan slept fitfully, Olivienne would wake to hear her lover's thoughts. The horrors and anxieties of Tosh's dreams were taken directly from their real experiences. The biggest one was of Olivienne being pulled down into the deep by the leviathan. She knew how it affected Tosh because waking on that beach to see the commander herself unconscious and gravely wounded was almost more than Olivienne could bear.

Their jobs were dangerous and worry was an ever-present weight across both their shoulders. And as a couple, Olivienne wanted to be better about shouldering her half of the load. Being too far away at the round table, Olivienne did what she could to show her love. When the spiced stekka medallions were served onto her plate, she discretely apported half of them onto Castellan's dish. They were the officer's favorite and Olivienne got a smile and an invisible caress for her action.

"You're remarkably sweet tonight. And so protective with your maman."

"Well, I have a remarkably sweet and protective lover. I have to keep up, you know. It wouldn't do to have a mere Shield Corp officer show me up in the business of love and devotion."

Castellan gave Olivienne's cheek another caress with her telekinesis and let the invisible touch move farther down the other woman's arm to her fingertips. Olivienne nearly dropped her eating utensil at the unexpected thrill of it and Castellan's voice sounded softly in her head.

"There is no competition necessary, love. You are everything I want and need in this life and all others."

Olivienne blushed at Castellan's tender words. The small looks and telekinetic touches continued throughout the meal and the only indication of their secret play was the flush that persisted on Olivienne's cheeks.

Later that evening, Kesharan came over as promised to sit with Olivienne and Castellan and learn all they had discovered and accomplished. He was thrilled about each new adventure they completed. Castellan could easily see that the young psi had a fire of curiosity inside him very similar to his sib's. One thing that was equally as obvious was that he was growing to be a thoughtful and loyal psero and she looked forward to the dae when she could call him parsib. He left near twenty-four hundred oors with a head stuffed full of stories about giant trees, black dirigibles, and the acid spitting drakes of Dir Nubila.

Olivienne shook her head as he wandered down the path toward the palace, with his own Shield guards in tow. She stood in front of Castellan within the officer's embrace and met her lover's eyes. "I'm not sure whether he will have dreams of adventure or nightmares of terror."

Tosh snorted and pulled away to lead Olivienne inside. "He seems like a brave enough young psi. I'm sure he'll fare just fine." As soon as the door was shut, she abruptly guided the Connate against the hard surface, pinning Olivienne in place with nearly her shear presence alone. The twinkle in Castellan's eyes let Olivienne know that all their interaction at dinner had put her in quite a mood. "Now you on the other hand…what sort of dreams do you wish for?"

Olivienne carded her hands through Tosh's hair, mussing it delightfully. "Well, that depends, Commander."

Tosh cocked a single pale brow. "On?"

"On whether or not we wake in your suite or mine."

"And what difference does our location make. What kind of dreams will you have in your own bed?"

Olivienne grinned mischievously. "I'm sure they will be beyond compare."

Castellan laughed. "And if you wake in my bed?"

"Tosh…" Olivienne pulled Castellan's head close so she could whisper in her ear. "Your bed is closer."

Pale eyes glinted in the low light of the entryway and Castellan abruptly bent to lift Olivienne up by the back of her thighs. The Connate was quick to wrap her legs around the strong officer's midriff. "My bed it is!" It didn't take long to make their way to Castellan's suite within the Connate's residence. She could have used her levitation to lift them both had she wanted it. But she knew that Olivienne secretly delighted in the strength of Castellan's body so the officer tried to oblige her whenever possible.

Once inside, she slowed but Olivienne was having none of it. Suddenly both women's clothing disappeared and reappeared on the lounge and Olivienne dug her fingers into Castellan's scalp. "Bed now, or I'll have you on the floor."

Castellan laughed but grew distracted as Olivienne's mouth wandered down her neck. She stumbled through the door of her room and collapsed with a gasp onto the bed. Their nudity became obvious by the heat slicked across Castellan's abdomen. She groaned. "You'll be my death." She ran her tongue from jaw to the hollow of Olivienne's throat and the woman beneath her whined and thrust upward.

"Please, Tosh."

Castellan raised her head to meet Olivienne's dark gaze. The black centers had grown large with the dimly lit room and Olivienne's desire. "I wish to take my time with you." Olivienne bucked again in an effort to seek friction where she most wanted it. Castellan pressed down on her shoulders to hold her in place. "Will you consent or must I hold you down to make you wait?"

"By the Makers! Do something, I'm begging you."

"Oh, no worries about that, love." Tosh pulled back and Olivienne whimpered. Then the Connate found herself immobilized with nothing more than the power of Castellan's thoughts. Her newly tested seven rating telekinesis meant that no one would be able to break free from her hold and Olivienne grew wetter thinking of it. "Tonight I get to be the adventurist, searching for your treasures." Castellan's lips settled lightly over Olivienne's nipple and the woman on the bottom strained to increase the pressure.

When Castellan took the hard bud into her mouth, a cry erupted from Olivienne's mouth. "Don't forget to use your teeth — oh!"

Castellan moved from one breast to the other, working her lover into a frenzy of passion, then made her way south. "I believe I see a clue here." Her talented fingers grazed down Olivienne's abdomen and made its way toward fine purplish-black hair. "Perhaps I should inspect it closer."

Olivienne struggled to control her breathing. "That...would be, uh, my pro — professional opinion."

As the commander's mouth descended into Olivienne's treasure, she lost words completely.

NEARLY TWO OORS later both women lay sated on Castellan's bed. After being thoroughly ravished, Olivienne had turned the tables and explored Castellan's body ince by ince. She paid back every iota of delayed pleasure Castellan had wrung from her, thrice-fold. Castellan blew out a breath as her heart pounded in her chest and Olivienne moved up to cling tightly to her. The winded woman welcomed Olivienne into the circle of her arms while she recovered.

Olivienne was quiet for nearly a meen as she listened to the rhythmic thump below her ear. She sighed. "I love hearing your heart beat so."

Castellan chuckled and the sound of it vibrated against Olivienne's ear. "Well, you are the one who is to blame."

"Was I too rough?" Olivienne met those heart-stealing pale blue eyes.

"Not in the slightest. I only meant that my heart beats for you. Perhaps I would have made my maman happy and settled down sooner had I met you rotos ago."

Olivienne laughed. "Or perhaps you would have never settled down at all. I'm well aware how I was even at the time we met but—" She idly traced a pattern on Tosh's bare sternum. "I don't know. I feel like I've taken a long journey between now and then and I've arrived a different person than when I left."

Castellan pulled Olivienne even closer as the depth of her feelings washed through her. "We are both different people. I'd like to think we are better together than apart."

"You make me better." Castellan made to protest but Olivienne quickly covered her lips with a single finger. "No, it's true. There is something about you, Castellan Tosh, which inspires everyone around you. Including me. I wish I had met you sooner."

"Fear not, love." She kissed Olivienne's finger. "We met at exactly the right time for each other and now we have the rest of our lives to revel in this romance."

Olivienne gave another dreamy sigh as she lifted her head to gaze upon Castellan's face. "Had the Makers themselves crafted me the perfect woman, she still wouldn't be half as perfect as you."

Bold laughter rang out from Castellan's mouth, which shook both of them. "Oh ho, you speak such pretty words now, my sovereign. Perhaps you'd like to switch to the Service Corp so you can go join the traveling bardes—"

Olivienne shifted above Castellan and covered her mouth with kisses before the other woman could finish her sentence. They had a rare spot of free time the next morning and Olivienne was going to do everything in her power to keep Castellan abed to enjoy it. Between the ever-present danger surrounding her family, the upcoming oathing ceremony, and the coming journey to search out the lost temple of Psiere, she knew they would bear the weight of responsibility soon enough. But in the meantime, the evening was theirs to enjoy.

Chapter Three

CASTELLAN HAD ORDERED the Connate's moto checked thoroughly by three different specialists before they made their way to the Tosh family residence the next night. Much the way Castellan had been the previous evening, Olivienne was a bundle of nerves at the thought of meeting Castellan's papan, sibs, and the rest of her family. The Shield duty roster for the evening included Lt. Madlin, as well as Specialists Soleng, Lear, Yazzie, Qent, and Penn. Madlin and Soleng would ride in the same moto as the commander and the Connate, while the other four would follow behind in a second moto.

Olivienne's knee jiggled as she fidgeted with the bottom of her corset. Her new outfit consisted of pants that were made from a fine dark cream-colored material. They were form-fitting at her waist and hips, but flared out at her thighs before tapering once again to disappear into knee high black boots that perfectly matched her black corset. Her blouse was light cream and loose, gathering only at her neck and wrists with rows of fine buttons. Of course she wore her ever-present pistol but it was in a different holster that allowed for a cross draw, to accommodate the ride in the moto. The altered position was necessary with the corset to prevent the pistol from pinching into her side.

Castellan placed a calming hand on the soft cloth and the knee stilled. "Relax. You are merely meeting with my family, not the entirety of the Imperium. No one will judge you in my parens' home. Besides, according to Yazzie and Devin, my maman loves you." She said the words with a sigh.

Olivienne laced their fingers together and took in her lover's second oathing dinner outfit. As much as she loved Castellan in the black uniform of the Shield Corp, even she had to admit that Castellan's current outfit suited her much better. The officer wore pressed black pants that were fashioned very similar to Olivienne's. They were the popular choice for many of the more active members of society as they allowed greater freedom of movement compared to the more traditional cut of trouser. While Tosh's pants, boots, pistol holster, and belt were all black, she wore a loose shirt of the palest blue that highlighted her fair hair and pale eyes. That combined with Castellan's tanned skin made for quite a head-turning sight. She let the image of her lover soothe her until their arrival at the Tosh estate.

While Castellan's parens lived in a nice home outside Tesseron, it wasn't grand or imposing the way some of the homes within Tesseron's more affluent districts. There were no fences or gates to get inside. Rather it was a long drive that led to a house sitting atop a slight rise. Outbuildings for the mining business were to the left and the right but they were surprisingly neat and tidy. Castellan interrupted Olivienne's musings as they slowly made their way toward the distant house. "You look perplexed."

Olivienne gestured out the window of the moto. "I've never actually seen a mining operation and I wasn't sure what to expect. I thought there would be great open pits in the ground. I swear I've seen some like that."

"Well for one, there hasn't been any mining at this site in tens of rotos. And while it's true that illeostone and other resource mining used to be done like that, things have drastically changed in the past couple decarotos or so. Some was due to the laws coming out of the Imperium, which limit the amount of damage that can be done to the land in the pursuit of raw material. But other changes..." Tosh gave a prideful smile. "Those are directly attributed to my maman. She made my papan realize that mining for illeostones could be approached much like farming."

A dark eyebrow rose with Olivienne's skepticism. "And how is that, exactly?"

Castellan laughed. "Tosh Mining has a strict policy that once a section has been depleted of stones, the area is filled in, terraformed, and reforested to restore the natural beauty and usefulness of the space. That is one of the things that allows us to mine large tracts of land because it's with the public knowledge that we will return the area just as beautiful as before we started. I have a feeling you'd know these things as well as the laws if you'd paid attention in your connate training."

"Sovereign course lectures were boring as spit. Just me sitting in a room with some advisors, and I fully admit to forgetting perhaps more than I learned in them." Olivienne looked up to see Castellan's eyes crinkled at the corners and a smirk that barely contained her laugh. "It's true, I'm telling you I came out of that course poorer of intellect!"

Castellan tried to imagine the overactive woman sitting solo in a room listening to lectures geared toward the duty of running all of Psiere. "Let me guess, you paced like a wild tigre for the entirety of every single class?"

"You may be right on that. However, I did complete the course with some knowledge."

"About your duties as a sovereign?"

Olivienne laughed aloud as they pulled up in front the Tosh house. "Well no, not that. But I did learn to keep three crunchy reds in the air for nearly twenty meens at a time without dropping a single one."

They both exited the moto and Castellan came around the front to link her arm with Olivienne's. "You taught yourself to juggle applets? And to think, the rest of us psi trust you to take on the mantle of Queen eventually!" She gave a teasing chuckle and shook her head in fond disbelief.

Olivienne's heart sped up as they approached the main entrance to the domicile with their Shield team in tow. Somewhat distracted by the dinner to come, she managed a pat to Castellan's hand and gave an easy answer. "Well lucky for Psiere, my appointment to the Divine Cathedra is tens of rotos away and I'm sure there will be a refresher between now and then."

"Even so, you will remain a queen in my heart until you become a queen in title, Connate Dracore." Castellan winked and gave a little bow as the door opened to reveal her maman with a small child on her hip.

Cassiene drew back in surprise and quickly bowed as best she could while clutching the little pale-haired girl. "Connate Dracore! My apologies, when I heard the moto I thought you were Tellesen and Aryn arriving." She stepped back and opened the door wide for the two women to enter.

Olivienne wagged a finger on the hand that wasn't holding the well-aged bottle of portea. "None of that now, Mamanar. You promised that you'd call me Olivienne after our lunch the other dae."

The older woman's smile softened her characteristically stern features. "So I did. Please come in and welcome to the Tosh home."

Castellan paused long enough to address their assigned Shield team for the trip. "Madlin, as we discussed...four to cover the exits and two with the motos. You've all seen and memorized stills of my family. No one but Toshs get through, savvy?"

"Yes, ser!" Lt. Madlin gave a crisp salute then marched back down the steps to assign individual locations.

As soon as they were both inside, a handsome older man rounded the corner into the foyer. "Cassie, have you seen the—" He paused when he noticed his daughter. "By the Makers, Castellan! It's been ages since I last saw you in person. Teleo calls are not the same, my girl." He grabbed the reticent commander in a great embrace and spun her around as if she were still the little girl he remembered. To Olivienne, it seemed as though his exuberant actions matched his youthful good looks. And Cassiene Tosh had certainly not exaggerated about her husband's attractiveness.

Rather than be put off at the rough handling, Castellan laughed heartily and slapped the man on the back. "Papan, put me down or you'll hurt yourself." When he settled her on the floor again, she gestured toward Olivienne. "Papan, I'd like you to meet my future par, Olivienne.'Vienne, this is my papan, Tello Tosh."

As soon as Tello saw the sovereign, he dipped into a deep bow, causing a forelock of pale hair to fall across one eye. "Connate Dracore, it is my extreme pleasure to make your acquaintance. You honor the Tosh house with your beauty and presence here this dae."

Charmed by the dashing man that looked so much like her love, Olivienne gave a shorter bow back to him. "I'm afraid the pleasure is all mine, ser."

"Oh, don't let his pretty words and face get to you, my dear. I warned you about those Toshs, did I not?" Cassiene swooped in and looped her free arm through Olivienne's. "Let's drop that portea off in the kitchen and you can meet Tessior and Temera—"

The little girl clapped at the mention of her parens' names. "Maman and Papan!"

"That's right, darling" Cassiene smiled fondly at her youngest son's daughter, then addressed Olivienne as they made their way through the house. "This bundle of brightness is Temiora. She is a handful but I love having her underfoot whenever they visit—"

They were interrupted by another voice coming down the hall. "Mamanar, have you been feeding her biscuits? There is a half-eaten and soggy one on the counter."

Cassiene winked at Olivienne before turning her attention to her son's par. "Mayhap. But Temera, you know that it is my solemn duty as avia to sneak the child sweets."

Castellan joined up with her maman and Olivienne around

the same moment Tessior and Temera came through the kitchen doorway. Greetings were repeated with Castellan's sib and parsib and the younger couple was obviously star struck by their sovereign guest. When Tellesen and Aeryn arrived less than five meens later, they were a little more settled. But their two boisterous children latched on to their famous amita immediately. Their cries rang through the sprawling house.

"Castellan! We missed you."

"The news vellums called you the 'Hero of Temple Beach,' tell us the story."

"Please!" Castellan's heart clenched at their words and she regretted avoiding her family for so long. She hadn't seen them in nearly two rotos and the children had grown so much. She promised to herself to do better in the future. They stood on either side of her in the middle of the entertainment room, clamoring for attention. Aelysen and Tellyn had always loved hearing her stories of adventure. It was only when she introduced Olivienne to them that they turned shy and quiet.

The ten-roto-old girl turned toward the Connate and gave a proper bow and her sib copied the motion, though not as skilled. It was obvious that Aelysen was the bolder of the two sibs as the little boy hung back behind her for the greeting. "Maman and Papan said you're going to be our Queen somedae. When I get older I'm going to be your Shield just like Amita Castellan. I already protect my sib when he gets teased for being too smart." Tellyn nodded behind her.

Delighted, Olivienne took the little girl's declaration seriously and went down on one knee. "Well, Aelysen, if you are anything like your amita then I have no doubts we'll be seeing you in the heroic black uniform soon enough." Aelysen's eyes danced with delight as Olivienne moved her gaze to the eight-roto-old boy. "What of you, Tellyn?"

His first words were an awed whisper. "She knows my name."

His sib gave him a light elbow to the gut. "Of course she knows your name, she's going to be the Queen somedae and knows everything."

Castellan barely stifled a snort of laughter and Olivienne did her best to ignore her future par. She gently corrected the child. "No one knows everything. Not even the Queen."

"The Makers knew everything." The boy's voice was so solid and sure.

Olivienne leaned over and tapped his temple with her finger. "Think about it, Tellyn. Have you ever met the Makers?" Both children shook their heads. "Now, since you've never met the Makers, it stands to reason they didn't know about you, right?" They both nodded. "And since they didn't know about you, but you know about the Makers...that means you know something the Makers didn't. Lots of things, as a matter of fact, because the Makers have been gone a long time."

Aelysen's mouth dropped open. "Wow."

But the boy didn't say anything at first. Tellyn stared at her with a look of intense concentration before he broke into a big grin. "You're really smart! I want to be an adventurist like you when I grow up."

Olivienne smiled and saluted them both. "Well then, I say the profession will be lucky to have you."

As she stood to give them space, Tellen clapped his older sib on the shoulder and whispered in her ear. "I think she's a fine match for you, Lanny. And Aeryn and I wish you all the happiness with your future par."

Castellan moved her gaze between her sib and parsib. Aeryn's smile was warm and welcoming as she nodded in agreement. The stoic commander was touched beyond words and could only smile in return.

The scene was broken when Cassiene called out from the doorway. "Now that we're all here, let's begin Castellan and Olivienne's second oathing dinner! After all, the sooner they oath, the sooner they consor, and the sooner this avia has more babes to spoil!" Both Olivienne and Castellan blushed at her words but held hands all the way to the Tosh dining room.

Olivienne was struck by how different the Tosh household was compared to that of the sovereign family. It was noisy, warm, and full of carefree moments. While Olivienne loved her maman, papan, and sib beyond the pale, the Dracores had always been more restrained in word and action with guests at the table. Most of that was due to the enormous pressure put on each and every member, as future or potential rulers of Psiere. That was why she loved the Tosh family so much almost immediately. They provided a much needed balance that she had been missing her entire life, and Olivienne couldn't wait for more meals and meetings in the future.

IT WAS THE morning after the second oathing dinner and
Gen. Camen Renou stared hard at the two Sovereign Shield officers in front of her. Captain Torrin of the Queen's guard was a
big, broad-shouldered man with a dark complexion and a shock
of black hair. He'd been in the Shield Corp since graduating
Academy. While the other officer, Commander Castellan Tosh,
was a fairly new recruit to the Shields. You wouldn't know it
from the ease with which she took on the Connate's team that
Tosh had spent the majority of her career in Psi Defense. The general thought that perhaps in that respect, one soldier was much
like another. But she'd seen Tosh in action enough times to know
that, late transition or not, the commander most definitely bled
the black and silvere colors of their corp.

Finished with her short perusal of the two officers tasked
with arguably the most important jobs of the land, she quickly got
down to the business at hand. "Captain, Commander, my apologies for the unexpected nature of this briefing."

"That's quite all right, General." Cpt. Torrin's voice wasn't
deep per se, but rather sturdy and had a resonance found in few
other men. He was someone to be listened to and Castellan
admired the man immensely. Nearly fifteen rotos her senior, he'd
been serving as the Queen's Shield Captain since Castellan was
still at Academy.

Gen. Renou shuffled a few vellums on her desk until she
found what she was looking for. She stood and handed it across
the desk to Cpt. Torrin, as he was of the highest rank. After he
read it, he passed the sheet to Cmdr. Tosh. Castellan paled as she
read printed words of something that was clearly a prescient premonition. "Captain Torrin, as I informed Commander Tosh, we
found no leads from the bombed moto of last weke. But I've
called you both here todae because of this new intel on the recent
uptick of rebel attacks."

Cpt. Torrin glanced at the sheet that remained in Tosh's
hand. "Was it Lieutenant Kensata, ser?"

Knowing that Cmdr. Tosh was new to the Corp, Gen. Renou
explained. "Kensata is the Shield Corp's highest rated in both
clairvoyance and prescience. Defense also has a six rating but
Kensata has been ours since straight out of Academy. Anyway, as
you're both aware, many clairvoyants and prescients are triggered by other events and he said that he had this premonition
after reading the sovereign announcements first thing this morning."

Castellan tilted her head even as her brow wrinkled. "Announcements, ser?"

"Yes. Last night I sat in a meeting with Queen Olivara, King Keshien, General Leniste, and Templar Aislyn, to discuss the best method to quell the discontent that seems to be emanating from the southern continent. As you're both aware, we have some known enemy agents at work, which no one in Defense, Shield, or Security has been able to locate. A few of us have suspected that Lord Pon Havington is the mastermind behind it all but as of yet we still have no proof. He is sly and will not easily be caught."

"Have you gotten any good intel from First Lieutenant Cando, ser? If you remember, I gave her name to General Leniste earlier this roto as a possible contact down in Ostium."

"Yes, your recommendation has been invaluable. Leniste has already instructed General Tenet to reassign two aids to Praefectus Havington with the intent of spying and reporting back to Tesseron. Unfortunately, your less-than-effective replacement in Ostium, Lieutenant Commander Bello, cannot be recalled at this time without arousing Havington's suspicions."

Tosh nodded. Having spent nearly five rotos overseeing Ostium's forces in Endara, she was very familiar with the elected official of the entire southern continent. But she had never liked the man as he'd twanged her six rating intuition channel from the moment they met. "He would go cautious. I'm certain of it."

"Exactly that. Anyway, Ser Enik Gannon is the top enforcer and right hand man in the rebellion, which we highly suspect is led by Havington. Known accomplices to Gannon are Camillo Binn and Gahmo Dek. Those three names and faces pop up across the two continents but no one has been able to lock them down. They stir discontentment and anti-sovereign sentiment wherever they go. We've even got witnesses that state Gannon and his crew of lackeys have gone so far as insisting Havington would be a far better leader for Psiere than the Queen."

Torrin's brows drew down at her words and he clenched his fists. "He has the audacity to insinuate such rubbish?" Captain Del Torrin was about as loyal to the Queen as one could get outside her family.

"At ease, Captain. Beyond reassignments and increasing efforts to locate Gannon, Binn, and Dek, the Queen has seen fit to make the grand announcement that the lost temple of Psiere has been discovered in a far off place and that the Divinity Corp is putting together a team that will attempt to reach the location."

Cpt. Torrin nodded since he was already aware of the news but Cmdr. Tosh had not known of the meeting that occurred while they were at her parens' house.

"Why would she do that, ser?"

"As you are aware, the mystery of the Makers has always received a high level of interest in Psiere. It is romanticized and built up, the citizens love it. We owe our very lives and way of life to whomever the mysterious people were that built the great temples and left them filled with schematics and devices. The Queen is hoping that the news of this great discovery will distract people and sway them to what the current government is doing for Psiere."

Tosh rubbed her forefinger across her lips in thought. "She's certainly not wrong. People love the mystery. I myself have always held a fascination for it and I follow the newest findings regularly."

Torrin laughed unexpectedly. "It was good fortune that put you in charge of Connate Dracore's Shield team then. I would have never thought to turn the team into a hybrid capable of not only protecting the sovereign but also assisting with her job as an adventurist. Well done, Tosh!" He clapped her on the shoulder and she took the praise with good humor.

Castellan inclined her head in his direction. "Thank you, ser."

"None of that, Tosh. We're on a level now. Both of us are in charge of sovereigns and technically equals in power, despite our disparate ranks."

"Be that as it may, your experience deserves my respect, ser."

Gen. Renou watched the two officers interact and was impressed by the words and sentiment coming from both. She had always suspected that Tosh would be a great Shield addition, and truthfully wanted her straight out of Academy. But due to some stupid bet with Leniste, she lost out on the initiative to recruit the intelligent and highly channeled woman. "Anyway, we've gotten a bit off track. As I was saying, Kensata's prescient episode was triggered by the announcement. We've had experts breaking down the lines in an effort to glean more details. 'In the darkness of the eighth lune, the blood of many will run while the cathedra sits empty. Two will falter while only one can heal. A new star will shine in the Psiere sky.' What does that mean to you?"

"Eighth? Octobra is next lune, ser."

"I'm well aware of how soon it is, Captain Torrin. Though we all know that sometimes the precision of such things cannot be trusted. And the rest, any clues?"

Tosh had a thought. "Ser, it sounds like a tragedy in the making. The blood of many...but beside that, I believe it will occur when the Queen is not performing official business. Perhaps in the evening?"

Renou nodded. "Ah yes, 'while the cathedra sits empty' seemed to indicate that to my eyes as well."

Capt. Torrin shifted nervously. "The last bit seems ominous, as though two people will be injured and only one will be healed. As much as it pains me to say it, the new star in the Psiere sky could refer to the Connate assuming the mantle of Queen."

Tosh froze as a wave of dread swept through her. The idea of something happening to the Queen or Olivienne made her blood run cold. Her thoughts raced as she said the first thing that came to mind. "Our oathing ceremony is this lune, as well as our weke long holidae after. Whatever is to occur will do so after we return, and shortly before we are set to embark on the adventurist mission seeking the Temple of Antaeus."

"Is there a ceremony planned for the start of this mission?" Torrin wasn't as up on the schedule of Olivienne's adventurist career so didn't know exactly what was planned for the mission to come.

"No, we were hoping to keep it a quiet affair. Unless that's changed?" She turned to Renou with the question.

"To my knowledge, no. The Queen wants to keep the details as top security as possible. So while the discovery of the third great temple was made public knowledge, she wants the mission itself to operate in the black. We don't need a repeat of what happened down on Navis."

Tosh sat forward in her chair. "Speaking of that, do you think the prescient event to occur could be another attack, similar to what happened to us there? The opposition already got their hands on one of the black dirigibles, it's possible they could get more through their sources. If Havington, Gannon, and their goons are determined, I'd look for another attack either in the air or on the ground."

Torrin laughed. "In Tesseron? They'd have to be mad! Our security in the city is top notch because of it being the main seat for all corps as well as Psiere's governing body. I don't think they'd sacrifice people like that."

"Sacrifice people...that's it!" Castellan slapped the arm of her chair. "They won't sacrifice people at all. Tesseron is a port city, just as Ostium is."

Renou knew exactly what she was referring to. "But Tesseron has never had a problem with prolonged attacks by the Atlanteens the way Ostium does. I'm not even sure we've ever seen some of the larger species they use this far north."

Tosh rubbed her temples, hating the thought that Atlanteen troubles would follow her so far from Dromea. "That's exactly why it would be a disaster. Tesseron is relatively unprepared compared to some of the southern cities, especially Ostium. They've always seen attacks from the deep. But Tesseron was built differently. There are no walled beaches, the ports and docks are open to whatever denizens should happen to come crawling up. Bindle Bay is an unprotected beauty just waiting to be despoiled by the Atlanteens and whatever matter of sea bug they send."

The General was quick to correct her. "We do have protections, Tosh. Defense Corp has stations and rail guns situated all the way around the bay within five mahls of the actual port."

"What about automatons or physical barriers? The residential districts are practically built right up to the water around Bindle Bay. My apologies for overstepping, General, but I know the Atlanteens and I know what it's like to be on the front lines against the creatures they send up from the deep."

Renou narrowed her eyes. "Is this your gut talking or your channel?"

Castellan pursed her lips. "I'd say it's a bit of both. My intuition works best when I'm closer to whatever is occurring, be it a person, a thing, or an event. But combined with my experience in dealing with the Atlanteens, I really think this is what we have to fear, ser."

"Very well. I will send a missive to General Leniste instructing him to have patrols increased as well as formulate a plan of engagement in case there is an attack en masse." She sighed and leaned back in her chair. "As for now, I believe your Shield teams are already running on high alert status. What I will do is increase unassigned Shield presence around the city, specifically near the royal residence and the Imperium campus." She stood and the other two followed. "As always, keep your sovereigns safe. You're dismissed."

Both gave Gen. Renou a crisp salute and spoke in tandem,

"Yes, ser!" before exiting the office.

Once outside in the corridor the two officers walked side by side. Torrin spoke unexpectedly, startling Tosh. "I don't know how you do it."

"Ser?"

He stopped in the middle of the empty hall. "I don't know how you can lead a Shield team to protect the one you love, knowing she is at risk every meen of every dae."

Castellan shook her head. "I thought so at first too but since taking over I've found it to be nearly the opposite. There isn't anything I wouldn't do or sacrifice to protect Olivienne Dracore. Any time we leave the residence I've got my full attention on her safety. It's true that she is the future heir to the Divine Cathedra and as such deserving of respect and protection. But more than that, she is my greatest love and I take my duty to keep her safe with the utmost seriousness."

"You don't find yourself torn between love and duty?"

"I haven't yet." Castellan smiled. "Between the two of us, I think you have the far harder assignment. Your responsibility is to keep the greatest person in all of Psiere safe. You too would lay down your life in an instant if it would mean the Queen's safety. I don't think the source of our love for the people under our protection makes as much difference as the depth of emotion. We care, that's all that matters."

Cpt. Torrin looked thoughtful for a few secs. "I suppose you have a point." They began walking again. With a side-glance to Cmdr. Tosh he admitted a bit more. "You know, I had reservations when I discovered they were bringing a lower level officer on board to head the Connate's Shield team. But I have to say that I think you're the best she's ever had and I'm glad to be serving with you in the Corp."

Tosh laughed. "Well I'm just glad that it was the Connate's team that needed a lead. I could never shoulder the load of protecting the Queen. Talk about nerve-wracking. The acid roils in my stomach just thinking of it!"

"Yes, well, pray to the Makers that you won't find out what it's like to protect the Queen for rotos to come."

She clapped him on the shoulder. "Too true!"

When they parted soon after, Castellan focused on the rest of what the dae would bring. It was their third and final oathing dinner, which would be held at the sovereign residence. Instead of eating with the entire family of one person or the other, the third oathing dinner was reserved for the future pars and their parens alone. Castellan would be lying if she said she had no worries about her intelligent and stubborn maman meeting with the Queen. But there was no changing the outcome of something so minor. At least the evening would be private. The following morning would bring the news of their oathing to the entirety of Psiere. And the event itself would happen in two wekes time, inside the grand chamber of the temple of Archeos.

Castellan remembered what the King had said two nights before and swallowed thickly as she pushed out into the suns' shine. "By the Makers, I hope I don't suffer a faint."

Chapter Four

CASSIENE TOSH SAT stiffly in her seat around a decent-sized round table within the Royal Palace of Psiere. It wasn't her location that was so off-putting, though admittedly it was much too grand for the Tosh matriarch. Rather it was the company. There were a mere two seats between her own and that of the Queen of Psiere, the person rumored to be the most beautiful woman in all the land. She glanced up again and grimaced before turning her gaze back to her soup. The rumors were certainly not off the mark. Tello Tosh was in an animated discussion with the King, so he was of no help for his uncomfortable par. It was actually Castellan who noticed her unease. She took in the tense set to her maman's shoulders and the slight crinkle between her brows as she precisely scooped broth into her mouth.

"Maman, is something wrong?"

The older woman glanced to her right and gave Castellan a smile that was more grimace than anything else, then answered before turning back to her soup. *"Nothing is wrong, dearest."* Since the question wasn't a deeper probe of information she could get away with a slight falsehood.

"I don't believe you."

Cassiene quickly glanced around the table then turned shrewd eyes on her daughter. *"Why ever not?"*

"You're wearing 'the face,' the one you always wore whenever Avia Tosh would start regaling us with stories of her stage daes. The very face that says you're not having a good time." The older Tosh woman sighed quietly, catching Olivienne's attention as well. Castellan noticed and gave a little shake of her head to prevent the sovereign from interfering.

"It's just that I feel so...inadequate sitting at this table."

Castellan wasn't used to seeing her maman less than bold and forthright. The older woman's admission took her aback. She reached over to cover her maman's hand with her own. Having caught Cassiene's gaze, she spoke calmly and resolutely mind to mind. *"You have never been inadequate. Never."*

Unknown to the Tosh women, their exchange wasn't as deep as they thought and the most powerful telepath in the room picked up part of it, as well as the emotional state of the two women. One of Queen Olivara's many talents was to use her channels to facilitate ease and comfort to those she dealt with. She could do more than read a person's emotional state with her empathy channel, she was also excellent at deciphering body language as well. She knew that sometimes people lost track of their own shine until she helped them to uncover that part which was brightest.

The table was set up so that Tello Tosh and the King were seated next to each other. Then continuing around the table at a right spin was Queen Olivara, Olivienne, Castellan, and finally Cassiene. The Queen spoke up between the soup and the next course. "You know, Psera Tosh, I believe we were at Academy at near the same time. It seems like a lifetime ago, doesn't it?"

Cassiene looked up, surprised that the Queen was speaking to her, and on a more personal topic. "My Queen?"

Olivara waved a hand through the air in dismissal. "Oh, none of that. We are about to become family through our daughters. Within the privacy of our family gatherings you may refer to me as Olivara."

The other woman looked aghast. "Oh no, I mustn't!"

"Please?" The Queen wasn't above turning up the charm with a smile and emotional nudge.

"Oh, um, very well. But only if you call me Cassiene. It is my honor. And to answer your question, I believe I was a few rotos ahead of you."

"Yes, I remember now. But you were only there a roto before graduating early. It was the talk of the Academy, because psi rarely graduate early. You were the one who solved Dreason's Equation!"

Cassiene colored at the Queen's words. "Oh, it wasn't much, my Quee—er, Olivara." She quickly amended her address with a squint from the sovereign.

"Not much? My love, you are being modest now." Tello gently grasped his par's left hand. "She didn't just graduate a roto early. She earned the highest proficiency scores across the divisions that the old Academy head had ever seen."

Castellan smiled and joined the conversation. "It's true. I was told during my time there that I came the closest but just missed beating her record by two points."

Cassiene Tosh looked at her daughter fondly. "You were still top of your class, darling. Not to mention you were an entire roto younger than I was when you graduated. You just advanced earlier is all."

The King's loud voice added to the rest. "Simply brilliant! Clearly Commander Tosh's intellectual proficiency comes from a superior source. I can't think of a better addition to the family."

After that, the conversation took on a more natural flow as the Queen and Castellan's mother engaged in conversation that ranged from children to Cassiene's thoughts on various official policies. When dinner was nearly complete, Olivienne looked at her future par. Her words were for Castellan only. *"I think that went well. Don't you?"*

"I'll admit, I was a little concerned with how stiff Maman was being but the Queen turned her right around. Your maman still amazes and intimidates me."

Olivienne rolled her eyes but smiled. *"By the depths, don't ever tell her that or she'll be impossible to be around!"* They both laughed and quieted again at everyone else's curious looks.

THE DAE OF the oathing ceremony arrived early for Castellan Tosh. It wasn't nerves that had her up and about before the first sunrise. It was an official missive from General Renou that pulled her from her warm bed and Olivienne's embrace. Her lover was most displeased but knew that Tosh had a duty to perform and whatever news it was would concern Olivienne's own safety.

"Return swiftly, my love."

Castellan finished straightening her black uniform and slipped her pistol into the holster. Then with a little grin, she gave the reclining woman a jaunty salute with her hand flourishing at chest level. "Yes, ser."

Olivienne apported the pistol into her own hand, knowing it would draw Castellan across the room one last time. "You're forgetting something."

The officer crossed the room in five long strides. "I've forgotten nothing." Castellan leaned in and gave Olivienne a deeply tender kiss before sliding the pistol from her hand and holstering it once again. "I'll be back as soon as I'm able. Until then, contact Savon if anything comes up."

Olivienne gave her own smirk and saluted. "Yes, ser." She continued to stare at the door for a few meens after Castellan left, then gave a great sigh and pulled herself from beneath the coverlets. "I may as well get up now as there will be no sleep in a bed gone cold." The ceremony wasn't scheduled until fifteen hundred oors so she dressed in comfortable clothing with the intention of getting a bit of exercise until Castellan returned. She thought about the ceremony to come and snickered to herself. "I hope she doesn't suffer a faint."

Across the city in General Renou's office, Castellan was surprised to see not only Captain Torrin, but the Queen herself. She gave a quick salute to all, and bowed to the Queen. "My Queen! General, Captain. What news?"

Renou waved toward the one free chair. "Have a seat Tosh. We had another prediction, a clairvoyant one about todae's ceremony."

"Was it Kensata again, ser?"

The short, gray-haired general shook her head. "No. It was one of the interpretists working at the temple. She also has a four rating clairvoyant channel and happened to arrive early todae. As she opened the main door into the temple, she got a premonition of pistol fire and screaming. She reported it to her superiors right away and they called me."

The Queen sat forward in her seat. "What is your plan, General?"

"I've initiated a sweep of all the public rooms in the temple. As you know, many areas are locked and require a high security level to access so I thought we would be safe to search only the public areas. I've made sure each team searching has either a prescient channel or clairvoyant channel specialist with them. My other suggestion is to close the ceremony to all but immediate family, Corp heads, and a few well-vetted broadsheet representatives. That way the news will still go out with the appropriate stills for the public."

Queen Olivara pondered the changed plans for a meen. "And what of the traditional weke long oathing trip? I want to be sure my daughter is safe and secure."

Cpt. Torrin laughed and when three pairs of eyes turned his way, he quickly explained himself to the group. "My apologies, but I'm having a hard time imagining the Connate sitting someplace safe and cozy for an entire weke."

Olivara sighed. "It's true. Olivienne doesn't idle well."

"My Queen, if I may?"

"Go ahead, Commander."

"I thought of the Connate's safety when I arranged our trip.

Rather than head to a traditional holidae location, I arranged a short adventurist mission on the Island of Instrucia. No one is aware of our destination save my team and all supplies have been checked by clairvoyants and canid teams before locking it securely away, to be sure no tampering has taken place."

"An adventurist mission you say?"

"Yes, General. There was a secure translation that came in from Interpretist Cadentia that she had flagged as interesting. It mentions the Temple of Antaeus, but also speaks of a cave or system of caves in the forested hills, north of Scola. While there are no coordinates for the cave, there were landmarks listed that I've cross-referenced with local maps of the island. Not only will the Connate be safe and isolated from potential ill-wishers, but she'll also be happy doing what she loves."

Torrin remained silent while General Renou sat back with a thoughtful look on her face. It was the Queen who actually commented on the plan. "That doesn't sound like much of a holidae to celebrate your oathing, Commander."

Castellan colored slightly. "While I was the one to set the plan in motion, I left the planning and security of it to my lieutenants. And to be completely honest," she glanced around the small office, "I enjoy the adventurist parts of our missions. As does my team. I think it will be a welcome break for all of us from the hyper-vigilant security we've maintained the past few wekes in the capital."

Renou rapped her knuckles on the top of her desk. "Very well then, as long as the Queen approves..." She glanced toward their sovereign.

"And she does."

"Then I'd say you're all set to go. Now you just need to make it through your Oathing Ceremony, Tosh."

Castellan swallowed nervously. "I'll try my best, ser."

They all laughed as they stood and three of them made their way out of the office.

THE GRAND CHAMBER, of both the Temple of Archeos and the Temple of Illeos, is comprised of the entire top level of the pyramid. Rather than be of solid construct, the pyramidion was an immense hollow room full of the suns' light. The initial vertical walls rose above the floor ten foot, and large windows were spaced evenly all the way around the interior at the same ten foot height.

The rest of the chamber was open until it met at a point, twenty yords above. The only design to break the surface of the pyramidion were giant skylights set into each of the four sloped sides. Each skylight was in the shape of an eight-pointed star. The longest points of the star, vertical and horizontal, were nearly thirty foot in length so the design was both beautiful and let in plenty of illumination during daelight oors.

While the majority of the great pyramids were comprised of basic Psierian materials, such as quarried stone and known composite materials, no one knew what the pyramidion was made from that allowed it to hold up for centuries under the immense weight with no supports beneath save the windowed walls.

The chamber itself was fairly bare inside. The only real thing to note was a large raised dais and altar in the very center. It resembled a much smaller version of the great pyramids with its stepped side, only the dais featured a flat top six-foot square. The altar in the center of the dais was a composite pedestal, with two smooth hand-shaped indentions. The altar, nicknamed the Sovereign Stone, was part of every major ceremony involving the rulers of Psiere.

When a female heir reached the age of adulthood, there was a ceremony to declare her a sovereign in her own right. The Queen and heir would both touch their hands to the indentions in the Sovereign Stone, while standing high above the gathered people in attendance. Each woman would feel a prick to their palm, then the space around their palm would glow so bright that neither woman could stare down. It was a simple exchange and as soon as the glow faded, the ceremony was complete. When a sovereign became Queen, there were two pricks to her palm.

It was not quite the same for oathing and consorage ceremonies. Those circumstances differed in that it would be the sovereign on one side and their future par on the other. At least the technical aspects were the same. However, each ceremony had its own unique dialogue, used for the length of Psierian recorded history. Phrases spoken by the head templar, and answered by the bonding pair in return.

Unfortunately for Castellan Tosh, she had forgotten her response. Olivienne watched as her commander grew pale and sweat formed upon Castellan's upper lip. The smallish crowd waited below but still Tosh froze.

Olivienne smiled. *"Have you forgotten your lines, darling?"*

Castellan's pale brow drew down. *"I may not have enhanced*

memory, but I am a level six intellect. I am surely capable of remembering a few lines of text." She paused her mental rant then sighed. *"Bollux. I've forgotten."*

At the realization, Castellan grew paler yet and Olivienne feared her par-to-be really would suffer a faint. She gave a mental push to the other woman to break her concentration. When Castellan's blue gaze met her own she prompted. *"In the dawn of daes, and deepest night. Six stars to the north and four to the right..."* She trailed off as Castellan repeated her words and filled in the rest.

"In the dawn of daes, and deepest of night. Six stars to the north and four to the right. We are all travelers and companions, seekers and sibs on another plane. In this life I pledge to you that my course will be steady and steerage firm. I oath to you, and give you my loyalty, honor, and truth, until that dae when we return to the temple's light and become bonded in full."

Templar Zane Aislyn smiled at the two women before her. "By the Makers will, and within the great temple of Archeos, when next the stars align you will be joined into a permanent bonding that can only be held by a sovereign and their par. Consentisne?"

Olivienne and Castellan answered as nearly the same voice. "Assentior." With that single word the gathered people in attendance let out a great cheer. As soon as the Connate and commander stepped off the dais they embraced and gave each other cheek kisses, as dictated by tradition and propriety. Lines of well-wishers congratulated them under the keen gazes of not one but four sovereign guardian units. Unlike the Queen, King, and sub-Connate, all of Olivienne's team was in attendance. Castellan asked for the special allowance from General Renou. She also assigned additional non-sovereign Shield Corp guardians to the Connate's residence and transportation they would be taking up to the island of Instrucia.

They had originally considered overnighting at the residence before boarding the railer early the next dae but after the issues broached that morning, both Renou and the Queen decided it was safest for them to head out straightaway after the ceremony. After sharing the joy of oathing with friends and family, the newly promised couple stood for the traditional interview and photography session. The official royal photos had been taken prior to the ceremony.

Olivienne was the first to get a question from the gathered broadsheet representatives. "Connate Dracore, can you tell us the destination of your oathing trip?"

The sovereign smiled and winked at the questioner. "I'm afraid that even if I knew the location, security would dictate that I couldn't tell you. However, I can admit I was assured that wherever we end up, I'll be doing what I love most." She spared a mischievous glance at Castellan.

Every broadrep in attendance laughed at her innuendo and Castellan flushed. "Commander Tosh, what does the Queen think about you flaunting official protocol to dally with Connate Dracore? Didn't your relationship pose a conflict of interest?"

Castellan frowned at the unexpectedly serious question and Olivienne gave her hand a squeeze. "As much as I hate to air my personal business — "

The broadrep interrupted. "Begging your pardon, Commander, but your personal business became public when you entered into a relationship with one of the sovereigns of Psiere."

Tosh grimaced. "So it did. To answer your question then, we initially met before I took over Connate Dracore's Shield Corp unit and my relationship had the approval of both General Renou and Queen Olivara."

As soon as Castellan finished speaking, she felt a firm hand settle onto her shoulder and saw the Queen out of the corner of her eye. "Actually, if I may correct Commander Tosh ever so slightly, the relationship was not approved by me — " Gasps went through the crowd until the Queen continued speaking. "I'm not sure if you've heard, but I'm an excellent judge of character and I know a good match for my daughter when I see one. So I didn't merely approve the relationship, I highly encouraged it." Quite a few people in attendance laughed at her subtle rebuke of the broadrep and Olivara looked around. "Now, in the interest of moving things along and letting the newly oathed couple begin their trip, they'll answer one more question. You there, in the back." The Queen pointed at one woman near the back of the small gathering of broadsheet representatives.

"Thank you, my Queen." The broadrep saluted her sovereign, then addressed Olivienne and Castellan. "Connate Dracore, with Commander Tosh to be the future King, and you the Queen, it seems quite dangerous to be running around on adventurist missions. Will either of you switch Corps or professions now that you've oathed?"

Olivienne smiled at her phrasing, though inside she seethed at the continued idea that sovereigns should settle in and be swaddled throughout their lives. "Neither one of us will change Corp or profession at this time, nor for the foreseeable future. But tomorrow isn't written in stone, my friends, only yesterdae. So Makers know what is in store for us." She glanced around, meeting the eyes of various people in attendance. Her sib grinned and made a genuflection of respect. Castellan's maman wiped tears even as Castellan's papan winked at both her and Castellan. She took a deep breath and let it out. "Now, if there are no other questions I'd rather like to board a railer and celebrate my oathing to the most amazing psi I've ever met."

A few snickers from the crowd met her words, and Castellan's youngest sib called out, "Don't break your Shield Guardian on the first dae...she's in charge of your safety!"

Castellan's face turned red even as Olivienne shook her head and wagged her finger at Tessior. "You're lucky that I'm taking your sib far away from Tesseron the instant we step out of the temple. Else she'd be sure to show you exactly why Shield Corp is the top line of defense for sovereigns." The entire chamber broke out in laughter and Tellesen gave a chuck to his sib's shoulder to stop him from speaking more.

As they were getting ready to make their way from the Grand Chamber, a group of musicians began playing the "March of the Sovereigns." It was a rousing musical composition that made heavy use of both horns and drums. The scene painted for all, especially the broadsheet representatives, was one of celebration, security, and competency. Every broadrep in attendance would go back to their broadsheets and report on the romance and unity of the sovereigns of Psiere, further pushing the agenda that all was well. The Queen was a wily one and knew that the oathing ceremony would tap into the nostalgia that people adored when it came to tales of love. She hoped it would be enough to turn the tides back on some of the anti-sovereign factions that were causing unrest across the continents.

"YOU KNOW, I initially wanted to begin our trip on my cycle, or a pair of them." Rather than a traditional officer's two-room segment like the one they initially met on, the Connate and her future par were given the deluxe model that featured a seating area and single large sleeping room, with a small sheltered deck at the very end of the railer. Castellan and Olivienne stood outside watching the city disappear into the distance. Arms around each other, they held glasses of portea in their free hands.

"That may have been interesting for the first hundred mahls or so, but ultimately much too far away from you for my tastes. We are oathed now, and within a span of one roto we will consor."

Castellan pulled the glass away from her mouth to give Olivienne a look of adoration. "One roto seems too long yet strangely not long enough."

Silence continued minus the clacking of the railer wheels on the tracks. Then Olivienne turned so she was facing her future par. "The ceremony will likely have a lot more people than todae's. I hope you're okay with that."

Castellan turned as well. "I'm okay with anything that allows me to spend the rest of my life with you. 'Vienne..." She stopped to think for a sec while Olivienne looked on. Then Castellan found her words. "Loving you is an adventure that I never grow tired from."

Olivienne smiled and her eyes narrowed playfully as she drained the remainder of her portea. "You know what *I* never grow tired of?"

Intimately familiar with all of Olivienne's looks, Castellan quickly drained her own glass. "I think I can guess." Suddenly both glasses floated out of their grip with the smallest exercise of Castellan's telekinesis, then she quickly bent down and picked up her lover. Olivienne wrapped her legs around Tosh's waist as she was carried through the door back into their room. Castellan set the glasses on a special tray and continued moving to where the bed lay freshly made.

Olivienne laughed delightedly as she was delicately lowered onto the coverlets. "We're going to miss evening meal."

"Says who?"

"Me if I have my way."

Castellan chuckled as she straightened and began unbuttoning the shirt of her oathing outfit. "Well, I say your way sounds absolutely divine and well worth a little hunger."

She made it as far as four buttons before Olivienne lost her patience and apported away all their clothes. When Castellan raised a pale brow in question, Olivienne explained, "We have better things to be doing than dressing and undressing. Now be a good soldier and come here."

"But the wait is half the fun."

Olivienne leveled a playful look at her. "Don't make me come off this bed to fetch you, Tosh."

With a smile, Castellan complied and floated up into the air, then over the bed. Grabbing the levitating woman's hand, Olivienne reeled her in until Castellan could settle her nude body between Olivienne's legs. Both women moaned as their skin pressed together. Olivienne's distraction only lasted for a sec before she threaded her fingers through Castellan's hair and pulled her into a deep and passionate kiss. When they finally broke for air, Castellan remarked, "I'm starting to appreciate the appeal of impatience."

"Perhaps that's why you love me so much."

Castellan placed smaller kisses at the corners of Olivienne's mouth, working her way down her neck, all the while dropping words as she went. "Mayhap I can think of hundreds of reasons why I love you more." She moved lower yet. "Any Psierian can be impatient, but only one holds my heart."

"I'd like to think I hold more than your—oh!" Olivienne gasped as her commander's lips pulled upon a hard nipple.

"What was that?" Castellan had released the nipple and continued to explore. Her lips met the flesh of Olivienne's breastbone and smiled at the wetness that painted her own stomach from Olivienne's excitement. She left a trail of kisses as she moved lower yet and Olivienne gripped Castellan's hair in anticipation. The sovereign knew what was to come and wanted it with every shred of her being.

Castellan continued down Olivienne's body until she was faced with all her womanly glory. She caressed Olivienne's quim with her full hand and let the palm put a bit of pressure against her clit. Olivienne moaned incoherently and thrust upward against Castellan's hand. "Darling, please!"

"You know, I once heard someone say that patience was reward in and of itself."

Olivienne opened her eyes wide and gripped Castellan's hair tighter causing the soldier to hiss. Seeing she had Castellan's full attention, Olivienne spoke in a low voice. "Whoever said that was a Maker-forsaken liar!"

Castellan winked back at her, turned on more than she could ever believe by Olivienne's tight grip and her obvious desperation. "Oh, I completely agree."

"Then what are—" Her words were cut off with another gasp as Castellan lowered her mouth and put her tongue to better use than merely spouting pointless proverbs. Some acts were reward enough.

Oors later, spent and starving, Olivienne lay in bed and marveled at how lucky she had gotten with such a noble and dashing companion as her commander. Tosh lay next to Olivienne, catching her breath from the last round of tupping. Suddenly from naught but the aether, Castellan laughed aloud, startling her future par.

Olivienne looked at her and gently smoothed the blonde hairs out of Tosh's eyes. "What is it? What's so funny?"

"You were right."

"About?"

Castellan's stomach rumbled loudly from the late oor and its own emptiness. "We missed evening meal."

Olivienne smiled fondly as she caressed the smooth expanse of Castellan's yowling belly. "I'm sure we can find you something." She sat up abruptly and apported the clothing back to the bed. "Come on. And while we eat you can tell me what we'll actually be doing on our oathing holidae. Are we going to Baen?"

Castellan grinned at how well Olivienne had kept her curiosity in check. The trip was meant to be a surprise, after all. "Actually, we're heading for the Island of Instrucia. We have a small adventurist mission with a treasure or information that supposedly concerns the lost temple." At Olivienne's gobsmacked look, she grew nervous. "I'm sorry if you would have rather done something else. I just thought that—" Her speech was cut off by a kiss.

When Olivienne pulled away, she smiled and tenderly caressed Castellan's cheek. "I know I've said it before but I'm just going to tell you again. You're perfect."

Castellan's stomach chose that moment to make itself known again and the commander blushed. She grabbed it in mock outrage. "Perfectly hungry is more like." She held out her elbow to Olivienne. "Shall we go see what the dining seg has to offer at this late oor?"

"Absolutely."

Just before they walked out of the room, Castellan pulled her to a stop. She cradled Olivienne's face between both her hands. "I just want you to know, in case I don't tell you often enough, you're the best thing that's happened to me and I love you."

"I love you too, darling. Now, let's go feed that beast of yours, Commander."

Tosh grinned. "Yes, ser."

Chapter Five

THE RAILER ARRIVED at the Instrucia switching station just past twenty-three hundred oors. The eastbound railer was primarily scheduled for a thirty meen stop to allow for passengers embarking and disembarking, but it was also necessary to de-couple the luxury segment so it could be stored at the station for the Connate's return trip.

The dirigible shipyard was within walking distance, which Castellan was glad for. Her oathing ceremony on top of the early meeting with the Queen, Gen. Renou, and Cpt. Torrin meant that it had been a long dae already, with many oors yet to travel. Olivienne turned toward the gates for the public sector dirigible. Despite the late oor, there were quite a few people headed to the platform for the overnight trip. Castellan quickly guided her in the opposite direction.

"We're over here."

Olivienne peered into the dark sky ahead of them but could only make out a slightly darker mass. "Are we not taking the general transport? It's only two and half oors across the Straights of Madrasa to get to the railer station on the other side. We can sleep on the railer up to Scola. Why the special conveyance?"

Castellan called to her first lieutenant who led the group down the cobbled walkway. "Savon? Can you give Connate Dracore the details? I only told her that our oathing trip was to be an adventurist mission, but naught all else."

He glanced back with a raised brow. "But ser, you told me in no uncertain terms that it was all your surprise to tell."

Castellan's smirk was barely visible in the evening light of the station. "Well, Lieutenant, it seems we were too busy on the railer for much conversation. Now if you please..."

Lt. Madlin gave a snort as she tried to hold back laughter but quieted quickly as Savon spoke. "Connate Dracore, we have chartered with Captain Velten to take us directly to the mission location. She and her crew will stay with us throughout until they drop us back here in five dae's time. We have maps of the area and a vellum of interpreted text that seems fairly straight forward as to the location of the Maker's cache."

They got their first good view of the transport as they climbed the steps leading to the loading platform. Olivienne craned her head back just as spotlights came on to light the platform and starboard side of the massive ship. "That doesn't look like Velten's dirigible."

Every Shield member immediately drew sidearms until Velten herself stepped off the gangplank and approached the group. She wore a smile as she bowed deeply to the sovereign. "Ah, Connate Dracore and Commander Tosh, right on time. I hear congratulations are in order!"

Olivienne smiled as the rest of the team relaxed. "Indeed they are, Captain. I see a few things have changed for you as well since we last met." She gestured above them to the new, and larger, ship.

"Oh yes, that is a story in and of itself but that can wait until morning. Why don't you and your team bring your gear aboard and get settled in your cabins. I'm sure you're all tired from the dae's events. Perhaps we can speak of all our changes and the coming mission over breakfast tomorrow? Say, zero nine hundred?"

"That sounds like a wonderful plan. Castellan?" Olivienne called to her commander, who was busy instructing the Shield team.

Castellan turned toward the conversing women at the sound of her name. "Actually, Captain, not to start this trip on such a serious note, but we've had some security protocol changes since my lieutenant spoke with you regarding the charter. Per direction from the Queen, we need to inspect the entire dirigible before the Connate can board. The alternative would be for the captain, you, to subject yourself to a trust reading."

Velten's eyes widened enough for Castellan and Olivienne to notice even in the limited lights of the platform. "Have things gotten so bad then?"

"I'm afraid so. General Renou's second in command himself verified the railer pilot before the trip north. So...your answer?"

The captain, with the sternly braided white-blonde hair straightened and immediately saluted Castellan. Her attitude was a vast improvement over the woman they met on their trip to the Isle of Navis. Back then she was a brilliant captain but also a disgruntled officer who resented the fact that a mere commander outranked her aboard her own ship. Despite being so put out, she managed to defend them when they needed it, thus earning the utmost respect from the Connate and her Shield team. "Commander Tosh, I submit to a trust reading with you."

Trust readings were a deeper connection than the more casual types of telepathy and neither person would be able to lie to the other, so the trust had to go both ways. "Thank you, Captain."

Castellan held out her hand to clasp with the captain's then gave the officer a mental nudge before posing her questions. *"Captain Seema Velten, who holds your pledge of service?"*

The captain's response was quick and sure. *"Queen Olivara Dracore."*

"Who is your direct report?"

"Previously Defense Corp, newly commissioned to Shield Corp, directly reporting to General Renou."

Castellan made a little grunt of surprise. *"Oh?"*

Velten smiled but continued speaking mind to mind. *"Yes, ser. After your personal report on the incident at Navis, the Queen herself requested that I and my crew switch Corps to work with Connate Dracore on the next mission. Something to do with security clearance, I imagine."*

While switching Corps wasn't out of the ordinary for individuals across a wide variety of careers, it was unheard of to convince a ship's captain and entire crew to switch. *"And you all changed Corps, just like that?"*

The captain's smile grew. *"Well, my crew and I are a bit mercenary at times and extremely tight knit. It doesn't hurt that we were also promised the finest ship to ever come out of Soflin. And I must say, the Queen certainly delivered on that promise."*

Castellan physically twitched as she came out of the deep communication, then smiled and pulled her hand away while speaking aloud for the rest to hear. "Well then, Captain, I look forward to many journeys with you and your crew."

"Same. Now if you'll all follow me, my chief mate can get you squared away in your cabins. As you can see, we have plenty of room for everyone and their gear."

THE CONNATE, COMMANDER, and captain all shared a table at zero nine hundred oors the next morning. The dirigible was about a third larger than the craft Velten previously commanded and the dining hall was significantly nicer. They enjoyed first meal as the captain told them of all the new ship's improvements that could aid in their missions.

"Apparently the notes from your previous adventurist trips were heeded closely and this vessel is equipped with not just an impenetrable bladder, but flame resistant materials all around. That includes the lines holding bladder to gondola."

Castellan smiled at that. "That's wonderful news! Now let's hope that the anti-sovereign faction doesn't acquire the same. What of equipment? Anything new on that front?"

Seema Velten smiled, proud of her freshly commissioned vessel as any new paren. "As a matter of fact, we have upgraded telemetry systems and have onboard a super-range voteo that can connect with nearly any city via signal jump."

Olivienne was intrigued. "Signal jump?"

"Oh yes! I'm aware that the two of you have been quite busy over the past roto but the Engineering Corp has been constructing signal stations around the two continents. They are able to receive wireless voteo signals and send them off to the next station toward their signal's destination." She shrugged. "Don't ask me how it all works, I'm just a simple captain after all."

Castellan laughed and shook a finger. "Oh ho! Captain yes, but never simple. I've read the reports of your career since our last encounter. You are highly decorated, as is your crew. I'm not surprised that Renou scooped you up. Now, what other wonders does your new vessel hold?"

They were interrupted briefly by the captain's voteo. "Captain, we've arrived at the conflux where Mir Pusilli meets with Mir Cognitia."

Captain Velten set her eating utensil down and smiled at her guests. "Connate, Commander, where to from here?"

Olivienne returned the smile. "Truthfully, I only just got to study the translated text this morning. It is vague, as all Maker's poetic texts are known to be. But I believe we should follow the Mir Pusilli to its origination point."

Velten cocked her head. "May I ask what the text says?"

"Sure, Tosh?"

Castellan nodded and pulled a folded vellum from the pouch that rested at her left thigh. She carefully unfolded it and pushed it as flat as possible against the table, then began to read. "Near the sanctuary of learning, the mother gives birth. The smallest child of earth, a name she is earning. Where the greatest step lay churning, there is a place of stone dearth. With a curtain concealing worth, a place for which the seeker is yearning. Beware of the lake, which hides the sun in the shimmering dark. Best not to slake, as the siren stuns, heed knowledge in the mark."

Seema Velten made a face. "Well that's not convoluted at all!"

Olivienne and Castellan both laughed but Olivienne was the one who answered her. "That is the nature of most of the Maker's texts, I'm afraid. Castellan and her Shield unit have already figured out that the beginning portion refers to Scola, and Mir Pusilli. It is the smallest river on Instrucia and the reference to giving birth led them to assume we need to head upstream to its origin."

"Well, I can't pretend to understand any of it but you've given me enough for now." Seema laughed. "The rest is for you adventurists to figure out. Let me take a moment to relay that to the navigator." The captain grabbed the voteo and responded. "Reduce speed to quarter full and follow the Mir Pusilli upstream until further notice."

"Aye-aye, Captain!"

Velten moved her intelligent gaze from the Connate to the commander. "Now, where were we?"

Castellan swallowed her bite and answered. "You were about to regale us with all the wonders of your new ship."

"Oh yes, that's right. Okay, to answer your question from before we were interrupted, the ship has a special storage room with standard adventurist gear. Now *our* ship, and our ship alone, also has increased illeostone storage and more powerful engines. While the new engines take more stones to run top speed, the one balances out the other so we still have a max range of fourteen hundred mahls per load. But," the captain winked at Tosh, "you asked me why we switched Corps so readily, well this is why...the new engines mean that the *Quaesitum* can run twenty mahls per oor faster than our old dirigible! No other captain in Psiere has such a powerful ship under their command."

"By the Makers! I thought such speeds were impossible because the pliable bladder material collapses with the wind shear? Wasn't it determined about thirty rotos ago that only rigid bladder ships could break the forty mahl per oor speed barrier and they proved too heavy for heliopus gas to lift?" Castellan had completely forgotten her meal with her surprise.

Olivienne nodded. "She's right. And while there are other, lighter, gases available, they are too unstable to be used safely."

"Truth is, the increased speed is all due to the new materials. Not only are they significantly stronger, but they are all a lot lighter. The new bladders withstand wind shear as well as they withstand fire and such. The engines have also been improved based on the redesigned cycle schematics of all things. Now *that* is an adventurist find that has legs. I wonder who was responsible."

Olivienne grinned proudly. "That was actually one of mine."

Castellan pointed at her. "That smile seems borderline disrespectful since I believe it was the very same set of schematics that led to your previous Shield team captain's medican discharge."

"But darling, it also brought us together. So, it's not all bad." Castellan flushed at the pet name that was said aloud in front of the captain. Velten smiled indulgently. She was about five rotos older than Tosh, and slightly jaded when it came to romance, but that didn't stop her from admiring a good match.

"I have to say that love looks good on you both. Well done! Now…if you're finished with your meals, and if you think we have time, I'd be happy to personally give you a tour of the ship before we head to the bridge."

Castellan nodded. "The Mir Pusilli is just under twenty mahls long from where it merges with Mir Cognitia to the point where it emerges from its underground beginnings.

The captain pulled a pocket watch from her waistcoat. "That puts us about eighty meens out from your destination so there is plenty of time. Unless you have preparations to make for the mission?"

Olivienne shook her head. "Actually, after reading through all the materials this morning, I'm up to speed now. Based on the text, we'll be looking for the largest waterfall along the river's length. According to the survey maps of the region, it is fairly close to the beginning. From there it will require basic searching for clues. Tosh was right, it does seem fairly cut and dry."

Castellan grunted. "Of course I'm right! I am a trained professional."

"You're not a professional adventurist, my love. But even I will admit that for a soldier, you make a mighty fine one."

"Oh be quiet you! Or I'll bribe the captain to tie you to the bow of the ship for the rest of the trip." All three women broke into laughter as they took care of their mess trays and left the dining hall.

TWO OORS LATER, at half past eleven hundred, the Connate and her Shield team stood in a clearing next to a small river. The dirigible floated twenty yords above and the entire team stood in its shadow. Instrucia was famous for its wild untamed tracts of forest and they were lucky to find a clearing large enough for the ship to fire its anchor line. Similar to the mission for the third key, all fourteen members of the group rode down the anchor line to the ground below. They were only a few hundred yords from where the beginning of the river was marked on the map. Unfortunately, it wasn't anything they could see from the air because of the dense treetops so they were going in fairly blind.

Each guardian carried a standard pack on their back, with the exception of Yazzie and Lazaro. Castellan chose Spc. Yazzie as the one to carry the medican pack for the Connate and team, with Spc. Holling carrying the smaller backup kit. The translated text specifically mentioned sirens and Specialist Gren Holling was one of the two animal empaths in the unit, as well as having a secondary specialty in animal biology. Tosh wanted Holling at the ready to deal with any non-Psierian threats that arose during the mission. While Spc. Lazaro and Spc. Penn were both in charge of team communications, Penn was also an interpretist so Tosh wanted her available for any quick translations that may be needed, which left the large long-range voteo on Lazaro's back.

They could hear the loud roar of Mir Pusilli, which seemed strange given its relatively small size. It was no more than three yords across where they stood, but the landscape meant it was swift-flowing and frothy with rapids. Unfortunately for the team, the prevalence of hills and rocky outcroppings, as well as a sharp bend in the river, made it so they couldn't actually see its source. Castellan called out orders. "The Connate is going to take the lead and I'll be with her. I want Qent and Lear on left wing with Dozier and Soleng on the right. Yazzie behind the Connate and the rest to fan out. Be wary of where you step. The entire island is made of layered soluble and insoluble rocks so caves and waterfalls are fairly common. You don't want to find a cave entrance on accident." She looked at Olivienne. "Anything else?"

Olivienne smiled as mission leadership was handed over smoothly. "Watch for anything out of the ordinary. It could be as obvious as a statue or carved post, or as subtle as a strangely bent tree." She motioned her hand in a circle. "If you could all humor me, I'd like you to do a three-sixty and look at the forest around you. If you see something that doesn't look like it belongs here or was unnaturally altered, immediately let me or Commander Tosh know."

The entire team saluted as one. "Yes, ser!"

They couldn't actually walk next to the river because it cut through a large rocky incline. Instead they opted to follow a game path that made its way up and over, watching as the river got farther away below them. It wasn't until they reached the bottom that they could see where the river hooked around toward another wall of rock that looked like a tiny cliff. Trees broke the skyline at the top but were unable to grow on the cliff face. The entire group stopped to look on in awe as they took in the splendor before them. The small river emerged from a hole about twenty yords up the rock surface and about five yords across. It tumbled down the cliff face in a cacophonous rush.

Lt. Madlin scowled. "We have to go up there? Doesn't look like much of an entrance."

"No actually." Castellan pulled the folded vellum from her pouch. "We are looking for the first large waterfall after the river's birth. Because we couldn't see the details of it from the air, we had a fifty-fifty chance at finding it whether we chose to head up or downriver."

Olivienne wiped the sweat that had formed on her brow with the exertion of their hike in full packs. "Sorry everyone, seems this was a wasted jaunt. We'll turn around and head the other way."

Spc. Lear laughed causing the rest to turn in her direction. "Begging your pardon, Connate, but I've traveled all over the two continents and this is one of the prettiest sights I've seen. It wasn't a wasted trip at all in my book."

The rest of the Shield team wholeheartedly agreed and Castellan grinned proudly at her future par. Olivienne smiled and discretely squeezed her commander's forearm. Her words were for Castellan's ears alone as she leaned close. "You did good work, Tosh. Thank you for putting this team together for me."

Cmdr. Tosh whispered back. "All part of my duty, ser. Just trying to keep my Connate happy."

"Well, if last night is anything to go by, you'll be due for a promotion in no time." Castellan flushed lightly but any response she may have had was interrupted by Lt. Savon.

"Sers, what are your orders?"

"Take a few stills of this," Olivienne waved her hand toward where the Mir Pusilli erupted from the land's gentle embrace, roaring like a newborn as the spray hit the light of the two suns. Glittering prisms floated in the mist, refracting every color back to their wide eyes. Spc. Leggett rushed to comply, though they all knew the recorded images could never compare with seeing such a beauty face to face. Once she was finished, they hiked back toward their original starting location.

Thirty meens later they passed the anchor point for the dirigible. Castellan had them voteo the ship and let them know the team was heading downstream. They went nearly an oor up and down the rocky outcroppings and over giant fallen trees as they followed the river. Castellan could have used her telekinesis to move the blockages but one of the main adventurist principles that she read about after taking command of the Connate's Shield team was to leave no trace. Because the missions often took historical adventurists out into the wild, they were taught to plan and prepare, minimize their impact on the environment, respect the land and wildlife, and leave no evidence of their passing if at all possible.

They were walking along a relatively calm stretch when they heard another great roar ahead of them. The entire group had been following yet another game trail that ran along the river merely a few yords from the rippling surface. They rounded a rocky outcropping, following the river as it disappeared around a bend and Olivienne, who had been in the lead, stopped abruptly. "Well then, I think we found what we were looking for."

Castellan peered around her shoulder at the drop-off only three foot in front of them. "Bollux! You could have gone right over!" The river traveled a bit farther along before dropping off to nothing, which was why they hadn't realized they were so near the waterfall, but the edge where they were walking had crumbled back, ending their trail abruptly.

"Nonsense. I would have done no such thing. I'm a professional, Commander, which is why I never barrel into places I can't see or out of them. Now if you would all kindly back up..."

Castellan gave a hand signal and the entire Shield team did an about face and marched back the way they came until they had an area large enough for them to regroup. When Olivienne joined them, she took off her pack and dropped it to the ground. "All right, we don't exactly have a good area to work with to anchor rappelling lines. I suppose we could backtrack farther and try to go around this big Maker-forsaken rock next to us to find a better way down. I don't know how long that will take though. And the river is much too swift and dangerous for any of us to cross at this point. Anyone have suggestions?"

"Seems like cheating a bit but the commander could just lift us all down!" The group all laughed at Yazzie's words.

Olivienne noticed that of the group, Spc. Dozier's gaze was intently focused above them and across the river. She had her own thoughts but Olivienne was really trying her best to comply with Castellan's request to encourage this strange mixed team of Shield guardians and amateur adventurists. "You have a thought, Dozier?"

Specialist Veva Dozier was only twenty-three rotos and one of the youngest members of the Shield team. But with a secondary degree as a historical adventurist and a specialty in caves and mountain training, Olivienne knew the psi would come up with something. "I believe so, Connate. While our path here doesn't have a good place to string lines, the other side of the river has large trees and a decent-sized staging area that runs right up to the drop off." She glanced up at the nearly vertical rock face next to them, then across to the other side. "I could climb the rock at our backs and shoot an anchor line across to the opposite rock face. Once we have a firm rope established we can use climbing harnesses and pulleys to make our way across. Then we can anchor another line and use that to get to the bottom of the falls." She looked nervously between her commander and the Connate.

Tosh wiped away any uncertainty the specialist had with a quick clap to the shoulder. "Excellent idea!" She looked toward the leader of their expedition. "Connate Dracore?"

Olivienne rolled her eyes at Tosh's formality. "Yes, I agree. All right, Dozier, make it happen. The rest of us will put on our harnesses while you take care of the crossing line." Dozier immediately stripped her pack and pulled out the harness so she could make the climb. The rest did the same a bit slower. Everything worked as expected and twenty meens later they were standing on the other side of the Mir Pusilli while Olivienne shot a second anchor into the rock face to tie off another line so they could rappel down to the base of the cliff. It was a damp decent but eventually they stood at the bottom and carefully picked their way across slick rocks so they had some distance between them and the spray near the pool at the bottom of the waterfall.

Castellan pulled out the folded vellum so she could consult with Olivienne. She read aloud the next relevant part. "Where the greatest step lay churning, there is a place of stone dearth. Like a curtain concealing worth, a place for which the seeker is yearning."

"Curtain concealing worth..." Olivienne glanced toward the fall, trying to peer into the darkness behind. "Could there be something behind it? Does it look like there is more water filling the pool than is coming from the river above?"

Tosh tried to see where Olivienne was pointing but it was too dark behind the fall of water. She glanced around until she spotted the person she wanted. "Specialist Qent!"

He jogged over. "Yes, ser."

"You've got the dowsing channel, right?"

Zed Qent was the other guardian with a secondary degree in adventurist training, and his specialty was with water training. "Yes, though it doesn't typically do me a lot of good. Pretty much useless ability, truth be told."

Castellan grinned at the stocky psi. "Not todae it isn't. Can you tell me if there are two streams converging here at the base of the falls? That would help us determine if there is a cave opening behind the water."

"Oh! Yes, ser, I can do that." He faced the waterfall and closed his eyes, then raised his arm to trace the water path with his pointer finger. "The greatest flow of water is coming from above, but you're right." He moved his finger down and pointed straight toward the rocky cliff. "There is a reservoir deep within, and a smaller stream that joins with the Mir Pusilli." He opened his eyes. "I'm afraid I can't tell you whether or not the stream has a passable path for the average psi, only that there is a stream that comes from deeper within the rock.

Castellan smiled at him. "Good enough, Specialist!" She looked at Olivienne. "What now?"

Olivienne sighed and grumbled. "Now we're going to get wet."

Castellan shook her head. "If our guess is right, there will be a cave behind the falls and the way will be cold and damp. Not the best place to be traipsing around in a wet uniform and boots so maybe we should limit it as much as possible." She glanced around until she spotted a large flat stone that was at least a yord across and two yords long. It would be heavy but well within her improved telekinetic limit. "I think I have a better idea." She carefully lifted the large stone until it floated just over two yords above the ground, then moved it steadily underneath the water-fall causing the spray to bounce off and around. Tosh grunted at the added weight of water pounding onto the stone. It was cer-tainly a testament to her greatly increased capacity that she could perform such a feat at all and the rest of the group stood in awe of their commander.

"By the Makers, there it is!" Olivienne pointed at the large opening that had previously been hidden by the "curtain" of the waterfall.

Theory confirmed, Castellan moved the stone and set it aside then turned back to Olivienne. "Before we head in to check it out, let's decide how to split the team. What sort of support will you need inside?"

The Connate glanced around at her Shield team. "I want Penn with us for her interpretist skills, and Qent and Dozier as our other trained adventurists. I'll leave the rest up to you."

Tosh nodded and called out her orders. "First thing, we're going to eat and drink something. Take a thirty meen rest then the following people will accompany us into the cave—Penn, Qent, Dozier, Savon, Yazzie, Holling, and Calderon. I want the rest of you to set up a quick camp out here. Madlin, you're in charge of the secondary group. If anything goes wrong, you've got two people with salvo and rescue training, so make use of Specialist Devin and Specialist Meza's skills, savvy?"

Madlin gave her a quick salute. "Yes, ser!"

Half an oor later the team had rested and eaten a meal of rations. Castellan had Spc. Lazaro send another update to their contact aboard the *Quaesitum*. If something went sideways with both teams, Captain Velten needed to know where the Connate was and the details of her endeavor. When the cave team was geared up once again and ready to go, Castellan addressed them all. "Is everyone ready?"

A chorus of, "Yes, ser!" was the collective response.

Castellan quickly lifted the stone back into place and held it effortlessly. "After you, Connate Dracore."

With a mischievous glint in her eyes, Olivienne quickly leaned close and kissed Tosh on the lips. "You amaze me, Com-mander."

The stone wobbled as Castellan blushed at the compliment as well as the unprofessional kiss while in front of her Shield team. She valiantly tried to recover by steadying the stone and clearing what she knew to be a lovesick look from her face. "Erm, okay then. Let's be off, shall we?"

The entire group laughed at the interaction but Lt. Madlin was the only one brave enough to comment. "Connate Dracore, best not kiss her again until you're into the cave proper. The next time she may drop the stone entirely."

Tosh sputtered. "I would never!"

Olivienne patted her arm reassuringly. "I know, darling." But even as she said the words, she turned to wink at Madlin. More snickering followed as the Connate's group picked their way carefully across the slippery stones to where the opening was located. Once they were all inside, Tosh set the large stone off to the side of the cave opening so Lt. Madlin's team could still get in if they needed to. They'd be wet, but the way was passable. The ones left behind took the opportunity to inspect gear and weapons, as well as rest and take in the beauty of the area around them. The compassionate side of each one of them hoped they wouldn't be needed, however the adventurist side of them all wished they'd be called to service.

Chapter Six

THE ROCK KEPT the group fairly dry on the path that led beneath the falls, but they still had to slog through water to get to the tunnel. Water resistant material only did so much, and it didn't take long for their boots and pant legs to soak through, squelching between their toes with each step. Olivienne grimaced as she slipped and felt herself caught by an unseen hand. She didn't turn back to look at Castellan since they all had their head lamps on and she didn't want to blind anyone, but there were other ways to show appreciation.

"Thank you, love."

Olivienne got an invisible squeeze to her arm. *"Anytime."*

The tunnel they were in was significantly larger than the small stream of water they followed. There was plenty of room for the group to walk along next to the water, though they had to be careful to duck under low hanging parts of the rock ceiling. They made it about thirty steps in when they came to a section where the wall had been smoothed and carved with familiar cypher code. "Specialist Penn, to the front please. The rest of you shut your lamps down to preserve the stones and our sight. Stay alert."

Ciera Penn quickly followed her commander's order and squeezed through the other guardians to make it to the carving. "Ser?"

"You have the new temple cypher memorized, correct?"

"Yes, ser!"

Olivienne nodded, her light wavering up and down while still pointed at the wall. "Good thinking, Tosh. We can't be sure which temple key is used here so Commander Tosh and I will each take the old keys while Penn works on the new one." She reached into her satchel and pulled out three blank cypher sheets that were different from standard vellum, as well as three black wax sticks. "These are treated to be waterproof and we can simply wipe them when we're done." Olivienne handed a sheet and stick to both Tosh and Penn.

The three psi got to work decoding and while Olivienne and Castellan had no luck with their translation, Spc. Penn was successful. That only solidified their belief that whatever was deep within the cave directly related to the Temple of Antaeus. "Connate Dracore, I've finished." The Shield Corp guardian handed the sheet and wax stylus back to Olivienne. The Connate and commander huddled together to read the paper by the light of their lamps.

Olivienne idly scratched at an itch where the strap of the headlamp rubbed under her jaw. "Okay, for those of you who don't remember their musical instruction at academy, the notation scale is Re Ga Ma Pa Dha Nie. The carved wall states that 'the siren sets the limbs to sleep, to counteract combine the three.' Then there are three notes written, Re Ga Nie."

"Hey, it all rhymes!" Spc. Qent was the youngest of the group and always met each new adventure with an abundance of enthusiasm. Castellan thought there were times the young guardian could perhaps use a bit more restraint.

Someone snickered in the group but Olivienne went into teaching mode, with only a small call out to his ignorance. "I'm not sure if you've been paying attention to the past roto, Specialist Qent, but the Maker's texts almost always involve standard metric lines that form some sort of rhyming pattern. As someone with adventurist training you should know that."

The specialist's voice came out of the group that stood in the dark behind the three translators. "Oh, right. I forgot. Apologies, Connate Dracore."

"As I was saying, we know the original translated stanza mentioned a lake and sirens that can stun so the three notes must tie into that warning. However, I've never read of any species with stun capabilities."

Castellan motioned for Spc. Penn to head back into the group. She gave a nod and shut off her headlamp to comply. "Specialist Holling, you've got a secondary degree in animal biology. Have you heard of anything like what was mentioned in the texts?"

"No, ser. Most of the beasts that have been discovered on Psiere have more defensive mental abilities, nothing that could be considered an aggressive or an offensive type channel. Empathy is most common, and a few of the more intelligent species have rudimentary telepathy. It's possible that this siren could be an entirely undiscovered species. The location is fairly remote. I'd wager there are thousands of cave-dwelling species alone that we've never seen because of lack of access to their environment.

And the ocean animals—"

Olivienne laughed. "Okay, Specialist. We get the point. So bottom line is that we don't know what is down that tunnel or if it can actually harm us."

Castellan adjusted her own headlamp so it sat more comfortably. "Is it possible that nothing is even down there after so long? I mean, how old could this carving be if the Makers left it behind? She covered her lamp with her hand and turned to look at the group. Holling, you've got a three-rated channel in animal empathy. Are you picking up anything down here?"

"No, ser."

"Yazzie, you've got standard empathy, anything?

She shook her head in the near dark. "No, ser."

The commander sighed. "And the Connate and I both have a five rating telepathy channel. I'm not getting anything."

Olivienne shook her head. "Neither am I."

Castellan deferred to the mission leader. "It's your call, Connate. What do you want to do?"

"Anything from your intuition channel, Tosh? Or your prescience, Savon?"

"No, ser."

The commander thought for a sec. "Nothing more than a vague sense of caution."

"All right, I say we proceed cautiously but let the other team know that we're heading farther into the tunnel and to stand ready."

Castellan pulled her voteo off her belt and depressed the alert button before speaking. "Lieutenant Madlin."

"Madlin receiving."

"The warning near the tunnel entrance states that the siren sets the limbs to sleep, to counteract combine the three. Carved next to the cypher are three notes, Re Ga Nie. Copy?"

"Yes, ser." Madlin repeated the important details to confirm. "Re, Ga, Nie. Leggett is copying as you speak. Anything else, ser?"

"With nothing twanging our prescience or intuition channels, we suspect that it's possible whatever this siren is that's mentioned in the warning has long since perished. The Connate has decided to proceed with the mission and we're getting ready to follow the tunnel farther in. Stand ready for orders or warning, copy?"

"Yes, ser."

"And Lieutenant, use caution and utilize all your resources in the event you need to initiate a rescue."

Castellan smiled as Lt. Madlin's firm voice came back to them. The woman nearly radiated surety and dedication. "You can count on us, Commander."

"Tosh out." The commander clipped the voteo back to her belt and addressed the rest of the team. "Line up the same way we came in. The Connate and I will take the lead and everyone keep your lamps facing forward. Savon, pick two for rear guard."

Lt. Savon gave a quick salute. "Aye, ser. I'll take the back with Dozier. She knows caves and my prescience may help give warning in the event that something comes from behind."

Castellan nodded. "Sorted." She turned to Olivienne and gestured into the darkness. "Connate, after you."

The tunnel beyond the carving wasn't very wide, maybe large enough for two psi to walk side by side with outstretched arms and touch the walls. The small stream was narrow enough for one big step across, though Olivienne had no idea how deep it was. The tunnel itself was cold and damp, as one would expect. Olivienne tried to see if it was something carved by the Makers or if at some point the stream had been a raging river that formed the space naturally. But even with the light of the lamps shining upward as she craned her head, it was impossible to tell.

About one hundred and eighty yords in, the tunnel abruptly opened to a large cavern. There was a rocky shore that followed the edge of the water but they couldn't see how far it went. The cavern was so large that their headlamps couldn't penetrate the darkness to the other side. Castellan called out to the rest of the team. "I want two illeostone lanterns placed on either side of the tunnel entrance, then shut down your headlamps."

The specialists carrying lanterns rushed to comply then all nine in the group shut off their headlamps. Savon reached up to itch where the strap was rubbing on his temple. "Can we remove the lamps, ser? These are about as ill-fitting as anything I've seen."

Castellan turned to their expedition leader, deferring to Olivienne's judgement again. She wanted to prove that she wouldn't interfere with the Connate's job as historical adventurist. "What say you?"

Olivienne glanced around the large space. The stream didn't sound as loud in the cavern, but there were a whole host of other sounds. Dripping water and their own echoing voices both filled the space and highlighted how large it seemed in the darkness. "Let's light two more lamps a little farther in and then I say sure. We'll make a pile near the tunnel so we can grab them in a hurry if necessary."

The commander gestured to the rest of the group. "As she says." Everyone, including the commander and the Connate removed the unnecessary gear and made a pile. "What now?"

Olivienne smiled. "Now I light it up and we see if we can find whatever the Makers have hidden here." She focused and suddenly the ceiling of the cavern glowed with fire from her pyrokinetic channel.

Someone at the rear of the group gasped and Savon murmured below his breath. "By the Makers!"

The cavern was easily three hundred yords across with a lake of dark water taking up much of it. "There!" Olivienne pointed to a rocky outcropping sticking up from the water near the center. "That has to be it."

Castellan raised a pale eyebrow. "You think so? I mean, it is the only bit that stands out in here."

Olivienne shrugged. "I'm fairly certain. Rotos of adventurist missions have given me a feel for where their caches are located but I have been wrong on occasion. It can't hurt to search around the shore first."

"How long can you keep that light going?"

While Castellan couldn't make out the violet of Olivienne's eyes, she could definitely see the arrogant squint. "As long as it takes, Commander."

Castellan coughed as she realized Olivienne's double meaning and two specialists laughed outright. "Fine. Since the team is in such high spirits, let's have them do the legwork, shall we? Savon, I want you to take Qent, Dozier, Holling, and Calderon around the left side of the lake. The Connate and I will take Yazzie and Penn. Follow Qent and Dozier's adventurist experience and call out if you find anything."

"Yes, ser. Come on you lot, let's go."

As Savon's group began their way around the left side, Olivienne led Castellan, Spc. Yazzie and Spc. Penn across the stream that flowed from the lake into the tunnel beyond. From there they picked their way around the rocky shore, searching walls and the cave floor for anything that would indicate a Maker cache.

They made it about halfway around the lake, each member of the team spread in proper search formation, when Spc. Holling called out from across the chamber. "Commander Tosh!" The Connate's small group looked across to where Holling held up a barely conscious Savon.

Suddenly the lieutenant gave a shudder and began to speak. "They come! Fear, fear, fear...the sound will stop us. The creatures feast."

He slumped and Hollings voice grew desperate. "Commander, there is something else in here with us!"

"Bollux!" Before Tosh could think to move, a sound filled the chamber, freezing them where they stood. It was as if every bit of willpower seeped out through the soles of their boots. Despite being as brave as any before her, Castellan quivered as the sound made her insides feel strange. No one could move, not even to speak. They could only stare wide-eyed in whatever direction they were facing as amphibious creatures crawled out of the water. They were pale, with large milky white eyes. Their ears and nose were nothing more than slits but the size was offset by their mouths full of long sharp teeth. The heads cast around as if they were blind, but the one nearest to Spc. Yazzie seemed to focus in on her and advanced slowly.

"Tosh! What do we do?"

The commander answered back the same way. *"It's the sound that prevents us from moving. But it started before they came up from the lake so it may not be the creatures causing it."* Following her instincts, she used her telekinesis and grabbed the siren that was heading for their medican and pitched it back into the lake. She opened a telepathic channel to the entire group. *"I'm not sure how they see but they have a sense for where we are. Those of you with hard channels will need to protect the rest."*

"Commander, I feel them in my head now. These sirens would be considered greater beasts."

Castellan tried to peer across to where Spc. Holling stood. A creature was slowly approaching him from behind. *"What are you trying to say, Holling?"*

"I believe the sirens would be covered under article twenty of the Psiere Legibus. It states that – "

"Lethal force may not be used upon a greater beast within their protected territory. I know, Specialist! But these are not a discovered species nor do they have a protected territory." Castellan quivered with frustration. She was about to respond to Holling's statement when a grunting cry echoed through the cavern. Even though their voluntary muscles seemed to be locked, they could still

blink and make sound in their back of their throats. Luckily, involuntary functions like breathing were unaffected.

"Castellan! It's Penn."

The commander couldn't actually see Spc. Penn because the woman was slightly behind her, but Olivienne had a perfect view and based on the expression on her face, Penn was in dire straits and the commander had a dilemma. She was unable to use her telekinesis on what she couldn't see. Castellan quickly pitched another creature into the lake that was approaching Qent, and one that was getting nearer to the Connate, then she had a brilliant idea.

With a quick focus of her power, she used her levitation to move herself backward until she bumped up against the cavern wall, where she had full view of the entire team. At once she saw that one of the sirens had a firm hold of Penn's calf in its sharp teeth. Blood sluggishly trickled from the wound and Castellan quickly pried its mouth open then flung it into the water. After making sure that the rest were safe for a few moments she called out to the team. *"Holling, those things can't be more than fifty punds, so your three rating teleportation channel should be sufficient to drop them in the lake. Olivienne, your telepathy is as strong as mine. Can you try to contact Madlin on the outside and hold your pyrokinetic flame?"*

Olivienne thought about how far away the other team was and the fact that they were currently underground. *"The distance may be too great but I'll see what I can do."*

"Let her know that they can't just rush in. They need to counteract this paralyzing sound first. As for the rest of you, stay calm. Holling and I will keep the beasts off you until the other team can figure out a solution to our problem." Even as she spoke, Castellan flung two more sirens into the far side of the lake. She knew Holling would tire fairly quickly, so the onus of protection would fall on her until Madlin and her crew could initiate a rescue.

Olivienne focused her mind outward, back the way they came in. *"Lieutenant Madlin..."* She paused and tried harder, expanding her thoughts until she felt a headache pushing from just behind her eyes. *"Madlin!"*

The response was faint but Olivienne heard. *"Connate Dracore?"*

Olivienne knew she wouldn't be able to maintain such a strenuous communication channel for long. *"Cave danger. Paralyzed. Need three-note defense. Hurry. Injured."*

"Yes, ser!"

Olivienne panted with her exertion and rapidly worsening headache, and her pyrokinetic flame dimmed.

"'Vienne? Are you okay?"

"I'm fine, Tosh. Just need a moment."

"Did you reach her?"

Olivienne glanced over to meet Castellan's eyes. *"Yes, I imagine they're scrambling as we speak. Hopefully she heeded my warning."*

"I have full confidence in the lieutenant." She looked to Spc. Penn, whose face had turned pale and sweaty. *"I'm concerned at the siren's bite. We don't know if they carry toxins but we need Yazzie to look at her as soon as possible. General Renou will never forgive me if I let something happen to her niece on one of our missions."* She called out to the young specialist. *"Stay alert, Penn. Just focus on the here and now and we'll get you out of this cave and treated as soon as possible."*

"Yes, ser."

Less than ten meens later, the sirens suddenly stopped their advance. Heads popped up from the water by the dozens, more than Castellan had even realized were in the chamber with them. It was disconcerting the way their milky eyes glowed in the light of Olivienne's pyrokinetic flame. Light emanated from the tunnel leading out to the falls, growing brighter by the sec. All at once a chord sounded on each of their voteos, as well as emanated from the tunnel. And just as quickly as the group had become paralyzed, they were all turned loose. The strange amphibious sirens made haste disappearing back into the water and Yazzie immediately rushed to Spc. Penn's side as the young woman collapsed to the cave floor, stripping Penn's boot and rolling up the trouser leg to see the bite.

Castellan called out to the rest of the group. "Savon, double-time your team back to the cave entrance." She looked around and realized that Yazzie and Penn were safe enough with the absence of the sirens. Then she turned to Olivienne. "Can you hold that light long enough to take a trip across the lake?"

The Connate pulled her commander into an embrace and gave her a quick kiss on the lips. "I can handle it if you can."

Rather than continue to yell detailed orders in the large cavern, Castellan chose telepathy. *"Madlin, Savon, the Connate and I are headed out to the island. Keep the rest of the group ready and facilitate Penn's evacuation once Yazzie has her stable."*

"Yes, ser!"

It didn't take long to levitate them both across to the small outcropping of rock in the middle of the dark water. They were disturbed by thousands of faintly glowing shapes below the surface as they flew across. Olivienne made a guess. "Are those...the sirens?"

Castellan shrugged as they landed on the three-yord diameter rock. "I have no clue. Maybe they're eggs. They seemed very amphibian-like, and don't froglets and such lay eggs? Either way, it's going to remain a mystery because there is nothing that could entice me to go in that water and find out!"

Olivienne smirked. "Nothing, hmm?"

The commander refused to be swayed. "Nothing."

A sigh, then the Connate gave in. "Fine. Let's check this rocky bit for buttons or hidden alcoves, shall we?" The rock they were on jutted upward so while they stood on the edges of it, it actually rose above their heads. Olivienne began to climb and Castellan followed suit. Near the top Olivienne found what she was looking for. "Aha!"

Castellan looked upon the series of clustered stalagmites with confusion. "I don't understand."

"Look above us." Castellan followed her finger. "Stalagmites are formed when water drips from above, depositing minerals that grow over time. Stalactites are obviously the same deposits left behind from above. However, look at these stalagmites. See how this big one in the center is dry?"

"Yes."

"Now watch." Olivienne used the heel of her hand to strike the dry stalagmite until it loosened. Then she gripped it, twisted, and the rock formation came loose in her hand. When she turned it over, it was actually hollow and contained a rolled up vellum.

"By the Makers, that's brilliant! How did you know?"

Olivienne tucked the vellum into her waist pouch. "I've seen similar false compartments before. Sometimes in a hollowed rock that doesn't look as though it belongs, sometimes in other things. It's a common Maker cache device."

Castellan just grunted, continually surprised by the ingenuity of the strange people that left behind so many questions. "Ready?"

"Absolutely."

When they reached the shore by the tunnel entrance, Yazzie had already assembled a litter from the composite joints and rolled fabric stored within her medican pack. Holling and Savon were helping the specialist to lay down so she could be carried out. "Everyone grab your headlamp and let's get out of this Maker-forsaken place."

"Yes, ser!"

Castellan looked around. "Where's Lazaro?"

Lt. Madlin pushed forward. "I had him stay outside and contact the dirigible. When Connate Dracore mentioned that someone was injured, I thought we may need a quick evac."

The commander clapped her on the shoulder. "Good thinking, Lieutenant!"

Luckily for Penn, the dirigible had made the short trip down river from where it was originally moored. Castellan could see evidence of a flare near where the new anchor line sank into the rocky cliff twenty foot from where the falls came down. The commander was even more impressed to see a caged rescue travois sitting on the ground near the anchor point, with a climbing driver already attached to the line and ready to go. The dirigible really did have everything an adventurist team could need.

Yazzie and Holling got to work loading Penn in the medican cage while the rest of the Shield team donned climbing harnesses and packed away what gear they'd brought. Yazzie found Tosh before they began their ascent. "I gave her a standard injection for counteracting toxins. She seems improved already. I don't think that was the siren's main offense, I believe it was the tone. Some species are fatal when their only weapon is toxicity, we got lucky."

Tosh nodded. "We certainly did."

Fifteen meens later they were all safely aboard and Penn had been taken to the ship's medican room for observation. The captain herself met the group and quickly pulled Olivienne and Castellan aside. "Connate Dracore, Commander Tosh, if you would both come with me, I have urgent news from the capital."

Olivienne paled. "What is it?"

The captain shook her head and remained silent until they finished the trip to the captain's room. Once inside, she secured the door then turned to face them, looking grim. "I'm afraid the news isn't good. There has been an attack on Tesseron. Atlanteens sent creatures up from the deep and, despite preparations for just such an eventuality, many lives were lost. The city's general doctore with telesana was killed in the second wave of attacks, so the Queen sent her private medican to help. He burned out his channels trying to aid the most critically wounded.

"No..." Olivienne tensed next to Castellan.

"The Queen's own doctore was assisting with injuries at the nearest hospital when dirigibles came in from the south and began dropping shells across the city. While in transport between the residence and a council meeting with General Leniste, the Queen's moto was caught at the edge of an explosion and thrown. Two of the Queen's Shield team are dead, one is critically injured, and Captain Torrin has a broken leg and two broken ribs."

Olivienne choked out the words. "And my mother?"

Velten sorrowed as she replied. "Queen Olivara suffered a shattered femur and pelvis, a dislocated shoulder, and currently lies in a coma. They are unsure if she will awake from such grievous injuries. I have orders to bring you straightaway to the capital."

The Connate sobbed and immediately turned to press her face into Castellan's shoulder. Castellan did her best to console Olivienne but was curious about captain's orders. "Grim news indeed, Captain. Would it not be quicker to drop us at the railer station on the other side of the channel, where you picked us up?"

Captain Velten shook her head. "I'm afraid I can't do that, Commander Tosh. My orders come from the King himself."

Olivienne abruptly pulled away from Castellan to face Velten. "What aren't you telling us?"

"Because of the Queen's condition and dire outlook, the Imperium has cast their vote early this morning." She spared Tosh a brief look of pity. "Queen Olivienne is to return to the city in its time of need and take her rightful place on the Divine Cathedra."

Olivienne covered her mouth at the news. It was one thing to hear that her own mother was critically injured, but it was another to find out that she'd already been chosen to replace her decades before she expected.

Castellan shrugged into that familiar mantle of responsibility and went into Shield commander mode. "How soon can we make it to Tesseron, at top speed?"

"We'll have to stop off at either the switching station on Instrucia or the one on Endara. We filled up on illeostones before we took you on, but coming here, then all the way back will put us over our fourteen hundred mahl limit." She did the math aloud. "Approximately twelve hundred mahls, will be about twenty oors, plus roughly another half oor to replenish supplies and fill the stone tanks. We'll run straight through otherwise so you can be back in Tesseron by tomorrow afternoon."

Castellan pondered the captain's words before responding. "In the interest of security, I'd like to recommend stopping for illeostones while still on Instrucia. The island is more insulated and we can't be sure where the attackers have placed their spies along the two continents.

Velten nodded. "That is what we'll do, then."

Olivienne pulled herself up to her full height as she listened to Velten's estimation. "It sounds like we have a plan. If either of you need me I'll be in my cabin." The newly made Queen of Psiere quickly walked away toward the berth she shared with Castellan.

The commander didn't follow, knowing two Shields would be waiting outside the captain's room to escort Olivienne. She sighed and turned back to the captain. "Are there no other tele-sana healers that can help?"

"My missive says that there was a conference being held down in Ostium, sponsored by Praefectus Havington, and all but the two senior doctores in Tesseron and one low level telesana medican in Soflin were in attendance."

"Makers *take* that blasted man! I will kill him myself when I see him."

Captain Velten was caught by surprise in a rare show of rage from the officer. "Commander?"

Tosh shook her head and pinched the skin at the bridge of her nose. "Get us to Tesseron as fast as you can and be wary. This dirigible now carries the Queen of Psiere and as such will be running with a target painted on its side. I trust you to keep us safe." The commander sagged beneath the weight of her new responsibility and Velten nodded.

"Yes, ser."

Castellan left the room to find her love and new Queen. Their quest for answers had just gotten more complicated.

Chapter Seven

"'VIENNE...' THE ONLY cabin larger than their own was the captain's. But despite the size of their berth, Olivienne was sitting on their bunk taking up as little space as possible. Her legs were drawn up tight to her chest and her right cheek rested upon her knees. Castellan didn't get an answer so she came all the way in and secured the door. She approached her lover slowly, worried at all the news that had been thrown at them in such a short amount of time. Castellan knew how much Olivienne adored both her parens, and despite their push-pull relationship, Olivienne was especially close to her maman.

"I didn't even get a chance to tell her I loved her. We just— everything happened so fast after the oathing ceremony and then we got on the railer..." Olivienne's voice faded away and Castellan settled on the bed next to her just as the new Queen's shoulders hitched with a stifled sob.

Castellan pulled her close and soothed her as best she could. "Shh, it's okay. I've got you, love. She knows how much you love her, never doubt that."

"Why did she send her private doctore away? Why? She'd still be fine."

"Because she's our Queen, and we both know that she would do anything to protect her people."

Olivienne clutched at Castellan's uniform shirt, desperate in her anger and grief. "I resent them all. I hate those that want to kill my family just because of our name. I feel embittered by the people who took my maman away, people who were more important than her life."

Castellan loosened Olivienne's dark hair from her braid and slowly combed her fingers through the strands. "But you *don't* resent them and you would have made the same choice."

Teary violet eyes looked up at Castellan, searching for some sort of proof in the other woman's gaze. "How do you know? I'm no Queen, surely everyone must see that!"

Castellan turned so she could cradle Olivienne's face between her hands, then gently wiped the tears away with her thumbs. "I know because they're your people too. And you are a

Queen as much as any sovereign before you. 'Vienne, you are amazing in your own right and will have your own legacy to pass on." Castellan leaned forward and placed a gentle kiss upon her Queen's lips, then lowered her hands and gazed deep into Olivienne's eyes. *"I love you and I have faith in you. And no matter what, we will guard you with our life."*

"I don't want to lose you too!"

"You won't. And you haven't lost Olivara yet either. Have faith in her strength. I think she would hold on just to make sure she has rotos longer to meddle in our romance."

Olivienne snorted through her tears, Castellan's words having elicited their desired reaction. But the mirth lasted only a sec before reality crashed down once again. Olivienne turned to sob into Castellan's shirt, heedless of the dirt and grime accumulated from their dae of adventuring. She cried out her fears, confident that with her lover she could still be herself and not have to don the mantle of the Queen just yet. All Castellan could do was hold her and verbally assure that everything would be okay.

After she had cried for a bit, Olivienne pulled away and wiped the tears on the shoulder of her shirt, frowning at the streak of dirt left behind. "I need a thorough washing."

Castellan sighed as she took in the state of her own uniform. "As do I. Unfortunately I still have to brief the team on the most recent events. Will you be okay for the moment?"

"I—yes. Can you let the captain know that I'd like to take evening meal in our cabin?"

"Sure. Do you need anything now? It's been oors since we last ate, you need sustenance in you."

Olivienne shook her head. "I'd just like some time to think, if that's okay."

"I'll brief Savon and Madlin first, then they can watch the door while I speak with the rest of the unit."

"I hardly think I need both of them guarding my door while you're gone."

Castellan ran a hand through her hair, mussing it in a way that normally Olivienne would love. But seeing her commander so agitated only served to upset Olivienne even more. "It's not that simple. I've read the entirety of the Shield Corp protocol manual. Part of my promotion as your unit commander was a requirement to memorize the priorities and mandatory practices for guarding a Connate *and* a Queen. Because only you have the potential to be both. The Queen is never to have less than two guards at all times. That's per entrance, 'Vienne."

"Things are different now, aren't they?"

Castellan took her hand and gave it a light squeeze. "Things are the same, just a little harder. I'm still your commander, and you're still my sovereign." Olivienne looked on the edge of tears again and Castellan pulled her into another embrace. "I promise that I'll do my best to not let duty take me away from you, just as I'll do my duty to make sure you aren't taken away from me. On my honor."

"On your honor."

"Yes. I pledge to you. Now…" Castellan kissed her on the forehead and gave her a nudge toward the facility. "I believe you wanted to wash."

A dark brow rose as a little of Olivienne's flirtatious personality came to the fore. "You could join me, Commander."

Castellan laughed at how predictable her lover was. "We may have one of the best rooms on the ship but it is still just a ship. There is barely enough room for one in the head, let alone two with healthy libidos. Perhaps we can explore this idea later after I've had my own rinse, hmm?"

Olivienne smiled. "Perhaps. Now go, talk to your team." Castellan took one step then hesitated. Her look said it all and Olivienne gave her a shove. "I'll be fine."

"I'll be back in a bit."

Olivienne watched Castellan leave the cabin, then made her way into the combined head and shower. Castellan was right, the space was much too small for such newly oathed antics. When the heat of her libido cooled with the water, it was replaced by thoughts and worries of her own future, and that of Psiere. If more than water ran down her cheeks while she rinsed off the dae, no one but her would know.

THE DAMAGE TO the city was obvious as they came in from the north and circled around to approach from the southwest side of Bindle Bay where the railer and dirigible stations were located. Docks were damaged, as were numerous buildings next to the port. Debris floated in the water and the carcasses of at least two denizens of the deep littered the streets closest to the waterfront. Some buildings near the center of the city still smoldered from fire caused by the explosive shells that had been dropped from the attacking dirigibles. The team had instructions to leave their gear on the *Quaesitum*, only bringing with them their personal weapons and satchels. The sole exception was that Holling would also carry his medican kit. With the state of things on the ground, Castellan didn't want to be caught unprepared in case of another attack.

She informed General Renou of their arrival time when they were a few oors out from Tesseron and was taken aback to see Olivienne's reception at the transportation hub. They were met with no less than a full troop of Shield Corp guardians standing at attention. Fifty soldiers seemed like overkill when the city was supposed to be stable but it wasn't as if Castellan were in any position to argue. While the Shield Corp standard uniforms were all black down to the very boots on their feet, the color seemed especially fitting on such a somber dae.

General Renou herself stood at the bottom of the dirigible platform and watched Olivienne's Shield team intently. She was impressed by their seriousness and attention to their surroundings, as befitting any unit assigned to a sovereign. She had to be sure of their steadfastness because Olivienne was no longer just the heir to the Divine Cathedra, she had become their supreme ruler and the team that protected her needed to be solid. Gen. Renou sorrowed that the couple's oathing trip had to be cut short, but she grieved more that her longtime friend lay comatose because of the greedy intentions of a few savage pseros and pseras.

Castellan saluted her general when they reached the line of motos. "General, you didn't have to meet us here. I would have given my report as soon as Connate — erm, Queen Olivienne was settled." Olivienne jerked her head around to look at Castellan, startled by her new title. She wasn't used to hearing herself referred to in such a way. When Olivienne looked up she saw a sea of black clad psi saluting, all ready to put their lives on the line to protect her. On one hand she was honored, but on the other she hated it with every shred of her being.

General Renou broke both women from their deep thoughts. "Actually, it was easier for me to meet you here. Queen Olivienne must go straightaway to the Chamber of the Imperium. A meeting has been called and the Queen needs to be in attendance."

"I will do no such thing. I need to see her." It wasn't necessary for Olivienne to explain who she referred to.

In a rare breach of protocol, Camen Renou reached out and clasped the Queen's hand. "Please, Olivienne. I know you want to see her but this meeting needs you, and Olivara's condition will not change in the next few oors."

Olivienne narrowed her eyes. "Why do they need me at this meeting so badly?"

Renou leaned closer so that only Tosh and Olivienne could hear. "They don't need you at the meeting, but *you* need you at the meeting. They are voting on your future and that of Psiere within the oor. And with the King in-absentia...we need a royal presence there."

Olivienne rubbed her forehead just above the bridge of her nose, then sighed. "Fine."

Both commander and Queen refused to leave their unit behind so a hauler was brought in that could transport everyone to the Imperium. It took nearly twenty meens to get across the city and all Olivienne could do was worry. Her heart mother wouldn't have insisted she attend the meeting first if it weren't of the utmost importance. When they arrived, the entire group was escorted through the grand halls to the doors of the main chamber where the Imperium met on a daily basis. Two Politia Corp guards tried to stop their group from entering. Before things could escalate too far, an aide slipped out one of the side doors positioned farther down the hall. He seemed a little too smug for Castellan's tastes. "Apologies, Connate Dracore, but the Imperium is in a closed meeting and none may enter. Perhaps you could retire to your residence until they call for you?"

Castellan's ire grew at the man's disrespectful attitude. She answered before either Olivienne or General Renou could utter a single word. Castellan's voice rang loudly in the grand hallway. "Your Queen is not called about like someone's pet canid. Salute her now then get out of the way, Administre!"

The man stubbornly refused, going so far as waving over more Imperium guards for added security. "I'm afraid I can't do that, Commander. I've had explicit instructions not—gerk!"

Lifting him and the guards didn't tax Castellan in the slightest. She raised them all to a decorative ledge that ran the entire length of the two-story hall. "I'll bring you down when I come back out. Until then—" She glanced at Olivienne and smiled. "Perhaps your new perspective will give you better insight on how to behave in the presence of the Queen of Psiere."

A few members of Olivienne's Shield unit cracked smiles but otherwise didn't laugh as they normally would. They were taking their duty to guard and protect to the utmost extreme. General

Renou was the one who broke the quick silence following Tosh's move. She muttered something beneath her breath about "the impetuousness of youth," before gesturing toward the door. "Ready?"

Castellan forced both twelve-foot wood doors open at once, announcing their arrival into the chamber with a loud bang. Each door was carved from the heaviest wood in existence and weighed close to thirteen hundred punds. Two psi were needed to open or shut just one and slamming them both open at once was just a small show of Tosh's power. One of the Capital Representatives from the southern continent stood. "What is the meaning of this? We left orders not to be disturbed."

Olivienne didn't yell, but she didn't have to. As soon as she stepped out of her protective group, the entire chamber fell into silence. "The Queen has countermanded those orders." She walked forward steadily, heading straight for the seat she had seen her own maman take more times than she could possibly count. Castellan followed and stood to the side and slightly behind as Olivienne settled onto the padded cushion of the Divine Cathedra. "Now tell me, what is it we are discussing in this somewhat rushed and secretive meeting?"

One woman stood from her desk near the center of the chamber and sputtered an excuse. "We weren't rushing — it wasn't — "

Another representative pulled at her tunic and whispered up at her. "Sit down!"

It was then that General Renou spoke loudly enough for the entire room to hear. "On the contrary, pseros and pseras, you should be standing to salute our Queen."

Suddenly the entire chamber was in motion, standing and saluting the most powerful woman in Psiere, their new Divine Cathedress. Olivienne gave the room a nod and the entire body of the Imperium seated themselves again. Then her eyes focused on one psera in particular, someone who was a good friend and associate of her papan. "Representative Ormie Tember, please tell me the nature of todae's private meeting."

Castellan watched everyone because it was her job. She was also counting on her channels to help warn of imminent trouble from anyone within the Imperium. The commander observed the called-upon woman who stood at the Queen's behest, and noted Rep. Tember's bright orange hair and pale eyes. The representative's tunic and trousers were as colorful as anything Castellan had ever seen.

"Queen Olivienne—" Tember paused and smiled at the woman she had practically watched grow up. "This emergency meeting was called by Representatives Sechena Keene and Gorman Dollek."

Castellan narrowed her eyes at the two representatives from the southern continent. She well knew Keene, as the woman was the capital representative for the region near Ostium and was known to be in Praefectus Havington's inner circle. *"They're both from the southern continent. Something smells rotten in here."*

Olivienne didn't outwardly acknowledge Castellan's warning and their mental conversation didn't last longer than a few secs, as telepathy was the quickest form of communication. *"I have already been briefed on the representatives for the Ostium and Soflin districts."*

"You have?"

"I know everyone has always been under the assumption that I'm nothing more than a feckless wanderer, but I've done my duty and stayed current on the politics of Psiere. No matter how much I despise it."

Castellan smirked and didn't care if anyone wondered what it was about. *"They will underestimate you."*

"Exactly."

Olivienne called out the two people in question. "You may be seated, Representative Tember. Representatives Keene and Dollek, please step forward and lay out the details of this emergency meeting so that I may have the most up to date information at my disposal."

Praefectus Havington's prime lackey, Dollek, answered. "Queen Olivienne, we were merely meeting to discuss our path forward from this incredible tragedy. We," he gestured around him, "the Imperium, have concerns about the security of Psiere. After speaking with the other representatives of Dromea, we have compiled a list of three items that could help solidify our political structure and return the people's confidence in the leadership of Psiere."

Castellan growled beneath her breath and Olivienne smiled to hear it. The Queen raised a single dark brow at the representative's declaration. "And what, pray tell, are these miraculous items?"

Representative Keene carried a file in her left hand and with Olivienne's question she reached inside to pull out a sheet of vellum and began reading. "Item one on the list requests that the

Imperium vote to reassign the current planned expedition to the lost Temple of Antaeus to a different adventurist other than, well, you...your Majesty. The second item is for the Imperium to vote on retiring you from the Divinity Corp active duty, as it is done with the career for all Queens of Psiere." She paused to clear her throat and Castellan didn't need to see her future par to know that Olivienne would surely be livid from the first two items read aloud.

Despite Castellan's misgivings and fears of an angry outburst, Olivienne's voice remained quite civil. "Go on, Representative Keene, tell us what the third and final item on your list is."

"Well the third item, my Queen, is in deference to your new and abrupt transition from the Connate to our Divine Cathedress. We thought that it may be a bit easier for you if the governance of Dromea is left solely to Praefectus Havington, at least until you feel confident to take on the full mantle of responsibility for the entirety of Psiere."

"Heresy!"

"Disloyalist!" Cries rang throughout the chamber as many representatives loyal to the monarchy jumped to their feet in dismay. Boos rumbled through the large room even as the other capital representatives of the southern continent tried to defend their counterparts.

Olivienne called to her commander as the Imperium descended into chaos. *"Castellan?"*

"Yes, my Queen."

Irritation colored the feel of Olivienne's words in Castellan's head. *"Don't call me that! And that being said, a Queen doesn't raise her voice. A little help please?"*

Castellan grinned at the Queen's directive. Suddenly, the same doors they had originally marched through meens before, slammed shut again and every person in the room felt the power of it through the soles of their feet. Silence descended upon the room as Olivienne stood and acknowledged the help. "Thank you, Commander. Now that I have the attention of the Imperium body..." She walked forward toward where Representative Keene still held the vellum. "First of all, there will be no transfer of power to Praefectus Pon Havington of Dromea. Second, my mother is not dead yet and as such there is no need for me to retire from my Corp profession."

"My apologies, Queen Olivienne, but the first item has some merit. With the adventurist mission set to take place in two weke's time, it is quite impossible for you to participate in such an undertaking while you remain as the Divine Cathedress. If you do not want to give up the mission, then it should at the very least be postponed until things are more settled or —"

Olivienne's disconcerting purple eyes bore into the representative from the region near Guin. "Or what? Until we see which side of the mortal coin Olivara Dracore falls on, am I right?"

Representative Kennet bowed slightly. "I meant no disrespect, my Queen. I'm only trying to suggest the most prudent course given the situation."

Olivienne clenched her teeth momentarily to keep from spewing the vilest of curses at the hapless man. It didn't help her temper one bit to know that he was right. "I agree that while I sit as Queen of Psiere, I cannot continue with any of my currently assigned missions, and that includes the one my mother personally handed to me involving the Temple of Antaeus. But as Queen now myself, I get to decide how or even when this mission resumes. And for now it will remain on hold until things are a little calmer here in Tesseron."

"Thank you, my Queen." Rep. Kennet nodded and returned to his seat.

"Now, if our business is concluded here todae—"

"I'd like to call a vote!" Someone gasped and muttering swept through the chamber as Representative Dollek held his right hand high above.

"By the Makers, what for?" Olivienne gave the man an incredulous look.

Dollek stubbornly continued with his request. "For the temporary power restructuring between Endara and Dromea, to assist the new Queen in acclimating to the nation's most important seat."

"Bollux, man! That is a power play plain and simple!" Olivienne recognized the speaker as the local representative for the region around Tesseron.

Unfortunately for Olivienne and all those who were most loyal to the monarchy, once the call for a vote had been requested, the Imperium needed to comply. Luckily though, the voting results split primarily along the continental division and the agenda item was quickly shut down. Olivienne was slightly reassured that at least a few of the representatives from Dromea joined with their counterparts from Endara.

When the furor of voting settled down, Olivienne stood from

her seat and the entire chamber followed her lead. "Now...with that bit of nonsense put to rest, I'd very much like to go see my mother." As one, all members of the Imperium bowed and Olivienne made her way out, followed closely by Castellan, General Renou, and Olivienne's Shield unit.

RATHER THAN TAX the medican facilities in an already overloaded city in the daes following the coordinated Atlanteen and dirigible attack, Olivara was being kept in a special room at the royal residence. A doctore came from the hospital twice a dae and two doctore's assistants were assigned to Olivara full-time. They spoke to the specialists in charge of Olivara's care when they arrived at the royal residence. Afterward Olivienne ordered no one to disturb them other than for regularly scheduled checks until they left Olivara's room again. She needed to see her maman in peace, to take in the full state of the elder Dracore's injuries.

Olivienne's first look at her maman brought tears to her eyes. Her papan sat slumped near the bed with his eyes closed. Based on the pallor of his face and the circles beneath his eyes, she sincerely hoped he was sleeping. A quiet beeping and hiss came from the machine that monitored Olivara's pulses. The bright white bandages on the previous Queen's head stood out in stark relief against her nearly black hair and tan skin.

Olivienne's words were a whisper. "Oh, Maman."

"I can wait outside if you like."

A hand blindly reached backward to grab onto Castellan's. *"I need you."*

Within the safety of the private room, away from prying eyes and talkative administres and other staff, Castellan wrapped her arms around Olivienne, cradling her from behind. She sent a quick telepathic message to Savon and Madlin before responding to Olivienne with another. *"You have me for as long as you need."*

Castellan went over the rest of the dae in her head. They had a meeting planned at nineteen hundred oors with General Renou, General Leniste, and Templar Aislyn concerning the transfer of power and the postponed Antaeus expedition. At twenty hundred oors they would be joined by the heads of the rest of the Psi Citizen Corps to discuss overall security of the city and managing resources to rebuild the sections that had been damaged.

It was sure to be a long night but all Castellan could do was be there to support Olivienne. She briefly spared a thought for her sib Tessior and his par, Temera. Castellan had contacted her maman and was told that little Temiora was staying with her avia and avus while the city was in turmoil. The Security Corp had Tessior on double shifts to help quell fears and assist in the cleanup efforts, and as a member of the Engineering Corp, Temera was participating in the repair and rebuilding of the city.

Castellan spared another glance at the King, or whatever Olivienne's papan was titled since the vote, and felt helpless. Her mind raced with all that would have to be done in the coming daes while her body gave in to its craving and pulled Olivienne in tighter.

Olivienne whimpered within the circle of Castellan's arms. *"I grieve for all of Psiere right now."*

"I know, love. But we'll get those responsible for this...and when we do, I'll dig the deepest hole on Iuvenis and stuff them all in. They'll never see the light of dae if I have my way."

Olivienne stiffened and turned her head to glance at her future par. *"Darling, such words do not befit a soldier of honor."*

"My words are my honor, and I pledge to you here and now that I will personally see these disloyalists brought to justice for the death and destruction they've caused."

Olivienne gave her a faint smile and squeezed the hand gently clasped within her own. *"I love you."*

Castellan sighed. *"I love you too. Now try to rest if you can, it is sure to be a late night."*

"Yes, ser." The familiar words were accompanied by the feel of humor, like a smirk, and Castellan held hope that they would make it through this newest challenge relatively unscathed. With another look toward Olivara Dracore, she knew they would need a miracle for her hope to see fruition.

Chapter Eight

DESPITE MEETINGS THAT ran late the evening before, they were up early the next morning. Most of the city was situated west of the river, following Bindle Bay along its north side. But much of the industrial and goods conveyance of Tesseron continued on the east side of the Mir Tessere, following the bay and railer line for a few mahls. During the attack from the Atlanteens, two armicrustes and a massive leviathan had done significant damage to the river barge docks, parts of the large railer station, and even a few dirigible platforms that were close to the water. Not only were the stinking carcasses a disease risk, but getting supplies and building materials into the city was severely hampered by the damage.

That was where Olivienne and Castellan found themselves as the first rays of Archeos broke over the horizon, followed by Illeos. At least two aides, one adminstre, and three city officials informed Olivienne that a Queen doesn't perform menial duties, and General Leniste cautioned her that helping in the cleanup efforts would be a nightmare for her security detail. She informed Leniste that she'd already cleared it with her unit commander as well as General Renou and Major General Treledon, who was the head of the Tesseron Security Corp force. The city Security Corp officers had locked down the sections the Queen would be working in. And while some broadsheet representatives would be invited to cover the cleanup efforts, no other private citizens were to be allowed in the area.

A group of engineers and numerous other workers stood a few yords away, and the lead engineer in charge of the shipping hub repairs approached cautiously and saluted Olivienne and Castellan. "My Queen, where would you like to begin?"

Olivienne knew that Castellan had overseen similar cleanup efforts when the then lieutenant commander was in charge of the defenses of Ostium, so the Queen deferred to her. "Commander Tosh? Didn't you deal with such down on Dromea?"

"Yes, specifically during the battle of Temple Beach. It's a shame cleanup is only just now beginning, else we could have salvaged the armicruste meat for the local populace. What's done is done, I suppose. Have a team remove the exoskeletons, they can be ground up and used for fertilizer. Just throw them on a hauler to be taken to the nearest Stock Corp processing facility. Make a pile with all the rancid meat somewhere away from the intact buildings or other areas that can be damaged by flame."

"Ah, I'm beginning to see where I come in here."

The commander continued with a grin. "And Queen Olivienne will have the enjoyable task of putting one of her infamous Dracore channels to work by incinerating the remains of the beasts."

Olivienne wrinkled her nose as Castellan verbalized what she'd already guessed. "That sounds absolutely vile!"

Castellan laughed. "Oh, it is! While you're waiting for the crews to separate the carcasses, you could probably begin on the leviathan that beached itself between here and the dirigible station."

The Queen smirked. "Oh, aye aye, ser!"

"Savon, Madlin!" Castellan yelled for her lieutenants who were conversing by the hauler they'd arrived in. They both approached at a quick jog.

"Ser?"

"Take the team and stay with the Queen at all times. Only the broadsheet rep and his crew are allowed near. Keep watch for disturbances on both land and water. We don't know if the Atlanteens have a way of monitoring the happenings topside, or how they are getting their information to coordinate attacks. Better to be safe than sorry."

"Yes, ser!" Madlin and Savon saluted smartly then followed Olivienne as she made her way around the waterfront toward where the leviathan lay stinking in the morning air.

The lead engineer cleared her throat. "Erm, and you, Commander Tosh?"

"Engineer Corbin, you mentioned that there was a team standing by to repair the dock supports and that you were waiting for one of the large block and tackle machines to lift them." Though it was phrased as a statement, Castellan's pale brow went up indicating she wished for confirmation.

Teza Corbin adjusted her stance and swallowed thickly when she bore the full weight of Commander Tosh's pale gaze. She had heard of Castellan Tosh's immense power, everyone had. After all, stories of the Hero of Temple Beach had come in shortly after the commander took over the protection detail for the Connate.

But there were whispers of greater feats that paled in comparison to that tale. Some were saying that the commander had even lifted an entire leviathan out of the water during one of the Connate's missions. Of course Teza didn't believe the woman was that powerful, but the stories made everyone wonder just the same. "Yes, ser. I was told that all available machines are currently assigned to the repair detail of two separate hospitals that were damaged in the attack. We were just going to work on repairing nearby buildings in the interim until one became available."

Tosh grinned. "Well, in lieu of mechanical means of support, perhaps you'll settle for a channel lift. How much do the dock sections weigh and how long will it take to fix?"

Still skeptical, Teza pondered the maths aloud. "Each dock section is nearly two tuns and has eight supports. It takes a pair of workers about ten meens to enact repairs on one support."

"How many pairs of workers do you have?"

"Enough pairs to do a full dock all at once. Ser —" The engineer hesitated at questioning the commander's plan but if a dock collapsed while under repair, her workers would be endangered. "The docks are quite heavy and if it goes under while my teams are repairing the supports, they'll likely be killed."

Castellan clapped the woman on the shoulder. "Have no fear, Corbin, I was tested a few lunes ago up on Instrucia. I've got a level seven telekinetic channel and can easily hold forty-two hundred punds for twenty meens before my reserves run low. Will that suffice?"

Teza Corbin's mouth gaped open for precious secs. "There is no such level!"

Tosh smiled kindly. "There is now."

"By the depths!" The commander didn't respond to the exclamation. She merely stood quietly while her news sunk in. After speaking at length with Olivienne about her increased power, Castellan knew that it would be off-putting to be standing in front of the most powerful telekinetic in all of Psiere. Soon enough, the woman came out of her temporary daze to once again wear the look of a professional. "I'm assuming you'll need occasional breaks. How long? Can we do all three docks todae?"

"Hmm, I'll probably need a ten meen break between the first and second repair, then longer between the second and third. I think a twenty meen rest would probably suffice while my reserves build again, then we can finish that last one."

The engineer nodded in agreement. "We can set up supplies for the next repair while you rest so all material is ready when we start each. I'll get my team sorted and let you know when we're ready to begin." She saluted and moved off to inform the rest of the repair group.

They worked steadily for more than an oor, with the promised small breaks in between each job. Olivienne had completed burning the dead leviathan to ash, as well as the bits of armicruste meat by the time Castellan's team finished repairing the third and final dock. Olivienne was looking a little pale when she returned to her commander's side so Castellan ordered an aide to fetch the Queen some food and water to help with her recovery.

Castellan reached up to smooth the stress lines between Olivienne's eyes. "You're going to have a headache later."

She got a tired smile in return. "It was worth it to help get this city back on track."

The two powerful women sat next to each other, leaning shoulder to shoulder. They were perched on a stack of construction material that would be used to repair various parts of the waterfront and shipping hub. The warm colors of the suns' rise had just begun to fade over the water as the oathed pair sat in silence to absorb the beauty of it. It painted the perfect image and the broadsheet photographer wasted no time in capturing the moment. The image would surely speak a thousand words that the broadrep would have no room to print. One photo told an entire story of heroism, love, loyalty, and dedication to the people of Psiere. After all, it wasn't every dae one saw their Queen work to near exhaustion performing such gruesome and thankless duty. Everyone on the docks fell in love with their new Queen in that moment.

The calm silence was broken a few meens before zero eight hundred oors when the incoming railer announced its arrival with a long and loud mournful whistle. Another team with haulers and pushers had done a bang up job clearing the side tracks so shipping segments could be loaded and unloaded for the much needed incoming supplies from cities outside Tesseron. Castellan watched for a meen as citizens disembarked from the passenger section, before standing and holding out her hand to Olivienne. "Are you ready to put your apportation channel to work on some of the smaller debris?"

Olivienne made a face and took her hand to be assisted up. "Gladly! Unfortunately, I don't think I'll ever be able to scrub the smell of burning sea beast from my skin!"

"Perhaps I'll give you a hand later." Castellan winked and was delighted to see a rare blush color her Queen's cheeks.

"Perhaps I'll let you."

Their private flirtation was interrupted by a cry from one of the workers near the newly repaired docks. "Leviathan!"

Everyone spun toward the water to see a long tentacle breaking the surface of the bay, reaching not for them, but toward the nearest railer platform where citizens were unloading. "Bollux!" Castellan watched the great eye rise above the water and she quickly looked around for something she could use to fend the beast off.

"Commander, what do we do? None of our personal weaponry is powerful enough to affect a creature of that size." Lt. Savon had come running full tilt and Tosh waved him toward Olivienne.

"We would need the big explosive shells to do any damage. Get the Queen out of here! I'll handle the beast."

Olivienne had a terrible flashback to the last time they had seen a leviathan, and the memory of Castellan nearly dying pierced her heart with pain. She clutched at the commander's black shirtsleeve. "No!"

Castellan turned to press a kiss against her lips. "It will be okay, I've got this." She knew she didn't have the capacity to lift it after spending the morning repairing docks but Commander Tosh was not one to give up without a fight. When her eyes flicked away, she spied exactly what she needed. "Never mind, stay right here. Savon, form a circle and guard the Queen." As soon as she stepped away, the rest of the team moved in to physically barricade their sovereign.

People were running away from the water and the questing tentacle, screaming in fear. Madlin was quick to point out the obvious. "Ser, it seems to be searching for someone."

"So it is, Lieutenant." Then with a minor flex of her mental muscles, Castellan picked up one of the stele beams nearby and sent it flying across the water toward that baleful eye. A tentacle came up at the last moment to wrap around the length so the commander let it go and picked up two more. Faster than the first one flew, Castellan sent the next two beams deep into the body of the leviathan. A strange keening sound emanated from the beast and its tentacles flailed about. The stele beam it had been holding dropped into the water and the long questing tentacle near the railer platform slammed into a hauler, knocking the vectura onto its side before falling to the ground, lifeless. The bay was deep enough that when the leviathan died it began to sink below the surface, dragging the few long tentacles that had made it to land back underwater with it.

Cheering broke out across the waterfront as well as from watchers that had been on the platforms of the railer station and the nearest dirigible station. Castellan flushed with embarrassment and the photographer snapped pic after pic of her and of the scene. Seeing a greater story than one about the Queen helping with the cleanup efforts, the broadrep rushed to Castellan's side from where he had been cowering behind Olivienne and her Shield unit. "Commander Tosh! Ser!"

After watching the water for another meen to be sure the creature was truly gone, Castellan turned to acknowledge the broadrep. "Yes, Lebben?"

Lebben smiled as he held his stylus to the book of vellum. "What you just did was amazing! Can you tell me what you were thinking when the tentacle first broke the water?"

Castellan humored the man. "I was thinking something needed to be done before he wrecked all our hard work on those docks."

He nodded and scribbled furiously before asking the next question. "And from where I was standing, you appeared quite calm. Is this...erm, do you have a lot of experience dealing with leviathans? We've all heard stories about Temple Beach, ser, but nothing has ever been written about a lone psi taking on a leviathan."

Olivienne caught Castellan's attention and pointed at the timepiece in her hand. Castellan nodded before turning back to Lebben. "I'm afraid this will be the final question as the Queen and I have matters to attend to. But to answer, I've only one experience with a leviathan. It was during one of Queen Olivienne's adventurist missions, over on Mater Island."

Lebben's eyes widened. "Ser, I know you said this was the last question but please, I've heard a fanciful story that you once lifted a leviathan straight out of the ocean. Was the tale based on fact?"

The commander gave a hearty laugh and clapped the man on the shoulder. "Of course that's not true, man!" He sighed, slightly crestfallen at hearing the fantastical rumor proven false. Then Castellan leaned closer and gave him a wink. "I merely pulled it ashore when it had dragged Queen Olivienne into the sea."

At that, the woman in question walked up. "I was trying to save a baby roc, Commander! They are a protected species, after all."

Lebben gaped at both of them and gave a quick bow to the Queen. "My Queen! I never knew your missions were so...exciting!"

She grasped his other shoulder and two of the guardians behind her snickered when it looked as if Lebben would faint from the casual touch. "Well, ser...now you know. If you're done here, Commander Tosh and I must find out where we're needed next."

Lebben held the stylus and vellum book aloft and gave them a big grin. "Yes, my Queen. I have all I need between my eyes and my words. And thank you, Commander, for sharing your story. I think the citizens will be excited to read about the heroics of their future King." With those final words, he turned on his heel and walked away, already composing the story that would be printed in time for the next dae's sheets.

Bemused, Castellan was left facing the railer that had just arrived, watching passengers disembark once again. For obvious reasons they had stopped when the leviathan made its appearance. A lone figure carrying a black duffel broke free from the crowd on the railer platform as security specialists began ushering people along to get the railer schedule back on track. The figure coming toward them was obviously a woman, but she was too far away for Castellan to see her clearly. Security Corp officers rushed to stop her, but let her through when she presented documents pulled from her waist pouch.

Olivienne moved to stand next to Castellan and shielded her eyes so she could see the approaching figure better. Being a crack shot with the pistol, Olivienne's eyes were notoriously keen at long distances and her dark brows rose with shock. "Is that..."

"Commander Castellan Tosh, what is it about you and those infernal creatures of the deep? Do they follow you to every port city in Psiere?"

"Gem!" Castellan called out excitedly.

Olivienne clutched the commander's belt, near her pistol holster. "*Tosh...Maman!*"

"*On it!*"

The commander wasted no time on pleasantries. "Savon, Madlin, round up the team. We need to get to the royal residence as soon as possible. Call the security hub and have them clear the streets between here and there, priority critical."

"Yes, ser!" Shield guardians scrambled to gather the small amount of gear they had brought along for the dae. Tosh and Olivienne jogged toward the approaching doctore.

Gemeda bowed to Olivienne when they came to a stop in front of her. "My Queen."

"No time for that Gem, how is your channel? Good for a healing?"

She gave Castellan a startled look as the commander took possession of her duffle. "Yes, of course. Was someone injured in the attack?"

"Not this one, but yes, my mother. Please, doctore, you must come with us."

Gem's gaze spun back to Olivienne as a hauler pulled up near them. "There are so many conflicting stories on the southern continent right now. We heard the queen died, others said she was wounded but would never recover."

Olivienne gave her a tight smile and gestured toward where the rear door had been opened on the waiting hauler. "Closer to the second than the first and Psiere needs your skill more than ever before, Doctore Shen."

"No need for dramatics. My heart, skill, and talents all belong to the Queen." They quickly loaded into the large vectura with Spc. Calderon driving and Lt. Savon in the front seat next to him. Lt. Madlin was on her voteo speaking rapidly with the local Security Corp office and her message was obeyed with abnormal speed. Less than two meens later, officers on cycles met up with and flanked their hauler as it sped down the roadway back toward the west side of the city.

CASTELLAN LEFT OLIVIENNE pacing outside Olivara's private room while Keshien sat nearby with a hopeful glimmer in his eyes at the prospect that his par was going to be healed. Dre. Shen warned that the damage to Olivara's mind may be too severe and the healing would only heal her body, without Olivara ever regaining consciousness. But she also wouldn't know until she began, which was why Olivienne was pacing off nervous energy.

Because of the attack and reason behind the unexpected arrival of the one person who had the best chance at saving Olivara Dracore, Tosh had set up a meeting with General Renou and Captain Torrin. Due to Torrin's injuries, they opted to meet in his private suite within the royal residence. She could have invited more but facts had become twisty of late and Castellan no longer knew who she could trust.

The first thing Castellan did was let the two officers know that Dre. Gemeda Shen had arrived first thing on the morning railer and was busy at that very moment healing Olivara Dracore. Torrin and Renou blew out sighs of relief but Renou was the more pragmatic of the two. "Does she know if the healing will bring her back? Sometimes coma victims never recover their mind, even when their body is healed."

"Doctore Shen told me she had no way of knowing until she started the healing."

Torrin spoke up. "And how is it that Doctore Shen happened to show up right when we needed her most? Didn't reports say that all the telesana capable healers were down in Ostium at a conference, save the two that were injured in Tesseron? Did she leave the conference early?"

Castellan had gotten the story from her friend during their ride in the hauler and was fascinated by it. "Gemeda was actually due to depart on the eight hundred oor railer yesterdae morning, heading back to her current home city of Gomen."

"But, she couldn't possibly arrive on the eight hundred oor this morn if that's when she left! It's nearly a forty oor trip."

Castellan nodded. "Yes, well Gemeda's companion told her that he had a dream two nights before where Doctore Shen was desperately needed in Tesseron. Gem said that he was a doctore's assistant that had also been attending the conference, and that he had a four rating prescience channel. So rather than question the man's dream, she changed her ticket to Tesseron for the eighteen hundred departure that very evening and let her hospital in Gomen know that she was taking an extended leave." Castellan leveled a serious look at the other two officers. "I trust Doctore Shen with my life, she is beyond reproach."

"Unbelievable!"

Torrin smiled at his general's exclamation. "More like lucky."

After that Castellan gave Cpt. Torrin and Gen. Renou her report on the happenings at the docks and they seemed especially taken aback. Renou shook her head in disbelief. "Until this attack we've never had a leviathan in Bindle Bay, let alone two within a matter of daes. And you say it appears to have been targeting

Doctore Shen? Not the Queen?" Castellan nodded.

Cpt. Torrin directed the next question toward the general. "You mentioned that you had a high level prisoner from one of the attacking dirigibles that Defense had brought down with shells. Who was it?"

Because of his injuries, Torrin hadn't been updated on the most recent events any more than Tosh. They were both eager to know the latest state of the anti-sovereign investigation. Renou removed a few sheets from the satchel she carried. They were security reports with included image stills. "Camillo Binn was the privateer leading the dirigible attack on Tesseron, though we're still not sure how it was so precisely coordinated with the Atlanteen attack. Someone has found a way to communicate with our enemies of the sea, and what's worse is that they appear to be working together. To what gain, we can only imagine."

Castellan cocked her head to the side, deep in thought. "Has anyone ever spoken with an Atlanteen? We've seen them from afar, sure. But have we ever communicated?"

Renou frowned. "What I'm going to tell you is the highest level of secrecy. The leaders of Psiere have kept the information sealed for many rotos to prevent others from attempting similar. Not a word of this gets out, with the exception of Queen Olivienne, savvy?"

Both subordinates nodded. "Yes, ser."

"Near one hundred rotos ago, we had a team of telepaths, as well as psi and animal empaths, join an expedition to make contact with the Atlanteens. Their expedition ship was just off the coast of Dromea, in the Solis Sea. They had a military dirigible floating directly above to observe and receive coded light transmissions that were relaying the team's findings from the ship's crew. It was well before the miraculous discovery of voteos. The dirigible is the only reason we know as much as we do about what happened. Now if you've ever taken one of the Greater Beasts classes at Academy, you'll know that in order to facilitate communication with many species, you need only to put your hand into their medium. It doesn't require a full immersion. Anyway, the expedition that went out to make contact included an experimental research vessel, one that was extremely advanced for the time."

Torrin sat up slightly in his chair. "And did they make contact?"

General Renou nodded gravely. "A platform was lowered to

the water so the group of telepaths and empaths could submerge their hands. One Defense Corp Lieutenant and two automatons stood on the small platform with the biologists while five artilleries of bombardiers lined the rail up on deck." She paused and leaned forward. "Twenty-six skilled soldiers and two automatons...and not one could stop what happened."

"Were they killed, ser?"

"Not all of them and not outright. They did make contact, much to their surprise and excitement. The Atlanteens informed the scientists that the oceans of New Atlantea, their name for Psiere, belonged to the people of the sea. Three hundred rotos of Oral history had promised that the two-leggers would never trespass else they'd be subject to execution."

Castellan's pale brows rose with surprise. "Who promised them? If the events happened a hundred rotos ago, that makes their oral history close to four hundred rotos old. Psierians don't even have written history that goes that far back! Our own records only go back to roto two hundred and sixty-two." She ran a hand through her hair. "We only know what roto it is now based on initial data discovered in the first translated texts."

"More mysteries that we don't have the answers to, I'm afraid. Unfortunately, the lieutenant in charge of the mission instructed the scientists to tell the Atlanteens that the two-leggers were the true rulers of Psiere and could go where they wished, while the people of the sea were relegated to the waves and below."

Torrin made a face. "I see where this is going now. What kind of insensitive git would say such a provocative thing during first contact with an intelligent race?"

"It was a man by the name of Pogon Havington, Pon Havington's avu-patruus. From what I've read, Pon's avus, Polestre Havington, was estranged from his sib. Their feud was well known at the time. The Havington feud had become infamous after one meeting between them caused a small riot in the main council chamber of Cordeesh." She gave a careless wave. "Information about the Havingtons is long-held public knowledge since both the feud and riot made the broadsheets at the time they happened. It's also in the historical records if you wish a better look at the Havington family history."

Renou grinned, knowing that neither of her officers would be interested in such things. "Anyway, that was probably how Pon Havington's particular branch of the Havington line avoided the scandal when Pogon was discharged from Defense Corp service dishonorably and sentenced to Aetate for five rotos. He got lucky because his actions happened only a few rotos after the creation of the Psiere Legibus, and the establishment of Aetate and Iuvenis as destinations for those committing serious infractions. Had it been a handful of rotos earlier, he would have risked being tied into a boat and sent out to sea for the Atlanteens to do with as they saw fit."

The general drank deeply from a nearby glass of water then continued her tale. "As you've both already surmised, his words were not taken well. The Atlanteens initiated an immediate attack on the vessel. The biologists brought the platform back to the deck of the ship to begin evacuations to the dirigible. What earned Pogon his discharge and sentencing was the fact that he was one of the first to grab onto the rescue line swinging from the dirigible and therefore was pulled to safety ahead of all the biologists and the rest of his team. When not one but two leviathans rose from the water around the ship, the dirigible increased altitude to avoid the questing tentacles, dooming the rest of the people on the vessel. The floundering research vessel was ripped completely in half."

Tosh drew back in surprise. "Is the entire Havington line nothing but rotting fruit? You said that the information was sealed, how many actually know about the contact?"

"Only three knew at the time what was said on that platform. Havington and the two biologists who were rescued with him. The information was recorded when they were debriefed and the sealed documents were passed on to the relevant Corp heads. The biologists were instructed to never tell anyone their findings, as was Havington."

Cpt. Torrin scowled. "Did Pogon Havington have any contact with his family before being sent off to Aetate? Though I suppose he would have plenty of contact after his return as well. You mentioned that he was only sentenced to five rotos."

Renou sighed. "He was only initially sentenced to five rotos for his actions on the expedition ship but when Queen Oletia, that's Olivara's avia, reviewed all the reports from the incident, she instructed him to be re-sentenced to Iuvenis, where he spent the rest of his life. However, you are correct to surmise that he did have contact with his entire family before the first sentencing. There was quite an uproar when Polestre Havington entered the Grand Arbitration chamber in Ostium. I read those old broadsheets. Apparently the common speculation was whether or not Polestre sorrowed for his sib or was happy to see the man put away after having such a contentious relationship with him. The entire Havington family in attendance that dae was allowed a half oor of privacy to say their goodbyes after sentencing was complete."

Castellan thumped her fist on the arm of her chair. "Which means that he could have passed along the intel on how to contact the Atlanteens as well as what was said that dae. And that knowledge was more than likely passed down to Pon's father, Polegane, then to Pon himself. I'd also suggest that the entire Havington family line would have reason to hate the sovereigns of Psiere after Pogon was sent off to Iuvenis."

General Renou nodded. "So it would appear."

"I'd also lay cred on the fact that Praefectus Havington is the one who has been communicating with the Atlanteens and has possibly instructed his lackeys on how to do it as well."

"But to what purpose? Why would the Atlanteens even listen to or work with him if they are as aggressive as we've seen?" Cpt. Torrin blew out a frustrated breath.

Renou stroked her lip in thought. "Well the first rule of any successful negotiation is for both parties to get what they want, or at least think they've gotten what they want. Question is, what do the Atlanteens want? It's not like they could make use of any of our resources or technologies. None of our aether tech is built to work underwater."

Tosh sat up. "They want the sea, the oceans, and every bit of space that's not land. That's what Havington would have promised them."

The captain of Olivara's Shield Corp unit looked at her with concern. "Can he do that? Is it feasible for Psierians to stay out of the oceans altogether? How much does the Stock Corp depend on ocean harvest to feed the citizens?"

Having learned much about the intricacies of Psiere governance over the past roto, Tosh looked toward Renou. "I know from Olivienne that the Queen has ordered many reports and fact finding sessions to see what the impacts of a successful uprising would be, should the sovereigns no longer hold power. Did any of it mention a population drop from war or conflict?"

Renou scowled tiredly and rubbed at her forehead despite the fact that it wasn't even middae. "There was such a report that broke down how many lives were predicted to be lost during an event of that nature. We'd have to look at Stock Corp reports to see what percentage the ocean haulers contribute to the nation's food supply. But if the population declined enough, I'd say it was entirely feasible to stop ocean harvest completely, for at least five deca-rotos."

"Ser, I..." Castellan closed her eyes to sense with her soft channels. When she opened them again she looked back and forth between Cpt. Torrin and Gen. Renou. "This feels right."

"Bollux to you and your intuition channel, Tosh! But you were on target with your warning about the nature of the attack on Tesseron, and I fear you are right about this as well. I'll get a team set up to do the maths and comparisons, meanwhile I know Leniste has his interrogation crew working on Camillo Binn. We need definitive proof that Havington is the head of this snake in order to move on him. We've put a lot of good clues together but it's nothing that will allow us to pursue the man."

"What are the odds that Binn breaks and leads us to the information we seek?"

Renou shook her head regretfully. "If Havington is as smart as I suspect, then I doubt he's ever had personal contact with Camillo Binn. My guess is that Binn will only give us the names that we already suspect, his known associates."

Torrin growled. "Ser Enik Gannon, and Gahmo Dek."

"Precisely. And unfortunately for us, the anti-sovereign factions appear to be operating in cells, without knowledge of what the other cells have planned."

Tosh frowned, feeling a touch of impotent rage build. "By the Makers, I hate all this waiting!"

Their discussion was interrupted by a tone from the voteo on Castellan's belt. "Tosh here."

The voice on the other end belonged to Lt. Savon. "Commander, the Queen is awake! I mean, um, Olivara Dracore...not Queen Olivienne."

Tosh couldn't help smiling at the flustered man. "I know what you mean, Savon. I'll be there shortly. Tosh out."

She clipped the voteo back on her belt and stood along with General Renou. She directed her parting comment at Torrin. "I'll be sure Doctore Shen stops here as soon as she has capacity to do more healing. If Olivara Dracore is up and possessing of all her faculties like we hope, she's going to need her captain at the ready!"

Torrin gave her a grateful smile. "Thank you, Commander."

Secs later, the two women were out of the room and heading back across the royal residence with Castellan hoping for that miracle.

Chapter Nine

THERE WAS NO one in the hallway outside Olivara's private room save a mix of Shield Corp guardians from both the previous Queen and current Queen's units. Despite being down four, including Torrin, there were still enough Shields to adequately secure a Queen who had not left her room. Castellan glanced to where the much shorter general paced down the hallway alongside her. "I don't see King Keshien, Savon, Gem, or Olivienne. I certainly hope that is a good sign."

"From your lips to the aether itself, I hope you're right."

Renou rapped on the door and it was pulled open by an excited Lt. Savon. "Sers, the Queen is awake!"

"Well, technically I'm not Queen until the Imperium votes to reinstate me. But yes, I am most certainly awake." Both officers entered with relieved smiles. Olivara Dracore looked tired and a bit pallid, but well enough to soothe their worries. She laughed lightly. "Maybe I can slip out for a little vacation before the vote. How much would it take for you all to keep hush about the end of my little nap?"

"I see that while your injury may have robbed you of a few daes of time, it certainly didn't steal away any of your wit and mischief."

Olivara held out her hand to her long-time friend. "My dearest, Camen, you know it takes more than spite and shells to keep me down. And my wit is eternal."

Castellan looked around. "Where is Doctore Shen? I promised Captain Torrin I'd send her his way once she was sufficiently recovered."

King Keshien stood on the far side of Olivara's sick bed, holding her hand, while Olivienne mirrored his position on the side closest to the door. It was Olivienne who pointed toward a low couch against the far wall where Gemeda was deeply asleep. "She stopped when she was three quarters through the healing and came to get us. Gem said that there was a lot of damage and she was surprised Maman held on as long as she had. She also warned us that she was likely to collapse and need immediate rest when she was finished with the healing."

Castellan glanced toward the couch where her long-time

friend had clearly been laid out. "Should we move her to another room?"

Olivara waved off the suggestion and spared a quick glance and a wink for her par. "I have it on good authority that the couch is comfortable enough. Just leave her there for now. She can move to one of the guest rooms later if she likes."

"What about you, my love? Is there anything you need?"

Keshien had moved closer as he spoke and Olivara took a few secs to lean her head on his arm. "Gozen eggs covered with textured crème, and with slices of seared panis on the side." Both Castellan and Lt. Savon stifled quiet laughter with their fists.

"Maman, why don't you try some broth first? Then later when your regular doctore arrives, we'll ask if you can have something more substantial."

Olivara gave an aggrieved sigh then smirked as a fit of humor came over her. "Is that an order, my Queen?"

"Oh, you!" Olivienne lightly slapped her maman's arm even as tears welled in her eyes. "I feared desperately that you were gone for good. I never got to tell you how much I love you."

Olivara squeezed her daughter's hand. "I know you do, my dear. And I love you as well. I know it wasn't easy to fill the seat of the Divine Cathedra, even if only for a few daes. When did you arrive and what has gone on since?"

Lt. Savon caught Castellan's eye from near the door as Olivienne launched into the tale of their arrival and her confrontation with the Imperium. *"Ser, would you like me to find someone to provide broth to the Queen?"*

"I think that is a wonderful idea. How many oors have you been on duty without a break, Lieutenant?"

He grimaced. *"Six, ser."*

"Why don't you call Lieutenant Madlin in and head to the guardian residence for some down time? As a matter of fact, I want you to switch everyone out. I suspect we'll be on the move again soon and I want a fresh crew with Queen Olivienne." He nodded and turned to leave but stopped when she added one more directive. *"Oh, and send for Queen Olivara's regular doctore as well."*

He tilted his head curiously. *"Are we calling them both Queens now?"*

She shrugged. *"Seems safest, don't you think?"*

"Yes, ser." With those last private words between them, he quietly slipped out the door.

It took nearly a half oor to relay everything that had occurred in Tesseron after Olivara was injured. She seemed just as shocked as the rest when Castellan informed her of their suspicion about Pon Havington and his long dead Avu-patruus. "Pox on that family! It seems the entire Havington line is rife with drama and deception. I agree with your suspicions. Camen I'd like you to get that report to me as soon as possible."

"Yes, my Queen."

The Queen's mind was racing with all the information she'd learned. "Someone needs to schedule another meeting with the Imperium for first thing tomorrow morning."

Keshien spoke up, feeling better now that he knew his par was going to be okay. "I can do it when I leave to brief Torrin's team. Would you like me to send out an official report on your health and awareness?"

"No. Not just yet."

Castellan merely raised a pale brow but Olivienne was much more vocal. "What? Why ever would you want to keep that quiet? The people need to know that their Queen is alive and well!"

"They already know that." Olivienne opened her mouth to speak, then abruptly shut it again as Olivara's words registered. "Think about it. Right now we know the Imperium is flush with Havington supporters from Dromea, and who knows how many of them may be contributors to the anti-sovereign movement. I suggest we surprise them tomorrow morning. Let them think they are getting their new Queen, and that the balance of power is still in peril."

"Do you need me there for that?"

Olivara gazed at her daughter, seeing a near twin to herself at the same age in the younger Dracore. "No, I think the King should be fine enough company. Why do you ask? Were you hoping to continue your aborted oathing holidae, or perhaps go over the findings from your last adventurist mission? However did that pan out?"

Castellan and Olivienne wore the same gob-smacked look as they first met each other's eyes, then turned to stare at Olivara. "By the Makers, the entire cave mission slipped my thoughts completely!"

Before anyone could respond to Olivienne's chagrinned statement, the door opened and a shaggy dark head peered in. Kesharan's eyes lit up when he saw his entire family inside. Rather than enter in a calm manner befitting of his status as sub-Connate, he burst into the room. "Maman!" Then without a word or glance at anyone else in the room, he threw himself toward the bed and wrapped Olivara in an embrace. "They told me you'd been gravely injured and put me on the first railer south once they had security sorted. There were rumors on the railer that you'd been killed and Olivienne was our new Queen."

Kesharan's voice sounded hoarse, as if he had spent a lot of time crying on the long ride from the island of Instrucia. He was barely into adulthood and Castellan sympathized with the youngest Dracore. Kesharan had just been to Tesseron for their oathing ceremony. He would have made the trip all the way to Scola the dae after Olivienne and Castellan's departure, only to be told of the attack on the Queen and sent south again. Olivienne stepped back to give her sib some room and Castellan took the opportunity to interrupt her future par's thoughts.

"Now that the Queen has reminded us of the document we retrieved on Instrucia, I'd like to go take a look at it. Do you wish to accompany me or would you prefer to stay here with your family?"

Olivienne didn't bother answering Tosh directly. Instead she addressed her sib. "Well, they got part of it right, Kesh. They did vote me in as Queen while Maman was gravely injured. However, she's going to rectify that tomorrow so I can go back to being a boring historical adventurist."

He laughed and the group ignored his wet cheeks. "Good thing. I'm not sure how I feel about my sib being Queen of Psiere just yet."

"Me either! And on the topic of adventurism, now that Maman has reminded us of the document we retrieved from Instrucia, Castellan and I are going off to translate it."

"Savon is also sending your personal doctore around to give you a once over. Maybe you'll get your eggs yet todae." Castellan smiled at her future mamanar.

Olivara had yet to let go of Kesharan so she merely smiled in appreciation over his head. Castellan and Olivienne passed the doctore on his way to Olivara's room but didn't bother slowing down.

Back in Olivienne's royal residence, the soon-to-be reinstated Connate didn't waste any time apporting her satchel from her specially designated location next to her bed to the stone-topped table in the sitting room. She laid out supplies enough for both of them and placed the coded document between. "Based on what we found in the cave, I suspect this document will require the Temple of Antaeus key. Why don't you take the top three paragraphs and I'll take the bottom."

"As my Queen wishes."

Olivienne scowled. "You are working your way into a sound thrashing later!"

"Promise?"

They had missed the playfulness over the past few daes and Olivienne was glad to see her beloved slowly bring it back into their dynamic. She winked at the handsome woman and waved her hand toward the document on the table between them. "Mayhap. I suppose it will depend on what we find here."

"Well then, let's not waste any more time."

Castellan finished before Olivienne, having a natural knack with the maths needed for code translation. She sat back dumbfounded by the words that lay in front of her. Some of them made no sense other than by inference and by the context of what else was written. Rather than say anything, she remained silent while Olivienne finished her half. When the sovereign's translation was complete, she looked at Castellan with shocked eyes. "I—" Olivienne stopped speaking and shook her head as if to dispel the strange things she had just read. Rather than attempt to speak her aborted thoughts, she merely waved toward Castellan. "Go ahead, we may as well read this out."

Castellan started reading her translated portion. "The first bit begins, 'Scientere Extremus T'kinsaa Flx'n. Log nine-eight-four-three-seven-two.' Bollux but that's a mouthful! Then the rest of the text translates as such." She cleared her throat and began the main passage. "With the travesty of our arrival on Psiere and no indications of rescue, it was voted by the captain and crew that we should make plans for a future on this undiscovered planet. Many people died when the Terra Halcyon two-four-seven-nine crashed north of the mountains on one of the western hemisphere continents. With the aid of ship transport shuttles, we scienteres have mapped out every habitable biome on the planet. In an effort to spare as many species as possible, we seeded Psiere with the most adaptable and least violent of our specimens. Sadly the rest were left to perish in their cells aboard ship."

Olivienne interrupted. "Darling, that ship we were on when looking for the third key. Could that be the one the text is referencing? And the cells with creatures left to die..."

"If you remember, according to the automated announcement in the truth spray room, we were trying to gain access to the Terra Halcyon two-four-seven-nine cargo storage room. But clearly it was no sailing vessel as we first surmised."

"Clearly not, and I'd forgotten about the announcements." Olivienne briefly lamented the loss of the vessel to the caustic lake before her natural curiosity moved to the fore again. "Continue please."

"We were thrilled to discover the mineral that imbued native species with extranormal mental capacity. After rotos of study and dissection, it was proven that only species having a pineal gland could develop conscious control of the psychic powers. Within three generations all the seeded species originating from the Terra Halcyon two-four-seven-nine were displaying power equal to the natives. Unfortunately for the expedition team, all of us are Tau Ceti. We are both long-lived and asexual so we have no progeny to develop these powers. Two of my fellow scienteres created designs for in vitro chambers to facilitate non-sexual reproduction and mineral inheritance to the Tau genetics but it has yet to be trialed on our race. Instead the captain ordered crew and staff to begin work on Tau temples, as was standard protocol whenever the Tau Ceti discover and inhabit a new land."

"Tau Ceti. By the sounds of this text, these Tau Ceti are none other than the Makers!"

"So it seems. Okay, so it goes on to say trouble began in the roto one hundred and six. The most dominant and intelligent species were thriving on every continent and ocean, but tragedy struck when Antaeus was destroyed by a passing asteroid called Torae. The first and most disheartening was that the explosion incinerated the one emergency beacon we managed to launch into orbit. While we have been able to pick up sub-space communications, including updates on all the species we've collected, we remain unable to send a signal outward through the atmosphere of this planet. The beacon was placed in attempt to boost the emergency alert to any nearby Tau ship."

The commander paused, considering the ramifications of travel beyond Psiere. It was an overwhelming thought given that as a society they hadn't even gone beyond the bounds of their two continents. She began again before Olivienne could get too impatient. "We did have a bit of luck in our favor as the impact force from the segments of the small destroyed moon had significantly less energy than if the planet had been hit by the asteroid itself, so there was minimal damage done to Psiere's surface. Unfortunately, a number of recordable changes occurred to the planet itself. Tides were reduced and the Psiere axial tilt became twenty-five percent more unstable. But most disturbing was the discovery of the amalgam stones formed when bits of Antaeus melded with those pieces of Torae to create entirely new rocks of power."

Castellan stopped reading, her part done. "Your turn."

Olivienne pulled her paper near and continued the translation. "It has long been hypothesized that homo sapiens were limited by their biological drives and diversity of personality when it came to their capability of species advancement. We tried to practice non-involvement with all our seeded creatures, letting nature take its course. But all our work was nearly undone when homo sapiens discovered the antoraestones. Within a hundred rotos, few of the original seedlings were left. A succession of poor rulers combined with the might of the powerful stones doomed their primitive society. A few juveniles remained as well as embryos in the Terra Halcyon two-four-seven-nine fertility bank, but obviously none could survive or mature on their own. We were forced to intervene else we lose the lot of them." She stopped reading and Castellan looked back at her in confusion.

"Are...could we be these homo sapiens? Is that who or what we are as a race?"

Olivienne shrugged. "That seems to be what the text infers. There are also some words I'm not familiar with in the next bit. Clearly their science is well beyond anything we have."

"Well, according to this, anything we have was all given by the Makers so it stands to reason we would not exceed them. Bollux but this is a convoluted mystery!" She tapped Olivienne's translation. "Continue please."

"Using technology aboard the Terra Halcyon two-four-seven-nine, we genetically engineered certain traits into one particular batch of DNA. The traits were inserted in such a way as to follow mitochondrial inheritance. That was to guarantee they would be passed on along the females of what we deemed the sovereign line. The females of the modified genetic strand were designated as the eternal rulers of the homo sapiens and would be physically distinguishable from the rest by their dark hair and violet eyes. With the completion of the temples, we rebuilt the homo sapien society, established a ruling family and central laws, and left coded texts in the main temples of the northern and southern continents. It seemed dishonest to guide them to such an extent but we scienteres became invested in the experiment to such a degree that we had no choice but to follow through. The strange and emotional race became the young we could never have. To protect their fledgling society, we gathered as many of the antoraestones as could be detected with our imaging equipment and moved them to an impenetrable chamber within the third temple. Then the temple was locked and its location well-guarded until the homo sapiens reached an age and awareness to warrant discovery."

The commander looked at her Queen in shock. "You!" Out of nowhere she laughed loudly, barely able to control her mirth.

"What could possibly be so funny about any of this?"

Castellan shook her head and smiled at the woman she loved above all others. "All those doubts you had...and the Dracores, *you*, were made to rule. You literally carry the traits within you to be Psiere's ruler. I think the time for doubts about your capability and competence as Queen should be put to rest."

Olivienne looked chagrinned. "You may have a point. But the rest—this is beyond anything I've ever imagined. Despite how fantastical it all seems, I can't deny the obvious proof we've lived with for countless generations. We currently have the in vitro chambers in both great temples. It's how same sex couples have children, or those couples who can no longer physically bear a babe. But to actually design a child with particular traits? To know that I myself came from such a line?" She let out a long sigh and read the last bit. "After three more generations it became quite obvious that there was no longer room on any of the main continents for the crew of the Terra Halcyon two-four-seven-nine. To avoid discovery by our recovered and seeded races, we have moved all personnel and equipment to a remote location on the planet, one that is not currently accessible by any of the species' technologies. With the launch of yet another emergency beacon, we simply await the dae when another Tau ship comes to our rescue."

"What? Read that last sentence again!"

"With the launch of yet another emergency beacon, we simply await the dae when another Tau ship comes to our rescue." Olivienne turned wide eyes toward her lover. "Castellan, the Makers, these Tau Ceti...if they are as long-lived as the text states, they may still be here on Psiere."

Tosh ran a nervous hand through her perfectly combed hair. "Son of a sint. We have to tell the Queen." She paused before inclining her head slightly at Olivienne. "I mean, the other Queen."

Without speaking, Olivienne gathered all the translations and supplies into a neat stack, slid them back into the satchel, and locked it. When it was closed tight, she apported the bag back to her room and turned to Castellan with a mischievous grin. "The first Queen happens to be resting right now and the information we discovered is not life and death to be imparted immediately. As for the second Queen...I believe we have a matter yet to attend before we leave this residence."

"Erm, what exactly is this matter? I wasn't aware of anything on your schedule todae."

Purple eyes twinkled with delight. "I promised you a sound thrashing, did I not? I wouldn't want it to be said that a sovereign of Psiere goes back on her word. Besides, this is still technically our oathing holidae."

Castellan wasn't about to argue with a Queen's orders. Instead she looked at her timepiece and threw out a suggestion. "How about this? We both used a tremendous amount of energy this morning clearing the shipping hub. I could certainly do with a good rinse and a bite to eat."

"But I'm not—"

Castellan leaned forward to quiet Olivienne's protest with a kiss. "You may not think you're hungry but trust someone who has used and abused their hard channels much too often. You need to replenish what you lost this morning."

As the mere mention of food brought a beast to life in Olivienne's belly, her stomach gave a great rumble. Olivienne grabbed the offending part of her person and made a face. "I suppose you're right." She lifted her index finger and tapped it against her lips in thought. "Hmm, how about a soak and lunch tray?"

The suggestion earned her another kiss. "I'd say you have the absolute best ideas. I need to speak with Lieutenant Madlin for a sec. Why don't you start the water and as soon as I'm finished, I'll put together something for us to eat. I'll be ten meens, tops."

Olivienne tilted her head curiously. "Why do you need to speak with Madlin?"

Castellan winked. "To let her know that after the events of this morning, the Queen is requiring a few oors of mandatory rest and that she should not to be disturbed for anything shy of an emergency."

A dark brow quirked up. "Rest? You'll ruin my reputation as a tireless historical adventurist!"

"Oh, I'd lay wager that Madlin will know the truth amidst the tale. I'll also guarantee that your exhaustion will come if I have my way."

"Just my exhaustion?" The commander laughed and gave her a telekinetic shove toward the stairs leading up to Olivienne's suite.

As promised, a little less than ten meens later Castellan came through the doorway into Olivienne's room carrying a tray full of assorted finger foods — fresh fruits, various meats and cheeses, as well as a bottle of vineo and two goblets."

Olivienne was already settled deep within the water and she smiled to see her lover arrive. "Ooh, is that bottle from of the case I got on my last trip to Ostium?"

Castellan shrugged and set the tray on a low table near the extravagant soaker tub. "I assume so. I recognized the label as a vinier local to that region. I've heard their blend is quite good." She stripped out of her uniform and joined her lover in the water. It could easily fit twice as many people so the newly oathed couple could spread out if they wished, not that they did. "Try this one. It's a new fruit the staff picked up the other dae, a crossbreed between stone fruit and applet." Castellan held a large slice of succulent pink flesh against Olivienne's lips and the Queen opened her mouth obediently. When she bit into the fruit, juice ran down her chin and dripped into the water. At first she giggled but the sound quickly turned to a moan as Castellan leaned forward and cleaned the mess with a kiss. She pulled away with a smirk. "Mmm, it is good!"

"Come back." Olivienne pouted. It was a look reserved for Castellan alone and the loyal woman appreciated it.

"Not yet. First we need to get you fed then we'll see about sating other hungers."

Olivienne splashed water toward her. "Tease." Instead of further protest she reached over to grab a pale slice of cheese and bit into it with a click of her teeth.

It didn't take them long to make short work of the platter. Castellan used her telekinesis to move the entire table it rested on farther from the tub, then they sat back on opposite sides to sip their vineo. "How are you feeling? I know it's been a tumultuous couple of daes for you and I want you to know you can lean on me for anything."

Olivienne gave her love a fond look. "And you can lean on me as well. You don't have to be the perfect commander all the time, especially not for me."

She got a smile in return and Olivienne was reminded yet again of how painfully attractive her future par was. Castellan's maman certainly had the right of it, the Toshs were hard to resist. Luckily, Olivienne didn't have to. With single-minded purpose, the sovereign set her goblet aside and slowly made her way across the large tub toward Castellan. "Would you really like to know how I'm feeling?"

"I never say anything I don't mean."

"Neither do I."

"'Vienne?"

Olivienne crawled across Castellan and perched seductively in her lap. Water sluiced down her body, running from her shoulders, breasts, and the tips of her hard nipples. Then she took the other woman's hands and placed them on either side of her hips. "Tell me, Commander...how do I feel?"

Castellan sucked in a breath and her fingers tightened unconsciously. "You feel like I haven't touched you in far too many oors." She leaned up even as Olivienne leaned down toward her. Castellan's next words were whispered against her lips. "You feel like a fire when I've spent daes out in the cold."

The kiss that followed was hot and wet as each opened their mouth to the other. Castellan nibbled lightly at Olivienne's bottom lip, eliciting a whimper from the woman on top. Water sloshed as Olivienne thrust down in the hopes of finding friction against her throbbing sex. It wasn't that she had suddenly become turned on. Olivienne's arousal had been building throughout the afternoon, since she found out her mother was going to be okay. They had both been under a lot of stress over the past weke and a good tupping was one of Olivienne's favorite ways to relieve building tension. Not to mention their romantic oathing holidae had been cut severely short.

When she pulled back for air, Olivienne rested her forehead against Castellan's. Both women were panting as if they were back in training at Academy. "Darling, you feel unbelievably good but I fear we're going to make a mess of the facility."

"I could care less about the facility. I'll clean up the mess tomorrow."

Olivienne laughed. "We have staff for that."

"Hmm, but do you have staff for this?" Castellan moved her hands up until her fingers brushed the underside of Olivienne's breasts. The sovereign held her breath until strong hands worked their way farther up to encase her breasts in full, taking special care to pinch and pluck at her nipples.

Olivienne groaned. "N—no, staff definitely doesn't do that."

She leaned into Castellan's touch. "Kiss me again."

"Yes, my Queen."

Even as Olivienne suckled at Castellan's bottom lip, the commander's right hand was in motion. It had left the soft flesh above and made its way down Olivienne's body toward the center of her arousal. "Yes." Olivienne's response was a muffled hiss since she refused to stop kissing. Knowing fingers worked their way between their bodies and swept through Olivienne's folds. There was a slickness there, heavy and fluid, one that couldn't be accounted for by the water in the tub. Castellan knew because she had the same between her own legs.

"Is this what you want?" Despite the angle and discomfort to her wrist, Castellan inserted two fingers and teased Olivienne's clitoral nub with her thumb. Olivienne pulled her mouth away and threw her head back. She didn't answer as her eyes fluttered shut with sudden aching pleasure. "If you don't answer, I'll be forced to stop."

Violet eyes suddenly opened, pupils dilated wide, and Olivienne gripped the back of Castellan's damp hair. "Don't you dare stop!" she panted. Olivienne moved her hips, timed with the rhythm of Castellan's thrusts. A flush moved up her chest and neck in a surprisingly short time and Castellan marveled that her lover was so close to release.

She stilled her movements, much to Olivienne's displeasure. "No, don't stop."

"I want to try something. May I?"

Fingers tightened in Castellan's hair momentarily as Olivienne locked eyes with her. "I don't care what you start as long as I finish!" No sooner had she said the words when Olivienne found herself lifted straight up out of the water, by the will and thought of Castellan alone. Despite the heat and humidity of the room, chill bumps washed across her flesh. But before Olivienne could protest the exposure and cessation of pleasure from Castellan's touch, she was pulled directly into the path of her lover's tongue. "By the depths!" With the angle improved, Castellan had no problems thrusting her fingers upward while she lapped at Olivienne's bundle of nerves.

"Oh!" As for Olivienne, she wasn't merely being lifted by Castellan's channel, she was completely immobile and at her commander's mercy. Her muscles trembled as she rapidly approached the end. "Castellan...Tosh, I—" Words failed her and Olivienne let out a small whine with each of Castellan's thrusts.

Rather than take time away from her solemn duty, Castellan reassured her future par in a different way. *"I've got you, love. Everyone's safe, you're safe and no one can hurt you. Let go, 'Vienne."*

Perhaps it was the reassurance of safety, or maybe it was the permission given, but something in Olivienne broke in that exact moment. "Tosh, I'm —" Without any further warning, Olivienne screamed loud and long with the force of her release. It was a rough and guttural yell as she twitched and jerked within Castellan's telekinetic grasp.

Castellan's own sex gave a twinge as she felt strong muscles clench and pulse around her fingers. She continued to lap lightly, waiting for the familiar sign from her lover indicating that she was truly done. She got it when Olivienne opened lazy purple eyes and met her gaze with a smile. Then with the utmost care, she gently lowered Olivienne back into the warm water of the tub, cradling the sovereign on her chest as the panting woman recovered.

Castellan ran her hands up and down Olivienne's back while inky black hair floated in the water above. "How do you feel now?"

Olivienne sighed. Her face was pressed into the crook of Castellan's neck causing her breath to rustle Castellan's damp hair. "Ask me in a meen. Right now I can't feel so much as my legs."

Laughter rumbled below Olivienne's cheek. "Do you need me to dry you and carry you to bed?"

Olivienne lifted her head slightly. "I will make it worth your while if you do just that."

"Oh ho, and how will you manage such a lofty promise when I've clearly exhausted my Queen?"

"I never said I was exhausted, I merely said I couldn't feel my legs. I think you'll find my mouth and hands in perfect working order and my energy more than sufficient for the task at hand."

Castellan grinned. "I'm going to hold you to your word."

"As you should, the Queen's word is law." The sassy response earned Olivienne a pinch to the rear and she let loose a peal of laughter. Castellan reveled in the sound. Most of the tragedy and sadness that had surrounded the sovereign had at last lifted with the healing of Olivara. Before Olivienne could completely render Castellan useless in mind and body, the commander sent one last thought into the aether. She wished for the rest of their troubles to be sorted as quickly and neatly as the Queen's health.

Chapter Ten

TWO WEKES AFTER Queen Olivara returned to her seat on the Divine Cathedra, Tesseron resembled a functioning city once again. Much to the public's pleasure, Olivienne and Castellan continued to aide in the rebuilding efforts. The newly reinstated Connate became a darling of her people partly due to her help with cleanup and repair, and partly due to the article written in the broadsheets that circulated throughout the two continents.

The citizens of Psiere had always loved the idea of a royal romance. They tittered and swooned many rotos before when Queen Olivara first oathed the dashing historical adventurist, Keshien Vincender. And their consoral ceremony was so highly attended, the Grand Chamber of the Temple of Archeos barely had any room to walk from one end to the other. However, the past fervor was eclipsed by the current excitement once the image of Olivienne and Castellan sitting at the docks near suns' rise circulated. People were practically salivating over every bit of news and information they could get about the Connate and her future par. So on top of planning the upcoming mission to find the Temple of Antaeus, they also had to sit through a number of interviews with broadsheet representatives, a fact which both Olivienne and Castellan found annoying and tedious.

They weren't the only ones to help restore Tesseron to its pre-attack state of beauty. Given the condition of the hospitals and treatment centers throughout the city, Gemeda also remained to help heal the multitude of people who were injured. She had taken a leave from her own home medican center before heading north to find the Queen in dire straits, so there was no need to rush back to Gomen and her previous post. Per the Queen's request and with Gemeda's consent, the Medi Corp had officially reassigned her to Tesseron until things were once again stabilized.

Even Capt. Velten and her dirigible crew made themselves useful while they waited to find when the mission to the lost Temple would take place. With the increased speed and capacity, the *Quaesitum* took regular trips to surrounding cities in order to bring in fresh supplies and other essentials to Tesseron.

The attack was a tragedy that Psiere had not seen in many rotos, if ever, and it warmed Olivara's heart to see her people come together to set things right. With so many things finally back on track, it was time for the Queen to address the last issue. She looked around her private conference room to meet the eyes of each individual seated at the table. Most were the usual attendees, such as her par, General Leniste, and General Renou, as well as Templar Aislyn, her daughter, and Commander Tosh. But there were two new people seated at the table as well, one of them looking quite confused. Once she had their attention, the Queen spoke. "I've brought you all here to discuss the upcoming adventurist mission to the Temple of Antaeus. I've officially announced it to the Imperium, after Olivienne put it on hold two wekes ago. Everyone in this room plays a vital role in that mission."

Never one to hold back when she had something to say, Gemeda chose that moment to speak up. "Pardon, my Queen, but why am I here? I'm simply a doctore who is temporarily reassigned to Tesseron. I have no real knowledge nor bearing where this mission is concerned." Captain Velten watched the doctore with keen interest. It was her first time meeting the woman who had brought the Queen back from certain death, and she was not disappointed by the visage across the table from her.

The Queen smiled kindly, but her eyes held a glint that said she knew more than she cared to. The problem with being such a strong telepath and clairvoyant was that she almost always knew more than she wanted. Olivara's power was a curse as much as it was a boon. "Concerning that...I've had a precog about the coming mission."

"Maman?"

Olivara inclined her head toward Olivienne. "Obviously it's not about you specifically, darling, since you know we don't have visions about those we are extremely close with. However, I have had flashes of forest and the dirigible trip, as well as great danger coming from the sky. And death, much death. While I don't know how it all ties together, I know with certainty that Doctore Shen must travel to the Temple of Antaeus with you."

"Come again? I'm certainly no adventurist. Why—I wouldn't fair a meen out there in the wilds!"

Castellan laughed. "Oh come off it, Gem! I know for a fact that your physical conditioning is top notch for someone who is not in one of the military Corps. Granted, you're no fighter but then not everyone is. You still know which end of a pistol to fire if worse comes to worst."

"I was told by Savon that you nearly kept up with my Shield Corp unit the dae they were sprinting to haul us from the river near Vesper."

Gemeda waved her off. "An adrenal reaction, I can assure you."

Olivara sat back and watched the news of her warning and request play out amongst the three women. "Bollux! You're plenty fit, Gem—" Castellan paused and a dark look came over her face. "And as much as I hate to dredge up unpleasant memories, the Queen has not been wrong with her warnings yet. She knew my life would be in danger when we went to Navis and warned us then. I think we should take heed and give this some serious thought."

The generals and lead templar remained silent during the exchange. The Queen knew it wasn't her trip to organize, but that didn't stop her from trying to guide things in her own way. Olivara raised a single dark brow when a new voice entered the mix. "Excuse me, I don't know you, Doctore Shen, but what exactly are your reservations with going on this particular mission? From what I have heard, you are one of the top medicans in either continent. Few people can do what you do. I can understand if you think the mission is beneath you, or even if you are frightened of the unknown qualities of it—"

Gemeda stood abruptly. "I am neither frightened nor above such a mission! But it is as you said, there are only so many people that can do what I do, to the extent that I can do it. I feel as though I'll be taking my skills away from the people of Psiere during a tumultuous time just to play traveling medican to a team that already has two." Realizing that her outburst was unseemly when in the company of the Queen, she sat back down with a dower look upon her face.

"Gemeda, while I do have two medicans as part of my Shield unit, there is only one *you*. And as much as it pains me to say, my mother is more often right than wrong."

"Don't you mean always right, darling?"

Olivienne shot her maman an annoyed look before continuing. "If she says we need you on this mission or risk failure, then I'm inclined to believe her with every scrap of my being."

"If it helps, you will be under the protection of myself and my crew. No other's safety will be more important, save Connate Dracore."

Gemeda gave the tall, stern ship captain a shrewd look. "I'm fully capable of taking care of myself, Captain...what is your name?"

"Oh, my apologies. I just assumed everyone knew everyone else at the table." Queen Olivara lied with practiced ease, used to dealing with the Imperium and less than respectable representatives on a regular basis. But there was no way she could tell the two women that she had visions about them as well. "Doctore Gemeda Shen, I would like to introduce you to Captain Seema Velten. She commands the *Quaesitum* and has been permanently assigned to the Shield Corp as part of the joint Divinity/Shield task force set to work with Connate Dracore on her missions."

Professional and charismatic, if a little stern on occasion, Seema Velten stood and gave a bow toward Gemeda. "It is my pleasure to make your acquaintance, Doctore Shen. Your reputation proceeds you across both continents but it no way prepares a soul for your beauty." Castellan rolled her eyes and Olivienne grinned. The older psi in the room just chuckled indulgently.

Gemeda sighed. The last thing she needed was a cocksure dirigible captain making a play for her favor. She learned back at Academy that missions were best kept platonic. She could see where it had worked out in Castellan and Olivienne's favor, but not everyone could have a romance fit for the broadsheets and children's stories. Gemeda glanced around at the expectant faces and finally relented, if only as a personal favor to the two people who had become good friends. She met Olivienne's infamous violet eyes. "I suppose I'll do it. After all, how often does one get to travel with good friends, while at the same time risk life and limb for Queen and country? I am due for a holidae."

Olivienne voiced her affront at the implication that her career could be considered naught more than a sabbatical. "Holidae! I'll have you know—"

She was quickly quieted by Castellan's hand grasping her forearm. "'Vienne, Gem was putting you on. She knows what you do isn't as easy as all that."

Gemeda's wind up of Olivienne earned a few chuckles. "Do we know how long the mission will take?"

The Queen gave a self-satisfied smile as the doctore capitulated. Olivienne yielded the answer to Captain Velten, who was in charge of transport. Velten pulled out a rolled map from her satchel and flattened it out on the table. Leniste, Tosh, and Aislyn were quick to provide drink tumblers to weigh down the corners. "Based on the document given to me by Connate Dracore, we know that the Temple of Antaeus is located on the Isle of Magna off the eastern edge of Endara. The coordinates mark out a location midway up the western coast of the island. Heeding security instructions from Commander Tosh, I've plotted a course across the northern continent that would allow us to avoid the major cities and potential interference from the anti-sovereign factions."

Tosh had her own questions since this was the first she had seen Velten's travel plan. "I know you told us that the *Quaesitum* has the same range as other dirigibles, despite its increased size and speed. When we've been on similar long missions there were stops to fill the illeostone tanks. What are your planned refill points?"

"The trip east will have four legs. I've selected two smaller towns that have enough dirigible traffic to warrant stone stations. Ora Maris is on the southern shore of Dir Nubila. It is situated on the river that leads from Dir Altum to the inland sea."

Castellan gave a subtle nod. "Yes, I know the place. I believe Specialist Holling hales from there." She looked around the table in acknowledgement of those that didn't know all the members of Olivienne's Shield team. "He is one of our medicans." She waved toward the map. "Please continue."

"The trip from Tesseron to Ora Maris is eight hundred and sixty three mahls, so roughly fourteen and a half oors. Illeostone exchange takes about twenty to thirty meens, then we'll make our way over the mountains to Montesilva. The third leg takes us from there to a limited transportation hub in the tiny town of Nusquam. It's the last bit of real civilization before railers make the long jaunt across the northern steppe to Baen. Nusquam is situated along the Latus Ocean and almost directly west of the coordinates for the Isle of Magnus where the Temple of Antaeus is said to be located. In total, we're looking at a little over three thousand, two hundred and fifty mahls and near two and a half daes of continuous travel, barring illeostone stops."

General Leniste scowled. "Have we discovered the reason why this Magnus Island has never been found before? It seems a bit easy to just jaunt over the way you say."

Renou inclined her head in agreement with her counterpart. "It does seem a bit too easy."

Olivienne had her suspicions on that exact unknown. "Captain Velten, how long is the journey from Nusquam to Magnus?"

"That particular leg is seven hundred and forty-four mahls long, from the illeostone station to the point indicated by the coordinates retrieved in your third temple key mission."

"So to go there and back..."

Velten frowned. "Would put us slightly over our maximum range for the *Quaesitum*. We will be significantly over if we run into difficulty along the way, such as storms, headwinds, or rogues."

The Queen sat back, troubled at the new information. "With no guarantee that we can bring you back, I don't think I can approve this mission in good conscience."

It would mean the culmination of Olivienne's life's work to find the lost temple of Psiere and Olivienne was nearly desperate to continue as originally planned. "No! We'll think of something when we get to Magnus but finding the lost temple of Psiere is too important to cancel it."

General Leniste was a lot more vocal in his opposition. "Unacceptable! While we may be able to put together a volunteer adventurist group for a mission into the unknown such as this, there is no way Psiere can do without any of her sovereigns at this time. *Especially* at this time."

Olivienne looked from her mother, to both generals, and she could see them begin to collapse under the weight of keeping her safe. In a last ditch effort, she turned to the man who had taught her the most about historical adventurism. "Papan—do you have any suggestions?"

Everyone looked at the King, who sat back and rubbed his chin in thought. "Let's break down this mission. What is our goal?"

Olivienne was used to his leading questions so she went along with it. "To find the Temple of Antaeus."

"Good. And what do you know of Psiere's temples?"

Zane Aislyn tilted her head, starting to catch on to the King's thinking. "Each temple is comprised of multitudes of rooms and corridors. They house encoded texts and Maker technology."

"And?"

"Archeostones!" Castellan thumped her fist on the table. If there was one thing she knew about, it was the illeostone charging rooms in the temples. After all, her own mother ran the ones in Tesseron. She looked at Olivienne excitedly. "Each temple has been found with a total of four archeostones set in the walls of the charging rooms. It stands to reason that the Temple of

Antaeus would be equipped similarly. So once we arrive at the island, we need only to recharge the stones carried over on the dirigible in order to return home."

Olivienne's smile couldn't be brighter if it shone from Archeos itself. "So we have a plan to move forward. Are any in disagreement?"

This time it was General Renou who expressed concern. "The plan hinges on two things: that you can get inside the Temple of Antaeus, and that it houses archeostones. But we don't know what the Makers did before they abandoned it. There is no certainty that you'll be able to come home."

"Captain Velten, I know from the tour that the *Quaesitum* has engines on each corner, the fore dextra and laeva, as well as the aft dextra and laeva. Can any of their drive props be disconnected for manual use?"

Velten looked at Commander Tosh curiously. "Of course they can be disconnected, though there is no one who can make use of them manually. The sole purpose of the disconnect feature is for repair and maintenance. Why do you ask?"

"I thought perhaps the Engineering Corp could come up with a device that could attached to one of the drives. Something that would allow a prop to be powered by telekinesis. It may be significantly slower than an aether-driven motor but as long as the push ratio is sufficiently balanced, I can maintain motion for quite a long time." She glanced around the table. "Obviously it would only be used as a worst case scenario if we couldn't get the stones charged at the temple."

Keshien Dracore looked upon his daughter's future par with newfound respect. She had a much keener mind than he originally anticipated based on her rotos as a Defense Corp officer. Most people in that particular service corp tended to be unyielding and singularly focused. A lot more like General Leniste. "I've never heard of anything like what you're suggesting but I don't see why they couldn't come up with something. I know the head of the research and development center here in Tesseron. I'll ring her on the teleo after this meeting. Provided of course the Queen approves the mission despite the slight chance that the stones cannot be recharged."

Everyone moved their focus from the King to the Queen. Olivara sat for a moment weighing the risks. She looked around the table and met each person's eyes. Castellan could feel fear and confusion pulsing faintly from her lover and questioned her silently. *"What is it?"*

Olivienne glanced at her in surprise. *"How did you know? My thoughts have been locked down tight, as they usually are in any room with my mother."*

Castellan gave a slight shrug. *"I'm not sure. Perhaps we are starting to empathetically bond?"* She referred to the fact that even when a psi didn't hold the empathy channel, often times they will develop a low rating in empathy if they are especially close to someone, such as a copy sib or a par. It only ever happens in people with the telepathic channel that spend a lot of time around each other. The doctores and scientists had never been able to explain it, only surmising that it had something to do with the telepathic connection and emotional conjunction.

"Perhaps we have. I guess I don't understand where all this reticence is coming from. Maman has always supported my career before. And she knows it's dangerous. Many historical adventurists have died trying to access Maker caches and tech."

Castellan thought for a sec while the Queen remained silent. *"If you were in the middle of a forest and you saw a handful of trees on fire and you were familiar with the terrain, would you be concerned?"*

"A little I suppose."

"What if tens of trees were on fire all around you and the terrain was completely unfamiliar?" She watched understanding wash over Olivienne's face. *"The Queen has never been here before. The goal and destination of your path has never been so uncertain, and the combined anti-sovereign and Atlanteen movements of late make any direction dangerous. She is worried for you, not as a Queen, but as a mother."*

Olivienne didn't respond at first. Instead she closed her eyes in acute understanding. After all, it was only a few wekes before she had thought she was going to lose her maman. Loss made you do strange things, think strange things. *"Thank you."*

Their silent conversation was interrupted when the Queen's gaze moved to Gemeda Shen and paused. Gemeda looked back at her curiously. "My Queen?"

Olivara began to respond but froze before a word could come out. Her violet eyes rolled back into her head as a vision overtook her. The King was quick to grab Olivara's shoulders to hold her upright as the Queen experienced a strong prescient episode. Her words came out in a monotone. "Deadly treasure awaits to be held by the honorable soul. The path forward leads to another path forward. The grays will watch our search but beware of beasts that ride your coattails in the wind. A great battle is coming and only the keeper of the stone can be the victor when thunder and flame fill the sky." She slumped forward and went still.

General Leniste shook himself. "The episodes are always so strange. I don't think I've ever seen a precog that wasn't odder than my oddest dream."

Keshien came to his par's defense, though Leniste wasn't attacking. "The prescient episodes *are* dreams of a sort. They're waking dreams that just happen to have a root in future reality." He grinned around the table. "I will admit that the ones she has while sleeping and records in the morning are probably the strangest of all. I don't pretend to understand it all, not possessing any of those channels myself. But I've learned over the rotos to heed Olivara's because hers are so strong." They all knew the strength of their Queen's visions. She was infamous for her ability to see future Psiere dangers and guide her people around them.

Everyone waited expectantly. The silence was only broken by the sound of Templar Aislyn scribing the Queens premonition on the back of a used sheet of vellum. Another meen went by before Olivara roused from her stupor and sat upright, patting Keshien on the hand for his help. She gave them all a wry grin. "Well, that was certainly one of the more powerful ones I've had." The Queen looked over to the head of the Divinity Corp. "Did you get it all?"

Zane finished up the last sentence and nodded. Her white-streaked hair was pulled back into a low bun and she wore the traditional light gray robes of her Corp, which contrasted nicely with her dark skin. "Yes, my Queen. As to what it all means, well I'm sure each of us could take a guess and be more right than wrong."

Olivara rubbed the space just above the bridge of her nose. "Well, I did glean something out of it besides a headache...one important thing."

"What is that, Maman?"

"My vision tells me that this adventurist mission is going to happen. *Has* to happen." She turned to Keshien. "Get Engineer Lemino on the line when we're finished here and have her start the research team on that manual prop drive immediately. Tell her I want a working prototype within a weke's time."

He raised his brows in question. "That seems like a short timeline."

"I want Commander Tosh to trial it before the mission. And I want the *Quaesitum* to disembark the first of Septa." She met Olivienne's eyes. "That gives your team two more wekes to prepare. Savvy?"

Olivienne mentally gave a sigh of relief. "Yes, ser."

"Now, if we have the details worked out for the mission to the lost temple, we can close this discussion. We'll review again in ten dae's time to see where we stand on the manual propulsion drive. Templar Aislyn, Doctore Shen, and Captain Velten, thank you for coming. Zane, Instrae Greene should be waiting outside. I would greatly appreciate if you could send her in for the next discussion."

Tmpl. Aislyn bowed. "Yes, my Queen."

Keeley Greene slipped inside the meeting room and took a seat at the table after the other three gathered their materials and filed out. She placed a large satchel on the table then removed a stack of velum and passed a multitude of sheets around the table. "I'm not going to waste anyone's time. It was a long trip from Scola so I'll just get right down to the reason I'm here."

Olivara held up one image of a gray humanoid with large eyes. It had four digit hands instead of the psi five. There were markings on the sheet to indicate height and the humanoid was strangely short. "Is this...?"

Ins. Greene gave her a solemn look. "Yes. I put my best forensic sculptistes on the project. Using skeletal analysis, our own psychometrist, and the accounts from Lieutenant Madlin's precognitive episode, we were able to construct a reasonable facsimile of what we believe to be one of the Makers. The Tau Ceti as your most recent document provided." She waited for the image to truly sink in before continuing with her findings. "We believe the Tau Ceti to be dark gray in coloring, with smooth hairless skin, enlarged head and eyes, and no physical sexual characteristics. The analysis was adjusted when it came to light that the Tau were asexual. We had previously assumed that the narrow pelvic region indicated a male of the species but now we suspect that to be the standard for all."

Leniste grunted, taken aback by the foreign looking creature on the page in front of him. "What about the other information, that the sovereign line was somehow created by the Makers? Sorry, I meant to say created by these Tau Ceti. Is something like that even possible?"

"As some of you may not know, the high security research department under my purview has one of the few familial coders in Psiere."

Olivienne gave her a confused look. "Familial coder? What is that?"

Inst. Greene answered easily. "The device is used to extrapolate a number of things about Psierians. Medicans take a sample of blood to feed into the machine. The familial coder then determines various health specifics. Everything from familial ties, to potential for disease, gestational risk, or even declining mental acuity."

Renou looked quite shocked at the notion. "I had no idea such a thing existed!"

Leniste surprised them all. "Oh, they're very useful. My youngest sib was diagnosed with a blood deficiency using the blasted thing. Her doctore got her on a proper supplement right away."

Renou looked to her counterpart, always surprised when he displayed an unexpected bit of knowledge. It wasn't that Germaine Leniste was a dull psi. On the contrary, he had a brilliant tactical mind and a knack for knowing who to trust in dire situations. But he also tended to be stubborn and hotheaded. "I guess I'm not as up to date on channel knowledge as I'd like. Why couldn't a doctore with the telesana channel simply heal her straightaway?"

Castellan knew the answer to that one, thanks to Gemeda, but she held her tongue as Ins. Greene answered. "A doctore with telesana can only heal you back to the state in which you were born. Sadly, they cannot heal any defects in your code."

Renou rubbed the bridge of her nose. "Huh, I guess you learn something new every dae."

Keeley shrugged. "It's not like Psierians display a high number of ailments at birth. They are pretty rare actually. So most would only experience telesana healing involving post-natal issues or injuries."

Olivara reined in the discussion. "We've gotten a bit off track. Continue please."

"Apologies, my Queen." Keeley Greene shuffled to the bottom of her stack of velum before addressing the people around the table. "Anyway, the familial coder gives us, for lack of a better word, health scores, for those who have previously been tested. And what most don't know is that there is a coder built into the pedestals in each of the temple Grand Chambers. The results are private, given only to the newly oathed pair if there is an incompatibility registered or another health issue is discovered with one person or the other. Each person gets an individual percentage, and the couple also gets a percentage together to see their match potential. For instance, both could carry a dormant issue in their familial line that would become active in their children if they were to procreate the standard biological way."

The Queen was nodding along with Instrae Greene's words, already familiar with the coder. Keeley stopped to stare into Olivara's eyes and Olivienne knew they were having a private conversation. A moment later, the instrae continued. "With the Queen's permission, I can tell you that all sovereigns throughout recorded history have tested at one hundred percent. Just that knowledge alone seems to corroborate the document found on Instrucia."

Camen Renou looked from Olivara to Olivienne then turned back to Keeley. "What does the average psi test?"

"The average test result for all non-sovereign citizens is ninety-two percent. That is of course eliminating the outliers on the bell curve."

Castellan's intuition channel jangled at the mention of citizen testing and she remembered another time she felt a prick similar to the one in the temple during their oathing ceremony. The commander turned to glare at Olivara. Her tone was somewhat accusatory and warm with unfamiliar anger. "You knew my score. Was that why you all but forced me and Olivienne together? Was I even the first choice to head up her Shield unit, or were you merely hoping for a bonding match?"

"Castellan? What are you talking about? How could she know all that before we went through the oathing ceremony?"

Olivienne's question was ignored as Castellan continued to press the Queen for an answer. "What was my score?"

Sensing that his former officer was on the verge of disrespecting their Queen with all out insubordination, he grumbled a low warning. "Tosh..."

Castellan Tosh would not be dissuaded from the truth. Her eyes never left Olivara's purple gaze but the commander slammed her fist onto the conference table as her voice came out at a near yell. "What was my score?"

The room filled with tense silence with everyone at the table having no clue as to what was going on save for three. Gaze unwavering, Olivara answered the question. "Ninety-nine percent."

Castellan gave a hoarse cry, hating the thought of manipulation nearly as much as betrayal. She had worked her entire life, dedicated it to her career. Serving Queen and country was what she had lived for since graduating Academy. Now everything she had earned was thrown into question. "Was our entire romance naught but a grand manipulation to find the best possible match for your daughter?" She ran a hand haphazardly through her hair, sending it into disarray. "How much have I truly earned on my own merits and how much of my career is owed to your mollycoddling? Your *meddling*!"

"Commander Tosh, you are out of line!" Leniste's gruff voice filled the room and his face took on the familiar shade of ruddiness as the wick of his anger caught.

However, it was the quieter voice of General Renou that carried the most menace. "You'd best be careful where you tread with the weight of those words, Tosh."

"Darling?"

Castellan turned her head toward Olivienne at the tender tone in her mind. But before she could answer, the Queen's voice rang through the room like the tolling of a bell. "She's right. I knew Commander Tosh's percentage before I ever met her."

"By the depths!"

"Maman! How could you?"

She gave Castellan a penetrating gaze, attempting to convey the sincerity of her words. "But I can assure you, Commander, your name had already been flagged for the position long before the score came to my attention. It was only when I began digging into your academic history and testing that I discovered the information in your file."

Greene easily confirmed the truth of Olivara's words. "It's true. I know all this seems a bit suspect but the Queen only came to me when your name was selected above all others to head the Connate's team."

"Tosh?" Olivienne placed her hand over Castellan's white-knuckled fist where it rested atop the table.

Castellan's voice was low, still full of angry warmth. "If you remember, my maman told you that I advanced a few levels in primary?"

"Yes, at our oathing dinner."

"Well I recall going through a series of tests, both channel and intellectual. And the last one must have been the coder because I remember the prick to my finger."

Ins. Greene pulled another sheet from her folder. "That was done by my predecessor but I did pull the file for the Queen when she requested all your background records from the Academy."

"Bollux, but Greene's right." Renou shot Castellan an apologetic look. "I completely forgot but an academic check is standard protocol when an officer is promoted to lead a Shield team for a sovereign. And the Queen is also right in that we'd all but selected you by the time those records were pulled."

Olivara could see the ire swimming within Castellan's eyes and she made a call that only she could. It was one that very few queens would make outside their immediate family. She got up and walked around the table until she stood right next to Tosh's chair. Then with calm surety, she held out both hands palm up to the commander. "To prove to you that I had no manipulative intent beyond what you already knew of, I'm offering you a trust reading. Do you consent?"

Castellan's eyes widened at the rare show of trust by a Queen of Psiere. It was too late to back down from her anger, and to refuse such an offer would be a refusal of Olivara's trust in her. Castellan had no choice but to stand and touch her palms to the Queen's. Everyone had different ways to do a trust reading. Some required a touch closer to the head, but stronger telepaths could touch any bit of skin. Olivara was one of the strongest psi currently alive. Sadly, Pon Havington also numbered among that small group of talented individuals.

Both closed their eyes as soon as their hands touched. The rest of the group around the table watched with two parts fascination and one part trepidation. Olivara's voice was strangely loud in Castellan's head. *"Do you see my truth?"* Then without warning, Olivara opened her thoughts. Ideas, plans, and machinations flew at Castellan almost faster than she could read them. And with every new thought or idea that flowed from the Queen's head to Castellan's, truths were revealed. Olivara was not lying, nor was she hiding any further plans when it came to Castellan's romance or career.

Castellan conceded within the privacy of their reading. *"Apologies, my Queen. But you can see my thoughts as well and you know that truth is something I value highly. I had to know if the path forward was set for me, or if I earned it myself."*

"It's quite all right, Castellan. I understand your need to know. And I pledge by Sovereign Oath, you have more than earned your place."

"I have been told that I'm full of many things, most especially honor. And as you're well aware, I have a hard time doing anything that I think would bring dishonor to myself, or those I respect."

"Noted. Now if we've settled this matter of truth and honor, I have one more bit of information to impart."

While Castellan's eyes didn't open, her head tilted curiously to the side and she appeared to take on a listening pose to those watching the pair. *"Yes?"*

"Heed my words, Commander. While I don't know what every part of my prescient vision meant, I do know two things. You are both the honorable soul, and the keeper of the stone. You'll know what that means when the time comes. And you need to be wary every sec you are in that dirigible with my daughter. I see a significant death coming. I don't know whence the danger will come, but I believe it will come either before or after you cross the ocean."

Castellan Tosh gave the most truthful pledge she'd ever given. *"I'll guard her with everything at my disposal. On my honor it will be so."*

With those words both their eyes opened and their hands retreated from each other. Tosh gave a bow and Olivara acknowledged it. "Thank you, Commander."

Once they resumed their seats, the Queen opted to get the meeting back on track. "Now that we've got that settled, let's go through the interpretation points on that Instrucia document one by one, shall we?"

It took nearly an oor longer but in the end it was agreed that the information about the Makers should remain with a select few. Leniste thought perhaps telling the people about the Tau Ceti, and that the sovereigns were specifically created to rule Psiere would help quell the anti-sovereign factions around the two continents but Olivara disagreed. She shook her head at his suggestion. "I would rather keep that information until we can bring Camillo Binn's co-conspirators to justice. Let's keep our news about the Tau Ceti safe for a while longer."

"My Queen, I fear if you wait too long, the citizens of Psiere will be concerned that you've kept other vital information from them and question your fitness to rule."

Olivara winked at her long-time friend. "Well, my dear Camen, it's a good thing we have definitive proof that I was born to rule, isn't it? Now I don't know about all of you, but I'm ready for a rinse and a meal. It has been a long dae."

General Leniste was the first to rise after the Queen. He

stretched backward, holding his back. "By the depths, but you aren't kidding. If any dae feels like a four sun dae, it's this one!" Everyone around the table nodded, agreeing that it certainly felt twice as long as any other with back-to-back meetings of such a serious and sensitive nature.

Olivienne embraced her mother and father before following Castellan out of the meeting room. "What would you like to do this evening?"

Castellan rubbed the back of her neck and attempted to straighten her mussed hair. "Well, I have to meet briefly with Savon and Madlin to give them the updated timeline for the mission. But after that I'm all yours. Any ideas?"

Olivienne turned and drew Castellan into a kiss. It wasn't a thing of passion as so many of their connections were. Rather, it was one of sweetness and reassurance and Castellan felt the love flow from her future par. They pulled apart a short time later and Olivienne stroked her thumb across Castellan's cheekbone as a departing tender touch. "How about we grab our own rinse then look into dinner and a show. I hear there is a new production about the Hero of Temple Beach."

"Absolutely not! While I'm open to dinner and a show, I never want to see *that* one, if it is really a real performance and not something you made up to taunt me."

Laughter echoed through the halls of the royal residence as the pair made their way toward the exit closest to the path leading to Olivienne's private domicile. "Oh, it absolutely does exist and from what I hear, the public is raving about it. Perhaps we should just have a quick meal at Konette's, then we can come home and I'll give you a *private* show."

Castellan barked out a laugh and walked through the door that was held open by Spc. Leggett. The commander took notice of the way the other on-duty members of the unit ranged out in front and behind them once they started down the path. Their eyes never stopped taking in the surroundings, anticipating trouble. Though a few smirked at the overheard conversation. Castellan gave a satisfied sigh and pulled Olivienne closer. "I'm going to hold you to that later."

Olivienne smirked at her. "I look forward to it."

Chapter Eleven

QUEEN OLIVARA MET with Castellan and Olivienne in the Queen's secured office in the palace just before they left Tesseron. There, she gave them her final orders and a stern warning. "After much consideration on the subject, I've decided that Psierians are not ready for such a power as the antoraestones possess. What this means —" she gave her daughter a stern look " — is that you should do everything within your power to guarantee they remain inaccessible."

"But, Maman!"

"Wise decision, my Queen."

Olivienne whipped her head to the left to stare at Castellan. "Seriously? Both of you are missing all the good we could do! We could clear out all the rebels if we put antoraestones in the hands of a few trusted people."

The Queen gave her an exasperated look. "Misinformation spreads daily, all coming from the southern continent. Who exactly do you recommend to hold something that gives them the power of ten?"

Olivienne immediately looked to her left, to the one person she trusted absolutely.

Olivara shook her head and frowned. "Even Commander Tosh cannot win a war on her own, not to mention she has more important duties within the Shield Corp. Believe me, 'Vienne, I have considered all the good and I assure you that the temptation is mighty. The risk is simply too great that the rebels will some-how get their hands on one. Can you imagine a telepath of my strength with evil intent?"

"But, Maman, you would never turn against the people."

"There are others with the same rating, one at least with nearly the same channel profile as my own."

Castellan put her hand on Olivienne's shoulder. "She's talking about Pon Havington. There would be no stopping that man if he had one or more of the stones. I shudder to think of such a thing."

Olivienne huffed. "The odds that would happen —"

"Are not nil! I refuse to argue over this with you. Lock away or destroy the stones. Bring me two samples if you can, but the rest must stay." When Olivienne looked as if she would argue further, she met the violet gaze that was almost a twin to her own. "You have your orders." The Queen moved her gaze to Castellan. "Both of you. Do you swear a Sovereign Oath to obey?"

Castellan immediately bowed. "Yes, my Queen. Your will shall be done."

Olivienne remained silent but Olivara expected as much. She knew Castellan would perform her duty should it be required. "And remember, for security purposes you should tell no one about your orders concerning the stones. Especially not if you secure samples."

That time both Castellan and Olivienne nodded, the Connate seeing the danger of advertising to anyone that they held such a valuable artifact. "Of course, Maman. We're not fools."

"I never thought you were, darling. Now, give me a hug before you traipse off into the unknown. And come back as soon as you've verified the Temple and taken inventory of the chambers within, savvy?"

"Yes, ser."

"Yes, Maman."

OLIVIENNE STOOD ON the observation deck at the back of the dirigible with her eyes closed to the sight of Archeos sinking below the horizon, knowing Illeos wasn't far behind it. They were currently aboard the *Quaesitum*, a few oors past Ora Maris and heading southeast toward Montesilva. There was a chill to the air as it whipped around her, fluttering the sovereign's hair like a flag in the rising darkness. She left Castellan to her official report a quarter oor before, searching for a little solitude.

Olivienne had many things on her mind, least of which was the somewhat overwhelming notion that her family had been created to rule Psiere. Not for the first time, she wondered whether the Makers did such out of altruistic need to protect her people, or if it were part of some sinister over-arching experiment. Perhaps Psierians were nothing more than a collection of caged mouses, set to perform tasks and observed from afar. Olivienne shivered at the thought. She was so deep into her mind she didn't realize she had company on the deck until strong arms wrapped around her from behind.

"Hello, love. Don't you know you're supposed to keep your

eyes open when taking in the glory of the setting suns?"

Olivienne didn't acknowledge Castellan's subtle tease. "How was your report?"

Castellan gave her future par another squeeze before releasing her to stand side by side at the rail. "Just another report, with one exception." She moved her gaze from the orange, red, and purple horizon to where Olivienne stood on her right. "Apparently the Queen wants me to give my reports directly to her for the entirety of this trip."

"Hmm. Maman has always been a little...overprotective of me."

Castellan sighed. "I never thought I'd see the dae, but I think the events in Tesseron over the past few lunes have her rattled. About you, the Makers, about the state of affairs in Psiere, and about what we'll possibly find on Magna."

Olivienne turned toward her love, watching golden light bathe the clean planes of Castellan's face as the soldier's hair was mussed in the wind. Olivienne caressed her cheek. "I haven't read any of that from her. How do you know?"

Castellan stepped closer, sensing a need for intimacy in the touch. Or maybe she just needed it for herself. She wrapped her arms around Olivienne's lower back and pulled them together, front to front, until only inces separated their lips. "I know because I got a peek inside her mind when we did the truth reading, and I understand her because I feel the same way."

"Have I ever mentioned that one of the things I love about you is your dedication to Psiere?" Olivienne leaned in to briefly caress Castellan's lips with her own. "You'll make a good King, somedae."

She got another squeeze for her words. "I just want to be a good par."

"Just be you and you'll be the best of both." Olivienne sealed her words with a kiss. After a meen they pulled apart to once again stand at the rail. Propriety dictated they maintain a certain appearance in public and it wouldn't do to get carried away where just anyone could walk out and witness. The sovereign couple would have to save those moments for the privacy of their cabin. Olivienne watched the sky turn indigo as the blue light of Illeos hit the horizon. "What do you think of Doctore Shen and Captain Velten?"

Castellan's pale brows drew together in confusion. "What about them?"

"Were you not listening to them at last meal?"

"They certainly bicker plenty. I don't think they get along at all, which is a shame because I was hoping Gemeda would have a fairly pleasant trip."

Olivienne's mouth dropped open in astonishment. "Don't get along?" She burst into laughter and took nearly a meen to get control of herself again. "Oh, my love! Have you never witnessed a courtship from the outside before?"

"Wha—courtship? Certainly not! Gemeda would never fall for someone like Velten with her, her...she's so..." Castellan trailed off, unsure how to put into words the things she thought certain her long-time friend would dislike about the captain.

"So what? Accomplished, dashing, strong, commanding?" She laughed again. "*I*, for one, can *definitely* see the appeal."

Castellan gaped at her. Hurt blossomed across her handsome features, then that emotion morphed into something darker. "You see the appeal of Captain Velten?" That only served to elicit more laughter and Castellan scowled. She hated the jealousy that clawed into her belly.

Olivienne took Castellan's hand into her own and spoke directly into her lover's mind so no more confusion could be had. *"I merely see the lure of such traits. I have my own accomplished, dashing, and strong commander. It's not in my heart to look anywhere else. Gemeda will have to make do with the captain."*

She continued aloud as the second sun slowly disappeared into the darkness of night. "You are missing the basics of romance. Right now Gem and Seema are feeling each other out, like two children in a play yard. Our captain is clearly taken with the good doctore, and Gemeda is more interested than she lets on. They are also two extremely stubborn women."

Castellan gave her a curious look, though she couldn't see much of Olivienne's face under the star's light alone. "Are you sure?"

"Tell me, how was Gem when you were back at Academy together. Did she show interest in anyone besides you?"

The commander sputtered for a few secs before getting control of herself. "She, I never...we don't—sheddech!" She ignored Olivienne's laughter and grumbled out her admission. "Yes, we dallied, you already knew that, but we were by no means committed. She—" Castellan growled under her breath. "Oh, by the depths, you're right! Gem displayed the same behavior back then when someone new would catch her eye."

"See?"

"I can't believe I didn't until you pointed it out," she groused. "Should we say something?"

Olivienne scoffed at the idea. "Absolutely not! Do I look like my mother with her penchant for meddling?"

Castellan chuckled and caressed Olivienne's inky hair. "Actually..." She got a shove for her pondering.

"Darling, just let it play out. They will either find personal common ground or they won't. That's not something that can be forced, no matter *what* Maman thinks."

"And if it all goes sideways?"

Olivienne tangled their fingers together. "If the worst happens, we can at the very least count on the fact that both Doctore Shen and Captain Velten are professionals and would comport themselves as such."

"Fair enough." Then before another topic could be broached, Castellan pulled away from the rail, tugging Olivienne with her.

"Where are we going?"

The commander smiled into the darkness. "Back to our cabin of course. I believe there is an urgent matter that needs attending to."

Olivienne remained unmoving but smirked. "Urgent is it?"

"Absolutely."

"Is this a professional matter?"

Castellan started laughing, unable to keep up the act. "Well, I've never gotten cred or commendation for it!"

Olivienne moved closer and took the lead in tugging them toward the door. She gave a nod at Spc. Meza, one of the two Shields on the deck with them. Meza opened the hatch so they could step through into the bright passageway beyond. Still laughing at Castellan's comment, Olivienne pulled her into a quick kiss. "I find that hard to believe. You're much too good to be an amateur."

One of the guardians choked on their own laughter, though the two inside had only heard half the exchange. It was enough to figure out what was being referenced. The royal couple swiftly made their way through the ship toward their cabin. They only passed a few of the ship's crew on the way there. Most were either on duty, in the rec room, or resting for an early oors shift. Even though Castellan and Olivienne were trailed through the passageways by the four guardians who had been keeping an eye on Olivienne, the women were left plenty of space for privacy until they arrived back at their shared cabin.

"Connate, Commander. All has been quiet this evening."

"Lieutenant Madlin, you're looking pretty sharp and serious. Did you expect it otherwise?" Castellan grinned to show she was teasing.

They got a salute from both Madlin and Qent. "No, ser. Will you be leaving the cabin again, or will the Connate be enjoying the rest of the evening in?"

Olivienne laughed delightedly at the glint in Auda Madlin's eye. The lieutenant had always been perceptive when it came to the interactions between her and Castellan. "Oh, you can be sure I'll thoroughly enjoy being inside this evening. As a matter of fact, inside is my favorite place to be!"

Castellan blushed and rubbed the bridge of her nose. "'Vienne..."

Sensing her commander was the more private of the royal couple, Lt. Madlin gave another salute and wiped the smile from her face. "I'll be sure to adjust the unit schedule once you're...um, in for the night. Lt. Savon will be on at zero eight hundred."

"That will do." Castellan opened the door to their cabin and turned to sketch a quick salute to the members of their unit while Olivienne made her way inside. "Have a good evening, Lieutenant...Specialists."

Castellan shut and secured the door then turned to find Olivienne standing near the bed wearing nothing but her bosair and a pair of tight trousers. She had to fight to keep the grin from her lips. "Must you tease me so in front of my Shield unit?"

Olivienne smiled back at her, a picture of innocence. "Whatever do you mean, Commander?"

Castellan strode a few short paces to her side of their bed then removed her pistol belt and hung it on a nearby hook. She untucked her uniform shirt and turned to face the woman who both vexed and challenged her daily. "If you had your way, both my honor *and* reputation would be in tatters."

Laughter spilled from Olivienne's darkened lips. "Oh my love. After the way we carried on during that very first trip north on the railer, I don't think *tatters* is how anyone would describe your reputation. I'm positive half my team heard me screaming your name in their heads." She smirked at her future par, happy that their passion of body rivaled their passions of heart and mind. "Though, you weren't much quieter on that trip..."

"You!" Castellan came around the bed, stalking slowly

toward Olivienne. "You're going to pay for that."

"Promise?" Castellan barked out a laugh as Olivienne spoke again. "Actually, I believe I owe you this time, so I guess I will be paying. But first things first—" Faster than Castellan anticipated, Olivienne was in her personal space and pulling them together for a round of frenzied and wet kisses.

When the commander drew back for air, she attempted to slow them down. "Shouldn't we talk about—" Her words were cut off by another hard kiss that was deep enough to elicit a moan.

Olivienne released her and began unbuttoning Castellan's shirt with swift and efficient movements. "No, we shouldn't talk about anything but what is going to happen over the course of the next few oors."

A pale brow rose as Olivienne finished with the shirt and pulled it off Castellan's shoulders. Cool air tickled the commander's back as Olivienne unfastened the other woman's trousers. "Few oors? You certainly have high expectations of me, Connate Dracore."

Olivienne kneeled at Castellan's feet, pulling both trousers and undergarments down with her. She apported Castellan's boots from her feet then waited for her to step out of the material before giving a quick nip to the soft skin of Castellan's lower belly. The officer gasped and Olivienne spoke directly into the reddened skin. "I have it on good authority that you can keep up."

Castellan sucked in a quick breath when the first two fingers of Olivienne's right hand found their way into her slippery folds at the same time the nails of Olivienne's left hand gripped her buttocks.

"Sheddech! An—and if I ca—can't?"

Olivienne smirked up at her, "I have full faith in you, Commander." Then she leaned forward to taste the woman she would spend the rest of her life with. Castellan moved her feet farther apart, which served to open her even more to Olivienne's ministrations.

She tried standing at attention, hoping muscle memory would keep her from an embarrassing fall, but it was all for naught. After a few meens, Castellan was left moaning continuously with her legs shaking. "I—I don't think I can stay upright any longer, love."

Olivienne pulled back but didn't stop her motion. She merely replaced her tongue with the thumb of her left hand, which made the shaky woman hiss above her. "Such an upright and strong soldier you are, Tosh. You better not fall down on the job or it will surely reflect poorly on your record." Then without so much as a warning, she moved her thumb and dove back in. Thirty secs of maddening circular caresses and a fair bit of suction had Commander Castellan Tosh seeing stars. She groaned and slumped forward with her release, but with a generous application of her levitation channel she didn't fall.

Olivienne pulled her mouth away but left her fingers in place to feel the way Castellan pulsed around her, twitching and whimpering with the strong aftershocks of her orgasm. Olivienne's own clitoral node throbbed with arousal and sympathy. After a few more meens, Castellan straightened and Olivienne made to move her fingers. "Are you ready?"

"By the Makers."

"I'll take that as a yes." Olivienne's entire hand was soaked from Castellan's arousal and she brought her fingers up to lick them clean while her lover watched with nearly closed eyes. "You are amazing."

Castellan used her telekinesis to lift Olivienne from the floor and move her to the bed. "And you are trying to kill me!"

Olivienne's violet eyes sparkled with a combination of mirth and deep affection. "Oh but what a way to go! And Tosh?"

Castellan followed her lover onto the bed and began removing the prone woman's trousers. "Yes?"

Olivienne apported them off to save time, her need was too great for delay. "I have thoroughly enjoyed my time inside this evening."

"As have I. But the evening isn't close to being done yet." Castellan moved up the bed until their nude bodies were completely pressed together and her narrow hips settled into the juncture between Olivienne's legs. She leaned in for a kiss but paused in the last moment to recite a familiar line. "We are all travelers and companions, seekers and sibs on another plane. In this life I pledge to you that my course will be steady and steerage firm."

Olivienne laughed and pulled her in for a deep and emotional kiss. When they separated again, little puffs of air from Castellan's panting exhales tickled the hairs around Olivienne's left ear. "Beautiful words that I hope to never forget. However, if it's all the same to you, I'm in desperate need of some firm and steady steerage right this instant."

The commander rolled her hips forward, grinding their bodies together in the most delicious of ways. The motion pulled a whine from her lover's lips. "As you wish."

NUSQUAM WAS BIGGER than Olivienne imagined it would be considering they were on the very edge of civilization as they knew it. They didn't see the city when the *Quaesitum* docked at the transportation hub a little after zero one hundred oors. Instead Olivienne, Castellan, and Gemeda got their first glimpse when they walked down the gangplank the next morning in search of a place to break their fast. A storm had delayed them coming over the mountains into Montesilva so Velten stayed behind to oversee minor repairs as well as the general restocking that was needed before undertaking a long journey across the ocean. Neither Castellan nor Gem had ever been to the far eastern end of the northern continent. And while Olivienne had traveled by railer through the small outpost city on the way from Guin to Baen for one of her adventurist missions, her passage was done in the middle of the night and thus unseen.

The Psierian government kept it stocked with charged illeostones as well as a variety of supplies for passenger railers and other local needs. For every ten passenger railers that passed along the line, one followed with the specific task of stocking the recharge stations. Those railers left the temples and spread throughout the two continents to deliver stones. Because Nusquam was the only railer stop between the major cities of Guin and Baen, they had a larger supply station than most other places.

Many homes and establishments received power from the copere lines that ran beneath the ground. The lines in turn received their power from collection stations that ran on water and wind energy. It was one of the greatest Maker schematics found in the past few deca-rotos. However, some places were still too remote, or needed the portable power that only illeostones could provide. Haulers left daily to deliver stones to the more remote areas within a five-hundred mahl radius. They delivered north as far as the valley of the Mir Orientem. And they delivered as far south and west as King's Marsh, which was an uninhabitable swamp that covered an area roughly three hundred square mahls. Even with Maker schematics and technologies, it took many rotos to build railer lines through the area, and they frequently had to be repaired.

Olivienne knew of at least two science stations that relied on the existence of the city to stay functional. There was no harbor for catching picis. Rather the eastern edge of Endara was composed of mahls of tall cliffs that looked out across an endless expanse of blue that was the Latus Ocean. The citizens could supplement their meals with long lines dropped from the shore but most of their meals came from locally grown produce or bovids that were pastured on the sweet grass plains west of Nusquam. While they didn't have much in the way of entertainment, and only a small selection of eateries, the local cuisine was rumored to be excellent. At least according to Cpt. Velten. The captain recommended The Permaneo, saying it was her favorite place to eat on the rare occasion she was in the area, so that was where the trio was headed.

"When did the captain say we were disembarking for Magnus?" Gemeda was wearing form-fitting trousers, a long-sleeved shirt, and a lightweight jacket to combat the chill of the breeze coming off the ocean at zero eight hundred oors. Olivienne was dressed similarly, only she also had her ever-present pistol strapped to her right hip. Castellan and the eight Shield guardians with them all wore the black uniforms of their Corp.

Even though Castellan's attention was split between scanning the streets and the important woman walking by her side, she had no problems answering the doctore's question. "Velten told me last night that she didn't want to approach an unknown island in the dark so she reconfigured the schedule to allow us to arrive around zero six hundred thirty oors at the coordinate location on the map." Motion caught her eye down a nearby alley but when she turned to look at it fully, it appeared to be naught more than a stray canid. "Anyway, with that in mind, she's scheduled us to leave here at thirteen hundred oors."

Olivienne pulled the chrono out of her jacket pocket. "That's not much time."

Castellan laughed. "If you listen to half the crew of the *Quaesitum* there's not much to do here."

"According to Seema, there is one local sight that we could see after morning meal. Apparently there is a feature in one section of cliff that causes the oncoming waves to explode straight into the air nearly forty foot. It's said to be quite the spectacle."

Knowing they had all gone their separate ways after evening

meal the night before, Olivienne was curious about Gemeda's knowledge of the local points of interest. "When did you speak with Captain Velten?"

Gem waved a negligent hand through the air as they approached the eatery. "We had drinks in the captain's private lounge, a few oors after our meal."

"Oh?" A dark eyebrow went up and Olivienne directed a sly smile toward Castellan when the commander held the door open for both women. Their conversation paused while one of the hosts rushed to help the group. Lt. Savon had already called ahead to be sure there was a private seating area available. While they didn't announce the Connate would be in attendance, the group of black clad soldiers were a giveaway to the diners already inside. The owner of the establishment came out nearly as soon as the trio entered the building. She was a brawny woman with dark skin and short blonde hair with pale green highlights. Her eyes were pale green to match the highlights in her hair.

"Connate Dracore! We didn't know you'd be joining us todae, just that reservations were made for our private dining room." She quickly gave a low bow to the sovereign. "My name is Jindee Fwentus and I'd like to officially welcome you all to The Permaneo.

Olivienne smiled kindly and gave a small bow in return. "We try to keep a low profile when traveling but we heard such marvelous things about your eatery that we had to stop in on our brief layover."

Jindee led Olivienne, Castellan, and Gemeda into a separate room on one end of the building. There were a handful of tables in the private section so there was plenty of room for Savon, Lear, Penn, and Holling. Halfway through the meal, they switched out with the four guardians outside so that Devin, Dozier, Lazaro, and Qent could come in and eat as well. Olivienne enjoyed the food so much that before they left, she used her influence to have meals delivered to the Shield guardians that had been left behind on the dirigible, as well as for the captain herself.

After their stop at The Permaneo, they spent a leisurely amount of time sightseeing and even made it to the natural feature named Fragor Hole. Unfortunately, they didn't anticipate the shear amount of water that would explode upward and the majority of the eleven-member group relied on Olivienne's pyrokinetic channel to dry out on the walk back to the transportation hub.

Castellan was more than a little distracted on their walk back and it had nothing at all to do with her wet uniform. Twice she caught glances of reflected sunlight off nearby buildings, but every time she looked there was nothing there. By the time they arrived at the dirigible, her intuition channel was jangling uncomfortably. Once loaded back onto the *Quaesitum*, she sent Olivienne and Gemeda off with the promise that she would join them soon. Then she gave mental directions to her lieutenants to take all on duty guardians and stay with both women, before heading off to find the captain. Castellan found her on the bridge pouring over maps of the region. While the whip-thin woman's blonde hair was still pulled back into the severe braid that Castellan was used to from their trip to Navis, one thing that had changed was the fact that the captain and crew all wore the familiar black uniforms of the Shield Corp.

"Commander Tosh." She sketched a quick salute to Castellan, which the commander returned. "We're nearly ready to take off, I'm just doing one last check of the area and coordinates before plotting our course to Magnus. I'm estimating about fifteen meens until departure." She paused for a sec then grinned. "Oh, and could you pass on my thanks for the meal sent by Connate Dracore? I'm sorry I missed out on your trip to the eatery this morn. Perhaps we can all stop in on our return to Nusquam on the way back to Tesseron."

Castellan frowned. "I'm afraid this isn't about our trip or the departure. Have we had any communications from the local Defense center?"

"No, all has been silent on that front. If I'm not mistaken, you sent out your morning report before you left for the eatery. Were you expecting a response?"

"No, but I'm uneasy. I didn't see anything specific to warrant caution while we were walking around the city, but something has my hackles up here. Are any other dirigibles showing up on the sonica? Can we see if there is anything else in the area?"

"Yes, ser." Velten motioned to one of her officers on duty and a large greenish-hued screen lit up in front of the woman. The captain pointed to an area where two dots were fairly close to each other. "This one is us, and the other was a dirigible that was already here when we arrived just after zero one hundred oors."

Tosh pointed at three blips that were south of their location, approaching at a fairly fast speed. "And those? Is it normal to have so many dirigibles pass through Nusquam?"

Velten's lips formed a thin line as she gave the screen grim regard. "No. Absolutely not." Impressively fast, she slammed her hand down on the ship wide com button. "Attention, attention, attention. Exit all external decks with haste and prepare for immediate disembark." She called out orders to other crew members on the bridge. "Jent, release the anchor line. Seben, spool the engines for fast take-off." Then she took a seat in her captain's chair and locked eyes with Castellan. "You may want to warn your team to hold on."

Using her telepathy, she contacted her entire team at once, as well as Olivienne and Gemeda. *"We've got suspicious dirigibles approaching our location at max speed. Departure at full power is imminent so hold on to something. Savon and Madlin, don't let the Connate out of your sight!"*

Savon's voice came back to her. *"Yes, ser."*

"Tosh?" Olivienne's mental voice was followed by a wash of worry.

"Listen to Savon, and stay near the center of the ship where it's safest."

"Okay, stay safe."

Castellan gave a small smile at her lover's words. *"Yes, ser."*

Three black dirigibles, very similar to the one that attacked them on the Cliffs of Navis, burst through the clouds within a half mahl off their location. "What's the status on those engines, Seben?"

"Eighty percent, Captain!"

A boom sounded and the dirigible rocked with an impact. "Sheddech!" Castellan wasn't sure which one of the crew said it but she whole-heartedly agreed with the sentiment.

Velten yelled to another man. "Open reserve canister one!" As soon as the man complied a great hissing sound echoed through the bridge and the dirigible abruptly shot straight up from their previous location. Castellan was forced to grab onto the bulkhead to stay upright. Releasing the anchor allowed for the dirigible to rise slowly. However, opening one of the light gas canisters directly into the bladder gave their lift an immediate boost and the next shell that boomed from the approaching dirigibles never hit its target.

"One hundred percent, Captain."

"Get us out of range of those rail guns, now!"

"Yes, ser."

The *Quaesitum* shot forward and it didn't take long to get up to their max speed, which was half again more than any other dirigible in existence. They quickly outpaced the approaching rebels. Everyone on the bridge blew a sigh of relief as the black ships grew smaller in the view from the aft observation window. Castellan ran a hand through her hair. "By the Makers, how did they know we were here? All our transmissions have been coded and no official announcement was made about the Connate's adventurist mission."

Velten rubbed her chin. "It makes me wonder how deep this disloyalist faction runs, Commander. How many people knew about this trip, and can you vouch they are all loyal?"

"Very few people knew about this trip, outside those of us on your ship. And of the few back in Tesseron, they have all had a truth reading by the Queen herself." She paused as another thought came to her. "Of course the alternative to an inside spy is that there are disloyalists posted in all the major recharging hubs around Psiere, with instructions to teleo whomever is leading the faction at the first sighting of Connate Dracore."

The captain stood from her chair and made her way back to the map table. With deft motions, Velten quickly removed the table weights and rolled up the map she'd been using. "That would make a lot of sense. I know if I were looking for someone, especially someone going on a mission to a place no one has ever seen, I'd do just that. I may not waste my time on the illeostone stations in the middle of the continents, but I'd for sure watch the ones along the coast."

Castellan made a pained face. "Unfortunately for us, that means we're going to have company when we make it back to Nusquam."

"You don't think they'll follow us?"

"No. Right now we're heading into the unknown with a ship that's bigger than anything else ever conceived. They have no idea where we are going or how far. No, we have the ship advantage so my intuition tells me that they'll wait here for us to come back. Perhaps call in reinforcements."

Captain Velten barked an order to her communication's officer. "Perde, get General Renou on the long-range voteo, before we're out of range and lose the ability to signal jump."

"Yes, ser." The officer flipped two switches but the panel remained dark. He turned to look at the captain and commander. "Sers, our system is down. My guess is that we lost it when the shell hit during the attack."

The captain swore and pulled the voteo from her belt. "First Officer Vex, what's the repair status?"

A voice came back over the handheld device. The sound of wind whipping by made it hard to hear the man Castellan had been introduced to shortly after their first trip on the dirigible. "One of the bladder lines took damage, Captain. We also lost the long-range antenna, two port side bumpers, and a water barrel. Requesting instruction, over."

The Captain rubbed the worry lines on her forehead before responding. "Restring that bladder line first, then work on the bumpers. While you're doing that, see if you can get Engineer Davine to rig something as a replacement for the antenna." She turned to Castellan with a grim look. "We'll be out of range within meens and we don't dare slow down for fear those dirigibles will close with us again. I'm afraid the general will have to wait until we return to the continent."

"It can't be helped, Captain." Castellan sighed and turned her gaze to watch the rapidly disappearing cliffs behind them. She knew the Queen would be beside herself with worry. The commander also remembered the warning given by her future mamanar that said danger would come from the air. She never specified which direction and it was almost certain that they'd be attacked and horribly outnumbered on their return approach to Nusquam. Castellan hoped they'd find something in the Temple of Antaeus that could help them in the battle to come.

Chapter Twelve

BOTH CASTELLAN AND Olivienne were jolted awake in the dark of their cabin. The dirigible gave a great lurch, which was followed by a clap of thunder. Gazing out the porthole, it was obvious that the *Quaesitum* was in the middle of a massive storm. "We've been hit!" Castellan's voice was loud in her attempt to be heard over the roar outside.

Olivienne witnessed an unusual sight in the flashing darkness of their cabin. Her lover's pale eyes were wide with anxiety and Castellan had a white-knuckle grip on the edge of their bed. Olivienne grabbed Castellan's free hand to calm her. "It's fine, I've been through storms in a dirigible before. The captain will more than likely drop us below the clouds to spare us the worst of it."

"And getting hit by lightning?"

The dirigible lurched again and Olivienne spared another glance toward the porthole. "I'll admit, that's never happened to a ship I've been in. Not to my knowledge anyway. But it can't be that unusual, I'm sure they have contingencies for such things."

A loud knock sounded at their door followed by the mental voice of Lt. Madlin. *"Commander Tosh, the captain asked me to relay a status report."*

"A meen, Madlin."

Castellan turned on the lamp next to the bed and used her telekinesis to grab her uniform from where it was folded neatly on the armchair. She stood and quickly dressed before straightening her hair and striding to the cabin door. She stopped just shy of turning the handle to look back at Olivienne. "Are you just going to stay there looking so..."

Olivienne grinned and raised a single dark eyebrow. "Debauched?"

"Well, I certainly wouldn't have used *that* word!"

Olivienne sat up in the bed and pulled the slipping coverlets higher then smirked when she noticed Castellan's wandering gaze. "If you didn't want a chair, Commander, you shouldn't have nailed legs on my seat."

Castellan snorted with laughter but quickly stifled it when

the ship gave another lurch and knocking sounded yet again. "Commander?" She abruptly pulled the door open, causing the startled Lt. Madlin to take a step back. "Ser!"

"Report, Lieutenant."

"Ser, Captain Velten says we've taken damage on the fore dextra engine. She's going to drop us to an altitude of one hundred yords. We don't dare go any lower due to Atlanteen interference."

"What about our arrival time?"

Buffeting winds rocked the ship again and both women grabbed onto the doorway to remain upright. "The storm has pushed us off course and that combined with the damaged engine means we'll see a two oor delay."

The turbulence leveled off abruptly and Castellan gave a small sigh of relief. "And she's sure there is no risk to the Connate?"

"She doesn't foresee any more issues, ser. We're still about five oors out from Magna."

"Very good, Lieutenant. I want a full list of ship damage before first meal. Savon mentioned speaking with you about a change of schedule after you began your shift. Will he be taking over again at zero eight hundred?"

"No, ser. Because of the imminent arrival time at Magna, the entire team is taking half shifts so we are all as fresh as possible when we make landfall."

Castellan gave Madlin a tired smile. "Good call. I'll see you in the morning, or if there are any more issues tonight." Castellan gave a crisp salute and Lt. Auda Madlin returned it just as crisply before spinning on her heel and marching down the passageway.

"I suspect our Auda has a wee bit of an itch for you."

"Come again?" Castellan spun toward the bed after closing and latching the door.

Olivienne laughed at the flummoxed look on her lover's face. "Darling, you'd be hard-pressed to find anyone under your command who *wasn't* a bit sunstruck."

The officer scoffed as she once again stripped her uniform, folding it carefully before placing it back on the seat of the chair. She waved her hand through the air as she rounded the bed, unaware of Olivienne's hungry gaze as she took in Castellan's nudity. "*Pshh*, that's a ridiculous notion! Lieutenant Madlin is an exemplary officer."

"Oh, I won't argue that point with you. But one can be absolutely loyal to their job and still fancy someone. I mean, look at you and I. As an officer you are the best—"

"You're partial."

"—and yet here we are, oathed to consor in less than a roto. Besides, I know what it looks like when a woman is attracted to another."

Castellan flushed darkly from the pale roots of her hair all the way down her neck and onto her strong chest. Her mouth opened and closed a few times before words finally emerged. "She's my subordinate and I really don't want to know who she looks upon with desire. The very notion of it makes me uncomfortable." She got back into their bed and switched off the stand light.

Olivienne quickly moved closer to resume the embrace they favored for sleeping, with Castellan cradling her from behind. "I wasn't trying to make you uncomfortable. I was merely stating an observation. She would never make anything of it, and I'm sure it's not serious. But you have to be aware that you turn heads wherever you go."

Castellan sighed and the push of breath tickled the hairs near Olivienne's ear. "Of course I'm aware that I've been genetically gifted by my papan's line. I just try not to think of it, because a person's worth isn't found on the outside."

Olivienne drew Castellan's arm tighter around her middle and smiled unseen in the dark. "You're worth everything to me."

"I love you too, 'Vienne. Now, get some sleep. Dawn and adventure are mere oors away." Castellan's words received no response because the sovereign had already slipped quietly into her dreams.

OLIVIENNE AND CASTELLAN were on the bridge with Captain Velten and Gemeda as Illeos chased Archeos over the horizon directly ahead of them. It was approaching zero eight hundred oors when one of the steersman called out. "Land ahead, Captain!"

Velten quickly removed a spyglass from her waist pouch and stepped closer to the fore observation window. "That it is." The captain handed the glass to Castellan when the other three women joined her.

"It's huge! I mean, we knew its approximate size based on the map but it's completely different seeing it full-life in front of us."

The spyglass made its way down the line until the doctore had her look and handed it back to Velten with a smile.

Olivienne pondered their view. "By your estimation, we're near the coordinates that we assumed to be the Temple of Antaeus, correct?"

Velten nodded. "Yes, Connate."

"Which means, if the temple were at the coordinates we'd be able to see it. Instead, I saw a tower unlike anything I've seen before. The temple could be anywhere."

Castellan rubbed the space above the bridge of her nose and turned to meet Seema Velten's icy gaze. "Blast it, but Olivienne is right. How long is your estimate on repairs?"

The stern captain frowned. "Honestly, I have no idea. We don't have everything we need to make a repair of that size aboard the *Quaesitum*. I'm hoping that wherever we dock we can forage for suitable materials. My engineer is good, but even he has limits."

"You know what they say about a beast with two heads compared to a beast with one..." Three faces turned toward Olivienne and she elaborated. "I have two highly qualified engineers on my Shield team, one whom I know for a fact has an uncanny ability to fix just about anything on naught more than a boot string and box of rubbish." She looked to Castellan. "That is, if my Shield commander thinks he can be spared."

Castellan stood with her hands on her hips, looking out over the ocean toward the rapidly approaching green expanse that was Magna. "While I don't have a concern about your safety in the Shield team sense, we are still entering into an unfamiliar land." She held up her hand to forestall Olivienne's imminent protest. "I'm not saying we can't do without Soleng. You're right, his engineering specialty focuses on engines and he'd be ideal to stay and help. But I think we need to belay this discussion until we actually arrive at the coordinates to see what we have to work with. With the dirigible in dire need of repairs, we will be forced to potentially make our way afoot to wherever the Temple of Antaeus is located, and while we know the size of Magna from the map, we have no clue of the obstacles we may encounter."

For the first time since they set off on the lost temple adventure, Olivienne looked truly worried. "Surely, it can't be too bad. The Makers have never set traps on the way to designated locations. I assumed from the start we'd only have to worry about getting into the temple and bypassing the traps inside."

Castellan gestured out the fore windows. "If you recall, the island is shaped roughly like a tilted eight. Worst-case scenario, the temple is on the far northeast end, which would put it nearly seven hundred mahls from the coordinates of that blasted tower ahead of us. It's not traps I'm worried about, it's things like rocs, sirens, or drakes." She listed a few of their previous worrisome encounters. "With no definitive location of the temple, we could be searching for wekes or more and we don't know what this island holds or why the Makers felt it was most secure."

"The commander is right. Uninformed decisions lead to rash actions. Let's see what we find at the landing point then go forward from there." The captain turned her head to the navigator. "What's our TOA, Gentz?"

"Time of arrival is fifteen meens, ser."

"Stay the course."

"Yes, Captain."

As predicted, the coordinates did indeed lead them to the strange tower situated along the rocky cliff of Magna. It was nothing like typical Psierian architecture, or even that of known Maker constructs. It was a sleek tower, wide at the base and tapering more toward the top. It featured a domed roof with a spire jutting farther upward, and a dark panel facing the ocean. Between the dome and the panel, it looked a lot like an observatory of sorts. There were five strange floating platforms situated around the tower at varying levels, like leaves on a stalk. None overlapped the others and the captain surmised that they were landing platforms for dirigibles. There were large Psi-made holes at the base of the cliff below, where water washed in and out at regular intervals with the waves. It was Olivienne's keen eyes that pointed out the beacon at the top of the dome's spire. "Look there!"

"By the Makers, is this island inhabited?"

Everyone on the bridge crowded forward as they slowly approached the strange Maker station. They were close enough that Castellan attempted to cast her mind forward, hoping to sense another with her telepathy. Olivienne must have had the same idea because both women answered "no" together.

Lt. Savon and Lt. Madlin had joined them on the bridge meens before, and it was Savon who brought up their adventure to get the last key. "Connate Dracore, perhaps it's some sort of automated system like with the lights on that sunken ship in Dir Sanguis. Maybe the Makers set it to come on for approaching ships."

Velten rubbed her bottom lip then broke into a grin. "That idea actually has a lot of merit. You've got a good head on your shoulders there, Lieutenant."

Savon flushed at the compliment. "Thank you, ser."

"Slowing for approach, Captain."

"All right, birds, if this is what we think it is, there should be fixtures and hooks for us to dock and reel in. Head for the highest platform and get the crew on deck ready."

"Aye, aye, Captain!"

Castellan looked from the strange floating platform to the lone adventurist in the group on the bridge. As they got closer, they could see it wasn't truly floating but the connector was so small that it didn't look as if it could hold a significant amount of weight. "Do you think it's safe?"

Olivienne grabbed the captain's spyglass, which had been placed upon a secured shelf nearby. She looked out at the platform that loomed in front of them, then put it back. "It's hard to say. While the Makers are notorious for their traps when it comes to caches and the temples, I'm not sure the same will hold true for a transportation hub. As far as the platform is concerned, I'd say that if it has stood for hundreds of rotos already, a few more daes won't collapse it." She turned to Castellan, her violet eyes wide with excitement. "This is the first of its kind anyone has seen. We are looking at history!"

Gemeda had been silent for much of the approach, not having a lot to interject as her specialty was primarily restricted to medican knowledge. But she too seemed excited about the prospects ahead with the large foreign structure. "It could very well be, Connate Dracore. But on that comparison, we are also looking at our future."

Castellan scowled as she thought of the possible dangers the island could hold, up to and including the antoraestones. A slight mental push nudged Castellan's mind and she acknowledged Velten. Castellan gave the equivalent of a mental sigh. *"Yes?"*

"Why don't you appear to be as excited as the rest? Do you know something we don't?"

"Intuition only on this one, I'm afraid. Whether we are looking at the past or the future, my gut tells me it could be trouble."

"How do you figure?"

The commander briefly spared Velten a glance out of the corner of her eye. *"The Makers left this island unknown and relatively inaccessible for what, hundreds of rotos? Why? Clearly they had a rea-*

son to hide it from the rest of Psiere."

Velten fully turned her head to look at Castellan and frowned. *"You know something."*

Noticing that Captain Velten's intent gaze had caught Olivienne's eye, Castellan was quick to reprimand her. *"Plain face, Captain. I don't wish to draw attention to this conversation."*

"Not even from your future par, who is a sovereign of Psiere?"

"Not even. She knows all of the classified information already, there are about ten of us that do. The eleventh will be you."

"Why are you trusting me?"

"Captain, the deck team is reporting standard docking latches. Shall we commence?"

Velten waved her hand distractedly at the woman on the coms. "Commence."

"I'm trusting you because after our reading, I know that you're loyal to Queen and country. There are stones of power hidden somewhere inside the Temple of Antaeus. Translated texts mentioned that they grant Psierians ten times their current channel power. They amplify us somehow."

Captain Velten sucked in a quiet breath. *"Sheddech. Ten times would be..."*

"Yes, exactly that. Now, think of the most powerful person you know, and multiply their channel by ten. Good or evil, that is what we're looking at here."

"By the Makers. And the Queen?"

Castellan rubbed her temple because the Queen's directive weighed heavily on her shoulders. She didn't need her intuition channel to know it would cause problems between her and Olivienne later. Castellan knew without a doubt that Olivienne would disregard those orders if given half a chance. *"My first priority on this mission is to protect the Connate. My second, given to both me and Olivienne by Queen Olivara, is to guarantee those stones are never found if they can't be destroyed."*

Velten glanced over to see Olivienne excitedly chatting with Gemeda. *"How does the Connate feel about such curtailing of her adventurist mission?"*

"Olivienne is diametrically opposed to our second task and I suspect has no intention of following the Queen's directive."

The ship gave a lurch as the anchor line winch began drawing the *Quaesitum* toward the platform. The captain suddenly turned and clapped Castellan on the shoulder and gave her a grim smile. "Well Tosh, I certainly don't envy you the task ahead.

Good luck, my friend."

"Luck?"

Seema Velten laughed and waved her arm expansively toward the fore observation windows. "Most certainly you'll all need it to find the Temple of Antaeus on the other side of that." They all gazed out the windows to take in the massive forests. It was green as far as the eye could see, even from their vantage point atop the high tower.

Olivienne drew herself up and straightened the lower part of her waistcoat. "All right people, no time like the present. I'm heading down to open that blasted tower door." She quickly turned to look at Castellan. "Not a word out of you, Tosh. This is my bit of the mission now, let's play our parts."

Castellan was loath to admit how attractive she found Olivienne's commanding side. But, perhaps she would disclose that bit of information later when they had some privacy to explore each other physically. She smiled mischievously and saluted her future par. "Yes, ser. Savon, Madlin, gather the team. It's time this adventurist mission started proper."

Five meens later they stood at the ramp leading down to the platform. "Should we bring the gear, Connate?"

"Not just yet, Savon. Let's see what treasure this tower yields first."

Castellan addressed the team after Olivienne finished speaking. "Keep your weapons at the ready."

A chorus of voices answered her. "Yes, ser!"

Gemeda opted to stay on the ship until Olivienne and Castellan's Shield team made sure the platform and tower were secure. Velten stood with the group on the lower dextra deck. "You'll contact us every ten meens?"

Castellan nodded toward the brawny guardian with the heavy communications pack on his back. "Lazaro will be our contact with the *Quaesitum*. Specialist Penn is our backup, but she's also our resident interpretist so we're keeping her hands free for this one."

"I'll make sure my com specialist knows. Good luck, Connate Dracore," Velten called out with a crisp salute to the sovereign.

Olivienne smiled and saluted back. "Luck is for the Psierian who is lacking in wit or wisdom, neither of which is a condition I suffer." With that, Olivienne marched down the ramp toward the nearby door set into the side of the tower.

When they were two yords away, a cylinder of light flashed

red next to the handle of the door and the entire group pulled up short. A mechanical voice, very much like the one on the sunken ship, sounded from a box above the light. "Station access is limited to authorized personnel only."

Castellan turned to Olivienne. "How do we get authorization to enter a tower that has not seen life for hundreds of rotos?"

Olivienne reached into her shirt and pulled out a familiar thong. It was the very same one that Olivienne strung the first temple key on during their adventure to Mater Island. Only instead of just one key, the thong held all three. "Maybe one of these will help. I'm going to move closer."

"Be careful."

Olivienne winked back at her. "Always." Savon stifled a cough at the word he'd heard from the Connate too many times before.

One yord from the door, the red light suddenly flashed three times. "Psionic resonance frequency of temple keys detected. Access granted."

The light turned green, then *click* and *clunk* sounds emanated from within the door itself. Without a backward glance, the seasoned historical adventurist took the last few steps forward and slowly turned the handle. The door swung open easily, and the corridor lit up from panels placed at regular intervals near the ceiling. Olivienne smiled in wonder. "This is *exactly* like the sunken ship in Dir Sanguis!"

Castellan called back to the rest of the guardians. "You remember the protocol in that ship and, by the depths, don't everyone go inside the same closed room! We don't need another situation like the one with polycyclon gas on that last temple key mission."

"Yes, ser!"

Just like the sunken ship, the hall was wide enough for four guardians to walk abreast. The corridor was fairly short, only a few yords to a large room, with no doors to seal them off from the outside. The overhead lights came on as they entered, highlighting plain gray walls all around and six doors at even spaced intervals. Next to each door was a panel as tall as a voteo and twice as wide as the communications device. The center of the room had a column about eight foot in diameter. The smooth stele surface was broken by two narrow doors with no handles, placed strangely right next to each other. Next to the door was a round button. Castellan motioned and the Shield unit spread out in the empty room. "What's the plan, Adventurist Dracore?"

Olivienne considered her options, spinning slowly in place to take in the large circular chamber. "Let's see what's beyond one of those doors."

Tosh moved her gaze between three of the specialists. "Dozier, Lear, and Holling. Your intuition is higher than mine, anything?"

"No, ser." Lear, the brash pilot, answered and the other two simply nodded.

The commander motioned toward the door that was closest to Lt. Madlin. "Madlin, put a hand on that panel and see if you can get a psychometric reading."

Lt. Auda Madlin was nervous but more excited to touch unknown Maker technology. Despite her relative age and seniority on the team, her response was an awed whisper. "Yes, ser." Surmising the black panel was the controller for access, she reached out to place her palm flat on the surface. She got no psychometric reading but the surface beneath her hand turned green and the door slid open to the left.

She stepped back while both Olivienne and Castellan strode forward to peer inside. Everyone else craned their heads to see. "It's nothing more than a sleep cube with a small lav." Olivienne glanced sideways at Castellan. "Perhaps it's sleeping quarters for the docking crew."

"I'd say that's as good a guess as any. It certainly makes logical sense." Castellan backed away from the door and motioned to the others. "I'd lay odds that the rest are the same. Do you want to verify or move on?"

Olivienne backed away from the room as well and turned to stare at the central column. "Perhaps we can come back to this later, but I'm ready to move on. The sooner we get a lay of this place, the sooner we can figure out where the temple is."

"Not to mention Captain Velten needs to begin those ship repairs or we'll find the journey home a bit challenging."

Olivienne returned Lt. Madlin's grim smile and walked over to stand in front of the doors set into the large column. "There is that as well. Now, if there are no other objections, I'm going to push the button." Castellan lined up next to Olivienne and three guardians flanked them as the Connate reached her hand out. The circle lit as soon as Olivienne depressed it and humming sounded inside the cylinder. Then before anyone could prepare, the two doors *whooshed* open, sliding away from each other into the walls of the column, much the same way the door to the sleep cube did. Inside was a small chamber, large enough for maybe ten.

Olivienne looked to Castellan, knowing her entire unit would not be able to fit inside, nor would that be the safest option. She peered inside cautiously and saw a panel with a vertical line of six buttons to the right of the doorway. The second from the top was lit. Castellan peered in the same way and her voice came out tinged with curiosity. "Since I've seen no stairwells, unless they are hidden behind one of the other plain doors, perhaps this is a lift." The lifts of the largest buildings of Psiere were not nearly so sleek, nor were the doors automated as such.

"Very astute, Commander. We'll make an adventurist of you yet! Unfortunately, there isn't room in here for the entire team."

Castellan sighed. "That's probably for the best anyway. The entire team shouldn't enter that cylinder in case there is an issue." She contemplated the twelve-member Shield Corp unit for a few secs before addressing Olivienne. "Do you want to go up or down from here?"

"Definitely down. If my guess is correct, I'd say the buttons represent the different levels of the tower. That would mean the top button takes a person to the dome, the middle buttons for the levels with docking platforms, and the lowest level for the rest."

Savon spoke up. "The rest, Connate?"

"Think about it, all of you. What do we know about societies, structures in particular? Our own transportation hubs are set up with sections that lead to whatever matter of transport is available. There are also buildings for storage, control rooms, communications, maintenance, and a slew of other parts. All that to make up something as large and complicated as a transportation hub. While this tower is unlike anything we've ever seen, it still would require the basics to function. Communications, control, maintenance, storage, and the lot. I don't want the transport related levels, I want the good stuff and possibly an exit to get a feel for this island. Does that make sense?"

Heads nodded around the room but only Lt. Savon answered aloud. "Yes, ser. Thank you for explaining." What he didn't say, but Olivienne was well aware of, was that as little as a roto ago, the adventurist would have never taken the time to explain the reasoning behind her decisions. She would have merely gone haring off in search of adventure and left her Shield Corp guardians to flounder and catch up. A lot had changed in a fairly short period of time. Olivienne looked at her future par and raised a single dark brow. She had to admit that one of those changes was the absolute best thing to ever happen to her.

Seeing the challenge in Olivienne's look, Tosh called out orders. "Here's the plan, guardians. First crew will take the conveyance down. That includes the Connate, myself, and Lieutenant Madlin. We'll take Specialists Dozier, Penn, Holling, Leggett, and Calderon. Lieutenant Savon will take Specialists Qent, Lear, Meza, and Lazaro to explore the tower, starting with the top floor. Keep us abreast of anything you find up there and contact Captain Velten with updates." Savon nodded. "Specialists Devin, Soleng, and Yazzie will stay on this level and explore the other rooms. They'll be our backup in case something untoward happens. Savvy?"

The entire team saluted, excited to finally begin. "Yes, ser!"

With that, Olivienne entered the cylinder, followed closely by Castellan and the other six specialists chosen to go with the Connate. Once inside, the doors abruptly *whooshed* shut, causing half of them to jump. Olivienne laughed, too excited for the adventure to come to be afraid. They stood there for a few secs before Olivienne called to the commander. "Push the bottom button, Tosh."

Castellan grinned back, feeling Olivienne's excitement through their empathetic bond. "Yes, ser." Then without further delay, she reached out to push the last button in the column.

Chapter Thirteen

THE FLOOR OF the cylinder hummed below the soles of their boots and the buttons on the panel steadily lit and unlit in a pattern down the panel. Other than that, there was no indication of physical motion. For all the team knew, they weren't even moving. At least until the last button lit up on the panel and the doors *whooshed* open again.

Spc. Dozier, one of the two guardians with secondary training as an adventurist, happened to be the first to step out. Giant panels of lights illuminated nearly ten yords above them, adding to the natural light from the windows along one portion of the giant space. Veva Dozier quickly moved out of the way of the door and gazed up and around her, spinning in a circle as she took in the grand chamber. "Sheddech!"

The main level was easily twice as high as the one they docked on. Not only that, but the tower tapered toward the top so the base was double the diameter as the section where they entered the station. The door of the lift faced a bank of windows that looked out over the ocean. To the left and right of the windows, walls featured large ornate full-color maps. The one of Psiere was obvious with recognizable islands, mountains, and temples precisely labeled. A few of Psiere's oldest cities were on the map, but many other large modern ones were missing. Olivienne surmised that some had either changed names in the hundreds of rotos since the stones were hidden away on the island, or they simply didn't exist when the map was installed.

The map on the wall to the north of the windows was smaller but then it only featured a single island. It was the same island noted on the map they retrieved from the sunken ship. Obviously Magna. There were no cities labeled, only notations for two dirigible stations and a temple. One station was on the western side of the island where they had docked, and the other was on the eastern side very near where the Temple of Antaeus was marked. The dirigible station and the temple were separated by a river running from a large lake to the ocean beyond Magna. The title above the first map was *Psiere*, but the title above the smaller one of Magna was *Cryptid Territories of Magna*.

The Shield guardians were exploring while staying close. Some observed one map or the other, while others took in the sight of the ocean from the windows. Castellan stayed near Olivienne and asked the obvious question as they stared intently at the map of Magna. "What is a cryptid? I've never heard that word before, nor have I read it in any texts."

Olivienne tilted her head and stepped close to the large map. She traced the dotted red lines where they seemed to outline different areas of the island. "I've seen the word a few times in translated texts, but it's one of the ones that we couldn't extrapolate a meaning based on context. However, 'territory' implies habitation and seeing this map, I'd hazard a guess that it has something to do with beasts."

Castellan shot her a curious look. "Beasts and not the Makers?"

"If it were Makers or even Psi, the station wouldn't be abandoned like it is."

"Fair point."

Tosh's voteo crackled with alert tones. "Commander Tosh, we've secured the top level. It appears to be a control hub of sorts. There are screens and a number of switches on panels on the workstations situated around the room. It is significantly more advanced than anything we've seen before. Requesting orders, over."

Castellan looked to Olivienne. "Is there anything you want him to look for up there?"

A dark eyebrow rose with the commander's question. "In a control room? I'm an adventurist, not an engineer. That room is definitely *not* my bailiwick."

"You pick and choose like a plucker at a feast."

Olivienne laughed and gave Castellan a pinch to the arm. "Send Soleng up to them. He's languishing on fifth level with Devin and Yazzie. For that matter, send all three of them. It certainly can't hurt."

"Hmm, do you think it's safe for the captain to bring her crew in?"

Olivienne gestured around her. "This is no temple or Maker cache. It's merely an abandoned transportation hub, just like the area we repaired in Tesseron."

"I wouldn't say *just like*, Connate Dracore. I mean, nothing in Tesseron is half as fancy as all this." Lt. Madlin walked up as they were talking. "But on the subject of transportation, there are two more of those automated doors farther around the north and south walls. One leads to a giant storage building that must be built right against the side of the tower. The other is closer to the front of the building and exits onto a railer platform."

Tosh pulled the voteo from her belt. "Savon, pull Devin, Yazzie, and Lazaro up to the top level with you and see if he can make heads or tails out of the controls. Have Lazaro contact the captain and tell her it's clear to send down a team to the bottom level to look for repair parts. Stress caution to Velten, savvy?"

"Yes, ser. Savon out."

The commander turned to her sovereign. "Are you ready to see the rest? We need to be on the lookout for some sort of conveyance that will take us across the island. After hundreds of rotos, I have concerns that anything will function. At least the temple is directly across, more or less. That should minus a few hundred mahls from the distance we need to cover."

"I too have concerns about the infrastructure." Olivienne looked back at the map of Magna. "And even though the key on that map gives us a definite distance, I also don't want to walk four hundred mahls from here to the temple, crossing through territories of unknown creatures." Both gave a shiver as they remembered the cave sirens of Instrucia.

"I agree. I'm sure Specialists Leggett and Devin can cobble something of use in this mess. Worst case scenario, we await the dirigible repairs, though I'm not sure how long that will take—"

"I don't want to wait."

Castellan gave Olivienne's shoulder a squeeze, understanding her need to keep moving toward their destination. "We'll figure something out. Let's start by looking at that railer station."

FOUR OORS LATER Olivienne and her team had a rudimentary plan in place. As predicted, the storage building had haulers but all were in such a state of deterioration that they were unusable for moving the group across the island. However, because of the far more simple nature of the railer and its various parts, it required only minor cleaning and repairs to function. The only problem was that they needed illeostones to operate it and the hub had no charging room as they hoped. The captain sent her own engineer as well as a few other crew members down to the storage facility and were joined by Leggett and Devin in tearing down existing equipment to find the items needed to repair the

Quaesitum's right front engine. It was a given that they wouldn't find exactly what they needed, but Velten was confident that between her crew and the promised guardian, Spc. Ben Devin, they'd be able to build something functional.

"While I'm happy that we have the means to continue my mission, how do we power the railer across four hundred mahls?"

Olivienne was seated between Castellan and Lt. Savon at Cpt. Velten's round table. Also seated were Dre. Shen, and Velten. Lt. Madlin chose to remain standing for the meeting. Madlin brought up the other major issue. "I would also think that given the state of the railer and motos, the railer line is sure to have suffered degradation as well. Hundreds of rotos of growth of the local flora is certain to uproot rails. "We could also run into trouble if there are any bridges we need to cross."

Gemeda made a face. "You certainly have a knack for gloom and doom, Lieutenant Madlin."

Auda Madlin gave a little bow and flirty wink, which elicited a scowl from the captain. "I'm afraid that I'm a pragmatist through and through, Doctore Shen. Never fear though, I appreciate a little sun when I see it."

Castellan raised a single eyebrow at seeing a side of her lieutenant that she'd never witnessed before. "While even *I* can't lift a railer engine, I can clear and straighten the line as needed. And I think I have a solution to our issue of power."

Captain Velten rolled her eyes at Castellan's slight brag. "What are you going to do, Tosh, shove the railer along with your TK?"

"Nothing as exhausting as that. What have you used of the *Quaesitum's* on-ship illeostone supply? A little over half?"

Seema Velten gave Castellan a curious lift of her brow. "About that, why?"

The commander leaned forward to rest her elbows on the table. "The way I see it, you don't have enough to get back to Nusquam any way we go about it, which is why we were hoping for a recharge station here on Magna. My intuition is telling me that we'll find stones and a charging room in the Temple of Antaeus. Here is what I propose: The railer won't take as many illeostones if we keep it to just the engine and one segment. That should leave plenty for you to get the *Quaesitum* from here to the Temple of Antaeus. Once there, we can either recharge or replenish the dirigible stones for the return trip back to Nusquam."

"Tosh, you're brilliant!"

Castellan glanced sideways. "I think you're just a bit biased, Connate Dracore."

"Ser, I've been working with you for nearly a roto now. I'm not oathed to you but I'd have to agree with her."

Tosh flushed at her lieutenant's words. "Erm, thank you, Savon. Now if we can get back to the discussion at hand." She looked across the table at Cpt. Velten. "While I have rank when it comes to the Connate's safety and mission, the *Quaesitum* is still your ship. The decision is yours alone on this. If you say nay, we'll find another way."

"*What?*" Olivienne looked at her in dismay.

Castellan didn't acknowledge her outburst, but reassured her mind to mind. *"Velten is prideful and I'd rather have her voluntary cooperation than involuntary following of orders. Trust me."*

"Okay."

"What say you, Captain?"

Velten sat back and crossed her arms over her chest. "As much as I don't like to take the wind out of my ship's rotors, figuratively of course, your idea has the most merit. My engineer, Davine, says repairs may take upwards of a weke. We've tools enough on board and with the raw goods and machine parts they're recovering from the station, he's going to completely rebuild the engine. I'm sure we can find something to haul stones from the ship to the first level where the railer is located. Once repairs are finished, we'll leave here and head across the island."

"Ser, what if we get delayed along the way? We don't know the exact route the railer line will take and you won't be able to see it through the forest from a dirigible's vantage point above. If the *Quaesitum* heads straight there, they may overshoot us and we will be stranded with no way to contact them. Even long-range voteos are limited to about fifty or sixty mahls, depending on terrain."

Gemeda chimed in then. "Still glooming I see, Madlin. And if it's all the same, I'd rather not be stranded with a rough and rowdy adventurist team in the middle of nowhere on an unexplored island."

Castellan looked at her long-time friend with concern. "I know your stamina is top notch, Gem—" Olivienne coughed to stifle a laugh and Castellan tried to ignore it. "But if you really would rather stay with the dirigible and meet us at the temple then I see no problem with that."

Olivienne nodded in agreement. "I concur. Castellan assures me that you're fit enough, a fact that I'm convinced of after our dunking in the river near Vesper. However, you are no adventurist and I cannot see a reason for subjecting you unnecessarily to the trip across this island."

Gemeda frowned. "Unfortunately for me, I was given explicit instructions by Queen Olivara herself to stay lockstep with you for this entire mission. That means if you're tramping across this aether-forsaken island, then so too shall I."

Before anyone could comment on Gemeda's announcement, the alert tone on Tosh, Savon, and Madlin's voteos sounded. Castellan was the one who answered. "Tosh here."

"Specialist Penn sending."

Savon whispered across the table. "She's down in the storage facility."

"Go ahead, Penn."

"Ser, I just found a separate room full of communications equipment. I was thinking about our trip across the island. I know our long-range voteos are still limited and we wouldn't be able to stay in contact with the *Quaesitum*. However, if we could take some of this equipment with us, I think I could set up small signal jump stations along our route."

Castellan raised a pale eyebrow at the new specialist's words. "You've been out of Academy for a handful of rotos now, Penn. I thought that was new tech."

"Yes ser, but I stay current on communications because it's a bit of a hobby of mine, besides being one of my commissions. I can build them from what I've found."

Castellan looked around the table. "It sounds like a good idea but I'll admit that communications isn't in my bailiwick."

Lt. Madlin called out from her spot near the windows. "How much power will she need? As we just discussed, illeostones are in short supply right now."

"Good point, Lieutenant." Castellan directed her question into the voteo. "Specialist Penn, how much power will you need per jump station? And what's the range for a jump station?"

"One stone per, and the range is about sixty mahls using the standard com packs we carry, ser."

"And you have enough equipment down there for at least ten jump stations? I want to drop them more frequently than max range, just to be safe. We know not what manner of beast may investigate the items left behind."

Penn's voice was confident when it came through the small speaker. "Yes, ser. I'd say at least twice that."

Castellan smiled around the table. "Well, that takes care of my greatest concern. We will be able to stay in constant contact with the dirigible. Should we run into trouble, or the *Quaesitum's* repairs finish early, you need only to stop and pick us up."

Cpt. Velten finally uncrossed her arms and smiled along with the commander. "I feel much better about this plan of yours to go haring across the island. I'm amenable to giving up stones for the railer and your communication stations."

Castellan depressed the voteo button. "Specialist Penn, carry out your suggestion. Enlist a few other guardians and take all the equipment you'll need to the railer station. Place everything at the rear of the first segment. That's where we'll store our gear for the trip."

"Yes, ser. Penn out."

Castellan clipped the voteo back to her belt. "I don't see any other questions that need answered before we fully prep for this trip. Anything else?"

A chorus of no's went around the table and Olivienne stood. Her excitement for the upcoming adventurist mission was palpable in the captain's small meeting room. The rest stood after her and Castellan called out orders. "Savon and Madlin, I want you to oversee the moving of our gear to the railer segment and report in with me again in two oors." She turned to Velten. "How do you want to do the stone transport?"

"I'll go with them so I can speak with my first officer. Davine can organize a few crew members to help your lot transport enough stones to meet your needs. When do you think you'll leave? Half of todae is gone."

Olivienne looked from the captain to Tosh. "As much as I want to get underway as soon as possible, I'm aware of the logistics involved with getting our gear and team prepped for the trip. I also don't want to travel across these cryptid territories after dark if I can help it."

Castellan nodded. "That's a good point. Fine, let's plan on leaving an oor after first sunrise tomorrow morning. The team can have a little down time once all the prep is complete for the trip." The last sentence she directed toward Savon and Madlin.

"Yes, ser."

After that the group broke up and filed out of the captain's room. As Castellan and Olivienne moved into the passageway,

Olivienne sent a private thought to Castellan. *"While I always love beginning a new adventure, I'll admit that our personal time suffers with these trips."*

Castellan glanced sideways at Olivienne. *"Too true. It is more challenging to practice bed sport while in the company of the entire Shield Corp unit. Do you have a solution to the problem?"*

Olivienne gave her a sly look. *"Mayhaps. Or rather, not a solution as such, but a suggestion for later."*

"Suggestion?"

"Oh yes. I think a private meeting for two in our cabin is an absolute necessity. And just to be sure we thoroughly cover all the finer points in said meeting, I'd suggest taking last meal in private as well."

The commander laughed aloud, startling Gemeda who was walking just in front of them. She paused and made eye contact with the oathed couple and Castellan flushed while she fumbled through an explanation. "We were, ah, discussing the need for a private meeting later to, uh—"

Gemeda held up a hand to stop her. "No need to continue, Tosh. Just be sure this *meeting* doesn't leave you too exhausted to function in the morn."

If anything, Castellan grew redder in the face. Olivienne laughed before coming to her future par's rescue. "Such pretty advice you give, Gemeda. Will you take it yourself when you meet with the good captain later?"

The medican laughed lightly and waved a careless hand through the air. "Absolutely not!" Then she turned down the passageway that led to her cabin.

Castellan paused to watch their friend walk away, then continued toward their own berth. As they pushed through the door, Castellan removed her pistol from the holster and placed it on a nearby desk. "We have two oors alone until Madlin or Savon reports in again. Whatever shall we do with ourselves?"

Olivienne removed her own pistol and satchel from her belt. "I have a question that I'd like you to answer before I get to yours."

"What is that, love?"

"How many oors sleep is recommended in the Psi Defense Corp manual of conduct?"

Two pale eyebrows went up at the random question. "Come again?" Castellan was thrown off by the odd change of subject.

"You heard me, how many oors?"

The officer thought for a few secs. "Eight is recommended

during standard duty situation but each individual is a little different with their requirements. Why do you need to know?"

"And how many do *you* need to function well and be fit for duty?"

"About six and a half, which you already know."

Olivienne stepped close to Castellan and ran her hands up the soldier's arms until they could caress along the sides of her neck. "For the next two oors, I'm going to show you how much I appreciate your presence in my life."

Castellan turned her head to kiss Olivienne's palm. "I don't think that's necessary. If it's half as much as I appreciate you, I'm content." She wrapped her arms around Olivienne's waist. "And what about this evening?"

The Connate gave her most playful laugh, the very one that Castellan loved to hear. "Well, later I plan on doing my level best to wear you out, thus guaranteeing you a hard seven oors sleep tonight."

"And what if it is I who wears *you* out?"

Olivienne moved her hands up to caress the fine blonde hairs near the nape of Castellan's neck. "I think either way, the meeting will be a success."

The words, "I suspect you're right," were lost in the depths of their kiss.

THE LIGHTS UNDER the canopy of the railer station were particularly harsh in the dim twilight of dawn. With only one sun above the horizon and a thick forest of trees all around the tower, Spc. Qent was quick to voice his thoughts on the island. "This place is eerie. It reminds me of Mater."

Lazaro walked up and gave him a quick chuck to the shoulder and squinted in humor. "I can't tell, are you wearing a black uniform, or one of the blue of Security Corp?"

He made a face. "I'm serious here, Laz. You telling me it doesn't remind you of Mater, even a little?"

"They're not even the same kind of trees!"

It was Lt. Madlin who settled it. "No, he's right. While the forest itself is quite different, there is a similarity to Roc Island. It's the silence."

"See?" Qent puffed out when the lieutenant agreed with him.

Madlin continued. "It's as though there is this sense of...waiting. Shouldn't there be more sounds, like birds and insects? That is what makes it so strange."

"Do you think it's safe?" Spc. Penn had just come back from rechecking her communication supplies stocked in the back of the railer seg. They were waiting for the Connate and commander to return from a last meen meeting with the captain.

Laughter met Penn's hesitant words and they all turned to see Gemeda Shen exit the tower onto the station platform. She had a large duffel over one shoulder and her medican kit in the opposite hand. "Do my ears deceive me? Are Shield Corp guardians seriously debating the safety of an adventurist mission, when literally every other dae of their lives are in peril from the sheer nature of their Corp career?"

Ciera Penn flushed and rubbed the back of her neck. "Well, when you put it like that, my worry seems absurd."

Olivienne and Castellan had exited in time to hear the communication specialist's words. "Never fear, Penn! With the incredible and stupendous Doctore Gemeda Shen along, we shall be all good and well."

Gemeda rolled her eyes and Olivienne laughed along with the other specialists on the platform at their commander's words. The scene was broken when the railer engine abruptly *chuffed* to life. Lt. Savon stuck his head out the door of the powerful machine. "Sers, stone and water tanks are loaded and the railer is ready when you are."

Lt. Madlin confirmed her portion of the checklist as well. "All adventurist gear as well as food and water rations are loaded too. I also took the liberty of having Specialist Lear make enough vellum copies of the Magna map to distribute to the entire team."

As if by unspoken order, or perhaps through telepathic one, both lieutenants and all the specialists came out of the railer and seg and lined up on the platform in front of Olivienne. As one they saluted the sovereign. Then Castellan took two steps away, turned on her heel, and also saluted Olivienne. "Connate Dracore, this mission is yours to begin."

Their unwavering dedication and absolute deference to her, not just as the Connate, but as the senior historical adventurist, nearly unraveled her. Olivienne smiled with pride and saluted them all in return. "Well, then. I say let's begin the most important mission of our lives. Let's find the lost temple of Psiere!"

As one, a cheer rang across the railer platform then the specialists filed into the long railer segment that was attached to the engine. All the seats had been stripped from the back half, leaving enough room for the gear and the entire team to bed down with rolls if needed. They were as ready as could be. Once inside with the door shut, Castellan called out to their pilot for the first leg. *"Take us out, Calderon."*

"Yes, ser!"

Chapter Fourteen

DESPITE ALL THE excitement of their newest adventure, Castellan was taking no chances with the Connate's safety. Spc. Calderon kept the railer at a slow pace. Assisting him in the engine compartment were two specialists assigned as spotters. The commander drew up the duty roster the night before to be sure that one spotter had the intuition channel and the other had enhanced awareness. The assigned pairs would work together for the duration of the trip, assisting either Spc. Lear or Spc. Calderon as their pilot. The psi with awareness would keep an eye on the track ahead of the railer, while the other would watch along each side for anything that could interfere with their trip. Because of the intensity needed for such work, she had the spotters rotating out on the top of every oor.

Twenty meens into their journey, the railer slowed and the alert tone sounded on the Shield team's voteos. "Tosh here."

"Specialist Calderon, Commander. Looks like one of the lines is pulled up about forty yords ahead of us. Dozier says it appears bent. Instruction?"

"Bring us as close to the spot as possible. We'll investigate then."

"Yes, ser. Calderon out."

A little over a meen later, the railer *squealed* to a stop as stele clamps and calipers grabbed onto the wheeled mechanism and the entire Shield team marched off the passenger seg. Castellan was pleased to note the lot of them appeared to be hyper-focused on Olivienne's safety. In just a short amount of time, the landscape had changed from heavy forest to forested-swampland on either side of the railer line. Vegetation was thick as ever but with the added annoyance of flying insects in search of a meal. More than one specialist slapped at bites on their exposed skin.

The reason for their stop became obvious when they moved up to stand in front of the engine. One line was still firmly pinned to the mounded track surface while the other was pulled up and bent into a slight arch. Olivienne stared at the stele beam in awe. "What in the deep sea depths could do *that*?"

Her words prompted a higher level of awareness from the

entire team and they quickly took up a ranged formation all around the Connate, facing outward toward the swamp forest. Castellan looked to the bent line then pulled the vellum map from her trouser pocket. "It says here that we're in the territory of something called a skunk ape."

"Ape...ape...that's a colloquial term for the mountain hominids down on Dromea. Could it be a relation?"

Castellan shook her head but Gemeda answered. "Even the most robust silvers wouldn't be able to bend that beam. Clearly this is something bigger or stronger." She shuddered.

With a simple mental signal, *"Brace!"* the entire Shield team unsnapped their pistol guards and made ready for trouble, including Commander Tosh. "If that is the case, I certainly don't want to stand around waiting to meet one. While I possess ferrokinesis as one of my channels, it's not good for much more than sixty punds. And though I can easily bend that beam back into place and lift it with my tee kay, I don't know the tensile strength or whether the structural integrity will hold up to the force of such an action."

"So what will you do?"

Castellan looked at her sovereign. "It's what *we* will do. I believe we can preserve the beam's strength and form if you heat the center section first, then I'll straighten it and lift it back onto the track."

Olivienne raised a single dark brow. "Oh, as easy as that?"

"Well, I wouldn't call it easy, but it's certainly achievable."

Before Olivienne could retort, twin calls came from Lt. Madlin and Spc. Holling. "Commander!"

Tosh looked to Madlin. "Yes?"

"Greater beasts are approaching, ser. I suggest we do this a little faster to avoid a confrontation."

"Aggressive?"

Madlin shrugged. "I'm picking up curiosity only."

Holling added his cred worth of info. "Ser, the silvers read the same way though and they turn aggressive fast."

"Fine, let's begin. 'Vienne, if you will?"

Olivienne quickly used her pyrokinesis channel to heat the beam enough for Castellan to bend it easily without worrying that she'd crack the stele. The commander let it cool for a few meens after it was finished before she lifted the line segment and set it in place. Castellan called out to Specialists Soleng, Dozier, and Devin who stood at the ready with large driving hammers.

They made quick work of pinning the line segment in place with spikes. Castellan circled her finger in the air. "Load up, I want us out of here before our friends get curious and leave the trees."

Calderon swung up into the engine compartment and was followed closely by the spotters. "Yes, ser." Less than a meen later, the railer was once again heading east.

At no more than thirty-five mahls per oor with occasional stops to repair the tracks, the entire team was getting antsy. Each stop warranted the highest level of concentration and Castellan ordered a break around ten hundred oors where the line passed through a small clearing. The break lasted only fifteen meens, causing no small amount of grumbling from Olivienne and a few of the more hyper members of the team.

"I'm sick of this railer already!"

Castellan smiled indulgently. "Need I remind you we traveled for daes on a railer when we first met?"

"That's different." Olivienne insisted. Specialists Devin and Meza both nodded.

"Really?" Castellan moved her gaze from the Connate to the other two. "And just what makes it so different, Meza?"

The woman straightened unconsciously in her seat. "Ser, on a normal railer we're moving along at a fast pace. There is a schedule and a pace set. There are no such guarantees on this heap of stele flake. We don't know where we're going or when we'll get there."

"Tosh," Castellan swung her gaze to Olivienne and tried to hold back a smirk. "What she's trying to say is that we're going so poxing slow on this wreck that time feels interminable."

"The Connate is right, ser." Spc. Devin's deep voice made him seem older than his twenty-three rotos. "I just wish there was something to break the monotony —" His wish was interrupted by the now-familiar alert tone on their voteos.

Unfortunately for the team, their current location was in the midst of heavily forested rolling hills. The railer line cut through the landscape like a scar heading steadily upward, exposing striated rock that had worn with time. The trees in the forest were as massive as only hundreds of rotos untamed could make them, though they were nowhere near the monumental size of the ones on Mater. Some of the trees grew close enough to the tracks that their branches rubbed on the top of the passenger segment as they traveled beneath the canopy.

It was the proximity of the forest proper to their railer that set Castellan on edge with the imminent repair ahead of them. She pointed at Devin. "Be careful what you wish for, Specialist!" With those words of warning, she led the way off the railer to deal with the next obstruction.

Olivienne gave a sigh of relief when she saw the issue. "Well, that's the luckiest thing we've seen all morning."

A large tree had fallen across the railer track, preventing forward motion until it was moved. It was an easy enough task for a seven rated telekinetic. But something about the scene set Castellan's intuition jangling. She glanced around. "Madlin, Holling, are you picking up any of those skunk apes nearby?"

"Yes, ser."

"I am."

Their replies only made her intuition clamor more, especially when Lear spoke up. "Something feels off, ser."

Dozier was quick to agree. Both had a four rating intuition and Castellan drew her service pistol. The rest of the team quickly followed suit and assumed the familiar formation of protection around Olivienne. "I want everyone back on the railer. We need to go as soon as I move this tree. I don't know how smart these beasts are but this feels like a trap to me."

Savon pointed out the obvious. "Ser, what happens if the track is damaged on the other side?"

"Then we'll have a problem on our hands. All right everyone, load up. Man the rail guns we installed on each side just in case. Lear, cycle the engine and standby."

"But Commander Tosh, what of Article Twenty of the Psiere Legibus about greater beasts?"

Castellan frowned and sighed. "Don't shoot to kill unless you have to, but keep in mind the Connate is our highest priority. Just be ready."

Castellan strode to the front of the engine to assess the massive downed tree while the team loaded onto the railer. Savon held back and called to his commander to get her attention. He pointed toward where the trunk was snapped off at the base, some distance from the line. "Ser, I think you were right about the trap. That tree is healthy and the break looks fresh. This was no accident of age or weather."

"I agree. I want to walk down the line a bit to investigate and since you're here, you can watch my back."

Savon grinned, proud at having his commander's trust. "Yes, ser."

Utilizing her channel, Castellan made quick work of the tree. She lifted it well clear of the tracks before walking forward and moving it away from the railer. Nearly one hundred yords down the line Castellan hadn't seen any other signs of malfeasance. She judged the distance far enough and turned the great tree parallel to the railer line and set it on the ground off to the side. The branches prevented it from rolling into the other tree trunks at the edge of the forest. Savon walked behind her the entire way, guarding her back as requested. She turned to him and grinned but noticed her lieutenant had a peculiar look upon his face. "Savon, what is it?"

"Do you smell something, Commander?"

She tilted her head curiously at him. "I smell nothing but the trees. Are you feeling well—" Her words ended as soon as the wretched odor hit her nose. "By the Makers, what *is* that?"

A reverberating *crack* sounded through the forest and before either of them could pinpoint the location something slammed into the side of the railer segment. Tosh and Savon spun toward the railer in time to see a tree trunk hit the ground and roll away from the line. Rather than waste time with the voteo, Castellan contacted Madlin directly as her and Savon ran toward the railer. *"Lear, full speed ahead. We'll catch you on the way by. Madlin, report!"*

The railer gave off a massive chuff of aether and started toward them, rapidly picking up speed. *"Ser, we see nothing. It's like that tree came out of nowhere. But I'm picking up a massive amount of greater beast activity with my animal empathy."*

Another crack sounded secs before a smaller tree trunk slammed into the opposite side of the seg. *"Tosh!"* Olivienne's mental voice was like cold water down Castellan's spine.

When the railer was upon them, Tosh telekinetically lifted Savon and stuffed him through the seg door, then boosted herself after him. Tosh yelled at Lear once they were in. *"Keep it steady, Lear!"*

Despite their movement, the segment rocked again when another tree trunk hit the side. The force was so great that it cracked the plexi window near the back. "Sheddech!" Hoping to see what they were up against, Castellan ran for the back of the seg. She exited onto the small observation platform and watched in awe as creature after creature emerged from the forest to stand on the railer line. Using the width of the rails as a reference, she calculated the size of the skunk apes to be roughly one and a half times her own height. And clearly they were exponentially stronger, in both odor and physical manifestation.

Olivienne walked onto the platform a few secs later. "Madlin says they still don't come across as aggressive, merely wary. She also says they are relieved we are leaving. I suspect the trees were a warning."

"So why the tree across the line to begin with?"

Used to dealing with puzzles in her dae to dae life and aware that not all could be solved, Olivienne shrugged. "I don't know. Perhaps they were testing us."

"Perhaps." Castellan pulled the folded map of Magna from the thigh pocket of her trousers. Keeping a tight grip, she unfolded the vellum. "At the rate we're moving I'd estimate we're about here." She pointed to a spot that was not far from the large lake in the center of the island.

Olivienne rolled her eyes and interrupted. "I forget how abnormally good you are with spatial relations and distance reasoning. Go on."

"As I was saying, we've been heading east southeast, which should bring us to the western edge of the lake."

"Nessie. Do you think there will be more than one creature like the skunk ape, or singular?"

Castellan studied the other marked territories on the cryptid map. "It's hard to say, nothing is pluralized on the map that I can tell. The north side of the territory we're traveling through is labeled hydra, and the south is chupacabra." She stumbled over the unfamiliar word. I don't even know if the railer will take us all the way around the lake."

Olivienne frowned. "Well, I certainly don't look forward to traipsing the rest of the way on foot through these territories if it doesn't, especially if the others are as dangerous as the skunk apes." She thought for a sec then traced some of the territories with her finger as Castellan held the small map steady. "Look at the size differences of each area. From what we know of the skunk apes, they're significantly larger than us, and there were quite a few of them. So it's possible that the smaller areas with griffin and hydra are either smaller species, fewer, or not a range animal."

"What would that say about the territory of the Sasquatch and the ringdocus? Those two alone take up the entire eastern coast and some of the north and south. Are they giant beasts or wide ranging?" Olivienne answered with a shrug and Castellan put the map back in her pocket, then wrapped an arm around her sovereign as they watched the railer lines disappear behind them.

The couple enjoyed the rare quiet of the moment, content in the presence of each other. Their tranquility was broken by the segment door sliding open behind them. Castellan sighed and Olivienne turned her head to kiss the commander's neck. *"Stolen moments are often sweet as they are short, my darling."*

Castellan stifled a laugh. *"I prefer my stolen moments sweet and long as a dae of two suns."*

Olivienne didn't bother hiding her amusement. "Now, where is the fun in that, Commander?"

Both women were conscious of the person behind them and Castellan released Olivienne before spinning on her heal. "How can I help you, Specialist Penn?"

"Actually, ser, it's Connate Dracore I'm here to see."

The infamous dark Dracore brow arched up. "Oh?"

"Yes, ser. I've translated the texts we found in the control room of the tower. I thought you might like to see them."

"Oh!" She turned to Castellan. "It completely slipped my mind that I had Penn bring the encrypted stack of vellum they found in a storage compartment on the top tower level."

Castellan nodded and addressed the specialist. "And?"

General Renou's niece cleared her throat nervously. "Well, sers, the stack contained a number of sheets relevant to our adventure. The various cryptid territories are documented, as well as all the transportation systems on Magna. There is another map, similar to the one we copied from the wall of the base tower floor, only this one has docks as well as the two dirigible stations labeled."

Castellan's mind raced with curiosity about the other creatures on the island. "Let's take this inside where you can brief us along with Doctore Shen, and Lieutenants Savon and Madlin."

The trio filed into the seg, shutting and latching the door behind them. One of the alterations they'd done to the segment was to remove a table and bench seats from a defunct dining car of the old railer. The table and benches were installed just behind the standard seats. Castellan surmised the team could alternate at the table for eating, or it could be used exactly as they were about to. Savon, Madlin, and Penn sat on one side of the table while Olivienne and Tosh sat on the other. Olivienne called out to Gemeda before they could begin. "Doctore Shen, would you like to hear about the different species on the island?"

Gemeda grinned at the invite and to show that her next words were teasing. "Sure, why not? I'm bored as spit over here. There is only so much a medican can do when you all remain so blasted healthy." She sat on Olivienne's right as Spc. Penn removed the first vellum from the stack and placed it on the center of the table.

"Here is the new map I found of Magna. As you can see the dirigible stations, temple, and docks are clearly labeled."

Savon peered closer. "Docks?"

Specialist Penn pointed at each end of the large lake. "The lake is called Lacrimise. According to the map, the railer line ends at the lake and I assume the second portion of the trip will be across the water."

Madlin spoke up. "What about going around the lake on foot?"

"According to descriptions of the area, the land north of the lake is mostly swamp. It's heavily populated by the skunk ape. That's one of the reasons given why the railer line doesn't continue around the lake.

"And how much safer will it be if whatever this Nessie is sinks us in Dir Lacrimise?"

Olivienne placed a calming hand on Castellan's clenched fist. "Darling, I trust the Makers to know what is safe. If their dedicated route to the Temple of Antaeus takes us across the lake then that is the safest way to go."

"Pardon my saying, Connate, but following the Maker's path may not even be possible until we see what is available when we reach the docks. Whatever ship or conveyance left over from their time here is most likely in the same shape as the haulers we found. Hundreds of rotos does no engine good."

Tosh rubbed the space above the bridge of her nose. "Savon has a point. We may be stuck once we reach Lacrimise and will have to await the repairs on the *Quaesitum* to go any farther."

"Um, that's actually another thing I'd like to bring up, Commander. I've been dropping off my pre-made antennas at every railer line repair stop. But based on the behavior we've observed so far from the skunk apes, I wonder if they will remain unmolested."

Castellan glanced up to search for her other communications specialist. "Lazaro, fire up the long-range and see if you can contact the *Quaesitum*."

He stood from where he was searching through his duty

pouch and moved over to where the long-range voteo had been placed. Less than a meen later he had it powered up. "Shield team to *Quaesitum*, do you read? Over."

Conversation paused in the seg as they waited impatiently for the message to go out via each of the signal jump stations they place along their route. The only thing that could be heard was the *clack-clack* of the railer wheels traveling down the line. Then a voice came over the machine's speaker. "*Quaesitum* receiving. What is your request, Shield team?"

Dante Lazaro turned to Commander Tosh. "Ser?"

Castellan waved a hand through the air. "Tell him it's just a test of our long-range booster antennas. Also, I want a similar test at the top of every oor."

"Yes, ser."

The group at the table returned to their discussion while Lazaro finished the transmission. "Now that we've got reassurance on that point, what else can you tell us, Penn?"

"Well, sers, I've got descriptions of every cryptid listed as well as the terrains of their territories."

Olivienne pointed toward the first one to the north of the skunk ape territory. "Start here and continue right-ways around the island."

"The next species up the coast from where we landed is the hydra. The territory seems to be a continuation of the swamps and marshes that the skunk apes prefer. Hydras live and breed in the pools of water and are extremely aggressive. They are large water serpents with seven heads and poisonous blood. An interesting thing to note is the fact that they have regenerative capabilities similar to that of salamandus and can even regrow lost heads with enough time."

Olivienne's eyes widened. "Fascinating."

"Not only that, but because of something the Maker's called advanced cellular meiosis, when they lose one head, two will grow in its place."

Castellan asked the only question she cared about. "How big are they, and do they have a weakness?"

"The text says that the average hydra is about three yords tall and they are extremely dangerous. Both territorial and aggressive, with fire listed as their only weakness."

Tosh nodded and glanced at Olivienne. "We can work with that if the need arises."

Madlin pointed to the next territory north of the hydra.

"What is a unicorn?"

Spc. Penn shuffled a new vellum sheet to the top of the stack and continued. "Unicorns are herd beasts, similar to an equine but slightly smaller. They have a single spiral horn protruding from their forehead. The history in the texts mentions that the horn was rumored to have healing or mystical properties but detailed examination of expired individuals debunked that theory."

Castellan tapped the map. "Please just continue through all of them."

Penn cleared her throat. "Yes, ser. So the largest territory is for the Sasquatch. There are multiple tribes so they need a lot of space. And they're big."

Gemeda tilted her head curiously at Ciera Penn. "Tribes? That implies a measure of intellect and societal structure beyond the base hominids, or even the skunk apes."

"Yes, Doctore. Sasquatch are very large hairy upright hominids, like a cross between the skunk ape and us. They range in size anywhere from three to four yords in height. They are non-aggressive, but will protect their tribe and territory if provoked. Their diet consists mainly of flora, but they do supplement with piscis. Nuts and river swimmers are their sole source of protein. Because they are more intelligent and wide ranging, they control the entire territory surrounding the Temple of Antaeus."

Castellan leaned forward. "Are they guarding it? Does it say if they will let people past to get to the temple?"

"Honestly, ser, it just says they were set to guard the surrounding area from any other species that stray out of their own territory. It makes no mention of temple guards."

"My love, I think if they are listed as non-aggressive then we probably don't need to worry about their presence around the Temple. Please continue, Penn."

"Sasquatch take up nearly the entire northeast corner of the island. Their territory extends all the way down to the Mir Aedes, which flows from Dir Lacrimise to the eastern ocean. South of Aedes we find the ringdocus, alternately known as shunka warakin in the texts. They are large canoid hybrids that live in packs somewhere between ten and twenty in size. They require a lot of territory for hunting, and will defend it. The text says they'll attack with little provocation and the southern bank of the Aedes should be avoided at all costs."

Lt. Madlin frowned at the warning. "I grew up in a river

town and it's not easy to avoid one bank or another if weather is bad or the current is treacherous. And based on the terrain, I feel like the Mir Aedes will be rough going. Let's hope that we don't have to follow the river to the coast for that reason alone."

Spc. Penn looked at her lieutenant curiously. "Why do you think it will be rough?"

Madlin pointed at the map. "We've been on this railer line heading inland, but the way hasn't been flat. The farther from the swampland we get, the more of an incline there is. Which leads me to believe the center of the island is much higher than the coasts. Flat rivers are significantly smoother than those flowing downhill, especially if it's rocky on the other side."

"That's a good bit of intel to point out. Thank you, Lieutenant." Castellan pointed at the next section on the map. "Now, we're almost done with the territories. Let's get through this so we can start planning the next leg of the trip. What is a griffin?"

The young specialist shuffled the pages of velum again until she found what she was looking for. "Griffins are fascinating and beautiful!" She shoved one page toward the center of the table so they could all see the illustration. "The body and rear of the creature is that of a large feline. The head, front claws and wings are all of a bird of prey, very much like the rocs on Mater. Their diet consists of both land and sea creatures and they are very long lived. Also like the rocs, the text mentions that they only lay a few eggs every couple rotos and the population is typically quite low."

Olivienne tapped her lower lip with her index finger, reminding Castellan of the Queen. "We have intel that this island has been abandoned for hundreds upon hundreds of rotos. Do you think that with so much time passed there will be less or more of a population?"

Penn's eyes widened at the expanded history of their world that went beyond Psierians' recorded one, but answered truthfully. "It's hard to say, Connate."

"We speculated much the same before heading into the sirens' cave."

Olivienne sighed at the way Castellan pointed out the obvious. She hated unsolved mysteries but the trip wasn't to explore all the creatures of Magna. It was to get inside the Temple of Antaeus and solve the mysteries of their people. "All right, last one is the chupacabra. What can you tell us about that?"

"They are roughly the size of a Dromean ursine in stature,

both smaller and heavier than a human. Chupacabras feature a row of spines reaching from the neck to the base of the tail. They will kill any prey they can subdue, preferring to suck the blood from their bodies."

Olivienne made a face and Lieutenant Savon pursed his lips. Castellan looked thoughtful. "The chupacabra brings us back around to the skunk ape territory. So, based on all that you've discovered, the best course to our destination is the one that the Maker's laid out for us."

"Yes, ser."

Olivienne looked at Gem and smirked. "Should I say it?"

Gemeda laughed. "Oh, absolutely!"

Castellan leaned forward to look at the two women seated to her right. "Say what?"

"Ser..." Madlin called across the table, and when Castellan met her eyes, she saw the same humor as what both Olivienne and Gemeda carried in their expressions. "I believe Connate Dracore said as much at the very beginning of this discussion."

The commander looked nonplussed for a sec, then shook her head and gave a laugh of her own. "So she did."

They only traveled for another fifteen meens before the alert tone sounded and the railer began to slow. This time it was Spc. Lear's voice that came over the voteo, having switched out with Calderon. "Ser, we're approaching a multi-story building and a large body of water. It appears to be the end of the railer line."

Castellan responded into her own voteo. "I'm guessing the water is Dir Lacrimise, the lake listed on the map we found. Pull us in and drain the water from the illeostone tank to preserve power. Join the group but make sure the railer is ready to reverse at any moment." She glanced out the window at the massive building. It looked like a large smooth cube with slight indentions where windows would ordinarily be above and below. Other than that, there was no discernable way in from the railer line side.

"Yes, ser. Lear out."

The rest of the Shield team stood and quickly donned their gear, having all heard the communication. Castellan walked to where both Olivienne and Gemeda were checking their pistols. "Connate Dracore and Doctore Shen...are you two lovely pseras ready to begin the next leg of our adventure?"

Olivienne smirked at her lover. "I'd say lead the way but you should probably let a professional go first." She finished speaking as the railer squealed to a stop, then before Castellan could wipe the gobsmacked look from her face, the Connate and half the Shield team exited onto the platform via the two doors on the passenger seg.

Gemeda didn't even try to hide the laugh that bubbled up. "She's certainly a lot feistier than I thought she'd be on adventure."

Castellan grimaced and prompted her long-time friend. "Is she really?"

Gem shook her head and smiled. "Truthfully, no. She's exactly as I pictured her to be. I wish you all the happiness in the world going forward, my friend. Now, we should perhaps catch up with the group before we get left behind. Though I sense no thoughts other than ours."

The lieutenant stepped onto the railer platform and scanned the space. "I agree, I cast my thoughts out as we pulled up in search of other minds. There is no one here."

"Commander Tosh!"

The call came from around the corner of the station, where the decking that appeared to run all the way around the building extended out over the water. The entire Shield team, minus the current pilot, met Holling at the overlook. "What is it, Specialist?"

Rather than answer, the medican pointed out toward the large expanse of water. There was no end in sight and the blue of the Lacrimise was only interrupted by one thing. The water's surface was broken by a humped back, which led to a long neck capped by a comparatively small head.

"By the depths!" Olivienne smiled delightedly as the large creature swam closer, well within fifty foot of where they stood on the observation deck of the station. Her words breathed out with a sense of awe. "That must be a nessie."

Every member froze when a deep and resonating voice sounded in their head. *"No, humans. I am simply called Nessie. I've been waiting a long time for you."*

Gemeda's jaw dropped open. "By the Makers."

"Yes."

Chapter Fifteen

"WHAT'S A HUMAN?"

Specialist Gar Soleng's voice was barely a whisper but the rest of the team heard it above the sound of wind and water gently lapping against the retaining wall below. They watched with equal parts trepidation and fascination as the great beast swam closer. Olivienne leaned toward Castellan and whispered. "What does it mean that it's been waiting a long time for us?"

Castellan called out to everyone. "Telepathic shields in place. We don't know what manner of beast this Nessie is and it's best to be cautious. The Connate's life depends on it." Olivienne frowned at her words but erected her own telepathic shield.

Nessie swam so close that the creature's head was above the level of their observation deck. Its skin was smooth, more like an amphib, rather than scaled like a pisci. They waited, and Nessie waited, but the deep voice didn't return to their thoughts. Gem was the first to break the silence. "I suppose that answers the question of whether or not our shields could hold against such a powerful telepath."

Castellan scowled. "Unfortunately, we won't know any more unless one of us drops our shield."

"Ser..." Spc. Holling stepped forward. "I'd like to volunteer. I've always held an affinity for the greater beasts, as we previously discussed."

Castellan nodded. "Go ahead, Holling."

"Tosh!" Olivienne gripped her commander's forearm. "What if it's dangerous?"

Castellan winked at the sovereign. "Well, we have one other medican, plus the very best doctore in all the land should the beast take him."

"Ser?"

Cursing herself internally, Castellan rushed to reassure the guardian. "Have no fear, Holling. I sense no aggression nor is my intuition telling me anything but to trust Nessie. And as awkward as it will be, please translate aloud your conversation for the rest of us."

The dedicated, nearly thirty-roto-old medican saluted

smartly, "Yes, ser." He then turned toward the creature that had swam closer and whose head hovered less than five meters from the group. It was larger than Castellan initially guessed from a distance. Nessie's head was easily the length of an average psi. Holling smiled with delight and turned to his sovereign and commander. "Oh! Nessie is female and asks that we address her as such."

Gemeda gave an awed sigh. "Fascinating."

"She also says that Commander Tosh is an intelligent leader and a fine match for Connate Dracore."

Suspicion crept into Castellan's thoughts with Holling's words. Either Nessie picked up a lot of information from the team before their shields went up, or she could read them through the shields. Both thoughts were disturbing but before Castellan could say anything Olivienne spoke up. "Ask her if she knows where the Maker's went."

Screeching rent the air and the massive creature opened her jaws wide and directed a blast of sound and pisci-scented breath toward the group on the dock. Everyone futilely clapped hands over their ears to block the aural assault but it was inside their minds as much as it was vocal. Accompanying the screech was a single repeated word. It was followed by a wash of sadness that nearly buckled Holling and Madlin's knees. *"Gone, gone, gone, gone —"*

Castellan aimed a telepathic shout toward Nessie. *"Stop!"*

The noise within their heads abruptly cut off even as the screeching faded away. Nessie huffed another massive breath that displaced even Castellan's locks. Secs went by with only the lapping of water against whatever material the overlook was built upon. Finally, Nessie spoke in a significantly gentler tone, through everyone's shields. *"My apologies, humans. I fear that hundreds of years of solitude have adversely affected my emotional state."*

Castellan looked at the creature curiously. "Years? We are not familiar with that unit of measurement."

"A year is one revolution around your binary suns."

"Ah, a roto then."

The great beast blew a breath through her nostrils but otherwise didn't respond. It was a massive amount of time to have passed, and they wondered just how long-lived this Nessie could be. Olivienne glanced at Castellan and held her gaze. They didn't need to speak mind to mind to know their best course of action should be a cautious one. They'd worked together long enough that they could read each other's subtle physical cues and expressions. Castellan called to one of her lieutenants. "Madlin, are you sensing any aggression from Nessie?"

"No, ser. I sense curiosity, sadness, loneliness, and resolve."

"Resolve?" Olivienne's trademark dark brow rose with her question.

"Yes, Connate Dracore. There is a reason she is here. Nessie carries an immense sense of purpose."

"Of course I do, humans. I was gifted this lake when we first arrived."

Olivienne tried again. "Who is 'we' and arrived from where?"

The great beast's head whipped around toward the group and as one they stepped back. Nessie gazed intently at Olivienne. Castellan was ready for interaction but relied heavily on her intuition channel, which gave no indication Nessie would attack.

"Questions, questions, questions...you humans are a curious race. I can see why the Tau were so enamored with you. Sadly, they are gone and you are not allowed to know too many truths. There are rules, you see. I cannot advance you beyond your current capability."

"Not even knowledge?" Castellan called out to garner Nessie's attention, not liking the way the massive water creature was so focused on their sovereign.

Nessie moved nearer yet and blinked. Everyone watched as a double film covered the eye, top to bottom and side to side, then opened again. Holling was closest to the creature. He reached a hand out, as if to touch her neck, but was stopped by a casual flex of Castellan's telekinesis. "Fascinating."

Gemeda snorted. "Word of the dae, it is."

Castellan called a warning to him. "'Ware, specialist. Remember your duty."

Gren Holling abruptly straightened and resumed proper diligence. "Yes, ser."

Olivienne addressed Nessie again. "Please, can you answer any questions for us?"

"Yes, I can —"

"Wonderful, where —"

"But I will not."

The Connate huffed at the creature's unhelpful attitude.

Nessie laughed into their heads at the same time the beast repeatedly wheezed short breaths. *"I like you. I'm surprised one of the human leaders has wandered so far away from your land. You are one of the Maker's Meddles."*

Gemeda looked from her longtime friend, to her sovereign. "Medals? Is the Connate supposed to be a prize then?"

No one else in the group, save the Connate and commander, knew what Nessie referred to. They had to make a decision then and there whether to share one of the greatest secrets discovered. Tosh looked around, then ordered, "Regroup, back fifty paces." All at once the group of men and women turned and marched away from the dock edge while Nessie watched curiously, tilting her head back and forth like a canid. When everyone was far enough away to be safe should the creature turn more than curious, Commander Tosh addressed the group. "What I'm going to tell you is of the highest security, cathedra oath. Do you understand the penalty if you break cathedra oath?"

Gemeda raised an eyebrow, very reminiscent of their sovereign but nodded. Everyone else gave verbal confirmation exactly as they'd been trained. "Yes, ser!"

"The blood of every Psierian is tested at birth, then tested again during oathing and consoral ceremonies."

Gemeda spoke up. "Even sovereigns?"

Olivienne smiled. "Especially sovereigns." She took over from Castellan. "The document we discovered in the cave of sirens states that our people nearly died out. Wherever we came from doesn't matter as much as who we are at this point in history. Hundreds of rotos ago our people warred with each other because we had no proper leaders."

Spc. Penn, one of the youngest members and the person with the least field and combat training, opened her mouth in shock. "Psierians?"

"Yes. Apparently the Makers weren't ready for us to go extinct and they –" Olivienne glanced toward Nessie before turning her gaze back to their group. "Meddled in our makeup, tweaking and perfecting one particular line until they had crafted perfect leadership material. That familial line is the Dracore line. We were..." She met Castellan's pale blue eyes and her oath mate took over.

"Engineered to be exactly what Psierians need in a sovereign. The Dracores were created to rule us."

Savon exclaimed, "By the Makers!"

Castellan pointed at him and winked. "Yes, exactly."

Gemeda caught on fast and her doctore's mind raced with the implications. "So by Nessie's statement...the Connate is one of the 'Maker's Meddles' and I misheard the descriptor."

"Yes."

Spc Lear burst out laughing and Castellan turned her gaze onto one of their pilots. "Is there something you'd like to share with the group, Specialist?"

"Ser, all those folks in the anti-sovereign faction...they've got it all wrong. There is not one person they could suggest who could do a better job at ruling Psiere than our very own Queen. Why not simply announce as much and be done?"

Olivienne shook her head sadly. "Do you think the people grasping for power would care one wit or iota about the truth? They'd simply say the documents were lies. There is already a push to declare that the Makers were a construct of the sovereign family to lead people along to ruin. No, my mother is saving that news for when it would best be received. That time has not yet arrived."

Savon's face was serious and thoughtful. "What do we do now, Connate?"

Olivienne moved her gaze around the group, touched on Castellan, then focused on the watching creature in the distance. "Nessie!" She directed the entire group to close the distance between them and the railing.

"Yes, bana-phrionnsa?"

Olivienne didn't bother trying to understand the creature's terminology. "So you can't or won't tell us where we came from or where the Makers went."

"That is correct."

"Can you tell us if our race and yours came from the same place?"

Nessie thought for nearly a meen, tilting her head back and forth again. It seemed to be a favored mannerism. Finally, her mouth dropped open, looking very much like a smile. A great, blunt-toothed smile. *"I can tell you that we came from roughly the same time and place, though that is not the case for all creatures on Psiere. We all left—me, the Bigfoot colony, and humans—during a great plague. It was a dark time and the Makers collected us to preserve our species. Though those of us on this island were never updated."*

"Updated?" Tosh found the term strange.

"Yes. Humans were fairly primitive in the time I came from. I know the Tau were receiving deep-space cultural bursts that pertained to any of their more advanced species. All collection ships received them. So you were either updated by the Tau, or you evolved your cul-

ture to its current form naturally. I learned this from the scienteres stationed here. They were surprisingly loquacious." Nessie seemed almost proud of her knowledge and in that pride forgot that she was withholding information from the group of Psierians.

"Collected us?" While Olivienne stored the information away to ponder at a later date, she was caught on a different word than her future par.

"Connate, could she be speaking of the menagerie in the ship below Dir Sanguis?" Spc. Qent's voice was tentative.

Rather than his connate answer, Nessie's voice boomed in all their heads. *"Why yes, that is the exact truth of it! And I wonder, wonder, wonder if you seek the truth or if the truth seeks you. The Tau scienteres were collectors, were preservationists. It is against their nature to see unique species die."* Nessie paused and blew another blast of warm, wet breath toward the group from her large head. *"Or any species really."*

"Please, Nessie. What we seek is the lost temple of Psiere, the Temple of Antaeus. Can you help us with that, at least?"

"Oh no, I cannot go there! The temple is beyond the lake and across the mount, but I cannot wander farther than the water mouth. If I stray too close to the sea, I risk the wrath of the Atlantee."

Castellan sent her tightest mind-to-mind communication to Olivienne. *"She's simply mad."*

"Mad I may be, but I won't go to the sea."

"Bollux!" Castellan made a face as even her best attempt at private communication was thwarted by the beast. "Can you at least help us cross the lake?"

Nessie leaned as close to Commander Tosh as possible and took a great sniff. Then she blew out a short, sharp breath, flipping Castellan's collar and hair into disarray. Both Olivienne and Gemeda snickered at the sight. *"You smell like a meddle, but you're not are you?"*

Castellan narrowed her eyes at the strangely insightful creature. "No, I am not."

"I cannot help you 'til you crack the code. Then I'll guide across the water road. Light the windows for me to see, and to you I'll bring the temple key."

Olivienne glanced around and pointed at the strange building they'd come around when heading for the dock. "I suspect the answers we seek are there."

Castellan called out to the rest of the group. "Savon, take the Connate and Doctore Shen to search for an entrance."

Olivienne gave her a concerned look. "Tosh? What are you going to do?"

"Nothing much. I just want a few words with Nessie in private while you puzzle your way into the building. Based on the two sides we've seen, I suspect it won't be as simple as a latched door."

Olivienne looked as if she wanted to say something but instead chose to hold her tongue. She nodded and followed where Lt. Savon waited for her.

Once the rest had moved on to gain entrance into the building, the commander addressed the great beast in a tight band of telepathic communication. *"Nessie, will you submit to a trust reading with me? You don't have to answer any questions you choose not to, but I need to establish a baseline of trust where you're concerned."*

The mental voice that responded sounded somewhat amused. *"I will, however, I will make the same demands of you. For every question I answer, you will do the same for me."*

Castellan considered her options and decided there was no information Nessie could demand that would obstruct her mission or Corp duty. *"I'd say that is a fair enough trade. How should we do this?"*

"Come closer and touch my neck." Nessie swam until she could lean farther over the wall separating the dock from the drop below. The commander approached cautiously until she could lay her palm upon the smooth surface of the creature's skin. It wasn't slippery as she'd originally thought it would be, but rather smooth and soft as a sharc skin coat. Nessie had plenty of time to dry while she spoke with their group and for that Castellan was grateful. As soon as they touched, Nessie's voice boomed within Castellan's mind. *"I am ready, human."*

"Too loud. Can you quiet your mind a bit, I'm afraid my mental volume is a lot less than yours."

Nessie's telepathic voice came back significantly quieter. *"My apologies, I shall comply with your wish."*

"Thank you. Now, my first question for you is: will you help us across the lake?"

Deep laughter rang through Castellan's skull. *"I already answered that for you, Commander, and it remains the same. I will help you across Dir Lacrimise."*

Clearly the creature was exceedingly powerful. Despite not having the empathy channel herself, Castellan could feel a bit of humor ring through Nessie's words. It made her consider her own phrasing of the question. *"Nessie, when you say 'you,' do you mean my entire team, or me specifically?"*

"You are a quick one, aren't you? But I don't have to answer another question until you answer one of mine."

Castellan frowned. *"You're not answering a second question, but rather clarifying your first."*

Surprise colored Nessie's response. *"You are correct and definitely too quick to be fooled by a mere play on words. To answer your first question in a more thorough manner, I meant you specifically but I could be convinced to aid more."*

The commander inclined her head. *"Thank you."*

"It is my turn. Which of your years is it in your recorded history?"

Castellan thought the question exceedingly strange. *"It is the roto five hundred and six."*

"Five hundred and six is divine! Did you know it is a square pyramidal number?" Nessie paused. *"Ah, but you probably aren't familiar with that term, are you?"*

Castellan huffed. *"As a matter of fact, I am. It is a figurate number that represents the number of stacked spheres in a pyramid with a square base. We have formulae that deal with such. Is the number significant to you?"*

Nessie gave a slight shake but didn't pull away from Castellan's hand. *"Not significant in any way other than as a placeholder for history. By your year calculations I've been alone in this water for two-hundred and thirty-four years."*

The commander sucked in a breath. By Nessie's very words, the Makers had left in the roto two hundred and seventy-two, much more recently than originally thought. She attempted another question that she suspected the creature wouldn't answer. *"Where did the Maker's go from here? Back to the stars from whence they came?"*

Hot breath bathed the top of Castellan's head. *"That question is not allowed! Ask another."*

"Fine then. Why don't you want to help us across Dir Lacrimise?"

Silence remained in both their heads for nearly a meen after Castellan's question. She assumed Nessie wasn't going to answer, as she had done for the previous question, but the noble beast surprised her.

"I am lonely, Commander."

"Lonely?"

A wheezing sigh hissed from Nessie's nostrils. *"Yes, lonely. Before the Tau left, the scienteres stationed here would speak with me often. They'd share their knowledge and discoveries. Being bound to this lake as I am, I have no way of exploring this world and count on the good will of others to share their adventures."*

"*Why were the Makers — erm, the Tau stationed here? Is there something significant about this location?*"

"*Is that another question?*"

Castellan made a face at the blasted creature's tit for tat accounting. "*I suppose it is and I'll have to owe you two answers in a row.*"

"*That exchange is acceptable. This location is a scientere engineering and research station. I was told they were studying genetics and biodiversity.*"

Not all the terms were familiar to Castellan, but she recognized genetics from recent Maker texts and could hazard a guess about the nature of the station. "*Thank you. I'm ready for your next questions.*"

"*What is your earliest recorded history?*"

"*Our temples have been unlocked for one hundred and fifty rotos and our own recorded history only goes back to two hundred and ninety-five. It is as if our entire society were naught more than a blank slate before.*" She stopped, remembering the document they'd retrieved from the cave on Instrucia. "*I see the truth of it now. We were a blank slate before, through more of the Maker's meddling I suspect.*" She pondered the problem of starting a society in the middle. "*How is that even possible? Were they able to bring an entire people to adulthood with society completely intact then, what...replace our memories with ones of their choosing? Are they responsible for the reason more Psierians aren't curious about where we came from as a people?*"

"*Enough! Your curiosity hammers at me and I grow weary of it when my own has yet to be assuaged.*"

Castellan rubbed her temple with the hand not touching Nessie. "*My apologies, great Nessie. I fear my excitement of discovery got the best of me for a meen.*"

Nessie gave a slight dip of her head. "*Understandable. Humans have always been as such. My second question for you is about your purpose on this island. Why do you seek the Temple of Antaeus?*"

"*Psierians, specifically those in the Divinity Corp, are tasked with solving the divine mystery. They strive to answer two questions: who were the Makers and where did they go? Olivienne, our Royal Sovereign Connate, is a historical adventurist who finds the texts and schematics left behind by the Makers and brings them into our society with the goal of improving all our lives. Many have assumed there was a third temple based on untranslatable texts found, but Olivienne discovered the proof of such during her most recent missions."*

"You've told me how you've come to be here, human, but not why."

Castellan grimaced. *"Quite right. We are here because we seek proof of the third temple."*

Nessie prodded. *"And? I sense more."*

"Connate Dracore wishes to find the rumored antoraestones."

"I can see your thoughts clearly. You don't wish these stones found, do you?"

Castellan thought about her best response. *"I — "*

Her mental words were interrupted by Nessie's louder voice within her head. *"Oh, but you're also under a directive from your supreme leader, your Queen. It is an order that your mate does not agree with."*

She glanced around furtively even though she knew the team was off exploring the perimeter of the building. *"No, she does not."*

"Your Queen has the right of it, you know. The stones are dangerous, which is why the Tau locked them away on this island. Are your people better prepared for the power this time around?"

Castellan had no choice but to answer honestly. *"No. Which is why Olivienne and I have the top secret orders that we carry. We are to destroy the stones or, at the very least, safeguard them from access or discovery for many rotos to come."*

Silence reigned in both their heads for another meen then Nessie responded. *"I will keep your secret, human. And I will aid you in your mission, but I demand a payment in return."*

Leary, Castellan eyed the beast above her, taking in the strangely blinking orb that stared down. *"What is the payment? If it will hurt any of my team or mission I will say nay. We'll find our own way."*

Nessie laughed in her head. *"It will neither hurt your team or your mission."*

"And the payment?"

"I'll let you know when the time comes, Commander."

Castellan sighed. *"Then I suppose we'll see if I agree to this payment in that moment."*

Their conversation was interrupted by Spc. Holling. "Commander Tosh, the Connate is requesting your presence at the far side of the building. Is there anything you need me to do here?"

Castellan pulled her hand from Nessie's neck and thought for a few secs. "As a matter of fact there is. Stay here and speak with

Nessie. I'm giving you security clearance to answer any questions she has for you."

Holling saluted and gave her a grin as if she'd bestowed on him the greatest of gifts. Perhaps she had. "Yes, ser!"

She knew the man had an affinity with the great beasts, one he'd demonstrated over and over on their missions. Tosh had an idea that if he could form a rapport with Nessie, then the creature would be more likely to answer questions or help them going forward. At least that was her hope. She returned his salute, then took off at a fast jog in the direction from which Holling had come.

When she found Olivienne and the rest of the team, they were on the side of the building opposite the railer. Lieutenant Madlin had her hands placed flat against what appeared to be a sealed door with no handle or latch. There were large panels of the same material along the walls around the building. If she were to hazard a guess, Tosh would say they were windows but they appeared to be some sort of smooth, opaque material.

Olivienne noticed her approach and sighed. "Finally! We've been trying to figure out how to get in to no avail. There is simply nothing to puzzle out, just expanses of smooth material with no buttons, holes, toggles, or anything else."

The commander looked at Madlin. "Anything?"

"No, ser. Whatever opens the door or building isn't located along this stretch."

Castellan glanced around the rest of her team, singling one out. "Meza, clasp hands with Madlin, and then both of you touch the door. See if the combination of your clairvoyance and her psychometry will trigger something."

Olivienne tilted her head curiously. "What are you playing at, Tosh? We've never been taught anything about combining our channels."

Tosh shrugged. "Sometimes we get a reading in the field. It happened the dae of the flash flood when Savon and I touched. Call it a gut feeling, but it can't hurt to try."

The lieutenant and specialist did as instructed while the entire team waited. They waited nearly a meen before the two women intoned as one, "pillar," and then dropped their hands.

"What in the deep sea depths does that mean?" The speaker was Spc. Soleng but most agreed with the statement. All with the exception of the Connate.

Olivienne snapped her fingers. "There must be an external

control to lock the building!" She looked around the area with dismay. "But how will we find this pillar in the midst of all the overgrown foliage?"

Castellan smiled, remembering their time over Dir Sanguis. "Leggett, remember when Madlin had you modify the sonica to differentiate between disparate types of matter? Can you do something similar to read a hard material through the vegetation?"

Spc. Leggett rubbed her lip then glanced over at her counterpart on the team, Gar Soleng. He held up his hands. "Don't look at me, I'm all engines with my sub-specialty. My papan always said I was a gear-head at heart."

The rest of the group laughed at his declaration. Madlin stepped forward. "Let's put my tinkerist training to work and see what we can cobble together back in the railer." As the two women jogged away from the group, Commander Tosh addressed the rest. "While they're working on a mechanical solution to our problem, the rest of you spread out and start searching the hard way. Be wary in the thickets, we don't know what manner of bug or beasts this island holds. Also, keep track of your gear as well." She leveled a solid look at one of the team's pilots, Spc. Dante Lazaro and the man blushed.

Not willing to let the opportunity go by to tease the man about his mishap the previous roto, Spc. Qent grabbed the voteo from his belt and made the classic howler face. The entire team laughed loud and long at the reference to the incident on the way to Navis, during the second temple key mission.

Castellan gave her team an indulgent smile. Before she could get them on track again, Savon spoke up and circled a finger in the air. "All right you lot, let's get to work. Lazaro, Lear, and Soleng take the railer side. Penn, Devin, and Qent on the water face. I'll take Dozier and Meza to the left adjacent wall. That will leave Connate Dracore, Commander Tosh, Doctore Shen, and Specialist Yazzie on this side."

"Yes, ser!"

The team went off in their assigned directions, leaving Olivienne and Castellan with a curious doctore and an attentive medic. The commander looked at the thick underbrush and made a face. "What I wouldn't give to have my company sword right now."

Gemeda gave her a strange look. "Did you bring it on this mission?"

"I don't bring it on any mission as it was something we only use in Defense Corp. It's hanging on the wall in my suite. Truth be told, the majority of the time I wouldn't need it for this post."

"Except todae." Olivienne stated the obvious.

Tosh sighed. "Except todae."

"Well, the area won't search itself, hop to it, Commander!"

Yazzie grinned but turned and began her own search, staying near the Connate just in case. Even Gemeda wandered into the underbrush searching for what she didn't know.

Less than ten meens later, Lt. Madlin and Spc. Leggett returned with the sonica. Leggett had it cradled in her hands. "Ser, we made the modifications and tested just outside the railer. Where would you like us to use it first?"

Olivienne thought for a sec. "If only we could raise you up so you could see a larger area with the scope. What if you climbed to the top of the structure?"

"As my Connate commands, she shall get her wish." Castellan bowed low and gave her future par a charming smile. Then she looked at her guardian with a general engineering sub-degree. "Ready for a lift, Specialist Leggett?"

"Yes, ser!"

With a casual flex of her telekinesis, Castellen slowly lifted Branda Leggett into the air. "Call out when you wish me to move you a quarter turn. Leggett nodded but didn't respond as she was focused on the screen held within her hands. The rest of the team had come back around the building to stand with the Connate and commander when they saw one of their own high in the air. A few meens later she called out. "Right spin, Commander."

Castellan obliged her request and turned Leggett until she was facing the thick stand of growth on the side of the station where Olivienne had been searching. The specialist called out almost immediately and pointed down, some twenty yords from their position. "There. I've got a solid reading, sers!"

The commander fixed the general direction in her mind then brought Leggett back down to the ground. "Take us in, Specialist."

Madlin and Soleng had retrieved long blades from the railer and began clearing a path for Leggett as she called out corrections on their direction. Olivienne, Spc. Dozier, and Spc. Lazaro also used their apportation channels to help. It wasn't long before the group found what they were looking for.

It was more of an obelisk than a pillar, with four sides and a pointed top. It looked as though it sprouted from the ground like any of the trees around the area. Olivienne used her apportation channel again to clear a space for all of them and remove anything obstructing their view of the strange object. It was roughly two yords in height and looked to be made of stone, though what kind could stand four hundred rotos of wear, they didn't know. As they moved around it to the far side, they found a stele panel with buttons and large numbered squares. One other curious thing to note was that the pillar had two lines carved around it, starting at two foot, with the second one just below the panel at four foot.

Castellan looked to their sovereign and adventurist. "What do you make of it?"

"It looks similar to what we found on Navis. I suspect another number puzzle."

"Ser, what are the lines carved in? Decoration, or something else?" Meza traced one line with her index finger.

Castellan glanced around the gathered guardians. "Anyone hazard a guess?"

Dozier spoke from the back of the group. "Sers, if you remember Navis, there was an ampule that filled when you entered in the wrong number sequence. That was segmented into three parts, much like the carved lines have done to this pillar. Perhaps it moves if the wrong numbers are selected."

Olivienne spun around and looked at Veva Dozier with a smile. "Simply brilliant! I think you're right." She turned back to the panel. "Now, we just have to figure out what the numbers mean."

Penn chimed in with her input. "Sers, I've always had a knack for number puzzles. I think there are maths involved."

Olivienne sighed. "I hate maths! And I don't see a pattern here." She pointed to the five squares that ran in a vertical line down the column. Four had numbers inside and the bottom one was blank. "There is no pattern that I can see to the numbers. One, five, thirteen, and twenty-nine. If we look at differences, it's four, eight, and sixteen. Nothing!"

Castellan laughed at how vexed her lover got when it came to calculations and received a scowl in return. Luckily she was saved further censure by Spc. Penn.

"It's a basic pattern, not too hard at all really." She paused as she realized that she was perhaps stepping on the Connate's toes with her statement. "I mean, if you're a student of the maths the way I am, ser. Starting at the top, you double the number and add three. So one becomes two, plus three…and you have five. Then five becomes ten and add three to get thirteen."

"By the Makers, she's right!" Olivienne moved her finger down the line of filled squares even as Castellan called out the missing number. "Sixty-one." She looked to the side where Olivienne stood transfixed by the panel. "What now, Connate Dracore?"

Olivienne reached out a finger toward the number pad. "Now, we hope the number is correct." She pressed the first button and a hissing sound emanated from behind the stele panel. The 'six' glowed with some sort of light, as did the 'one' when she pushed it. A rumble below their feet put the entire team on alert as all the buttons flashed green. Suddenly a stele cover slid across the panel of buttons and the pillar slowly sank into the ground. Everyone jumped away from it, afraid to be caught by any edges. Olivienne looked around at her team. "Well, what are you waiting for? Let's see if it worked."

The group turned and jogged the short way back to the large structure and were relieved to see that the doors and windows that were once obstructed by smooth covers were now clear. Along with the doorway, a panel similar to the ones they found in the tower was also cleared. Olivienne reached out to touch her palm to the pad and the door *whooshed* open. Knowing how concerned Castellan was about security, Olivienne didn't enter the building. She turned to her commander and inclined her head. "I want to enter. What are your requirements for safety?"

Castellan called out her orders, ready to get their team moving forward and closer to their goal. "Madlin, take a team of six to maintain the perimeter of the building as well as guard the railer. I also want you to check on Holling but don't pull him away from Nessie."

Lt. Madlin looked at her curiously. "Are you hoping to distract the great beast, Commander?"

"No, I'm hoping to sway her to our side and Holling's fascination and eternal optimism is the best way to accomplish that goal. Take five meens with Lieutenant Savon and sort teams. Savon, meet us back here when you're finished."

"Yes, ser." Both lieutenants saluted her, then moved off to the side to confer.

Olivienne turned to Castellan with an excited look on her face. "I'm very glad to be sharing this adventure with you." Gemeda discretely ignored the private conversation from off to the side.

Tosh smiled. "As I am with you. I suppose I got my wish of all those lunes ago, didn't I?"

"Wish?"

"Yes, if you recall, I was jealous of you embarking on such an amazing adventure and I idly wished I could go off in search of fame and fortune, solving the mysteries of the world."

Olivienne smiled tenderly at her. "You're doing just that, my love."

Castellan shook her head. "No, *we* are." She noticed Savon coming back with seven specialists following behind. "Are you ready to continue?"

The Connate glanced from the team, to Castellan, then at the dark doorway. "Without a doubt."

Chapter Sixteen

OLIVIENNE PULLED AN illeostone-powered torch from her waist pouch and shined it into the darkness as she slowly crept forward. She needn't have bothered since panels illuminated on the ceiling as soon as they entered the building, showing them a wide hallway about twenty yords in length. It was similar to the tower near the dirigible entrance in that regard. Olivienne, Castellan, Gemeda, and Savon's half of the Shield team moved forward into the space proper as Lt. Savon pointed to doors on their left and right, as well as a large double door at the end of the hall. "Connate Dracore, should we split up like the tower or stay together?"

Olivienne looked from Lt. Savon to Tosh. "What say you?"

Castellan considered the eight people standing around her. "Our primary objective here is to secure a way across Dir Lacrimise. Our secondary task is discovering what we can about this building. Nessie mentioned that it was a research station for the Tau scienteres. She said they were looking into biodiversity and genetics." At the group's curious look, she amended her statement. "Neither are words in our regular vocabulary. But genetics is one recently seen in translated Maker texts. I think they are scientere or medican related terms and have to do with Psierian biology."

"All that to say we can split the team?"

Castellan sighed at her sovereign. "Must you be so purposely difficult?" Gemeda snickered.

Olivienne smiled knowingly. "I believe the phrase you were looking for there was, 'must you be so obviously right,' darling." That remark elicited a stifled laugh from Spc. Qent.

"Fine. Savon, take Penn and Yazzie through the right door. Devin, Qent, and Lear will check the left. Connate Dracore, Doctore Shen, and I will take the lift."

"Lift?"

Castellan addressed her future par. "I may not be an adventurist but my memory is fairly accurate. And, while these seem to be significantly larger, I recognize the doors from what we discovered in the tower."

Olivienne made a face at her commander's sass. "Fine."

Yazzie spoke with concern in her voice. "Ser, shouldn't I stay with the Connate?"

Tosh appreciated her medican's commitment to duty. "Doctore Shen will come with us. That will be plenty of coverage should an emergency arise. Plus you'll be able to better help the team on the first level." Yazzie nodded and Castellan addressed the rest. "Let me know if you find anything of significance, savvy?"

"Yes, ser!"

Olivienne didn't wait any longer. She impatiently strode down the hallway as Spc. Lear reached out to touch the panel next to the left-hand door. Gemeda saw the woman jump as it *whooshed* open and hid a smile behind her hand until they were safely in the lift. Inside there were three buttons arranged vertically. The trio assumed the center one was for their current floor, which meant there was one above and below. Olivienne's finger hovered over the panel and she glanced at Tosh. "Is your intuition giving you anything?"

"Not a bit. Chooser's choice, so it's up to you."

Olivienne hesitated a sec longer then touched the top one. There was a rumble right after the button glowed white then the doors *swished* open. The simultaneous simplicity and fantastical nature of the Maker's technology was wondrous. They stepped off the lift and glanced around. The second level appeared to be a living space with open windows on three sides. There was a lounging area and something that appeared to be a kitchen, though the chairs and other furniture was strangely low. To the right of the lift exit, there was a wall that featured three doors. Castellan walked over and put her palm on the access panel for the first. She called out to Olivienne and Gemeda. "It appears to be sleeping quarters—" She moved into the room farther and out of their sight, then they heard another *whooshing* sound. "—with an attached lav. Come take a look at this, both of you."

Curious, Gemeda and Olivienne entered the room and moved into the lav. Castellan pointed to something that resembled a waste-seat. With the touch of a button the bowl glowed blue and water sprayed upward before falling and draining down again.

"What in the two temples is *that*? I've never seen the like in all my adventuring. Did the tower have these?"

Castellan shrugged. "No one thoroughly investigated the individual berths on the top level once it was determined they were simple sleeping quarters. I suppose it did though."

"It's brilliant!"

"Gem?" Castellan's pale brow rose in surprise at her friend's outburst.

The doctore pushed the button again and pointed at the resulting water spray. "Look, with this technology there would be no need for cleaning paper. It would be significantly more sanitary that our current method."

Olivienne looked thoughtful. "What is the light?"

"I'm not sure. The Makers have tech beyond anything I've ever seen. If I were a tinkerer with Maker methods, I'd build something with a sanitizing feature to cut down on all the sick bugs." She pushed the button again. "Tosh, put your hand down there and tell me if the light gives off heat."

Tosh frowned but complied. "It does. Perhaps there is no fantastical explanation after all. It's merely to dry the water from one's seat after the rinse is complete."

"Is it illeostone powered, or from natural energy? I didn't see any wind generators and there are no rivers nearby."

It was Gemeda who answered. "The Makers only know how their gadgets and devices work. It appears more fantastical than science most of the time to me."

Castellan began laughing. "And you a woman of science, too!"

Gemeda sniffed. "Say what you will, Tosh. But not even your big brain knows how this all works so you can stuff your aether!"

Olivienne lost her composure at hearing the same retort from a highly bespoke doctore as she'd heard from her own much younger sib. She laughed and left the room. "I'm going to check the rest."

All three doors were confirmed to lead to identical rooms. Shortly after that, both the other teams checked in. Savon said the first level section facing the water appeared to be a partitioned laboratory of some sort. Castellan told him to look for any vellum or other documents they could gather data from. Lear checked in right after that and said the other section was for storage, with a larger door leading outside that opened easily with a touch to another hand pad.

"Can you tell what is being stored?"

"Ser, the containers were activated by hand pads and we opened one. It appears to be dried foodstuffs, and still good based on initial sniff. Though how it would last for hundreds of rotos is beyond me."

"Good to know, Specialist. I want your group to take the lift to the lower level and keep searching.

The upstairs team continued to inspect the last room. There were no coverlets on any of the beds, but after pushing buttons to open a few cabinets, they found plush covers made from an unknown material. Olivienne was awed. "How long ago did we determine the Makers left Magna?"

"From what Nessie told me, two hundred and thirty-four rotos."

Olivienne rubbed her face against the supple fabric. "Impossible."

Gemeda looked around the third room they'd entered, then glanced at the door leading to the lav. "I'd say there is little that is impossible for the Makers."

Castellan glanced at Olivienne. *"Should we tell her the mystery?"*

"And which mystery would that be, there are so many."

"Where we come from, who the Makers really were."

Olivienne thought for a few secs then gave a nod. She turned to Gemeda. "What I'm about to tell you is classified on orders of the Queen. You may have already ascertained by now, based on Nessie's comments, that the Makers are actually a race of beings called the Tau Ceti. They are small gray sentients who look quite different from the average Psierian. We actually found a skeleton on the island of Navis and Instrae Green had a team analyze it."

Gemeda's mouth dropped open in shock. "Truth?" She glanced at Castellan, who nodded. "So what, there are three intelligent species that developed, us, Atlanteens, and these Tau Ceti? And they, what, brought us here from another continent on Psiere?"

Castellan answered. "No, Gem. None of us are from Psiere. The Tau were explorers from the stars and crashed here. They'd been collecting species from all over and when the scientere ship became stranded roughly where Dir Sanguis is now located, they seeded Psiere with as many creatures as would adapt."

The doctore staggered back at the world-changing information. "I wasn't sure what Nessie was talking about earlier, I assumed she meant we were relocated from one place to another here on Psiere. I surely had no clue we had come from beyond. And they, what, sailed the stars the way our dirigibles sail the skies?"

"Near as we can understand based on the translated texts."

"But our language, our culture...the things we know and the way we know them...is it all a construct of these Makers? Were our people's lives naught more than a game to them? An experiment?"

Olivienne grabbed Gemeda's hand. "I don't think it was. The writings we found mentioned that the Tau considered Psierians the children they could never have. They were very protective, which was why they couldn't let us die out after a succession of power-wars. I think they made the best of a bad situation until they could be rescued."

Castellan looked at her curiously. "Do you think they were? Is that why the Makers disappeared more than two hundred rotos ago?"

"Truthfully, I don't know." She looked back at Gemeda. "The document also said they put a beacon in the space around our planet, to call for help. While they couldn't send a signal from the surface of Psiere, they were able to continuously receive a stream of information about all the species they were carrying. I have no idea how that is possible across an immeasurable distance like the stars above. I suspect most of our technologies, language, and culture are from those updates, exactly as Nessie stated earlier. They either left our continents to find a place where they could observe their 'seeded' species from afar, or they were able to return to the stars and their people."

Gemeda held up a hand. "I need a meen." She backed up to sit on the bed and gave a little bounce. "Oh, this is surprisingly comfortable!"

Castellan laughed as her friend was easily distracted by the more creature comforts. "Ah, Gem...you never change."

They were interrupted by the voteo tone. Castellan responded. "Tosh here."

"Lear sending. Ser, the lower level has a water ship inside. There is a launch of sorts and a door leading out to the lake. What should we do?"

Castellan glanced at her two companions. "Can you determine how it is powered? We can take the illeostones from the railer if we have to."

"Not yet, ser. We'll continue looking but this isn't like anything I've seen before and I've flown, drove, or rode nearly every sort of conveyance there is."

Olivienne laughed at the indignant specialist's tone of voice.

Tosh answered the woman. "Psierian conveyance, Lear. This is a Maker building so the old knowledge we hold won't necessarily apply. Keep searching."

"Yes, ser."

Castellan spoke again. "Savon, what is your status?"

The lieutenant's voice was strong through the little speaker. "Specialist Penn found a cabinet of vellum records and is trying to determine the full nature of this station. Yazzie is cataloguing tools and implements that seem familiar. Do you have new orders, ser?"

"Yes. I want Penn and Yazzie to continue what they're doing while you go down and assist Lear's group. We'll join in five meens."

"Yes, ser. Savon out."

Castellan looked at Gemeda, then moved her gaze to Olivienne. "Have we learned everything we can here?"

They walked out of the room and into the living space. "I think so. If nothing else, I'd say a fully functional and well-stocked living facility is a good resource to have. We'll need to inform my mother upon our return. She may wish to station a group of scienteres here full time."

Gemeda brightened. "Imagine being part of a group of volunteers that would come to Magna...living at the tower, here, or even the Temple of Antaeus. Simply marvelous!"

Castellan clasped her long-time friend on the shoulder as they headed for the lift. "Look at you! We'll make an adventurist out of you yet, Gem."

The three women were surprised to see that the center of the lowest level of the building was a large enclosed lagoon with a sleek ship bobbing with the motion of the Shield member aboard. The space was well lit from far above and Tosh realized they had gone much farther underground than she initially realized. But then it made sense since the lake level was far below the station itself.

Lear's bright red hair and dark skin could be seen up in the pilot's nest, Savon stood on the far side of the lagoon searching through cabinets, and Qent was walking the perimeter of the large space with eyes intently focused on the hull of the ship. Tosh assumed that Devin was probably in the ship as well. She called out to her lieutenant. "Anything yet?"

Savon spun from the cabinet he'd been facing and sketched a quick salute. "No, ser. Lear found what appears to be a key hole on the ship but we can't find the match for it. Perhaps the Makers hid it somewhere."

Gemeda pointed at the craft. "I don't understand. If this has all been sitting here for hundreds of rotos, how isn't it rotted away by now? Is the hull made from stele or the like?"

The pilot's head popped up from where she'd been leaning down. "I've felt a lot of materials, Doctore Shen, and none of them are like this one. It's very lightweight. At least I'm assuming it is because there are benches that clasp down to the decking. It's definitely not stele."

Olivienne rubbed her bottom lip. "I'd wager the Makers wanted this vessel to serve dual purpose between transporting people and goods. Or perhaps it was converted into a floating laboratory for the scienteres here."

"That makes a lot of sense."

The trio thought on the issue for a meen longer. Finally Gemeda broke the silence. "Do you think the key could be upstairs in the living quarters somewhere?"

Castellan shrugged. "We only gave it a cursory search. However, I think the key would be more likely located in the lab on the first level. This craft is a work tool so they'd have it someplace easily accessible. Whether that means down here or in the lab, I don't know. Say the word and I'll bring the entire team inside. Now that I'm thinking about it, I don't think we need guards in this location. My only concern would be that there are more of those skunk apes somewhere nearby."

Olivienne gave a casual wave. "Sure, call them in. They can use the facility if needed. It would probably be significantly more comfortable than off in the brush. I can tell you that while I love adventuring, I sorely miss that particular perk of civilization when I'm on my missions."

Gemeda laughed and Castellan merely smiled and grabbed the voteo from her belt. "Madlin, bring everyone inside, including Holling. Penn and Yazzie are through the right hand door from the main hall. Assign a team to search their area for something to fit a keyhole. The rest of you take the lift at the end of the hall to the lower level."

"Yes, ser. Bringing the team in now."

"The facilities appear to be working as well. Instruct Holling to test the water and if there is no contamination then fill all the flasks and the barrel from the railer."

"Copy that, Madlin out."

It was only a few meens later that Savon called out to them. "Ser, there is another palm pad over here, along with a display of some kind."

The trio of women walked to the back of the large space, which by the commander's estimation would have them directly below the storage portion of the first level. There they found not just a screen as Savon mentioned, but an entire console. It was smooth like an angled designer's table, only near six foot long. "What in all the deep sea depths is this?"

"Ser, there is a button on the side."

Olivienne leaned over to look, then without warning her commander and lieutenant, she reached out and pressed it. A *thunk* and *psshht* came from behind the console, then the face abruptly dropped down and flipped along a central horizontal access until a panel of buttons and screens on the underside was displayed. With another *psshht* and *thunk*, the panel raised and locked into place. Gemeda jumped back, startled at the motion while Tosh and Savon assumed protective stances of alertness.

Olivienne raised a dark brow. "That was curious."

"And fool hardy. You can't simply push buttons wherever and whenever you like, 'Vienne."

The Connate sighed at her love's concern. It was both reassuring and stifling. "Look around you, Tosh. This isn't a Maker's cache full of lost or hidden schematics and devices. This building isn't a location likely to be riddled with traps. The Makers, correction, the Tau Ceti, lived and worked here. While I may understand protections for a room full of treasures, I certainly wouldn't put deadly fail-safes in my own sitting room or office. I've done this for many rotos now, trust me to know what I'm doing."

Castellan rubbed the bridge of her nose and Olivienne knew her well enough to know she was capitulating to her experience. "Fine. You're correct in your assessment and I apologize for overstepping my bounds —"

"I love it when you tell me I'm right, even more so when you admit to your own error."

Gemeda hid a grin behind her hand.

The commander grimaced. "Maybe give me some warning next time?"

Olivienne realized her own error in that moment. She lay a hand on Tosh's forearm. "I'm sorry, and you're correct. I worried both you and Lieutenant Savon unnecessarily. I'll give you a heads up if I suspect I'm going to activate something."

The commander inclined her head slightly. "Fair enough."

"Now, let's see what this bit of tech does, shall we?"

The panel itself was a little too short for easy use by the Psierians. Olivienne looked around for something to perch upon and Castellan spied a number of roughly foot and a half cubes, comprised of some unknown material. Rather than an entire hand pad on the cube, it had a smaller one. Castellan gestured toward the small pad and Olivienne waved her on. "Go ahead, Tosh. Let's see what's inside."

The commander placed her fingertip to the pad and the cube gave a *hiss* before the top popped up. Gemeda commented, "Looks like an airless seal of some kind. I suppose that could be how the items in this station have stayed so pristine."

Castellan opened it fully and raised both brows in surprise. She pulled one of the items out. "Small rubbery suits. Could they be protection?"

"Maybe for the water. And look, this clearly highlights the size and shape differences between the Tau Ceti and us."

"By the Makers, you two weren't kidding when you said the Makers were strange beings from beyond the stars!"

Castellan immediately quieted her friend. "Gem, that's classified knowledge, even among our team. You must not speak of it aloud, savvy?"

Gemeda gave her a wink and directed a telepathic reply to both Castellan and Olivienne. *"Yes, ser!"*

Olivienne laughed. "You're certainly a lot feistier than I thought you'd be on adventure."

Gemeda leveled a humored gaze on her sovereign. "Truthfully?"

Olivienne shook her head with another laugh. "No, not at all. Nice to know that someone kept Tosh on the straight and narrow all those rotos at Academy."

"Oh, you know better than that, Connate Dracore. Tosh has always been the one keeping everyone else in line."

Savon politely ignored the exchange while Castellan let out another aggrieved sigh. "Do you think we can get on with our exploration now? Discussing the history of my upright demeanor in front of me sits poorly. We have a job to do."

"Oh, Tosh. Lighten up. We are safe here and it wouldn't be the worst thing to spend the night in this station and continue on in the morning. That will give the captain longer to effect repairs on the *Quaesitum* to be at the ready should we run into difficulty."

"Yes, Tosh. Listen to your future par, she is wise indeed."

Castellan snorted. "You just want to sleep on one of those beds upstairs tonight rather than on a bedroll in the railer."

Gemeda gave a sniff but deigned not to answer.

With the strange suit stuffed back into the cube, Castellan used her telekinesis to move it over by the console. Olivienne gave her a grateful smile and sank down upon it. "Okay, let's see here..." She searched the entire thing, then moved her hand out to flip a switch and the entire panel lit."

"Ser, it reminds me a bit of the strange panel in the sunken ship from our adventure below Dir Sanguis."

Olivienne flipped a few more switches and black screens lit in front of them, showing images of the area outside. Gemeda stepped closer and reached out a hand. "The stills are incredibly realistic."

"Those aren't stills, Gem." Castellan moved closer as well and pointed at the screen showing the railer. The trees nearby were moving. "I think we're looking at live images."

Savon smiled. "That's certainly beneficial, isn't it? I was concerned about bringing everyone inside, in case we had more of the creatures from the island approach us unawares. But this solves the issue of security monitoring quite nicely."

"And look here, this is very similar to the sonica display on the dirigible. Could some of the other gadgets," Gemeda waved her hand at the rest of the large console, "be used for communications as well? Seema was showing me her private tech in her quarters the night before we left."

Olivienne laughed aloud. "Oh, is that what we're calling it now?"

Gemeda flushed with the teasing and the entire scene provided too much for the hapless lieutenant. "Ser, I'm going to check on Lieutenant Madlin and the rest to see if they've found a key on the first level."

"Go ahead, Savon. Maybe have the other specialists rotate with the ones down here. A fresh set of eyes never hurt any problem. Meanwhile," she glanced down to where Olivienne sat staring at the multitude of screens, "we'll see if we can get this room opened up so the ship can enter the lake proper."

Lieutenant Savon saluted the three women before smartly spinning on his heel and heading for the lift. He called out as he went along. "Lear, Devin, Qent, we're going above. You can use the facilities and take thirty before switching with the other group." The specialists scrambled to obey, as excited to be leaving the moist lower level as they were to be getting some downtime.

After they left, Castellan gazed at Olivienne. "You know, if they haven't found the key down here by now, it's probably not on this level. It seems strange though since we have a ship, we have water gear, and we have a console of Maker monitoring tech." Olivienne reached out to flip two more switches and a great rumble sounded through the large space. Then a long vertical crack of daelight split the wall on the opposite side of the room where they assumed the waterway led to the lake. Olivienne gave a *whoop* and jumped up from her makeshift seat. "That's it!"

The gap continued to grow wider as the doors slid apart to the left and right side. When it was all the way open, a great head peaked in from the other side. *"I see you've found their lake craft. This will carry you comfortably across the way. The Tau used it many times when they were studying aquatic life. I usually had to wander far from the ship on those days as some of the fishes are afraid of me."*

Castellan looked curious from Olivienne to Gemeda. "Fishes?"

Gemeda tapped her bottom lip. "Could Nessie be referring to piscis?"

"Yes, Doctor Shen. I am referring to the species you call piscis, or swimmers. Such a strange way your language has evolved. Lucky for me I'm fluent in a number of ancient languages, including Latin."

Olivienne frowned. "Half of what she says makes no sense whatsoever!"

There was a twist of humor in their heads as Nessie responded. *"On the contrary, Bana-phrionnsa, my sense is easy enough to understand if one holds the history of their land."* She paused and swam until she was inside the entryway. There wasn't room for her to come all the way in because of the size of the ship. She tilted her head to look at the trio. *"Which you do not."*

"We—"

The voteo alert tone interrupted whatever Olivienne was going to say. "Tosh here."

"Ser, Madlin is on her way down now. They discovered a cabinet on one wall of the research room with a multitude of items hanging inside. Leer recognized one of them saying the end would match up with the keyhole on the ship."

"Very well, Savon. Tell the team to prep for some downtime.

If the ship doesn't start, we'll have to suss out an alternative. We'll stay here tonight and hopefully start across the lake tomorrow morning."

"Yes, ser. Savon out."

The lift opened. Lt. Madlin stepped out along with Specialists Calderon and Lear. Madlin was all smiles as they approached the group by the console. Castellan leveled a hard gaze at Spc. Lear. "Aren't you supposed to be on downtime right now, Specialist?"

Lear grinned at her, not at all intimidated by her commander. "Yes, ser. But I'm the only one that knows where the keyhole is. I had to slide a panel out of the way to access it. I figured it would be easier to show than tell when it came to the location."

"Fine." Madlin held out the object that Castellan assumed was the key. The commander took it and inspected the small item. Like so many other Maker things, it was made from an unknown material. Rather than have teeth or other such protrusions to move tumblers, it was a long, slim, rectangular shape, flattened along its length. She glanced at the leader of their adventurist mission and her ruler in all things. "Do you want to wait or try it now?"

Olivienne aported the key into her own hand to study. Finally she looked up at the group. "No time like the present I say!" She called out to their pilot. "Lear, catch! Let's see if you can get this Maker-forsaken craft to function."

"Yes, ser!"

The pilot led the group at a fast clip toward the ramp leading up to the ship. Once onboard, she climbed the stairs leading to the pilot's nest. Gemeda balked. "Doesn't look like much room up there. I think I'll stay down below and wait for you all to do your thing."

"Ser, I'll stay below with Doctore Shen as well. It makes more sense for the pilots to go up."

"Very well, Madlin. With any luck we'll only be a meen."

There was enough room for all four in the pilot's nest. The steerage was very similar to their own ships, which both pilots remarked on right away. Spc. Lear slid the protective panel to the side to reveal a small rectangular hole, which she inserted the key into. Nothing happened, even when she reached out to push the button above the panel.

Spc. Calderon pointed at the panel. "Perhaps that has to be shut to protect the area where the key is located with the ship in operation."

"Good thinking." Necole Lear slid the panel shut, then pushed the button and the ship came to life around them. Screens that resembled the ones from the console below lit and *pinged* regularly.

Olivienne looked perplexed. "What energy does it operate on?"

"I saw a cable running from the decking to the ship on the other side when I first began investigating." Lear gestured toward the side opposite where the lift was located. When the group of four leaned over the wall, they could see a thick black cable leading to a thick pillar on the floor that circled the small lagoon.

"Curious."

"What you're seeing is probably a charging cable to load the onboard batteries."

Castellan moved back to the pilot's station and peered over the bow of the ship. "What are charging cables and batteries? Speak plain, Nessie."

"Maybe we'd be better served to ask how she knows so much about the Maker's technology when she's been stuck in this lake for hundreds of rotos."

"Sovereign, if the Makers knew it, then so too did I. Language is no barrier when I glean the information straight from their thoughts." The creature paused and blew a loud breath from her nostrils. *"You Psierians have been trained and instructed to use the local mineral to power your devices and gadgets. However, you also use wind and water generated electricity to power stationary items and places. Batteries are merely a way for that power to become portable."*

Calderon's jaw dropped open. "Power portability without the weight of the stones? That could change so much of our society!"

"Calderon." The pilot looked to his commander. "This is for all of you really and I'll be sure to announce it later to the entire team. Everything we learn on this mission is to be top secret. There will be a debriefing when we return but even after, not a word of our findings get out. Savvy?"

Calderon and Lear straightened with the seriousness of her words. "Yes, ser."

Castellan nodded and gestured to Lear. "All right, Specialist. Shut it down. I'm going to assume the plug is easy to remove. We'll plan to leave at second sun rise tomorrow."

Lear opened the panel and the engine cut off. She removed

the key and held it out to the Connate. "The mission is yours, Connate Dracore. I'll give this to you for safe-keeping."

"Thank you, Necole." The pilot blushed at the informal address.

"Let's join the rest above, shall we?" When they'd all climbed down to the main deck of the ship, Castellan spoke with Lt. Madlin. "Do you know if Savon has the team spread out inside or if they're all on the second level?"

"I know most where headed up to the second floor but I think a few wanted to stay on the first and continue exploring."

Olivienne smiled at the capable and dedicated team that Castellan had put together to assist and protect her. It was more than she could have ever imagined and she pushed a wash of love through their fairly new empathic connection.

"What was that for?"

"I love you and I'm grateful for your place in my life every single dae."

Castellan gave her a light telekinetic squeeze. *"And I'm grateful for you. Let's head above and relieve everyone of duty for the evening. I'm sure after the past few lunes the team would appreciate a few oors of worry free downtime."*

"I know I would." Olivienne gave her a wink and Castellan wondered how sound proof the sleeping rooms were.

The commander called out to Nessie who had remained in the doorway to the lagoon during their engine test. *"We're going to shut the door again. You may want to back out so you avoid injury. We'll speak again before suns' down, Nessie."*

"Well enough. I'll remind you of our agreement at that time, Commander."

While Castellan hadn't forgotten about their private conversation, the details of it had slipped her mind during the discoveries of the past few oors. *"Until that time then."*

The great creature swam out of the Maker-created lagoon and Olivienne hit the switch on the console that would close the doors. They shut with a clang, indicated metal of some kind though not one any knew of that could resist hundreds of rotos of time without decay. Curious indeed.

Chapter Seventeen

LATER, AFTER THE entire group had eaten their last meal of the dae, Castellan kissed Olivienne on the temple and stood from her seat on the low couch in the second floor living space.

Olivienne looked at her curiously. "Where are you going?"

"Nessie insists we can't get into the Temple of Antaeus without her help so I promised a favor in return for the aid—"

"A fav—"

Castellan held up a hand to stay her lover's concerns. "As long as it doesn't harm our team or mission."

Olivienne frowned. "And you have no idea what it is?"

"I'm going to find out now. Would you like to come with me?" Castellan held out her hand and it was immediately taken.

"Of course."

Lt. Savon stood as well, quickly placing the remainder of his meal on the table. The commander waved him off. "Stay with the team and finish your food. We're taking a quick walk down to speak with Nessie and need no accompaniment. But when you're finished eating, I would like you to send another update to the *Quaesitum*, informing them that we'll leave at second sunrise. Give them the coordinates for this station as well as the destination marked on the newest map, on the other side of Dir Lacrimise." He nodded and made to resume his seat until Castellan snapped her fingers. "Oh, and find out if they have a remaining time to repair so we can better judge our options."

Savon gave her and the Connate a salute. "Yes, ser." Then he sat down again and picked up his tray and utensil. Castellan glanced around at the rest of the large space and smiled to see Gemeda in an animated discussion with both the medicans for the team.

It was near dark when they stepped outside the research building. Archeos had already slipped over the horizon and Illeos was slowly following. Castellan and Olivienne made their way around the structure and out to the area that looked over the lake. Castellan realized at that point that the overlook was built above the doorway into the lowest level where the ship was moored. They each gazed across the water that reflected a multitude of colors from the setting sun behind them. Suddenly Olivienne pointed off to the distance. "Tosh, look!"

Both made out the shape of Nessie's head as she rose from the depths and swam closer. *"Greetings, humans."*

Olivienne reached out when Nessie leaned over the wall around the decking. She delighted at the smooth, damp skin. She knew Nessie could understand their audible speech so she didn't bother using telepathy. "You amaze me with each meeting and keep me humble for the future."

Nessie tilted her large head. *"Humble?"*

"Yes, this entire adventurist mission has not only taught me more about Psierians and the Makers, but it has taught me that not all greater creatures we share our land with are violent or lacking in intelligence. You are a delightful being and I only wish my maman could have met you."

"Ah, your Queen. I can imagine the conversations I could have with such a ruler as only the Tau could make. Delightful indeed." She paused. *"But I sense you aren't here for the conversation alone. You wish to learn of my price for entry into the temple?"*

Tosh spoke. "Yes."

Nessie reiterated what she'd told Castellan earlier in the dae. *"I'm lonely. I miss conversing, learning, and sharing life experience with other intelligent beings."*

"What exactly are you asking of us?"

"I want you to staff the station here at Lake Lacrimise."

Castellan frowned but Olivienne merely looked curious. "You mean send Psierians here after we return to Tesseron?"

"No, 'Vienne. She wants us to leave people here now."

"What?" Olivienne turned from Castellan to Nessie. "We can't simply leave our members behind. This is our team, *my* guardians!" She spun back to Castellan. "Tell her, Tosh."

Castellan gazed up into Nessie's pervasive stare. "We have the keys for each temple as well as a way across the lake. Are you implying that even holding all that, we cannot get into the Temple of Antaeus? That we're still missing something."

"Keys you have, even three. But there is no better key than me. You are missing the Key of Nessie."

"Key of Nessie?"

"Yes, Commander Castellan Tosh. You cannot enter the temple without Nessie. The Tau made it as such, as the last bit of security. They left it to me to determine if the seekers are worthy."

Olivienne looked skeptical but couldn't say yay or nay

whether the great beast was being truthful. "And you deem us worthy?"

Nessie gave a low dip of her head. *"You are, though I cannot say the same of the rest of your race. However, I trust that you are steady leaders and will know what to do with the power when the time comes that you hold it within your hands."*

The sovereign raised a dark brow. "How do we know you're not lying? You're a very powerful telepath, it's possible you hold your truths deeper."

Nessie gazed at Olivienne and leaned farther across the short wall. *"You are free to do a trust reading, just like your mate."*

Olivienne reached out and touched Nessie's neck, unknowingly mimicking Tosh's actions from earlier. *"Do you swear that it is not possible to enter the Temple of Antaeus without your help?"*

"I swear it is so. You will need Nessie to get inside."

"And where is the Key of Nessie located?"

Nessie blew out a damp breath. *"The key is in Lacrimise."*

Olivienne removed her hand and looked at her commander with concern. "What do we do? We can't leave our people here just because Nessie is lonely. But if we don't then we cannot complete our mission."

Castellan moved her gaze toward the water that had turned black as shadows rose from the ground with the setting suns. She thought for a meen then met Olivienne's eyes in the light shining down from the second story windows of the building. "Let's ask them. We can complete this mission if a few wish to stay here at the Maker's research station. It shouldn't leave us too short-handed. Truthfully I was planning on two staying behind for leave on Endara but the team surprised me with their drive and dedication to your missions."

"What are you thinking?"

"I'm thinking that I know my team inside and out and I believe one or two would enjoy the opportunity to stay and keep Nessie company while the rest continued on. There is still a lot to explore here. It could take rotos to catalogue all that the Maker's left behind."

Olivienne frowned. "And what about when we return to Endara?"

Rather than Castellan, it was Nessie's voice that sounded in their heads. *"My deal would be concluded at the end of your mission. I would not put undue hardship on your people, Sovereign. However, if some wish to stay longer until your people return to this island, I would aid them to the best of my abilities while they live here."*

Castellan recognized a fair deal when it was presented and she nodded. "We need to discuss this with the Connate's Shield team. We'll let you know what we decide at first sunrise. Will that suffice?"

"Yes, Commander. I look forward to your decision."

Nessie slipped away into the dark water as the two women strode back into the research building. Castellan sent a mental call to the entire team. *"Shield team meeting in the main living space in five meens."*

Olivienne looked to her future par as they rode the lift up. "Do you really think some will stay?"

"Yes."

"And do you have a guess as to whom?"

The lift stopped and the doors *whooshed* open in what had become a familiar way. Castellan turned to her sovereign and gave an enigmatic smile, while holding her thoughts behind a light shield. "Certainly." She gestured out of the lift. "Which you'll find out soon enough. After you, Connate Dracore."

Olivienne narrowed her eyes and stalked into the room proper. She took a seat on one of the low couches with Gemeda, and Castellan continued on until she stood with her back to the large bay of windows on the lake side of the building. She looked around the room at her assembled guardians, the team she had painstakingly put together when she took over her sovereign's protection. Her gaze moved from her lieutenants, to the medicans, pilots, and engineers. She briefly paused on Holling and Penn before moving on.

"I called you all to this briefing because there has been a new development, which will alter the plans of our mission."

Savon stood and looked at her with concern. "Ser?"

"At ease, Lieutenant." She waved for him to return to his seat. "We have discovered news that entry into the Temple of Antaeus requires another key that we do not possess."

"But, Ser! We have the three temple keys! What more could we need?" Spc. Qent seemed particularly affronted by the information. Maybe it was because of his near death experience when they retrieved the Key of Illeos from the island of Mater. They barely escaped with their lives when Olivienne, Tosh, and Qent triggered a trap inside one of the greatwood trees.

Castellan gave him a reassuring smile. "According to our friend outside, there is another key and only that one will allow us entry into the third temple. She called it the Key of Nessie and says it's in the lake." She paused to look around the group before continuing. "And she will retrieve it for us but requires something in return."

"Ser, she's lonely."

Olivienne turned her head in surprise to look at her longest serving medican. "Holling?"

Spc. Holling looked at his sovereign, then his commander, and Tosh nodded at him to speak. "I conversed with her for a while earlier and I could feel it loud and clear in both thought and empathy. Nessie has been here a long time and I honestly don't know how she hasn't gone mad being by herself that long. I feel quite bad for her. Why, I can only imagine the history and breadth of knowledge that she possess!"

"You know, it's funny you should mention that..." The commander trailed off as the other sixteen members of the group stared in anticipation.

Olivienne's eyes went back and forth between Holling and Tosh. "By the depths, you knew!" She started laughing, leading the Shield team and one dedicated doctore to think that the Connate had gone as mad as the lake creature.

Castellan pointed at the passionate medican. "You, Specialist Gren Holling, are exactly on the mark. Nessie is requesting we post a few people here at the research station until we return to Endara." Murmuring began and Castellan held up a hand for quiet. "I know what this mission means to you all, which is why I will not force anyone. I'm asking for two volunteers to stay here until we pick them up on the way back."

Lt. Madlin spoke up. "Ser, what happens if no one volunteers? How will the Connate get into the lost temple?"

"There is always another way, Lieutenant. It just may not be as fast, efficient, or practical. But I will not simply abandon any member of my team, no matter how good a cause it is. You have my back and I have yours. That's how the Shields work, savvy?"

Madlin stood a little straighter and smiled. "Yes, ser."

Castellan looked around the large room, certain she had everyone's attention. "If it helps with your decision, we've ascertained that this facility is well-stocked with acceptable foodstuffs. It is safe, secure, and fully functional. Nessie has also pledged to assist in any way possible. Are there any questions?"

Spc. Penn raised her hand. "Ser, what would our duties be if we stayed here?"

The commander smiled knowingly. "In truth, I'm hoping we won't be gone very long, maybe a few daes, possibly as long as two wekes. However, there is plenty to do besides keeping Nessie company. According to yours, Holling's, and Yazzie's reports, the lab alone is full of Maker artifacts, documents, and other information. I'm assuming there is plenty to catalogue and translate." Ciera Penn seemed satisfied by her answer so Tosh continued on. "Now, if the questions are finished, I'm going to ask...are there any volunteers?"

Holling practically jumped from his seat. "I'd like to stay, ser! I think Nessie is fascinating and I'd love to make a record of history and stories about her."

Penn stood too. "I'd like to stay as well. My amita taught me to never let an opportunity pass me by if I were capable of grabbing it with both hands."

Castellan's laugh startled the rest of the team. Unlike her, they didn't know Ciera Penn's famous family. "Your father's sib is also my general and she'll kill me if you fall in love with this place." Everyone knew that she was referring to General Renou and all but Olivienne was surprised at Spc. Penn's powerful ties. She never said a word to her Shield mates.

The commander glanced around again. "Anyone else?" She moved to look directly at Spc. Qent and he shrugged.

"I'm not going to lie, the idea does intrigue me. But if I'm completely honest, I want to see the lost temple more than explore this area." The tan skin of his neck and face flushed red. "Is that okay, ser?"

Castellan smiled and strode forward to clasp the man on the shoulder. "It's more than okay, Specialist. And for the two of you staying, remember that this mission isn't about one person or one action. It's about all of us working as a team. The two staying here are just as vital as the ones continuing on. I'm very proud of you for the decision you both made, it couldn't have been easy."

"Thank you, Ser."

"Thank you. Now if we're finished here —"

Suddenly Spc. Branda Leggett stood from her perch on a makeshift stool. "Ser..."

"Yes, Leggett?"

The woman swallowed and her gaze moved around the room until it settled again on her commander. "If it's okay, I'd like to stay as well so I can examine the Maker technology in the sub-level, as well as investigate their ship. I could pilot you across the lake, then bring the ship back here. I suspect the dirigible will be repaired by the time you're finished at the temple so you won't need another transport across Dir Lacrimise."

Castellan smiled at her unexpected volunteer. "Wonderful idea, Specialist. While you're poking around, remember one important thing..."

"Ser?"

"Don't break anything. Also, you may want to team up with Specialist Penn and see if you can initiate communications from this location. I'd wager the Makers had a way to contact that tower of theirs, and if the signal can go that far, I don't see how it couldn't be boosted even farther yet."

Nearly in the same voice, Leggett and Penn answered. "Yes, ser!" Then they turned to each other and grinned.

The commander circled a finger in the air. "With that settled, the rest of the evening is yours. No watches, take the opportunity to enjoy a rare bit of free time. The sleeping room farthest from the lift will belong to Connate Dracore, and Doctore Shen will be assigned to the room closest to the lift. I'll leave it to the lieutenants to decide who gets the privilege of the third room, if any. The rest can bunk in any of the common areas. Dismissed!"

As the team disbursed and their attention wandered from the woman at the front of the room, Olivienne approached her lover. "It seems you've given away all three sleeping rooms...wherever will you bunk down, Commander?"

Castellan pretended serious thought. "Hmm, I suppose I can pull rank and take the middle room for myself. Or..."

Olivienne stepped closer and put her arms around Castellan's neck. "Or?"

"Or, I can beg my sovereign for a place at the foot of her coverlets, like a trusted and loyal canid."

"There is only one problem with that plan, my love."

"And that is?"

Olivienne smirked. "Canids lay above the coverlets and I most certainly want you below."

Castellan raised a pale brow, clearly intrigued by Olivienne's mischief. "Oh? How far below?"

"If you two are finished with your excessively ostentatious display of verbal coquetry, I'd like to take my leave."

Olivienne laughed. "It's a little early for sleep, don't you think? Not to mention, you interrupted us just to tell us of your evening plans? You can do what you wish, Gemeda."

Gemeda sniffed. "I've brought a book with me on the journey, my favorite. And the main purpose for my informational visit was mostly to warn you not to be too rambunctious with your tupping this evening."

"Oh ho, old friend. Is that the doctore's orders?" Castellan got a grimace for her question.

"No, it's a plea from someone sleeping two rooms over. I'd like to actually sleep comfortably, not wound up from a randy royal couple's domestic display."

Olivienne teased her. "Poor Gem, you wouldn't be so opposed if the captain were here to keep you company."

Gem waved a careless hand through the air. "As if I would need to wait on one woman for a proper night's tupping. Why I have an entire unit here to choose from and I'm certain at least one or two would be glad for the company. Take that Madlin, for instance, she was certainly flirtatious the other dae—"

Castellan wagged her finger at the doctore who had a reputation for casual dalliance. "Oh no you don't! Leave my guardians be, my team cannot afford to be distracted on this mission. 'Vienne's life may depend on it!"

She got an eye roll and her finger pushed away. "Oh, don't be such a serious budge-bird! I was merely putting you on. I know very well our sovereign duty in this regard, Tosh."

The commander sputtered. "But...she...you..."

"It was a joke." Gemeda moved her gaze to Olivienne and gave the Connate a wry smile. "I tried to lighten the mood and it seems as though I've broken her. Perhaps you should administer a few doses in your room to see if she comes around."

The woman being teased flushed red as Olivienne burst into delighted laughter. "Perhaps I should." She grabbed her commander's hand and pulled her toward their sleeping room. "Come along, Tosh. Doctore's orders now."

The last thing Tosh saw was Gemeda smiling slyly as she waggled her fingers in a goodbye motion.

When the door *whooshed* shut behind them, the first thing Castellan and Olivienne noticed was the complete silence in the room. It had clearly been insulated against sound in a superior manner as only the Makers could manage. "Well...we never considered *this* marvelous possibility."

Castellan smirked. "It helps not with the volume of your mental shouts, love."

She was shoved backward onto the bed in a fit of the Connate's pique. "Oh, you! Perhaps I should leave you to read a book this evening as well."

Castellan used her telekinesis to pull Olivienne on top of her. With faces mere inces apart, Tosh smiled at her future par. "And what will you be doing if I'm relegated to whiling away my attention in the pages of an adventurist novel?"

"I'll have you know that I do well enough on my own!"

"On your own? As in..."

Olivienne gave her a sly smile and wiggled where the seams of their trousers were pressed together. "Yes, that is exactly what I'm referring to, darling. Perhaps you'd like to see my technique?"

Intrigued and aroused, Castellan swallowed hard. "Indeed, I would."

The night had gotten chilly but inside the research station, the tempyrature was quite comfortable. Olivienne forced herself up so she was sitting on Tosh's lap with her legs on either side of the commander's hips. Then with precise and methodical slowness, she began apporting items of their clothing from both their bodies. First it was her own shirt, then Tosh's. Then Olivienne apported her bosair and belt, along with her pistol and pouch of small tools and devices. All Castellan could do was lie there in anticipation, gripping her lover's hips tightly. One by one, each garment disappeared and reappeared on a bench in the surprisingly well-equipped sleeping room.

Castellan found herself panting as if she'd run a race. "You've not even touched me yet and still I burn for you."

No sooner had she said the words when Castellan's side began to warm significantly. Olivienne laughed and soothed the warmth away with cool hands. "Be careful what you wish for when in the company of a pyrokinetic, darling."

"I would like very much to kiss you now, 'Vienne." Castellan made to sit up but was pushed back down by a hand to her bare sternum.

"Not so fast. I believe I owe you a demonstration of my technique."

Castellan groaned. "I fear such a demonstration will surely kill me faster than any shell sucker or deep-sea beast."

"Oh *pssh*, you are as dramatic as a Service Corp entertainer!"

The commander found Olivienne's bosom entirely too distracting and shut her eyes in an attempt to cool her ardor. Despite her self-inflicted blindness, she found the energy to scoff at Olivienne's declaration. "Service corp, never!" Meens of silence reigned and the commander's curiosity grew stronger with each sec that ticked by and by Olivienne's occasional jostling against her own pubis and mons.

"Tosh..."

Olivienne got no answer and tried again. "Tosh."

Castellan didn't open her eyes, suddenly afraid of what her lover had planned. "Yes."

"Won't you look at me?"

"It's best I didn't—" Castellan's mouth snapped shut as she felt increased rhythmic movement above her, sliding and grinding in a circular motion. "What are you up to, 'Vienne?"

"Open your eyes and find out, love." The sovereign's voice was breathy and hitched at the end of her statement.

Against her better judgement, Castellan did indeed open her eyes and was nearly struck blind again at the sight that assailed her. Olivienne sat with her head thrown back in all her nude glory, her hand working slowly between the folds of her sex. A flush that Castellan well recognized worked its way up Olivienne's chest to her neck and cheeks. Olivienne was surprisingly close to release considering the relatively short amount of time she'd been at it. "Oh, bollux! This is what you get up to when I'm not around?"

Olivienne's eyes opened a slit to take in her dashing commander where Castellan lay prone on the bed. "Mayhaps."

"Do...do you need a hand, my love?"

Rather than answer, Olivienne's eyes flew wide open and Castellan was struck by the intense gaze from those purple depths. Olivienne arched her back and jerked against her own hand over and over again until she finally slumped onto Castellan's chest. Knowing her lover quite well at that point, Castellan raised Olivienne up with her telekinetic channel and positioned the Connate above her own lips.

"Tosh, what are you—oh! By the depths, don't you dare stop."

She wasn't completely immobile. Olivienne gripped Castellan's pale hair as she rode the pleasure that Castellan served with lips and tongue. When her commander inserted two fingers, she knew that she would prove Castellan correct with the volume of her mental shouts when release took her a second time less than a meen later. Olivienne slumped forward once again and Castellan used her channels to move them both so they lay along the length of the bed rather than crossways. She gently stroked the dark hair with purple highlights, then moved it away from Olivienne's face.

An intense wash of love swelled within Castellan's chest creating a pressure inside her head that she was unable to keep in. The massive feeling moved to Olivienne along their fairly new empathetic bond. It was followed quickly by mental words. *"You amaze me."*

Olivienne's eyes widened at the onslaught of warm and filling emotion. *"I amaze you? My love, my beautiful and handsome darling...you are everything I've ever wanted and I can't wait to spend each dae proving as much to you."*

Castellan's voice was low and soft. "You already do that. I cherish you, 'Vienne."

The Connate rose from where she lay at Castellan's side. "Good. Now let me do the same for you." Then before Castellan could ask what she meant, Olivienne slid down the strong body and took a nipple into her mouth. Castellan arched her back as she was assailed by arousal and hypersensitivity. They were safe and had a one night reprieve from the rigors and responsibility of their mission. The two oathed women spent oors of their evening cherishing each other and unknowingly strengthening the bond of their future union.

BEFORE THEY LEFT the next morning, Castellan informed Nessie of the three Shield guardians that would be staying while the rest of the team continued on to the Temple of Antaeus. The large creature swam out a hundred yords and dove under the water, returning five meens later. She then leaned over the railing and let something small and hard drop to the decking from her mouth.

"What's that?"

"Remember, Sovereign, the Key of Nessie will get you into the temple, and naught else."

Olivienne nodded solemnly as she picked up the nondescript stone. It didn't look like much at all. "I understand."

"Nessie," Tosh called out.

"Yes, Commander?"

"Do you know anything about the other side of the lake? There is a terminal point marked on the island map but we don't know if it's another station like this one or if it is just a dock for the ship. Will there be another form of land conveyance like the railer?"

Nessie leaned closer and blew out a wet blast of air toward Castellan. *"The other side is a mystery, the other races dislike Nessie."*

"Other races?"

"Sasquatch, skunk ape, and ringdocus. Their territories merge at one locus."

The Shield guardians shuffled impatiently and Castellan sighed. "Nessie, you're rhyming again and not making much sense."

Laughter echoed through their heads. *"I make plenty of sense if you care to listen. You're much too serious, Commander. My final parting advice is this: beware the bird's lament."* She turned her head in the direction of the three specialists that would be staying at the station. Nessie had been officially introduced to them shortly after the group finished unloading the gear from the railer that they would need to move to the boat to complete their mission. *"I will give you three, Gren Holling, Branda Leggett, and Ciera Penn, a day to settle in. If you have wish to speak with me before tomorrow's suns' rise, you have only to cast your thoughts into the lake. As I'm the only lady here, you'll get conversation over a rusted piece of war trapping."* None of the group understood much beyond the fact that Nessie wouldn't be back until the next dae.

Holling stepped forward and gave the great creature a low bow. "Thank you, Nessie. We shall look forward to your return." Leggett moved off to join the rest of the team heading across the lake. Just as planned, Spc. Lear would instruct her while piloting them across, then Leggett should be able to safely bring the craft back for the trio assigned to the research station to use and study.

The trip across Dir Lacrimise wasn't noteworthy. It took a little over three oors before they approached a large dock wall on the other side. It was made from the same strange material as the research station building and docks. Clearly the Makers possessed superior materials for the structures to be able to last for hundreds of rotos with little to no degradation. Tosh looked around with a frown as Lear pulled the ship up to the large dock and the specialists went to work tying it up in order to unload the equipment.

"What's wrong?" Olivienne was ever-sensitive to her commander's moods.

Castellan waved a hand in a half circle. "Look around, what do you see? Or rather, what don't you see?"

Gemeda walked up and sighed. "I don't see a bloody railer or anything else for that matter. Are we to walk the rest of the way then?" She cast a glance at the short range of low mountains that had been steadily growing larger the closer the group got to shore on the far side of Lacrimise. On the opposite side of the mountain range from their docking location was a swift and deep river that they knew flowed onward to the sea. According to the velums, Spc. Penn translated it was the Mir Aedes, a rough river that was clearly impassable to the Maker ship. "How many more mahls did you estimate to the Temple of Antaeus?"

"Based on the maps we found? A little over one hundred mahls as a dirigible flies. Though it may as well be across the ocean, pinned between the mountains and river the way we are."

Olivienne walked up and clapped her on the shoulder. "Fear not, Tosh. We'll find a way. Perhaps there is a structure nearby that contains a conveyance inside. We should probably search the area." She pointed to numerous locations that could hide such a thing, such as a bend where the river entered a steep canyon, and a large stand of thick trees farther along the lake where the elevation began to rise.

Savon walked up to the group after squaring away the unloading. "Ser, what are your orders?"

Castellan looked at Olivienne, then glanced at the two places she suggested. "Leave the gear here on the dock and take the team to search the trees for any Maker buildings. Look for anything out of the ordinary, just as Connate Dracore taught you." She watched as Savon spoke briefly with Madlin before directing the rest of the team toward the thick woods.

"What was the message back from Captain Velten this morn? Did they give an estimate for repairs on the dirigible? And I'll admit that I'm a little concerned that we've lost all hope of contact now that we've crossed Lacrimise."

Olivienne, Castellan, and Gemeda walked toward the trees, following the rest of the team, while Castellan answered the Connate's question. "We got a response late last night, but nothing this morning before we set out. First Officer Vex said the engineer, Davine, had created a part that they thought may have the engine online but they wouldn't know until daebreak. So, my guess is that they'll hit this area in a few oors."

Olivienne grimaced. "That helps us not, now."

Roughly ten meens after the entire group began searching the forest, a great roar echoed through the trees. Lt. Madlin stumbled.

"Ser, greater beasts are approaching and they feel extremely aggressive with my animal empathy."

The entire Shield team froze and Castellan yelled out an order. "Pull back to the Connate and prepare yourself for anything."

"Tosh, that sounds like a Dromea silverback. Could the skunk apes be this far around the lake?"

Olivienne's eyes widened. "Oh bollux! That map had three different territories —"

"Merging at one locus. Nessie warned us about this very possibility in her inane rhymes before we left." Castellan thought for a sec before giving another shout. "Retreat to the docks!" Before they could move a single step, a large rotted tree trunk hit the ground very close to the Connate and exploded into a shower of wood pieces and fungus. Castellan attempted to shield Olivienne and Gemeda with her own body. She gagged when a strong odor wafted through the group and they caught sight of a massive furred body not less than twenty yords away. "Run!"

Everyone made haste toward the edge of the woods nearest the dock wall and their gear. Castellan made sure Gemeda and Olivienne were in front of her at all times. Olivienne kept glancing over her shoulder to make sure the commander was still close. Before they could exit the forest proper, screeches, squawks, and a lone lamenting wail echoed around them. The skunk apes paused and the group of guardians slowed.

"What the depths is *that*?" Gemeda stumbled and fell and Olivienne immediately stopped to help her up. Seeing the danger of their delay, Castellan sent her thoughts out to the group.

"Shield your sovereign!"

Chapter Eighteen

THE ENTIRE SHIELD team scrambled back to the doctore and Connate and formed a circular wall around them. Bred to be a woman of the people, Olivienne had thrown herself over top of Gemeda, unsure of what was to come. Tosh remembered the rest of Nessie's warning a moment too late. She mumbled the words aloud to herself. "Beware the bird's lament—sheddech!" She searched around for something to protect the group as a whole but a hail of small darts rained down on them from above, Psierians and skunk apes alike. All the great beasts fell where they stood. The guardians fared slightly better as many of the darts had hit thicker bits of armor or gear.

Unfortunately for Castellan, she was one of the ones who were hit. Her vision blurred and she dropped to a knee, trying her hardest to remain upright and conscious through the burning pain and dizziness. Whatever had been shot at them was fast acting and strong. Castellan squinted and watched as more massive creatures dropped from the upper canopy. They were thickly furred and wore vines and leaves woven as belts and covers. All held long, straight tubes. "What..." Even kneeling as she was, she estimated the creatures to be nearly twice the height of a Psierian.

Lt. Madlin called out to her commander. "I don't sense aggression like I did in the skunk apes, but they are definitely protective. I'd say this attack was in response to trespass into their territory. Should I make contact?"

Castellan tried to stay conscious but her sight was growing darker by the sec. "Negative, Lieutenant. Do not...engage." She collapsed forward as the creatures returned to the trees. "Protect...the...sovereign..."

Gemeda quickly crawled out from under the unmoving body of Olivienne and stood to take in the scene. "What's happened?" She missed the action, covered and surrounded as she was, and didn't see the hail of darts that rendered many unconscious, including Olivienne, Castellan, and Savon.

Madlin answered her. "Doctore Shen, other creatures attacked our group and the skunk apes. They've gone back into the trees but not before damage was done."

"Ser, the Connate's pulse is erratic! I suspect poison."

Gemeda dropped to Olivienne's side, opposite where Spc. Yazzie crouched. "Go check the others, I've got her." Yazzie had already pulled out the dart so Gemeda immediately placed her hands on Olivienne's forehead to begin healing with her telesana channel. She called out to the rest of the abled-bodied Shields. "Pull those poxing darts out if you haven't already!"

Though the poison was a relatively small amount from its location on the dart tip, it was very strong. Despite that, it only took Gemeda a few meens to get Olivienne hale and healthy again. The Connate sat up and looked around perplexed. "Tosh? Where is Castellan?"

Madlin and Yazzie were dragging a groaning Specialist Qent over to lean against a log with Calderon. Both men were still conscious, if in pain. Madlin pointed to where Castellan lay in a line along with Savon, Lear, and Lazaro. "Connate, she was hit by two darts. We've laid her out with the others in the same state." Gemeda glanced around. Devin, Soleng, Dozier, and Meza stood at attention with pistols in hand and their backs to the group.

Yazzie dusted her hands and pulled out a syringe. "I've injected the unconscious four with a standard anti-venom, but not knowing what the creatures used means it may or may not work properly. I'm going to do the same for these two now."

Olivienne gripped Gemeda's arm tightly. "You have to heal her!"

Gem didn't ask whom Olivienne was referring to, rather she quickly made her way to Castellan's side. Two meens into the healing, the commander roused and quickly took in her surroundings. She tried to sit up but was forced back down by Gemeda. "Lie still, you're not fully healed yet."

When Castellan saw the unconscious bodies to her left and right, she used her telekinesis to forcibly hold the doctore away. "Finish me last, take care of the rest first."

"Tosh—"

"That is an order, Doctore Shen!" Castellan stood, then swayed slightly, gripping a nearby tree limb to prevent herself from falling. "Get this team hale then come back to me. I'll be fine enough for now."

Olivienne wanted to protest but knew her stubborn lover wouldn't change her mind so she opted to pull her pistol and help guard the guardians instead. It was a strange twist to the norm. Within twenty meens, everyone had been fully healed, including the commander, but Gemeda dropped unconscious in a state of exhaustion as soon as she finished with the recalcitrant woman. Castellan caught her before she could hit the ground. She easily lifted the small-statured doctore and called out to their remaining medican. "Set up the litter, we need to pull back to the water and determine the best course of action from here." She glanced around until she spied Spc. Lazaro. "As soon as we regroup, I want you to fire up the long-range and see if you can get anyone on the mic. This situation has gone sideways and we need an extraction as soon as possible."

Once the entire group was back near the water and their gear, Olivienne approached her lover. "Tosh?"

Unnerving yips and howls could be heard in the distance on the far side of the Mir Aedes and Castellan held up a hand. "Give me a few meens and we can discuss how we move forward from here."

"What are you going to do?"

The powerful commander didn't answer but rather let her actions speak for themselves as she pulled large stones from along the water's edge and placed them in a protective circle around the group. Easily five foot in height, they made a good enough shelter to hole up in. When she was finished, she wiped the sweat from her brow and turned back to Olivienne. "Now we can talk about what to do next."

Olivienne glanced across the river and though she couldn't see what was making the noise she had a good guess. "The translated text mentioned that the ringdocus is naught but a canid, do you assume them dangerous to us as well?"

Castellan sighed and rubbed her right eyebrow. "I think that none of the beasts on this Maker-forsaken island should be underestimated."

"What now? We know elevation of Magna increases significantly the closer to the coast we go, as the eastern end is naught but mountains and tall plateaus. And the river flows right down the middle, at least according to the map. I wonder though..."

"Yes?"

Olivienne pulled from the pocket of her trousers the map Spc. Penn had copied. She traced the Mir Aedes to its mouth where it flowed into the ocean east of Magna. "The Temple of Antaeus is shown on the north side of the river and the dirigible station is marked on the south side. How did they travel from one place to another with a canyon and fast moving river between?"

"You're asking me questions I have no answer to. My guess is that we'll see when we see and not before."

Another howl sounded and Castellan called out to the lieutenants. "Savon, Madlin, post guards around this wall. Don't let anything get near us, savvy?"

They both saluted. "Yes, ser!"

Castellan walked over to where Gemeda's litter had been placed next to their gear. Olivienne followed her. "How long until she wakes?"

"Based on my past experience with her? Oors most likely. I'd feel better if we could get her to some shelter. It was a lucky thing she was with us for this portion of the journey. I fear we'd be permanently down a few members of our team without her. While the skunk apes were a brute force to be reckoned with, the Sasquatch had an intelligence about them that makes me wary. Territorial defense or no, I've no wish to ever face them under such circumstances again."

Olivienne shook her head. "There was no luck to Gemeda's presence, it was all due to my maman. She's the one who was certain that Doctore Shen must travel to the Temple of Antaeus with us."

"So she did. I wonder—"

"Ser, I've picked up a signal!"

Castellan and Olivienne turned to see Spc. Lazaro waving from where he'd propped up the long-range voteo against one of the large boulders Castellan had moved to fortify their location. They quickly made their way to him. "Is it the research station?"

"No, ser. It's the *Quaesitum*! Captain Velten says she got word from Specialist Penn that we'd gone across Lacrimise. Penn even gave them the heading for the dock on this side. They should be in sight within thirty meens."

Olivienne's mouth gaped as she looked from Castellan to Lazaro and back. "How? I thought they were still working on the engine and wouldn't know if their fix was successful until they attempted it after suns' rise? That wouldn't be nearly enough time to fix it and get here from the western dirigible station."

Lazaro grinned. "One of their steersman had a prescient vision that warned they should attempt their repair last evening because the Connate would need them sooner rather than later. The fix worked and that's what they did. The *Quaesitum* left before first light."

Castellan raised a pale brow at their lone communications specialist. "You got all that while we were conversing just over there?" She pointed a thumb at where they'd been standing after Castellan built the rock wall.

The guardian flushed. "First Officer Vex is quite chatty on the coms, ser."

"So it seems. He's also quite a flirt from what I remember." Dante Lazaro blushed even darker but elected to remain silent.

Olivienne stifled a laugh with her hand but otherwise didn't speak.

The commander gave her guardian a smile. "Keep up the good work, Lazaro." She turned to face the rest where they ranged around the rock wall, watching intently in case any of Magna's native denizens wished to make another appearance. "Attention," she waited while everyone turned to face her, "we've just gotten word that the *Quaesitum* is in route and should arrive within a half oor. Stay sharp just a little longer. We'll continue on to the temple the easy way."

A chorus of "yes, ser" met her news, and more than a few cheers.

Savon and Madlin approached but Savon was the one who spoke. "Ser, what are your orders when the *Quaesitum* arrives?"

Castellan tapped the communications specialist on the shoulder. "Lazaro here is going to voteo the dirigible and tell them to drop an anchor line to be tied to one of the dock cleats, rather than shoot a bolt into the ground. We can lift Doctore Shen to the ship using the same litter basket from the Instrucia adventure. Until they arrive, I want you to bundle the rest of the gear as best you can to make loading easier."

The lieutenants saluted. "Yes, ser." Then Savon called out for two of the guardians to begin bundling the gear while the rest continued watching.

Within forty means the entire team was back aboard the dirigible, leaving nothing behind but a strange ring of boulders near the docking wall. The captain herself met them at the staging deck outside. Her face registered surprise then concern when she caught sight of Gemeda on the litter. "Doctore Shen! Is she injured?"

Olivienne smiled to reassure her. "Fear not, Captain. We were attacked not long before you arrived and many of us were poisoned. Gemeda is merely exhausted after healing the lot of us. She simply needs to rest a few oors in her cabin."

Relief stole across the stern captain's face before she once again pulled a serious look down to mask her emotions. "Good to hear, Connate Dracore." She turned to two of the crew members who were assisting in stowing away the Shield team's gear. "You and you, take Doctore Shen and her gear to her cabin. Lay her on her bunk and secure her with the netting."

"Aye, Captain!"

"And be gentle, Bellen!"

The man at the head of the litter gave a little nod as his hands were full. "Yes, Ser!"

Satisfied they would perform their duties, she turned to the other two important guests. "We should retire to the captain's room and discuss your plan from here. Do you require anything?"

Castellan sighed at the thought of how close their morning had been to disaster. "I could stand a bit of refreshment."

"Scotch if you've got it, Captain. This morning has been simply dreadful."

"Follow me and I'll make sure you're both taken care of."

Castellan sent a mental order to both lieutenants. *"Do an inspection of the gear as you stow it. I don't want any surprises that can be prevented when we get to the end of this sea-soaking river."*

"Yes, ser." Their voices overlapped within her head and she turned to follow Velten and Olivienne.

It didn't take long before the trio sat on low couches with glasses of scotch in hand. The couches themselves were lightweight and bolted to the floor, the requirement for most furnishings in an airship. "We received a short update from the crew you left behind at the research station. Tell me what happened when you landed."

Olivienne recapped their adventure after they docked on the eastern end of Dir Lacrimise. When she finished, Castellan spoke up. "The Sasquatch are clearly more intelligent than we anticipated and I'm not sure what kind of long-range capability they possess. Because of that, I'd rather not provoke the creatures more than necessary as the temple itself is within their territory. My request is that we follow the Mir Aedes to the sea. There is another dirigible station, you can dock there while we consider our options. Is that amenable to you?"

Velten swirled the scotch in her glass. "That sounds like as good a plan as any. Give me just a sec." She grabbed a voteo from her belt and alerted the pilot bridge.

"Steersman Sidditch receiving."

"Follow the river full speed to the coast and dock us at the dirigible station listed on the new map."

"Yes, Captain. Will there be anything else, ser?"

"Configure the distance and give me the anticipated arrival time."

"Give me just a meen." It took less than that for the woman's voice to come across the voteo again. "Two oors and ten meens, give or take, Captain."

"Thank you, Sidditch. Velten out."

Olivienne raised a brow. "She's quick."

The captain raised her glass and smiled. "Only the best for my ship. Now, back to the matter at hand. Do you think these Sasquatch will interfere with you on the ground? Should I send some of my crew as added protection?"

Castesllan considered the captain's suggestion, thinking on the problem from multiple directions as she was trained to do. After nearly a meen, she turned to Olivienne. "Of the trained adventurists on the team, who would you say is senior?"

"Well between Qent and Dozier...he has more oors logged with me in an adventurist capacity but Dozier has logged quite a few before joining my Shield team. You read her transcripts, can you confirm?" Castellan nodded and Olivienne gave her a penetrating stare. "What are you thinking, Tosh?"

"I'm thinking that without Specialist Penn here with us, we may want to leave a small team, or one person with a few members of the *Quaesitum* to search the dirigible tower the way we did on the other side of the island. We found valuable stacks of coded velum there, perhaps there will be something that gives better insight as to where the Makers have vanished."

Velten looked at her shrewdly. "What makes you say that?"

"It's listed as a transportation hub on the map of Magna we retrieved. If that is the case, it was most likely the last place the Makers touched before leaving. Not the temple, not the research station at Lacrimise, but the dirigible station."

Olivienne appeared startled then smiled. "That's quite a brilliant deduction actually. I wouldn't have thought to look at the situation quite like that. What do you think of the problem I posed earlier? How are we to get from the dirigible station to the temple? I don't think the distance is too great, based on map markings, but between the topography of the land and these beasts, it could prove risky to the extreme."

Castellan burst out laughing. "What's this? Is Her Royal Sovereign Connate Olivienne Dracore suddenly adversely inclined to a little risk? Where is the daring-do that ran so many of her captains into the ground, hmm?"

"That was before meeting you, and before I took the time to walk in my guardians' boots and see what things were like for them." She paused and glanced at Velten, aware that she was spilling personal information to a woman who, while not a stranger, wasn't a close acquaintance. She moved her gaze back to Tosh. "I've changed a lot over the past roto and have come to realize having the right team and Shield commander can make all the difference for me and my missions. I have enjoyed working with all of you in the course of my adventuring."

There was a meen of silence after her long declaration, then Castellan spoke in a quiet voice. "You honor me, 'Vienne."

Velten sighed. "You two are overly-sweet like portea with your romantic inclinations. Despite how happy you appear, I'm still glad my anchor never stays long in one place. I don't have time for such bondings."

"Are you so against love then, Captain?"

Seema Velten thought for a meen while gazing into her nearly empty glass. "I wouldn't say I'm against it, but you see…my life is regimented and precise because that's how I prefer it. There are things I can depend on and other things, amorphous things such as love, that are not so dependable. They make a person distracted and distraction gets a crew killed."

"That's a very harsh way to look at it."

Seema smiled. "Not to mention, it would take a very special sort of person to put up with a wanderer like me. Things never work well for bonding when one is constantly on the move. It makes it hard to put down roots."

"I thought the same once as a Defense Corp officer."

Tosh and Velten both looked at Olivienne and she shrugged. "It's no secret that I never expected to settle down. A decision that was no doubt facilitated by my adventurist career."

The captain laughed. "You seem to have acclimated quite well to oathing, despite your previous aversion." She glanced to where Olivienne's right hand rested upon the thigh of Castellan's trousers. Castellan blushed but didn't bother denying the comforting touch.

"It helps that I seem to have found my perfect match in a certain Commander Tosh."

"Pardon my saying, but you two seem quite…different. Opposite nearly in some ways."

That elicited a peel of laughter from the Connate. "Different in ways that make things interesting, Captain. But we are remarkably cut from the same cloth in all the ways that matter most. Head, heart, and dedication to our duties, as well as our love for each other."

Castellan nodded. "It's true. Olivienne vexes me daily but there is never a moment I don't respect her or wish to be by her side." She got a poke to the ribs for her remark but nothing more than that.

They sipped their drinks for another meen before the captain spoke again. "Do you two fancy a game of cubes? There is naught we can do but wait while the good doctore recovers and we make our way to the next destination."

Olivienne smiled. "I'm certainly amenable." She turned to look at her future par. "You know, I've never asked...but do you play, Tosh?"

"Not for rotos now but Gem and I used to play with others in our time back at Academy. I'm sure I could dust off my rolling hand for the occasion."

Velten had already stood to fetch the set of cubes. "Yes, but were you any good?"

Castellan stood as well and drained the remainder of her scotch. "Mayhaps."

The Connate followed the other two over to Velten's meeting table and sighed. "Knowing your brain, you probably scooped cred from the lot on the regular."

She got a wink for her comment. "It may be possible I won a few cormi each weke."

They sat around the table and Velten leveled a steady finger at Castellan. "No channels, Tosh! Not all of us are so Maker-gifted as you."

The commander looked affronted. "I would never!"

"She's putting you on, love. We know you'd no more cheat in a game of cubes than you'd be caught derelict in your Shield Corp duty."

"I hate that you know me so well."

The captain snorted and dumped a bag of small stone cubes onto the table. "If you two are finished seducing each other with words and wit, I'd like to get on with the game."

Olivienne laughed heartily and grabbed a single cube to roll for start. "Spoil sport."

A LITTLE OVER two oors later, the trio's highly competitive game was interrupted by a tone on the captain's voteo. "Velten here."

"Ser, we've arrived at the end of the Mir Aedes. You may want to send Connate Dracore up to see this. It's....I have no sufficient words...it's beautiful, ser."

"I'll inform them, Vex. Velten out." She clipped the voteo back onto her belt and looked at the other two women, frowning momentarily at the pile of pintas in front of Castellan. "Shall we put our game aside and see what has stripped the words from my highly talkative First Officer's mouth?"

Castellan laughed, remembering Lazaro's comment near the dock wall. "May as well since the two of you seem to be on your last few cred. Good thing we were only playing for legume seeds."

As they made their way toward the door, Castellan grabbed her own voteo. "Tosh to Madlin."

"Madlin here."

"We've arrived at the dirigible tower. I want you to check Doctore Shen's status and have the rest of the team stand ready to disembark."

"Yes, ser."

Castellan checked her timepiece then addressed Olivienne as the three of them made their way down the passageway toward the captain's bridge. "It's nearly half after fourteen hundred oors. It would perhaps be best to explore the tower todae and put off heading to the temple until tomorrow morning."

Olivienne gave her a curious look. "It would give us an opportunity to see if any more coded velum sheets have been left behind. But is there a reason you wish to delay our leave-taking?"

"It makes basic sense since we still need to find a way to the temple and I suspect the Makers would have made provisions for getting from one place to the other. Beyond that, the Queen specifically stated that Gemeda must accompany you for the entirety of this journey. And for her to be any good to us, she needs to fully recover."

"How long will that take?"

Castellan thought for a sec. "Gem has nearly as high an overall channel rating as me even though, barring the telesana, it's almost all soft channels. However, from what I've observed, she builds energy incredibly fast, which probably helps her to heal more people and longer."

"Fascinating. Okay, I'll cede to your wishes in this because you are frustratingly correct much of the time." Castellan smirked and started to answer but Olivienne held up a finger to forestall the response. "Not a word, Tosh."

They arrived at the portal to the bridge and Castellan bowed with a flourish, gesturing her sovereign forward. "Your request is my order, Connate Dracore."

Both were laughing as they entered into the fore room that was surrounded on three sides by windows. Laughter stopped as they took in the wonderous sight before them. It was only a few oors past middae and the light of the two suns shone bright upon the land below. The river cut deep into the canyon to their left. High upon a cliff to the right stood the dirigible tower, built in a mirror image of the one on the other side of the island. The spires and platforms gleamed in the bright light but that wasn't what truly drew their attention.

To the left of the canyon on another high plateau stood the Temple of Antaeus. It was similar enough to the other two Psierian temples that the entire group on the bridge knew what it was, but there were obvious differences as well. For one, Antaeus looked significantly more defensible. There were no openings that Castellan could see. The Grand Chamber of both known temples takes up the entire top level of the pyramid. Only with Antaeus, instead of large windows all the way around the base of the pyramidion, there were only marked blank spaces, similar to what they found on the research station before it was unlocked. And though they couldn't see all four sides, the skylights that were visible appeared to be closed off the same way.

The land itself was untamed, thick and green with a forest that had been left to grow for hundreds of rotos, perhaps longer. There were low clouds and groups of small flyers swooping and diving in the breeze coming off the ocean. It was as unspoiled and beautiful as anything they'd ever seen. "By the Makers, it's glorious!" Lieutenants Savon and Madlin had come to the bridge and both were as awestruck as the rest. It was Savon who was unashamed to remark on the beauty aloud though.

Madlin was a little more pragmatic. "But how do we get in?" She moved closer yet to Tosh. "Ser, Doctore Shen continues to slumber so I left orders for Yazzie to check on her at the top of each oor until off-shift, then Meza will take over."

Castellan clapped her on the shoulder. "Good thinking, Madlin. Well done."

The sense of awed wonder eventually faded as Velten turned away from the sight to address her sovereign. "What are your orders, Senior Adventurist Connate Dracore?"

Olivienne smiled as only she could when the next adventure waited just around the corner. "Take us in to dock at the tower, Captain."

Chapter Nineteen

THE CONNATE AND her Shield team followed the same protocol for the second tower as they did the first. As Olivienne suspected, they did indeed find more stacks of coded velum that they could take back to Tesseron with them. She had a feeling that the secure interpretists at the Temple of Archeos would be very busy upon their return. Unfortunately, the ravages of time had made many of the motos with degradable parts no longer functional. It was the same issue they found in the motos and haulers located in the storage buildings at the first station, not that they would have been able to drive them anywhere with the trees so thick around the tower and temple.

One thing to note was that unlike the other dirigible station, there was no railer sitting ready at the base of the transportation hub. Instead, the tower incorporated two dirigible platforms near the very top, easily twice as big as the rest along the length. Upon investigation, the team found that the eastern tower's observation window faced the sea, just as the western tower. Because of that, Castellan speculated that perhaps the inhabitants of the island regularly saw ships come in from that direction. The Shield team stared at her in awe as they realized her full meaning — that they weren't the lone occupants of Psiere and that it was possible to travel even farther from Endara. Olivienne wasn't awed so much as she was giddy with excitement at the thought.

Another difference between the two towers was that the second-to-lowest button on the lift took them to the main floor of the tower, indicating that there was a sub-level, below that of the base. They had no idea where such would take them but by the time Olivienne was ready to explore the depths of the Maker-created place, it was nearing last meal.

"Connate Dracore, may I recommend that the team break for evening meal and some downtime? We've been going steady for oors."

"But I'm not tired yet. We're on the cusp of great things, Tosh, I can feel it! Let's just—" She stopped speaking at the look on her oath mate's face. "I'm obsessing again, aren't I?"

Tosh smiled. "Just a bit but it's completely understandable.

To be dead honest, I am too. However, it's my job to look after you and your Shield team and we all need to rest and reconstitute. I suspect we'll think and work better on full bellies, even you."

Olivienne sighed. "You're right and I know it, but *bah*, it galls me to slow down when we're so close!"

"Even so, slow we must go."

Castellan got a shove for her rhyme. "Now you sound like Nessie!"

"Speaking of, you've got the key she gave you for safekeeping, right?"

Olivienne pulled the object from a sealed trouser pocket. "I've had it right here, but honestly, Tosh, it looks like naught more than a lake stone. How is this supposed to get us into the Temple of Antaeus?"

Castellan gazed at the smooth, palm-size rock in Olivienne's hand. It was dull grayish-brown, like most other lake stones. Certainly nothing of excitement to look upon. "I don't know, but we didn't think the pendants could be keys either so we'll simply have to trust that Nessie knows what she is talking about."

"True enough."

After an oor for the team to eat and rest, including Olivienne, Castellan called out new orders. "Listen up. The Connate and I will be taking a team down to the last unexplored level. Savon, Qent, Yazzie, Lear, and Calderon are with us. I want Lieutenant Madlin to oversee a thorough exploration around the tower, searching for a possible way across to the other side of the river valley. Be especially wary as the region surrounding us belongs to the ringdocus." She paused to make eye contact with Madlin and the rest that would be staying. "And by the Makers...don't fall down the cliff."

"Ser..."

Castellan glanced to where her specialist with mountain training stood with a hand lifted. "Yes, Dozier?"

"I studied the rock striations along the river valley where it cut deep into the rock on our approach. I believe the stone walls are highly unstable and prone to crumbling near the edge. It's a good thing the Makers built the tower as far back as they did or it may have fallen into the river valley or the sea at some point."

The commander gestured toward her and looked to Lt. Madlin. "This is the Shield you want to coordinate with for your search. Set lines and don rappelling gear if need be but I want your team safe. Savvy?"

Madlin met Dozier's gaze and gave a slight nod, then turned her attention back to Castellan. "Yes, ser. You can count on us. If there is a way over the ravine we'll find it."

"Good, now if we're ready, let's head out."

The smaller group of five guardians followed Olivienne and Tosh to the lift. They had standard gear packs for a general adventurist mission, plus their weapons. No one was sure what they would face but Castellan mentally prepared herself just in case they found a Maker trap. Olivienne placed a hand discretely on Castellan's forearm and spoke mind to mind as the lift decended. *"Relax, Tosh. I don't suspect any traps or puzzles within the tower. As with the other side of Magna, this is a transportation hub."*

Castellan narrowed her eyes at her future par during the unusually long ride down. *"But you suspect something, don't you?"*

Olivienne smirked. *"We're going very deep into the land, wouldn't you say?"*

The commander's eyes widened as she realized what Olivienne was implying. The lift was still in motion, much longer than any standard floor change. *"You think the way across is under, not over?"*

Olivienne shrugged. *"As Dozier pointed out, the rock above is much too unstable. But we'll find out soon enough—"* Her words were cut off as the doors *whooshed* open, displaying nothing but darkness beyond.

"Sheddech!"

The Connate laughed at Spc. Qent's startled exclamation. She made to step forward but was held in place by a wall of Castellan's telekinesis. She turned to look at her overly protective commander. "Fear not, Tosh. Watch." She waited while Castellan dropped her channel then stepped forward once the way was clear. The tunnel beyond immediately lit, going on for a good twenty yords. It was mostly round and close to twenty foot in diameter. The walls looked like the same strange metallic material as the ship and the dirigible towers.

"Connate, do you think this goes all the way across to the temple?"

"Only one way to find out, Savon." Olivienne started forward but was brought to a stop again by Castellan's plea.

"Connate, a moment please. Let me verify something before we go haring off into some unknown tunnel into the Maker's know where."

The Connate rolled her eyes, but waved a hand for Tosh to do whatever it was she intended.

"Specialist Qent, I'd like a dowsing. Point to the strongest source of water, if you will."

He saluted, proud he could be of service again with such an inconsequential channel. "Yes, ser!" Zed Qent closed his eyes and held out one arm, spinning slowly as he got a feel for the various water pulls around him. Finally he stopped and oriented his arm upward at a roughly forty-five percent angle. He opened his eyes again and smiled. "That's the river. It looks like it's directly above the tunnel, but farther down along the way."

"Exactly as we suspected!"

"Do you think it will exit below the temple, or another entrance in the grounds nearby?"

Olivienne thought for a meen. "I think below. It would be most convenient."

Tosh nodded. "Not to mention the safest and easily defensible for security."

She got a sigh for her added observation. "Always the soldier, hmm, Tosh?"

With the new information in her head, Castellan calculated the distance between the tower and the Temple of Antaeus, then estimate the speed they'd travel on foot. She glanced down at her timepiece a made a decision. "Connate Dracore, we're about twenty meens at best from wherever this tunnel exits. Might I suggest we begin the journey first thing in the morning with Doctore Shen and the full Shield team?"

Olivienne's first reaction was to discount the commander's suggestion, as she'd done with all her captains in the past. She could feel how close they were and loathed to stop when the lost temple of Psiere was a mere twenty meens away. Then she remembered her maman's request about the doctore and tempered her expectations for the evening. Savon and the seasoned guardians of the team waited in anticipation, knowing exactly how their sovereign had reacted to being reined in during past adventurist missions. She surprised them all with a gracious smile. "You're right—"

Castellan cut in. "Come again?" Savon stifled a cough and Castellan gave the man a knowing smile.

Olivienne huffed at her lover's teasing. "It *would* be best to start this newest phase of the adventure fresh after suns' rise tomorrow. Now," She gave the tunnel one last glance before turning back to the lift. "Let's go give everyone the good news, shall we?"

The five guardians gave a *whoop* of excitement and Castellan gazed at them indulgently. Once in the lift, she met Olivienne's eyes while Yazzie pushed the button for the main level. *"Thank you."*

"I expect you to make it up to me later, perhaps in another sound-proof room, yeah?"

Castellan sniffed and glanced around to make sure no one noticed her blush-stained cheeks. *"Seems the least I can do for my sovereign."*

THE MORNING DAWNED clear as one sun then the next broke over the ocean's horizon to the east. Gemeda roused a few oors after the Connate's team had returned from the tunnel discovery the evening before. She declared herself well enough and that she'd be fit for duty after a good night's rest. The doctore went on to prove her words by being up and ready before the rest of the team the next morning. Because they had so much time to explore the tower the previous dae, Olivienne decided it wasn't necessary for anyone to stay behind. Instead, Captain Velten assigned her own team to investigate, instructing the crew members to log anything of interest or potential use.

It took three trips for the entire adventurist team and their gear to arrive at the tunnel entrance. Both medicans, Spc. Yazzie and Dre. Shen, carried med gear packs, though Yazzie had her base kit as well, which included a water container, a voteo, and her weapons. The entire group of fourteen was wound like timepieces, excited to finally see the inside of the lost temple. Castellan held up her hand to forestall everyone, including her future par, from starting down the tunnel.

"I know you're all anxious to get underway, as am I. However, I would like to stress caution. Now is not the time to be lax in our training. Follow Connate Dracore's instruction and guidance. While we assume this tunnel is a basic corridor, much like we found in the towers and the ship below Dir Sanguis, we know nothing for certain. If you remember, the ship had been left for a long time and we nearly sank with it. And here we are below an entire river. Look, listen, and feel for *anything* out of the ordinary down here, savvy?"

"Yes, ser!" Her instructions were met with a loud response and more than a few grins.

Commander Tosh spun on her heel to face Olivienne and gave her a crisp salute, quickly mimicked by the rest of the Shield team. "Senior Adventurist Olivienne Dracore...the mission is yours."

"Thank you, Commander Tosh. Now, if you'll all follow me, ranging exactly as we did in the ship below the lake."

Gemeda rolled her eyes at the formality of it all, though even she had to admit there was a weight to the moment that she'd experienced few other times, if any.

They didn't walk particularly fast because even though Olivienne was nearly certain there would be no traps along the length of the tunnel, it was considered adventurist best practice to always check your way forward. The tunnel appeared to light and dim in approximately twenty yord sections, dark farther off in front and behind them but light where they walked. Olivienne assumed it was to conserve energy. Though with the river above them, it seemed a given that the Makers would have utilized water current to power generators, the same kind that Psierians had found schematics for in both great temples. And just as with the first tower, the second one also featured massive holes in the cliff face at the water's edge and were assumed to be intakes for power generation, though Olivienne didn't feel it necessary to confirm.

After a careful twenty-five meen walk, the team faced the end of the tunnel. It was a massive wall that took up the entire twenty-foot diameter of the space. There was a rough indention that appeared to be the size and shape of the double doors of the lift at the other end. Next to the smooth indention was a panel and keypad of buttons, one for every Psierian letter of the alphabet, similar to keyboards for a typist's machine. Above the panel was a familiar-looking horizontal tube mounted to the wall, no more than a finger's width in diameter. It was identical to the one in the Navis cave where they found the Key of Illeos.

Olivienne reached into her sealed trouser pocket and pulled out Nessie's stone. She looked at Tosh with raised brows, clearly confused. "I don't see a place for the stone, do you?"

"No. Perhaps if you move closer, as with the pendants."

Even after moving closer, so close she could place her hand on the wall, nothing happened. She glanced over her shoulder while the rest of the team stood in anticipation. "Clearly something needs to be entered into the keypad. I'd like to say I've seen this before but this is truly a first for me in all my rotos of adventuring. It's very progressive tech and I'm at a loss."

Castellan looked around at the Shield team. "Does anyone have a suggestion? This is where we display our flexibility as a group of experienced and intelligent minds."

One deep voice came from the back. "Ser, what did Nessie say when she discussed the key with you?" While many would discount Gar Soleng's intellect simply because of his size alone, an underestimation he encouraged, Castellan knew better. The specialist was an extremely talented engineer on top of being a highly decorated Shield.

Olivienne looked at Tosh. "What were Nessie's words, exactly?"

Gemeda laughed. "You're asking Tosh? Keen she's always been but there is a reason she does everything by rote. It's because her memory is aether-washed."

Gem got a frown from the woman in question. "I do well enough, if you please. Not all of us can have an eidetic memory channel. As for what Nessie said, I believe she told us that we couldn't enter the temple without Nessie, that the Tau made it the last bit of security."

"That's right! She also said the Makers left it to her to determine if the seekers were worthy."

Madlin looked at the commander and Connate. "Is that all she told you?"

Castellan thought for a sec. "Erm, no. She also said we would need Nessie to get inside."

"May I touch the stone? Perhaps my psychometry can tell us something."

Olivienne handed the stone to Lt. Madlin as she moved forward. The lieutenant closed her eyes and her auburn brows drew down in concentration. "Intelligence...age and wisdom. I sense Nessie, a displaced wonder. Secrets." She opened her eyes and handed the stone back. "I'm sorry Connate, but that's all I'm getting."

"When you say secrets, does that mean lies? Could Nessie have been lying to us?"

Madlin shook her head at Olivienne's question. "No, merely secrets."

Gemeda brought up a point the rest had missed. "Why was she speaking *about* herself, rather than *as* herself? Doesn't that seem odd to anyone else?"

Olivienne and Castellan's eyes met at the same time as they both blurted out, "The stone isn't the key!"

More than a few specialists laughed at the simultaneous outburst and Savon, who had yet to catch on to the answer, spoke. "But sers, if not the stone then what is the key?"

Olivienne smiled at her loyal and steadfast lieutenant. "Why, Nessie herself is the key, of course. I believe we have to punch in the corresponding letters to her name. What say you, Tosh?"

The commander gave a nod. "Yes, that is what I surmised as well."

Rather than wait any longer, Olivienne moved back to the keypad and pushed each letter in order as *hissing* sounded behind the panel with each. They waited for something promising, instead the horizontal indicator mounted above the buttons flashed and red liquid filled the first of three segments of the glass ampule. "Bollux, I hate seeing that! What now?"

Dozier spoke from just behind Gemeda. "Ser, I saw something similar on an adventurist mission during my training. Not fancy like this keyboard, but we had to translate a word into code using the Illeos temple key. Perhaps you have to translate Nessie with the Antaeus temple key first."

"Brilliant! All those oors of adventurist training before joining our Shield team have finally proven useful, yeah?" Veva Dozier grinned brightly with her sovereign's praise but she didn't get a chance to answer before Olivienne was speaking again. "Tosh, I need your maths brain."

Castellan rolled her eyes but stepped forward to accept the cipher velum and wax stylus that Olivienne pulled out of her left trouser pocket. She immediately went to work writing out Nessie, then translating it into coded text. When Castellan was finished, she read aloud the new text. "O-C-I-E-I-N."

Olivienne pushed each letter as Castellan called them off. *Hissing* once again emanated from behind the panel with each press. After the last letter had been pushed, the indicator flashed again and the red liquid drained out of the glass ampule above the panel. It was a familiar site indeed for Olivienne, Castellan, Qent, Dozier, and Yazzie, the original ones to open the top secret drawer containing the Maker skeleton on Navis.

But rather than hearing a series of *clicks* and *clunks*, the entire group felt a deep rumble begin below their feet. Olivienne stepped back as the indention across from the door moved back a quarter ince and slid out of the way, opposite the side with the panel. The rumbling continued for two more meens until it finally stopped above and below them, after which, the group of Psieri-ans stood staring at the plain looking lift doors that would take them up to the Temple of Antaeus, the lost temple of Psiere. Oliv-ienne turned to Castellan. "By the Makers, we've done it, Tosh!"

Castellan looked back toward the doors and kept her deepest thoughts shielded as she contemplated the troublesome antorae-stones lying somewhere above. Her gut told her that Olivienne would prove difficult when it came to following her maman's orders. "So we have."

There wasn't room for the entire team to go up in the lift as it was the same size as the one on the other end of the tunnel. For security reasons, Castellan chose a strong initial group to go up first. "Savon and Lazaro will go up with Connate Dracore, Doc-tore Shen, and myself. When we're certain the topside is clear, Lazaro will use the long-range voteo to contact Lieutenant Madlin to bring up the rest." Castellan leveled an intense gaze at her lieutenant that would be staying with the main group. "Savvy?"

"Yes, ser." Auda Madlin swallowed down the disappoint-ment at not being chosen to be one of the first to step into the Temple of Antaeus.

On his way by to the lift, Savon glanced back at her in under-standing. "Don't worry, you'll be first next time."

"That hardly seems likely with you as first lieutenant. Besides, do you really think there will be another time?"

They both paused to look at where Castellan and Olivienne stood speaking with Gemeda just inside the lift doors. Savon turned strangely serious. "We perform a dangerous job and you never know what the future will hold." Then just as quickly, his smile returned and he clapped her on the shoulder. "Besides, with those two? I think this is only the beginning of our great adventures."

She smiled back, somewhat mollified. "I think you're right."

Ten meens later the doors of the lift *whooshed* open to show another dark passageway. The air was musty as only hundreds of rotos unstirred could leave it. And there was a stillness to the place that awed the small group. Olivienne stepped forward and the pas-sageway lit from above, like all the other Maker edifices on Magna. The floor of the passage ramped upward toward a doorway and Olivienne paused to look at the rest as they stepped out.

Savon immediately instructed Lazaro to contact the team below as Castellan and Gemeda gazed at Olivienne. Gemeda gave a sniff then immediately sneezed. "It's not dusty so much as stale. I would imagine they had the temple sealed quite tight to protect it from the ravages of weather and vermin alike."

Castellan gave her long-time friend an indulgent grin but directed her next question at Olivienne. "What are your orders? Assuming this temple is set in roughly the same layout as the others, is there a room you'd like to explore?"

"I want to personally explore everything but I suppose I have to be realistic. While I would like for us to at least step into every room, there are a few things we should confirm first and foremost."

"The charging chamber."

"Exactly. We should probably get some reassurance that we'll have aether enough to return home again. Once we confirm that, we should immediately inform Captain Velten of the room so she can start transporting stones for charging. I'm sure they'll have a cart or some such around here."

Gemeda tilted her head in thought. "What about document stores, and equipment? I read that the temples on the other two continents had an entire room full of coded velum sheets. They also had storage rooms with devices and schematics."

Olivienne nodded, a great student of all things related to the temples. It wasn't just because she was a member of the Divinity Corp, it was her lifelong passion to study the Makers and their knowledge. "Quite true, Gem. Tosh, it makes the most sense to split our teams into smaller groups to aid in searching and cataloguing each room. Wouldn't you agree?"

Their conversation was interrupted as the first group of specialists arrived in the lift. Lt. Madlin sent it back down for the rest once everyone had disembarked. Castellan hesitated at Olivienne's suggestion but admitted the idea had merit. "I agree that it makes the most sense. And you're certain there will be no traps or tricks here?"

"Certainty is found with sovereigns and seekers. I'm merely giving you my educated guess." Olivienne intoned an old saying by an unknown psi from long ago.

Gem pointed out the obvious. "You're also a sovereign." She got a wave for her suggestion.

"*Bah*, todae I'm only an adventurist." She glanced toward the lift as Specialists Qent, Meza, Dozier, and Devin stepped out. "If that's everyone, let's get started." She led the group down the passageway and as luck would have it, the doorway on the other end led to a familiar chamber on the bottom level. It was near the main entrance in the front of the temple. From there they followed the route that they assumed would take them to the temple charging rooms on the opposite corner of the immense structure. Olivienne gave a *whoop* of joy when she used a palm pad to open a large set of doors and found a two-story room with four fist-sized archeostones placed in the walls. She immediately wandered into the room to look around, as did the rest of the Shield guardians and Gemeda.

Castellan called out to Spc. Lazaro. "Inform Captain Velten's crew that we have a charging room here in the temple. Tell her to send a team with a cart of spent illeostones over. It shouldn't take more than a dae or two to charge them all once they're here."

"Won't she want to bring the dirigible over here, ser?"

"She mentioned last night that she'd prefer to keep the *Quaesitum* docked at the tower because of search efforts of her crew. However, I know she'll bring it around to anchor on this side of Aedes if absolutely necessary."

"Commander Tosh!" She turned to see Savon pointing at a small chest. "Something about this seems important. It's as if there is a vision waiting to come but it never arrives."

Tosh yelled out for her other lieutenant as Olivienne turned to see what the commotion was about. "Madlin! Lay your hands carefully on that chest."

"Yes, ser."

She jogged over and arrived at the same time as both Tosh and Olivienne. She intoned what she saw after placing a single hand in the center of the top. "Stones." She looked at her commander and sovereign. "I'm sorry but that's all I've got."

Olivienne's voice was for Castellan alone. *"Do you think it's the antoraestones?"*

"It seems likely, though I'd have thought there would be more of them."

The Connate reached out her hand toward the clasp but Castellan's hand was faster and she grabbed the daring woman's wrist. "Do you think it would be trapped?"

"I'm fairly certain it won't be."

Castellan smiled. "I trust you implicitly as the professional in this situation but why don't you let me open it with my telekinesis to be safe?"

Olivienne didn't respond, rather she waved her hand toward the latch for Castellan to have a go at it. Everyone stood back as the simple clasp turned and gave a *click*, then the lid swung slowly upward. Rather than finding a chest full of antoraestones as Castellan had feared, the container was filled to the brim with familiar looking palm-sized iridescent archeostones.

Spc. Soleng was close by and gave a little shout. "That's just a bit of brilliant luck, isn't it?"

Tosh raised a pale brow at the big man. "What's that, Soleng?"

He ducked his head briefly. "Well, ser, with those stones the captain won't need to bring the spent illeostones all the way here, she can place that chest in the illeostone room aboard the *Quaesitum* and they'll charge while onboard." He paused for a meen then his face split with a big grin. "If you modify the stone storage rooms on any ship, you would never have to offload to charge. Why...you could go on forever. Think of it, sers, it may even be possible to travel all the way around Psiere!"

Olivienne found his exuberance contagious and clapped him on the shoulder. "I like the way you think." Then she turned to Castellan. "He's made an excellent point. I wonder if this is how the Makers were able to explore so much of Psiere."

"Hard to say, maybe so." Their communications specialist wasn't nearby so Castellan sent a mental message. *"Lazaro, inform the captain that we've got a small chest of Archeostones and she should be able to use them to charge the ship's stones without offloading. Tell her I'll send a specialist over immediately."*

Dante Lazaro came from around a corner in another room. "Yes, ser." He placed the heavy long-range voteo on the ground and fired it up to contact the ship's crew.

While he was sending the message, Castellan spoke to Soleng again. "Do you think you can carry that all the way back to the *Quaesitum*? I'd rather get it there as soon as possible so the stones in their spent hold begin charging before we have to depart for Tesseron."

Spc. Soleng grabbed each side of the chest and lifted it before setting it down again. "It's heavy but nothing I can't handle. I've carried a pack easily three times more."

"True, but the pack sits well on your back for ease and portability. This will be awkward."

Soleng closed the lid and lifted the chest to hold it one-handed atop of his brawny left shoulder. "Then I'll switch it up, ser."

Castellan nodded. "Well enough, then." She called out to the lieutenants. "Savon, Madlin, I'm sending Soleng back to the dirigible with the stones."

"Yes, ser."

Olivienne looked around the chamber. "Tosh, I'd like to split those of us left into pairs to begin searching and cataloguing the temple. Three teams will work their way down into the lower levels, searching each room, while the others will work their way up. Since we have an odd number with Soleng heading to the tower, I'll have two people with me initially."

"Myself and Doctore Shen—"

"Already ahead of you, darling." A few specialists snickered at the nickname but wisely got their reactions under control. "I assumed you'd want to be my companion in this." She looked around the group as the rest of the Shield unit drew in to hear. Olivienne had been paying attention when she got to know the team during the time Castellan was going through retesting up on Instrucia. "You will be paired as follows. Dozier with Lazaro, Madlin and Qent, Lear and Devin, Yazzie and Calderon, and finally Meza and Savon. However, when Soleng comes back then Meza will join him and Doctore Shen can go with Savon."

Castellan stared at her in shock at first. She knew her team inside and out, all their strengths and weaknesses, but Olivienne wasn't privy to all that information in standard practice. "Did you just split everyone by channel ability, pairing the ones with enhanced awareness with those that don't have it?"

"I did. Surprised?"

"Pleasantly." They shared an intense stare until Gemeda snapped her fingers.

"If you two are finished mentally noshing each other, I'd like to get started."

Tosh grimaced at her friend's teasing before she straightened her uniform and pulled her eyes away. "Fine. See the Connate for your specific sections."

"I personally want to start with the lower levels. Let's send...the first eight names I mentioned up once the main level is clear. That will leave myself, Tosh, Doctore Shen, Meza, and Savon to check below."

Castellan gave her a scrutinizing look. *"Is there a reason you want to head below?"*

Olivienne motioned for the guardians to disburse while answering Tosh in her head. *"Historical adventurist records show that the most valuable finds were always in the lower levels of the temples, which tells me the antoraestones will likely be found down there as well."*

"I see."

Olivienne caught a flash of some emotion through their empathic bond, one that she couldn't quite identify. *"You're with me on this, right Tosh? I know we've clashed in the past but certainly you've come to see all the good these stones can do."*

Castellan smiled even as she cut her eyes away to give the team their last orders. "Savon and Madlin, I want oorly status checks for each team, savvy?"

"Yes, ser."

Then she turned back to Olivienne and made a solemn vow. "I do see all the good the stones can do, I always have. But 'Vienne, we both made a pledge to do our sovereign duty if and when we stumble across them."

Olivienne frowned. "Let's just see what we find before we decide on a course of action."

Both could sense the coming clash and Castellan felt naught but sick inside. Rather than speak of it aloud, Castellan nodded to Olivienne as the others followed along to check the next section, on the east side of the charging rooms. "Well enough."

Chapter Twenty

IT TOOK AN oor for Soleng to return from the dirigible. When he arrived, Castellan informed him of his assignment, and the group working their way toward the lower levels shuffled teams to accommodate the new addition. Gemeda left Olivienne and Castellan's small group to go off with Lieutenant Gentry Savon while Meza and the returned specialist paired into their own team.

Madlin had voteo'd that she and Qent found a room full of machine schematics one floor above the main level of the temple. Castellan sent Soleng and Meza above so the engineer could have a good look. All in all, they managed to investigate and record contents for nearly half the levels above and below on the first dae of exploration. Olivienne instructed the Shield team to bring various cases of coded documents back to the dirigible for storage. Some velums could be easily recognized as to their subject by symbols in the top left corner. It was common practice with Maker texts, though it was usually only used for things relating to process or industry.

Olivienne also had anyone with mechanical knowledge, meaning the two with tinkerist training, Savon and Madlin, as well as their remaining engineer, Gar Soleng, pick out various machines and devices they thought should make the return trip to Tesseron as well. The amount of space was limited on the airship but they had accounted for some extra storage when preparing for the journey. As they made their way back down the tunnel toward the tower lift, Olivienne threaded her arm through Castellan's. "I feel as though we've had a good dae's work. I can only imagine what new discoveries all the documents will lead to in the coming rotos." She gazed at her future par, violet eyes wide with excitement.

Castellan smiled back, happy to see the person she loved above all others so joyous in the midst of realizing her life's dream. But there was still that part of the commander, hidden deep down, that despaired at the decision she would have to make in the coming daes. "I feel as though Psierians are on the precipice of great change, a place we wouldn't be without your tireless dedication and perseverance to solving the mystery of the Makers."

That evening, Olivienne, Castellan, Gemeda, and Seema sat around the captain's table for last meal, discussing all they had found in both the temple and the tower. Olivienne estimated that they'd probably finish exploring the temple within the next two daes, most likely less. When the meal was cleared away, they moved to Velten's low couches with glasses of scotch. After a short moment of silence, Castellan brought up her concerns for their return. "Now that we have the issue of charged stones solved, we need to figure out how to avoid the ambush that awaits us in Nusquam. Does anyone have any suggestions?"

Gemeda looked to Velten. "Seema—"

Olivienne snorted at how familiar Gemeda was with the severe captain.

Gemeda resolutely ignored the slight tease and continued her train of thought. "How long can the *Quaesitum* safely and hygienically run without waste removal and restocking supplies?"

"Seventy-two oors is design, but we can go as long as a weke if we ration and dump overland."

Gemeda wrinkled her nose. "That's vile."

Velten looked mildly affronted. "We wouldn't do it in a populated region."

Olivienne laughed outright and Castellan attempted to get the discussion back on track. "Did you have a point, Gem?"

"I did, actually. Why do we need to stop in Nusquam at all on the return? With the archeostones aboard ship constantly recharging the illeostones, hypothetically we have the power to return straightaway to Tesseron. Though we would have to stop for necessities as you just pointed out."

Velten sat forward and looked around the group. "She's right! Let me check the map and see if I can plot a better course back that would help us avoid those bloody rogues that await us." She stood and walked over to a side desk and withdrew a large rolled map of Psiere from a cubby, a straight rule from the drawer, and a scrap of velum and stylus. Then she brought the items over to the table and unrolled the map. The other three joined her and used their glasses to hold down the corners. "We can take the same route back to the western edge of Magna, picking up your Shields and any other findings from the research station on the way. That's roughly..." She trailed off, measuring the distances and writing down each figure.

Castellan, with her head for numbers and spatial distance, watched the captain write everything down and called out the answer. "Four hundred and twenty-seven mahls. So a little over seven oors travel time at sixty mahls per, minus maybe forty meens to load Specialists Holling, Penn, and Leggett, and their gear. It will also give us a chance to give a proper farewell to Nessie."

Olivienne nodded. "That sounds about right."

Velten moved the straight rule to show a direct route between Magna Tower, as they had taken to calling the first dirigible tower, and Montesilva. "We can stop for basics in Montesilva. It's roughly one thousand eight hundred and fifty mahls, which makes it about thirty oors out from Magna and well within our range for supplies without dumping or rationing. From there we can travel straight through to Tesseron, which is another twelve oors."

"And look," Gemeda traced the straight edge from the tower all the way to Montesilva. "This route takes us well south of Nusquam, and perhaps out of the rebels' detection."

Velten made a little mark on the map where the straight edge passed south of Nusquam, then measured the distance down. "Looks like just over a hundred mahls."

Castellan frowned. "If they're ranging out from the city like they did before, it may not be far enough to avoid detection. As much as I want to say let's divert farther out of our way, my intuition is telling me that we need to return to the capital as soon as possible."

Everyone looked at her with concern but Olivienne was the one who spoke up. "Any specific reason?"

The commander shook her head. "No. Besides the Queen's orders for a speedy return, the rest is a gut feeling only, I'm afraid."

"Well, we should probably follow it then, eh, Tosh? So, total it looks like the return trip from here to Tesseron will be about...fifty oors, minus a little over an oor for the research station and Montesilva stops. Factoring in the three oor time difference between here and Tesseron, we can arrive around zero six hundred, two daes after we leave." Velten moved the implements out of the way and the others grabbed their glasses so she could roll the map up again. "I'll inform my pilots of the new return course and stopping points in the morning. I'll also be sure we have all hands on deck when we get within a few hundred mahls of Endara so we can be ready for any attacks. And make no mistake about it," she paused to meet Castellan's eyes, "we *will* be ready. My crew is top notch and we take our sovereign duty seriously."

Castellan smiled and inclined her head. "I never thought any less, Captain. Now, if that is all the planning we need to do for the evening, perhaps we can pick up our cube game from last night."

"What's this, you were playing cubes with these poor souls? Tosh, you're a cad!"

Olivienne looked to her oath-mate in surprise. "Oh ho, so last night wasn't a *strange run of luck*, as you put it?"

Gemeda laughed. "She used to strip all her fellow officers out of cred at least once a month. Tosh's skill with numbers and prediction makes the game a little too easy, if you know what I mean. She would never cheat but the bright ones don't need to."

Velten looked from Gemeda to Castellan before grunting in annoyance. "Perhaps we should try a different game then, if you're all amenable."

Castellan smiled benignly. "Sure, if that's what you wish. I'll play whatever you like."

Olivienne rolled her eyes, suspecting her lover was good at any game involving maths, skill, or prediction. But her retort was for Castellan only. *"I'll hold you to that later, my love."*

Castellan gave her a wink. *"I'll look forward to it."*

Gemeda interrupted their moment with a shove to Tosh's shoulder. "Enough! Your gaze holds more weight than the tallest mount of Zha Dromain. If you're going to take my cred, I'd like to get it over with as soon as possible. Please and thank you."

The entire group laughed and the captain went to one of her storage cabinets to find a different form of entertainment for the evening.

THE SECOND DAE of exploration went very similar to the first. Around fifteen hundred oors, Olivienne, Castellan, Gemeda, and Savon at last reached the lowest level. Madlin had voteo'd earlier that the rest of the Shield team was currently scouring the Grand Chamber. She reported that it looked the same as both of the ones in the Temple of Archeos and Illeos. Olivienne grabbed Tosh's hand. "I think this will be it for the temple exploration. Honestly, I don't see any other reason to stay here longer, I've accomplished my mission."

Gemeda looked happy at the Connate's declaration. "Do you foresee us heading back in the morn, then?"

"Anxious to leave us so soon, Gem?"

"The company has certainly been top notch, but I'm not prone to roaming as you seem to be, Tosh. I enjoy the creature comforts of home a bit too much."

Olivienne gave her a sly smile. "You don't think a certain captain will convince you to travel more often?"

Gemeda winked. "Well...I wouldn't mind the occasional dae trip, but I'm no more inclined to long ports than she is so our dalliance has worked well as what it is. I will say that I'm contemplating asking Medi Corp for a long-term placement in Tesseron. Something is telling me that Queen and country will need me there in the coming daes and lunes."

"Oh? Given the political environment of late I don't doubt it. And I think having you transfer to Tesseron is simply aces! I'll be glad to see you on the regular, as will Olivienne, I'm sure."

The woman in question rolled her eyes at Castellan. "I can answer for myself you know." She turned to Gemeda and gave the doctore a squeeze on the forearm. "I am happy at the news as well. We will need to get together more often to discuss Castellan's past behaviors. I'm sure you have stories."

Gemeda winked. "Makers *do* I!"

Olivienne was conscious of her trailing lieutenant and with her newfound empathy toward the entire Shield team, she didn't want him to feel left out. "What about you, Savon? Any big plans for your future?"

Gentry Savon was used to overhearing the casual conversation of those above his rank. Part of what made him such an excellent Shield and officer was knowing when to stay silent and when to speak up. He never expected the Connate to include him but he had no qualms about speaking of his newest decision. But his silence wasn't merely born of being amongst his superior officers. He'd had heavy thoughts on his mind since they arrived at the second dirigible tower, not that he would admit as much to the Connate or commander. He would plot and plan as if his thoughts and dreams were nothing more than standard fears. "Sers, all this travel has made me more focused on my role here as Shield lieutenant."

Castellan gave him a curious look. "Yeah?"

"Yes, ser. As my schedule allows, I've decided to pursue

adventurist training to complete an additional sub-degree."

She leaned over and clapped Savon's back. "That's wonderful! I will be certain to make sure the team can accommodate your lessons, and I bet the sovereign herself can give you training on the side to help you accomplish your goals." She looked to Olivienne who gave them both a pleased smile.

"You may not remember, Savon, but before I got as busy as I am now, I sponsored a few adventurists in training for the Divinity Corp. I will personally sponsor you and give you private instruction. I love the initiative you're taking. Your dedication does more than improve your own standing, it also improves the team as a whole."

Castellan nodded and glanced at the blushing man. "She's right. This is the exact kind of thing I was hoping to instill when I put together this cross-function team. Thank you for leading by example."

He shrugged. "Thank you for giving me the opportunity, sers."

The group of four were in the last hallway of the lowest level. They had to take a separate lift to reach it, different than the one coming up from the tunnel. Savon pointed out that it looked more industrial, heavier duty, and speculated that the lowest level would be for storage of larger items. The passageway itself was wide and straight with doors lining the walls to each side and one massive door at the end. His suspicion was proven true when they started opening doors. Castellan and Olivienne took the rooms along the right side while Gemeda and Savon took the rooms on the left. Each team would enter, investigate, and record the contents and purpose of the room, then move on to the next. The very first rooms opened were full of the same storage cubes of non-perishable supplies that they'd found at the research station. The next was full of large machines that they had no clue as to the purpose.

The Connate and commander finished their rooms about the same time as Gemeda and Savon. Their destination was a little farther down the corridor and the four approached it together. Savon was nearest to the touch pad so Olivienne waved him on. "Go ahead, Savon. Open it up."

He touched his hand to the pad but it flashed red and a voice intoned from behind the panel. "Access denied." The door didn't open.

"Apparently it's locked, ser. I don't see any place for a key, and no buttons to push either."

"Tosh, can you lift it?"

Castellan focused her channel, nearly gave herself strain, but it still wouldn't budge. "No. Though I have no idea if the cause is actually because it's locked, or if its weight is beyond my capacity." Given the appearance and location of the door, Castellan suspected what the room held and her mind raced with the conflict she was sure would erupt between her and Olivienne. Senior Adventurist Olivienne Dracore was quick with a solution to the locked door.

Olivienne pulled the three temple keys that had been looped together and tied with a thong around her neck, then walked over and stood near the pad. She touched her palm and less than three secs later, it flashed green as a voice intoned from behind the panel. "Psionic resonance frequency of Archeos, Illeos, and Antaeus temple keys detected. Access granted."

Tosh tensed and stepped closer.

There was no sound of unlocking once the touch pad flashed green, but the size and weight of the door was easily discovered when it began to lift. It was two yords thick, as were the walls to either side of the entryway. As the Maker text from Instrucia stated, the chamber was truly impenetrable. When the door was all the way up, lights came on to illuminate the large room that was piled high with iridescent black stones. Castellan had approached the panel to stand next to Olivienne when she opened the door. The commander stared with dismay as her final moment of fealty had come.

Gemeda spoke with confusion coloring her voice. "I don't get it, what's with all the stones? They're not archeo or illeostones based on the color alone."

Olivienne turned her head back to give Castellan a wide smile. "Tosh, we found them!"

Castellan frowned, shaking her head slowly. "We have our orders. You know the door must be shut again."

"Oh, pox on your orders! We can't seriously be expected to leave such a find behind."

Castellan stepped around Olivienne so she was close enough to touch her hand to the panel. "We swore a Sovereign Oath. I must obey." She looked at Savon and Gemeda. "Please step back." Both complied immediately, sensing and not liking the tension brewing.

Olivienne made to step forward anyway and Castellan knew

she had to act. A few things happened in rapid succession. Commander Castellan Tosh slammed her palm over the touch pad and the door began to drop at the same speed it had been rising. Then she raised her left hand into the air and gave a quick pull of her telekinesis at the same time she used her channels to move both her and Olivienne back by Savon and Gemeda. Her last act was to pull out her pistol and shoot the touch pad, rendering it useless as the massive door dropped the rest of the way to the ground. She then holstered her pistol and faced the other three.

Everyone stood in shock at her actions, perhaps Olivienne most of all. She had clearly forgotten that one of her mother's directives was to retrieve samples and missed Castellan putting her hand out to catch them. Instead Olivienne made the assumption that with the door pad destroyed, it would be a long time before the room was opened again, if ever. With its metallic makeup, Castellan had proven that it was tons more than even she could lift with her increased channel strength. And while Olivienne could apport something inside, she was unable to bring anything out due to the fact that she couldn't see her target. She turned to look at Castellan in disbelief. "What have you done?"

Rather than look away from Olivienne's hurt and angry stare, Castellan met those violet eyes. "I've done my sovereign duty. Nothing more, nothing less."

"Your sovereign duty is to protect and aid me! What you've done is, is...a travesty!" Her temper was rapidly rising and all in the corridor knew it, if not by the look on her face then by the rising tempyrature around them. Olivienne took a step toward her oath-mate.

Castellan threw up her hands in frustration. "My sovereign duty is complex, only part of it is fulfilled by my role as your Shield commander. The other is to carry out orders given to *both of us* by the Queen. These are facts you already possess. You stood in front of the Queen when she gave us the orders. You swore a Sovereign Oath—"

"I swore nothing!"

The commander ran a hand through her hair, weighed down by duty in the moment. "*I* swore a Sovereign Oath then, and followed the Queen's orders for both of us."

She barely heard Gemeda's whisper from where the woman stood next to Lieutenant Savon. "Oh, Tosh."

Olivienne took another step forward. "You knew what this meant to me! And yet... you," she paused to swallow and look away. When she turned back a moment later her eyes were a lot harder. "How could you?"

Castellan's own passion had risen with Olivienne's hurt and accusation. "She is right about the stones and you know it, 'Vienne. The current mood in Psiere is no place to bring something of such power. There are factions, entire groups of people, actively seeking to disband the current governing body, seeking to *kill* every Dracore! I would never forgive myself if this discovery found its way into any of those rogues' hands and you were to die."

"How very good that you have followed your conscience in this, Tosh. But if forgiveness is what you seek, you certainly won't find it with me. Perhaps you can find it with the Queen, your oath-holder."

Castellan tried one last time. She held her hand out to her oath-mate, hoping to gain at least a little understanding. "'Vienne, please..." Olivienne remained stiff and unyielding, fury still etched upon her face.

"We're done here." She turned toward Savon. "Let's go."

He gave her a concerned look. "Connate?"

She waved angrily toward the door. "We were tentatively planning to leave in the morning anyway if we found nothing else of consequence here at the temple, which clearly is now the case. Contact the rest of the team and tell them to return with their findings back to the dirigible. And tell Captain Velten we can leave first thing on the morrow." She gave Castellan a hard look. "After all, the Queen instructed us to return as soon as possible after the temple rooms were documented and we must *always* obey the Queen." With one final furious look at Castellan, Olivienne spun in place and stalked down the corridor toward the lift. The heels of her boots beating a rapid rhythm against the hard floor of the corridor. "I'll be in my cabin if anyone needs me."

Savon looked from Castellan to Olivienne, clearly torn. Castellan gestured toward the angry woman's departing back. "Go with her, don't leave her alone in this place. Standard guard posting for the rest of the trip."

"But, ser, won't you be with her?"

Castellan clenched her jaw. "Did she look like she wants me with her right now, Savon?"

He didn't answer but opted to jog and catch up with his sovereign. That left Castellan and Gemeda in the silent passageway. Gemeda gave the stoic woman a moment to reflect then spoke softly. "You know me, Tosh. I'm neither calling your decision or orders into question, nor do I want to know what was in that room. But I ask, was that your only option, or your best one?"

Castellan sighed and closed her eyes. When she opened them again, they shimmered with unspent emotion. "Both. Queen Olivara demanded a Sovereign Oath from both of us in this task. What would you have done?"

Gemeda didn't bother to answer since she didn't have all the facts. Instead she soothed her friend. "She'll come around."

Castellan didn't want to talk about the rift that she'd opened between her and Olivienne, not even to her long-time friend. "Go on, Gem. I can see Savon from here, he's holding the lift for you."

Gemeda looked at her in concern. "And you?"

"I'll be along later. I've clearly got some thinking to do."

"All right. Be well, Castellan. I trust your judgement, always have. Perhaps you should too."

Castellan didn't answer. She watched Gemeda walk down the long corridor and enter the lift, then the doors closed and they disappeared from sight. Once the other three were gone, Castellan raised her left hand and opened the fingers of her fist. Two small stones sat in her palm. They looked beautiful but harmless. It was very similar to the glassy black natural mineral, obsidae, but with a wash of colors reflecting in the depths when she turned each in the light. Then she gripped them tightly and looked back at the door. With a flex of her telekinesis the massive barrier began to rise. Castellan let it drop quickly and turned to glance behind her at the empty corridor.

Strangely enough, the brief display of power only served to settle her emotions. It convinced her that what she'd done had been for the greater good, even if it ruined the trust she'd built with Olivienne. Olivienne's life, the whole of Psiere, they were certainly more important that the happiness of one Shield commander. Sadly the knowledge that she and Queen Olivara were right didn't make her circumstance hurt any less. All in all, she rather she had been shot again than have to make such a decision.

BY THE TIME Tosh arrived back at the dirigible, evening meal had passed. Lucky for her, she didn't have much of an appetite. She found her lieutenants outside on the staging deck, deep in discussion. They quickly pulled apart when she approached. Both gave her a smart salute. "Any issues coming back?"

Savon cut a side-glance at his fellow officer before answering. "No, ser. The Connate informed us that she didn't want to be disturbed. She declined evening meal as well."

Castellan sighed. "All to be expected, I'm afraid. Did you confirm our return with Captain Velten?"

"I did personally, ser. Begging pardon, but what happened down below todae? Are we in danger?"

The commander stared thoughtfully at her other lieutenant, Auda Madlin. She'd always been a little less tense than Savon. Perhaps that was what made her such a good balance for the dedicated man. She debated how much to tell them considering the level of security that the stones were under, per the Queen. She herself could be punished severely for disclosing sovereign secrets, but on the other hand, these were handpicked and verified personnel that were tasked with guarding Olivienne when she herself was unable. Tosh made a decision to trust her judgement. "Let's go find Captain Velten and clear up your confusion."

Fifteen meens later, Castellan, Velten, Savon, and Madlin were seated on the couches in the captain's room. The commander requested whatever spirit the captain had that was strongest. From that alone, Velten could guess what happened. Once seated, she dove in. "I heard Connate Dracore came back raging."

Savon sat forward and immediately defended his sovereign. "Begging your pardon, ser, but Connate Dracore most certainly wasn't raging!"

"At ease, Lieutenant. Think on it, when Olivienne is angry, does she not rage?"

"Yes, ser, but the Connate was silent all the way back from the temple."

Castellan smiled sadly. "There are different ways to rage. Olivienne herself has two. One is that which I think we are all familiar with by now. It involves volume, words, and oft times excessive use of expletives. But when she's hurt, Olivienne rages inside. She turns her anger to silence, and her expletives into disconnection."

Velten took a sip of her scotch. "I'm guessing that you found that which you feared most?"

Savon turned to his commander. "Ser?"

Castellan took a sip from her glass, shuddering at the burn of it as it flowed down her throat and coiled like fire in her belly. "Do you remember the first time we met, Savon?"

"Yes, ser. It was on the railer north from Ostium."

"Exactly. During that trip Olivienne and I translated a text from the Makers, the very text that sent us off on the quest for the temple keys and ultimately Antaeus itself. There was a part of that translated text that wasn't released to any but a handful of people. Psiere used to have a moon in the sky."

"What?" Madlin nearly spilled her drink in surprise and Velten cocked her head curiously, not getting that bit of information during their approach to the dirigible tower when they first reached Magna.

"It's true. The moon was called Antaeus. Just as our other two temples are named after celestial bodies, so too was the lost one. The actual text stated that: On the sixth dae of Septa in the roto one hundred and six of Psiere, a great astaeroid by the name of Torae struck Antaeus." She paused to remember the rest then continued as best as she was able. "Those pieces of the moon that hit the surface of Psiere intact are actually what we call archeostones. And as you all know, they charge the illeostone mineral. What you may not know is that our own bodies, and that of all living creatures on Psiere, contains the illeostone mineral."

Savon whispered. "The power of our channels?"

Castellan nodded and let that sink in for a meen before taking another sip of her drink and continuing. "Besides the archeostones, a number of rocks thought to be an amalgam of the astaeroid Torae, and the moon Antaeus were found. Those antoraestones hold the power of amplification, by a factor of ten. This means that anything running on illeostones could run for ten times longer. It also means that a Psierian in possession of the stone would have channels that were ten times stronger."

"Son of a sint! But that's..." Savon fell to silence while Madlin sat in serious contemplation.

Castellan held up a hand. "I'm well aware of both the benefits and adversities that such stones would have to our society. But know this, the Makers locked them away because nearly all Psierians were destroyed in a great war, fueled by poor leadership and the antoraestones. That was how the Dracore line came to be, if you remember our discussion at the research station. And that is why they hid and secured them in such a remote location, protected not just by the hidden temple keys but by a powerful telepath, Nessie."

Savon spoke slowly, with dawning realization. "It was Queen Olivara, wasn't it? She directed you and Connate Dracore to keep everyone from the stones. I gathered that much from down in the tunnel."

"Yes."

"And the Connate didn't want that?"

Castellan looked up at her two lieutenants. "The Connate was completely opposed to our orders."

"Sheddech. What a quandary, Commander."

The somber woman raised her nearly empty glass to salute a statement that perhaps didn't deserve such regard. "Isn't it though?"

Velten used her own fairly low rated telekinesis to fetch the bottle of liquor from her secured shelf, then brought it to float near Castellan's hand. The commander tried to wave it away. "I shouldn't—"

"Bollux. You've got good people below you and one night won't matter. We're perfectly safe on the *Quaesitum*. Sometimes a little sauce is good for the heart, Commander."

"You should listen to the captain, ser. Mads and I can handle both the team and Connate Dracore for the night. You can trust us."

Castellan looked from Madlin to Savon. "I do. I trust you both, which is why I shared classified information with you. And know this, no matter what happened here todae with my orders from the Queen, I will always do my best by you. I protect my people."

Gentry Savon stood, quickly followed by Auda Madlin. "We know that, ser. I think that's why I respect you so much." He looked at Madlin and came to a private mental agreement. "I think we're going to take our leave now. Thank you for your hospitality, Captain Velten."

The captain nodded. "No thanks are necessary, Lieutenant Savon. And never fear, I'll be sure your commander is taken care of."

They both saluted then made their way out back into the passageway. Velten turned back to Castellan. "What would you like to do now?"

Castellan took another sip and sent her thoughts out to the one person who she knew didn't want them. *"Would you like me to take duty outside our quarters tonight?"*

Olivienne's reply was fast but mentally firm. *"I need some time, Tosh."*

"Well enough. Call for me if you need me."

"Blasted woman, I'll always need you. But right now...I can't bear

to look at your face. I'm too angry, at you and my maman, and I'll say something unforgivable. I need time."

"*Fair enough. I'll beg a berth from the captain.*" Castellan didn't get an answer but found it promising at least that Olivienne was talking to her. She moved her gaze up to Velten's. "Looks like I need a berth for the night."

"Has she booted you then?"

"Not like that, but she's hurt, angry, and self-aware enough to know that having us in the same room will cause tempers to flare. I respect her decision."

"I don't have any open berths but if you lift the seat of the lounger, you'll find a coverlet. While it's not as good as a real bed, it's fairly comfortable for a night or two."

Castellan sighed and finished her second glass of liquor. "Thank you, Captain."

"Do you wish another?" Seema gestured toward the empty glass.

"No, thank you. No matter how safe we are, we're still far away from home and I remain ultimately charged with Olivienne's safety. I've no wish to be impaired under such circumstances."

"I respect your dedication." Velten stood. "If that will be all, I think I'm going to retire to my own cabin for the evening. I have something to look over."

Castellan smiled, though it wasn't as bright as normal. "Tell Gem I said hello."

Velten returned her smile but didn't answer. Instead, she put her glass up in a secured bin to be collected by a porter in the morning. Castellan floated hers over to the same bin when the door shut behind the captain. Then she pulled out the two black stones from a secured pocket on the thigh of her trousers. The strong liquor made her question everything yet again, wondering if her decision was worth it. Then she remembered the heavy door and put the stones away. Looking back never did anyone good. She resolved to only look forward in the morning.

Chapter Twenty-one

THE NEXT DAE found Castellan no worse for wear, at least not physically. She did a brief bit of exercise in the open space of the captain's room before putting herself together in the facility and heading out to her own cabin. On her way there, she mentally called for her lieutenants. An answer came right away.

"Madlin here."

"When are we scheduled to leave and is the Connate still in our cabin?"

"Captain Velten has us departing in about...forty meens. She said she wants to leave with the second sun's rise in case the island has large flyers that come this far north. Connate Dracore is currently at first meal with Doctore Shen."

"Thank you. I'll be returning to our quarters to change then I'm heading to the bridge. I'm assuming Savon is off shift right now?"

"Yes, ser. He opted for nights until we near the mainland. We plan to switch up to shorter shifts for everyone when we get closer to Endara, like what we did when we neared Magna. That way all the Shields will be fresh in case we see enemy engagement."

"Very well, Madlin. I'll find you both later." Castellan opened the door to their berth to see a neatly made bunk. Everything was in order, but then she knew it would be. Olivienne only got messy when she was deep in the planning and implementation of a mission, or when she was outwardly raging as they had discussed the evening before. But when she was hurt...Castellan knew that was when Olivienne pulled into herself physically and emotionally.

Thirty meens later, Castellan was clean and hungry and headed resolutely into the ship's mess hall. She discretely verified that Olivienne had left before entering to give her lover the space and respect that had been requested the evening before. Once the commander finished eating, she made her way to the bridge. Madlin saluted when she came through the portal. "Ser, we're about five oors out from the research station. I've got Lazaro on standby to start sending messages on the long-range once we get a few oors out. He'll send them every fifteen meens until someone picks up. That way they'll have some prep time to get their gear together, as well as anything else they feel needs to come with us."

Castellan smiled at all Madlin had completed while she and Savon slept. "Well done, Lieutenant." She paused and tilted her head to take in the auburn-haired woman. "You know, I've never shied away from telling Savon how much I appreciate his capability and competence. I believe I owe you the same praise. I'm very pleased you agreed to join this team. I think you make a fine addition."

Lieutenant Auda Madlin wasn't prone to embarrassed blushes the way Savon was. Instead, she fairly glowed with her commander's praise. She stood a little straighter and her dark eyes took on a familiar glint of pleasure. "Thank you, ser. I've said it before but I'll say it again. This is the best post I've ever had and I can't wait to see where adventure takes us next."

Castellan laughed and clapped her on the shoulder. "Let's hope that it doesn't take us back to any siren caves, yeah?"

"No, ser."

During the oors the ship traveled to the research station, Castellan kept herself busy speaking with all on-duty specialists. She liked to have one-on-one time with the men and women on her team. It helped her understand their deeper motivations and needs, which in turn helped her to lead them better.

Gemeda had to leave halfway through first meal because one of the captain's crew cut himself on a storage bin that had been damaged in the rebel attack at Nusquam. Rather than wait to see if Gemeda returned to the mess hall, Olivienne went back to her cabin after eating. She saw right away that Castellan returned as well, if only briefly. Her commander was always tidy so her presence wasn't given away by a mess of any kind, but Olivienne found the previous dae's uniform folded carefully on Castellan's duffle.

Just knowing of the rift between them brought tears to her eyes. Olivienne crossed the cabin to grab the neatly folded shirt and pulled it to her face. It smelled vaguely like liquor and something that was undeniably Castellan. She returned the slightly wrinkled shirt back to the stack and dashed the tears from her still-swollen eyes. Olivienne was perfectly content to mull and brood over all that she'd discovered and lost in a short span of time. Her anger wasn't just about the issue of the stones themselves. It was equally about the fact that the woman she'd oathed to had acted alone with no regard or discussion on the matter. How could they be a team if one acted as such? Olivienne felt herself grow angry again, but before she could begin raging, her thoughts were interrupted by a knock at the door.

"Yes?"

The muffled voice of Gemeda came through the other side. "Connate Dracore, I apologize for leaving our meal early. May I come in?"

She thought for a few secs, then crossed the small room and opened the door. "I assure you, no apology is necessary. And you may as well, it's not as if I'm planning to do anything productive at the moment."

Gemeda and both specialists posted at the door politely ignored Olivienne's red-rimmed eyes. The doctore looked around. "No stacks of velum to translate?"

Olivienne gave a broken laugh. "No, I'm not currently in the mood. Is there something you needed, Gem? I'm afraid I won't be the best company right now."

"Let's sit and talk for a spell. Do you mind?" She gestured toward one of the sitting chairs in the room.

"No, go ahead." She followed Gemeda to the seats and took one herself. "What would you like to talk about? If you're here to defend her—"

"I'm here to do naught but talk. Do you remember that awful dae on the bridge near Vesper?"

"You mean when we were pulled up like half-drowned swimmers?"

Gemeda pursed her lips. "Or in Castellan's case, full-drowned."

Olivienne frowned at the memory of jumping in the Mir Altaq to save the woman who had both frustrated and intrigued her early on in their acquaintance. "I remember."

"I told you then that Castellan was a soldier's soldier, through and through. She has always been...regimented. You could no more take duty from Castellan than you can pull her from duty. Truthfully, I don't know if Castellan even knows who she'd be without the Corp. Her identity is tied up completely in her career. That's how Castellan is within her own head."

"I think I've always known that. It's not like she pretends to be something or someone she's not."

Gem smiled. "No, it's true. Castellan is exactly what you see at first meeting. I'm not going to drag this out or circle around what I came here to say. I think Castellan is struggling right now with her posting and her relationship to you."

Olivienne leaned back, her dark brows furrowed with dismay. "Me? Are you saying she doesn't want to consor?"

"Don't be daft. I've known that psera a long time and I can see plainly that she's never wanted anything more. As you should well know by now, Castellan doesn't do anything halfway. When she devotes herself to something, be it Corp or love, she goes all in. Castellan struggles because she is trying to balance those two things in her life. It's not a problem until the two collide and pull her in separate directions. That is what happened with whatever business you two had in that room below the temple."

Gemeda paused for a meen to take in Olivienne's wide violet eyes. She could certainly see the beauty that had ensnared Castellan so fully upon their first meeting. "Put yourself into her boots for just a sec. How would you choose if your Queen gave you an order and you knew it was diametrically opposed to Castellan's wishes?" She paused, then added, "*And* if the Queen wasn't your own maman."

Silence between them grew, lifted and held up by the muffled drone of the airship engines that was ever-present. Olivienne let out a long sigh and leaned back again in her chair. "I would be hard-pressed to find my way. But that doesn't excuse her from treating me as she did. There was no discussion, merely action with very permanent consequences. She held her own counsel on this and I thought we told each other everything. As a matter of fact, we agreed long ago that there would be no secrets, and in return I'd give her full compliance when it came to her duty as my Shield commander."

"Did the Queen not give you both orders?"

Olivienne was ready to give a hot retort but paused as she realized what Gemeda was saying. "She did."

Gemeda gave her a kind smile. "It sounds like she's not the one who veered from the plan then."

"But still..." She slapped her palm against the arm of the lounger. "Sheddech, but I hate being taken by surprise as I was! I feel so uncertain right now and off balance."

"That's what happens when one of your legs has been kicked under. But you don't have to remain that way. You know what you have to do."

The sovereign sighed again, feeling the weight of her station pressing down on her. "I need to speak with her."

Gemeda reached over and gave Olivienne's hand a squeeze. "No. First you need to listen. Castellan was never a woman of many words, and she won't speak at all if no one is listening. Get her side and explain how it makes you feel. No matter where you two go, or where you've been together, communication is key. Savvy?"

Olivienne gave her a curious look. "You know...you're pretty wise about matters between two hearts."

Gem touched the side of her nose. "You don't have to want to do something to have knowledge of the doing. Just because I've no interest in settling down doesn't mean I don't have the basic skills to turn someone's head to oathing. Not to mention, part of my advice is born solely from knowing Castellan for many rotos. She's stubborn as anything and difficult to understand sometimes, but a person couldn't ask for a better friend or ally to have, all things considered."

"One could say the same about you, Doctore Shen."

"One could." Gemeda gave her a sly smile. "Or you could simply put in a good word for me in Tesseron. Sometimes Medi Corp gets a bit stodgy when it comes to allowing transfers. Especially for someone in high demand like I seem to be."

Olivienne pointed at her. "Lucky for you, I happen to know that the capital is currently without a regional doctore in possession of the telesana channel. I'm sure they'd have no problems moving you into the open role...especially if you have a recommendation from a sovereign of Psiere."

"Ah, it pays good cred to have high friends destined for hard seats."

Olivienne laughed. "For what it's worth, I'll gladly give my word for you. I'd rather like it if I had another friend close by to speak with on occasion."

Gemeda smiled and patted her arm. "I'd like that too." They conversed for a little while longer until Gemeda returned to her own cabin. She had left Olivienne with much to think about. While she wasn't quite ready to speak with Castellan, she knew that time was fast approaching. Olivienne thought it best to have the conversation before they neared danger at the edge of Endara.

OORS LATER, THE *Quaesitum* was moored safely near the research station. In total, the team that volunteered to remain with Nessie during the Antaeus exploration had chosen three cases of documents and one case with various devices, ration samples, and other implements to bring back to Tesseron. Olivienne inspected all the items and agreed with the small team's assessment of each.

Once they were loaded, Castellan and Olivienne walked out to the water to say goodbye to Nessie. The creature swam near enough to lean her long neck over the rail of the viewing deck. *"I wish to thank you for leaving people here for me to converse with. It has been an enjoyable few days."*

Things were still clearly awkward between Castellan and Olivienne. They showed none of the casual comfort in each other's presence that was normally displayed. As if to highlight the emotional rift between them, they stood nearly two yords apart while saying their goodbyes. Despite the emotional upheaval of the previous dae, Olivienne wasn't afraid to call the large beast to task. "While I'm happy that you've had some time to speak with the Shields on my team, I'm less pleased that you tricked us with your reference to the Key of Nessie."

Nessie dipped her head down to give Olivienne a light nudge to the shoulder. *"I meant no harm. It was one part test and two parts humor. I meant it to be a light-hearted jest yet,"* she tilted her head left and right to study the sovereign, *"you don't at all seem light of heart."*

Olivienne glanced off to the side where Castellan stood stoically beneath the light of the two suns. "No, I'm not." She didn't bother using her telepathy to speak. The spoken words weren't anything the great beast couldn't understand, nor were they anything Castellan didn't already know. However, when she considered the next bit of information, she felt it necessary to switch to a silent method of speech to prevent anyone on the ship from overhearing. *"And in case you were worried, the antoraestones were sealed away, perhaps permanently."*

"All is as it should be, I suppose. There is a saying by the people from the time and place I left behind. It is that burnt bairns dread the fire."

Olivienne frowned. *"I don't understand. What is a bearn?"*

"Just a word that means nothing to you here. But the essence of the saying is that when a person has been burned once, they'll worry twice the next time they see flame. Your commander worries most about security and your reaction to the orders you were both given. I can see in your mind that you've often disagreed with your mother over policy or prudence."

"I have, but still — "

"Human, trust Nessie in this. Communication is a salve that helps heal the wound, but silence will only cause it to fester. And in case you

wondered...she cannot hear us right now. I've made our conversation private."

Olivienne gave a weary sigh. *"Thank you. And I promise to let the Queen know upon our return that we need to post someone to Magna, this research station specifically. I think it would be of great benefit to our people."*

Nessie gave a dip of her head and spoke into both Olivienne and Castellan's minds. *"I pledge to take care of them and teach all that I'm allowed."*

Olivienne gave a respectful bow and switched back to verbal speech. "Fair enough. Now as much as I regret leaving you behind, we must go. Things will be dangerous for us upon our return and I know my maman will worry until I set foot in Tesseron whole and hale."

"Tha e na nàdar màthair a bhith draghail airson a pàisde."

"I'm sorry, but I don't understand that."

"It means she will worry, it is her place to do so."

Olivienne didn't respond, instead she gave Castellan one last look, then spun on her heel and headed for where the dirigible had winched down to the ground for ease of loading the cargo. That left Castellan to turn and face Nessie. The creature gave her a penetrating stare as those strange vertical membranes closed occasionally over her eyes. Castellan was to the point as always. *"I know you're aware of more than you let on. I'd wager there is no telepath in all of Psiere that is as powerful as you. Do you have something to say to me?"*

"You are not incorrect with your assessment, Commander. As for advice, you already have the information you need."

"You gave us the key to the temple, which means you must have deemed Psierians worthy and responsible enough to handle the antoraestones. Did I err in my decision, and in doing so risk the wrath of my future par and Queen?"

Nessie exhaled a stream of damp air. *"The wrath of one Queen is much like the wrath of the next. Either could find you in the gaol."*

Castellan huffed at Nessie's non-answer. *"You're words are slippery."*

"To answer your question, I didn't give you the key because I judged Psierians 'worthy and responsible,' as you say."

Castellan's brows drew down in confusion. *"I don't understand."*

Nessie lowered her neck so her head was less than a yord in front of Castellan's. It was then that the commander realized the full size of the greater beast of Magna. She would have been hard-pressed to wrap her arms all the way around Nessie's neck and the head was larger yet. Castellan found herself mesmerized as the sole focus of such a strange and intent stare. *"Commander Castellan Tosh, I judged you worthy and you alone. Especially now in the aftermath of your decision."* She backed away as realization broke across Castellan's features. *"The power of honesty is worth ten times that of a lie, though a lie is heavier beyond measure. Your heart is honest, Commander. I trust you to know what is right and just in the world."*

"I..." Castellan's thought trailed off, suffering a strange loss of words. She blew out a breath and tried again. *"Thank you. I needed to hear that."*

"Good luck, Commander." Castellan saluted the magnificent creature and made to turn away but was stopped by another message in her head. *"Castellan Tosh."*

She looked at Nessie over her shoulder. *"Yes?"*

"Use those stones wisely."

Castellan's eyes widened at the fact that Nessie had picked up the deeper truth within her mind, even past her formidable shields that the Queen herself had complimented on one occasion. Castellan nodded and continued back to the ship. She knew she had to speak with Olivienne, but she also didn't want to approach the woman before she was ready. Olivienne had proven volatile in the past when they'd disagreed.

Sadly, even if they worked out Olivienne's displeasure on the way to Tesseron, Castellan knew it would surely return once she stood in front of the Queen again.

VELTEN WAS GENEROUS enough to allow Castellan and Olivienne the use of the captain's room to debrief the three specialists. Spc. Holling gave the most pertinent details of all the things that Nessie was willing to share with him, about herself and the Makers. He recorded everything in a book of velum that he handed to Olivienne. When he was finished with his debrief, he added one last bit of personal observation. "Ser, I sincerely hope I get the opportunity to speak with Nessie again. She was one of the most interesting and complex entities I've ever had the pleasure of meeting. It gives me greater insight to the rest of life here on Psiere."

That was a request that Castellan really had no comment for,

since their team was at the wills and whims of Olivienne's schedule. But Olivienne herself didn't shy away from responding. "I
will admit that I feel the same way about Magna. And if it is
within my power and ability, I too would like to return. So maybe
you'll get your wish, hmm?"

"Yes, ser." He grinned and accepted her answer for the promising response that it was.

Leggett told them that the panel in the sub-level containing
the ship was beyond her understanding, as was the propulsion
system of the vessel. "Ser, I couldn't even begin to tell you how
far the craft would go, let alone what fueled it. What I wouldn't
give to have a full set of tools to take that shell-cracker apart..."
Leggett trailed off, her head still stuck within the Maker's
machine mechanics. Even without understanding of the big
equipment, she was able to find a number of devices and small
machines within the research station to make her stay worth-
while. Some things Leggett put in the container to bring back to
Tesseron, while others she did her best to take stills or make engineering sketches for any who were interested in the Engineering
and Academic Corps.

Castellan leaned forward in her chair until she could clap the
specialist on the shoulder. "What you've found is top notch and I
bet those over at Engineering Corp would sell their last stone for
a chance to read over the schematic drawings you made. You've
done more than enough."

Spc. Penn opened the satchel she had slung across her chest
and pulled out a sealed sheath of vellum. She then held the
sheath out to Olivienne from where she was seated on the
lounger. "Connate, these were locked away in what we think was
a metallic desk. Not finding a key, Leggett was able to use her ferrokinesis to get it open. We found them right before Lazaro sent
word you were on the way, so I didn't have time to open the
packet, let alone translate the velums within. I speculated that
they could be of importance based on the secured location."

Olivienne took the sealed sheath and rested it on her thigh
then gave Specialist Ciera Penn a grateful smile. "Thank you, this
sort of thing is exactly the stuff adventurists look for. I've found
over the rotos that the stuff left lying around is usually of little
importance. But those items and texts that were hidden, locked
away, or trapped are frequently more valuable than a railer of
illeostones."

It didn't take long to finish the debriefing. Castellan stood from her chair and was quickly followed by the three Shield guardians. "Report to whichever lieutenant is currently on duty. I know they were due for a shift change soon. They'll have special instructions and duty rosters for the lot of you. Double check your gear and weapons as we'll most likely be facing enemy airships when we approach the mainland. Be ready, savvy? Your sovereign's life depends on it."

The three specialists saluted her and Connate Dracore as one. "Yes, ser."

"Good." Castellan waved a hand through the air. "Dismissed."

Castellan watched as each filed out while Olivienne stood off to the side, strangely quiet. The commander, seeing that her duty was done, and not wishing to subject Olivienne to her presence longer than necessary, took a step toward the door to go back to the bridge. She abruptly stopped as three words hit her ears.

"Don't leave, please."

As always, Castellan's first thought was about her duty. "What's wrong? Did they say anything that would cause concern during the debriefing?"

Olivienne took slow, measured steps toward her love. "This has nothing to do with the team at the research station. This has to do with us. I desperately need to speak with you, to shine a light upon a few details."

Leary but still open, Castellan returned to her previous seat, as did Olivienne. "Okay."

A meen later both women sat stiffly in their seats gazing at one another. Finally, Olivienne broke the silence. "I'm still angry and I think I will be for a good long time."

"Olivienne, I—"

"Please, Castellan, let me say what I need to say."

The commander gave a slight nod. "Go ahead."

"I haven't changed my mind about the good of the stones. It is a topic that we remain diametrically opposed. But I'm aware enough to understand your side of the argument. Yes, locking them away made me angry—"

"As I assumed it would."

Olivienne held up a hand and continued. "But not nearly as angry as learning that you hold my mother above me within your heart and actions. It made me furious."

Castellan leaned forward and rested her elbows on her knees. She scrubbed both hands through her neat hair, sending it in disarray. "I'll admit that I knew you would be angry, acting in the moment as I did. Justifiably so. Your mother also knew you'd be angry as well, but she knows my dedication to duty better than anyone else after our trust reading in the meeting room. Even as early as last roto, long before that meeting, she suspected that you'd try to talk me out of performing as directed. But that is neither here nor there."

"Why do you say that?"

"'Vienne...she's not your maman to me. Neither is she my future mamanar, at least not in this instance. She's my Queen. She rules my home, the people, the land, and me and you. I don't hold your maman above you, I hold the Queen above all."

Olivienne frowned. "I still hate it. I'd like to think that I hold you above others, regardless of rank or orders."

Castellan shook her head and sighed. "I suspect that is only one of the reasons you serve in the Divinity Corp and not Defense."

The Connate finally cracked a smile. "Mayhaps." She paused for a sec then her expression abruptly changed. "Wait, maman gave us two directives. One was to seal away the stones, the other was to gather two samples. Unfortunately for her, your quick action on the first prevented us from following through with the second."

"Actually..."

Olivienne narrowed her eyes. "Actually what?"

Castellan unfastened her sealed trouser pocket and pulled out the two stones. She held one out to Olivienne between her thumb and forefinger. "You didn't really believe I'd fail on either duty, do you? What kind of soldier do you think I am?"

"Wait, you *did* retrieve samples? But that means..."

Castellan sighed and rubbed her eyes with the thumb and middle finger of her right hand. "Yes, once I pulled those two stones in my hand I could and did easily lift the door. Though I'm not sure anyone below a six-rated telekinesis channel could. Even so, that would defeat the purpose of locking the stones away."

Olivienne took the stone that was held out and inspected it carefully. "It's hard to believe this shiny bit of bauble is capable of so much."

"Try it and find out. You're teleportation rating is what, a two?" Olivienne nodded. "And have you ever used it, could you use it?"

Olivienne grimaced. "Not with a capacity of just under

twenty punds. But sure, I know the theory of teleportation and everyone has told me it's nearly an identical feeling to that of apportation, just a harder pull."

Castellan gestured to the open area near the captain's table. "Do it now then, from here to there. The stone magnifies ten times your power. It should be nothing to move yourself."

"Fine." Olivienne's brows drew down in concentration, then sudden as can be, she disappeared from her seat and reappeared in the same position near the table. Given her previously seated position, she promptly fell onto her rear with nothing beneath her. "Oh, bollux! I forgot about that little detail. You can't change position during teleport."

"But you still did it."

Olivienne's mouth dropped open as she was dusting off her trousers. "Son of a sint, I did!"

After Olivienne returned to her seat on the couch, Castellan continued. "Rationally, what would you have me do, save follow the Queen's orders?"

The cushion of the lounger gave a muffled *thump* as Olivienne slapped it in a stubborn reutterance of her previous statement. "As your future par, I should be first in your heart."

"'Vienne, you will forever be first in my heart. But the safety of all must be first in my head, as is the reigning sovereign of Psiere."

Olivienne grumbled but her protest was losing steam in the face of Tosh's logic. "I'm a sovereign."

Castellan pleaded for understanding with her eyes as much as with her posture, and leaned over with her hand held out in entreaty. "If you were Queen, it would be your orders I'd fulfill, even if I thought them unwise as you seem to feel about your maman's decision. But the Queen outranks you."

Olivienne rubbed her own eyes, hating the way the conversation had once again brought her tears to the forefront. "Oh, Tosh. You know...one of the things I've always loved about you, admired, was the fact that you are such a noble and honest soldier. Brave, brilliant, and dependable to carry out any orders no matter how difficult. But..."

"But?"

"But those traits I admire are also the ones that frustrate me the most at times."

Castellan leaned forward and placed a hand on Olivienne's knee. "It may mean nothing to you, but I believe that the Queen's primary motivation in locking the stones away wasn't out of fear for herself or even the rest of Psiere. Her main reason was out of fear for you. She knows that you are in as much danger from the rebels as she is. I think we both know that she doesn't always do things the way we expect or even want her to. Your maman knows you well but she doesn't know you or I as well as she'd like."

Castellan stood and took a step closer to where Olivienne sat on the lounger, then she dropped to a knee. "I am deeply sorry for the upset that I've caused you. We both know I had to do as directed, but I could have gone about it a different way. We should have paused there in the temple, perhaps sent the other two topside so we could have a private discussion about the stones. I was just..." She swallowed and looked away.

"You were just what?"

Castellan brought her eyes up to meet Olivienne's, taking in the redness that she'd caused. "Yes, orders were orders, but I was afraid to disappoint you by going against your wishes. This was your mission, the culmination of your life's work. I may believe in the necessity to hide away the antoraestones and in my duty to the Queen, but that doesn't mean that I don't feel a temple's worth of guilt for stealing that bit of your discovery."

"Oh, my darling, Tosh." Olivienne reached out to run her fingers through Castellan's pale hair, straightening the strands as best as she could. "If we are to succeed together, if we are to place our hearts into one another's hands, then we must be open, communicative, and not be afraid to tell the hard truths. You promised me no secrets and in return I gave you my cooperation in all things related to my security. I understand that you had to follow orders and believe me, there is a part of me that hates my maman for putting us in this position. But I'm also upset with you because I want to be the one that you are ultimately loyal to, not my maman. It's irrational, I know, because when I'm Queen I would expect ultimate loyalty myself."

"Anger isn't rational and you are entitled to the way you feel. I would never say otherwise."

"Where do we go from here?"

Castellan searched Olivienne's face for some clue as to what she should do. She was caught between temple and stone, with no good way to proceed. "Do you...um, would you like to keep hold of the stones?"

As future ruler of Psiere, a role Olivienne was genetically

bred to, she was wise enough to know who was the strongest between them. Not to mention, even she was tempted by the power of the antoraestones. But Tosh...Tosh was as pure of heart and steadfast in her loyalties as anyone she'd ever known. "No. Returning the stones to Tesseron was a task my mother gave to you personally and in this instance, I agree with her wholeheartedly."

Castellan thought for a sec. "I'd offer to split them between us but I think we'll have more of a guarantee of getting them to Tesseron safely and secretly if they're kept together. And remember," she met Olivienne's violet gaze, "while Velten, Savon, and Madlin all know there were stones of power found below the Temple of Antaeus, none are aware that I possess samples. Under no circumstances are we allowed to divulge the existence of these stones."

"Again, I'm well aware of what my mother's orders were on this subject. And as much as it pains me to say it, I agree to stay silent and let you hold them." Olivienne gave her stone back to Tosh, who sealed them away once again in her trouser pocket.

Tosh moved to sit on the lounger next to Olivienne, then cradled Olivienne's right hand between her own palms. "If the rebels found out that something like this existed, they'd never stop trying to retrieve them. Worse yet, they'd make a concerted effort to reach the Temple of Antaeus and I fear they would not be as considerate of the life they found there."

"Darling, you don't have to convince me. I know that it makes logical sense. As much as I would love to take one of those stones and play with a channel I've never gotten to explore, as future Queen I also know how important security is, especially in times like these. I concede to maman's wishes in this as well, but expect the three of us to sit down and have a discussion in the near future. I'm getting very tired of my mother's machinations when it comes to my life and future." Castellan huffed, a familiar sound of agreement to Olivienne.

"As am I." The honest soldier sighed, recognizing that Olivienne had softened on the subject for the time being. Castellan had come to the understanding that she herself was both right and wrong in the situation. "While I wouldn't change any part of me following my duty and orders, I would go back and be more open with you about my intentions ahead of time if I could."

"But you can't. And even if you could, you'd be torn in two, opposite what you are now."

"No, I cannot. But at least with the other way, you wouldn't be so hurt."

Olivienne brought her free hand up so all four of their hands were clasped together. "I'm not going to lie or placate you by saying this ill wind will blow out by tomorrow. Though I can try, I will always wonder what other decisions you'll keep your own counsel on where your duty is concerned."

"I assure you, these are the only ones! I had a feeling that I'd be forced to step in and perform our sovereign duty for both of us and I was afraid that if given the chance to speak, I'd be swayed by my love for you. That was why I acted as fast as I did. Other than this one mission, I've been open and honest with you about my duty."

"Tosh," Olivienne chastised. "You've always tried to shield me from some of the harsher realities involved with protecting my sovereign self. Have you already forgotten the hauler incident the dae I met your maman?"

"Uh..."

Olivienne leaned forward and kissed Castellan. "Very eloquent, darling." She kissed her again and practically fell into the embrace when Castellan brought her arms up and tightened them around her shoulders. "Can we agree to work on this aspect going forward? You need to find a better balance between protecting me and loving me or we'll all go mad."

The strong soldier loathed admitting weakness of any kind. But the dae wasn't one for stoicism and solitude, it was a dae for concession and forgiveness. "I'll need your help."

"You'll have it."

They kissed, deeper than the previous time. It was a reconnection of sorts, with both women desperately seeking reassurance that they held the other first and foremost in their hearts. When Olivienne finally pulled back for air, she let out a breath that rustled Castellan's fringe of hair that she had been straightening earlier. "Can we go back to our cabin now? I've missed you something fierce."

"My love, it's only been a dae."

Olivienne clutched at the back of Castellan's uniform shirt. "One dae without your regard feels like an eternity. I dislike quarreling with you immensely."

"And I, you." She stepped back from Olivienne's embrace, then held an elbow out to loop through Olivienne's. "Come along, we've got..." Castellan pulled the timepiece from her trouser pocket with her free hand. "Looks like a little over an oor before we're expected to arrive at the first dirigible tower and people start looking for us. Perhaps even longer as I don't think the captain plans to stop there. I believe she'll continue straight on toward Endara."

Olivienne took Castellan's arm and smiled. "See? This is the kind of honesty I love to receive."

In another quick moment of seriousness, Castellan gazed at her with shimmering pale blue eyes. "I will do my best to be better when it comes to balance and communication. Officers in Defense weren't taught to share the reasoning behind every decision, but I'm in a different sort of Corp now and need to adjust my method of managing the orders given to me."

She got a blinding smile and a gentle squeeze to the hand for her comment. Olivienne met her gaze solidly. "I plan to do the same. Now, we should probably grab what little free time is available. We'll be busy enough once we get closer to the mainland."

Castellan snorted. "Your lips to the Maker's ears...er, or whatever it is they have."

They walked out of the Captain's room lighter of heart and with no small amount of laughter.

Chapter Twenty-two

OLIVIENNE AND CASTELLAN were in their room naught more than forty meens when the dirigible gave a great shudder and rocked back and forth. "What the Makers was that?" Castellan's eyes were wide and Olivienne dashed from the bed to their portal, opening it to get a better view.

"Ah, looks like we're in for a big storm. We've got to be near the first tower by now, I'd wager the captain will choose to moor there until the worst of this blows out."

The dirigible rocked again and dropped suddenly as they were buffeted from above. "Sheddech!"

Olivienne couldn't keep from smiling as she watched her lover's reaction. It was such a strange thing to see Castellan fearful of anything. She found it endearing and oddly enough, it instilled a protectiveness that she rarely felt for the strong soldier. Before she could attempt to soothe her, pounding sounded against their cabin door. Then a voice came through, pitched loud enough to be heard over the sound of wind, rain, and thunder.

"Commander Tosh, Connate Dracore, the captain says to inform you that we'll ride out the storm at Magna Tower. We're to continue on our way once the worst of it blows over. She also advises that all non-active personnel should remain in their cabin for safety's sake while the winds are so unpredictable."

Tosh stood from the bunk wearing a hastily wrapped coverlet and called back. "Thank you, Qent. We'll remain as directed until informed otherwise."

"Yes, ser."

Castellan verified that the specialist had left the immediate vicinity of the door then turned back toward the bunk, pulling the coverlet higher.

It was more than the Connate sported, which was naught but a mischievous smile. "It appears as though we have some uninterrupted time on our hands and we've been confined to the cabin by the captain, herself. Whatever shall we do to while away the oors?"

"I'm certain you've already got our time filled."

Olivienne winked. "If you're lucky it will be more than

time." Castellan's blush ran from her neck all the way up to her hairline.

All in all, the two dallied for oors while the wind and rain raged around them. Their activities distracted the storm-leery commander from fretting too much. They were safe enough from the lightening since Captain Velten had initially pointed out a catcher rod on the tip of the tower. She said lightening would strike that and go safely to the ground, or wherever the Makers meant it to go. If anyone knew about such things, it would be a woman that made her life in the sky.

Because of the delay, they didn't approach the coastline of Endara until nearly zero six thirty oors local time, which meant the rising suns were at their back. Everyone aboard the dirigible was up and ready for possible engagement. Castellan, Olivienne, Velten, and Gemeda were all standing on the bridge waiting to see what, if any, enemies would find them. Lt. Savon, Lt. Madlin, and First Officer Vex were stationed around the ship, ready to dole out orders at a moment's notice.

Velten peered into the distance with her spyglass then turned to her steersman on bridge duty. "Sidditch, anything on the son-ica?"

"There!" Steersman Sidditch pointed to the edge of the screen where three dots had appeared, on a trajectory that would inter-cept their own. The man grabbed a straight rule and held it up to the screen to confirm the group's path. "Looks like they're on track to intercept us shortly after we reach land."

Castellan moved to stand by the captain. "How far out does this machine detect other ships? And can we evade them?"

"Same as stationary points, about fifty mahls or so but between our two speeds, they're only about twenty meens from us at our current heading. We can turn farther south and see if our greater speed will take us around them —"

"Ser, two more!"

Sure enough, the lower left edge of the screen showed two more dots moving slightly faster than the three to the far right. "What's this...are they matching us for speed?"

The captain peered closer yet. "By the Makers, they are! How is this possible?" She gave Castellan an incredulous look. "The Queen assured me that we'd have the fastest ship available, that none other would be built with this new technology."

"Tosh, aren't the dirigibles produced in Soflin? That's on the southern continent."

Captain Velten moved her gaze to Olivienne. "What does that have to do with all the shells in the sea?"

Castellan gave the screen a worried glance. They were wasting time trying to find the whys of their situation, rather than come up with a plan. "In short, the Queen suspects a corrupt element emanating from Dromea. *If* that corrupt element has taken control of Soflin and their shipyard, then we are all in trouble in the coming lunes."

"Ser, what are your orders?"

The captain spared the steersman a glance then slammed her palm over the com switch nearby. "Prepare for battle stations. Enemy ships approaching from the north and south, ready rail guns on both sides. All non-combat personnel are to report to the mess hall at the center of the ship."

Castellan sent a mental missive to her entire team, as if the captain's orders hadn't given enough of a warning. *"Lieutenant Savon, take your half of the team north side of the dirigible, Madlin and hers take the south."*

Nearly identical responses came back. *"Yes, ser!"*

They watched the sonica for the next fifteen meens until the first dirigibles came into sight in the distance, growing larger as they rapidly approached. Castellan turned to Olivienne and Gemeda. "You two need to head to the mess, as the captain directed."

"Absolutely not!"

"They'll need my telesana in the coming fight."

Frustrated, Tosh's voice was a near shout. "This isn't up for debate!"

"Tosh is right, you," Velten pointed at Olivienne, "are our number one priority. Our sole purpose is to protect you and it will all be for naught if you hang your sovereign carcass over the staging rail shooting that pistol of yours."

"Sovereign carcass—" Olivienne's voice rose with incredulousness.

Velten interrupted before the Connate could begin raging at her orders. "And Doctore Shen is a civilian and will remain out of the coming battle as well."

Olivienne crossed her arms. "Sovereign or no, I will not be banished to the center of the ship."

Castellan gave another look to the screen and realized time was nearly out. "Fine, it's not as if I have the Shields to enforce the captain's order anyhow. At least tell me you two will stay here on the bridge?"

Both women nodded and Olivienne reassured her. "We will stay here until directed elsewhere. But where will you be?"

The commander waved toward the plexi windows surrounding the bridge where they could see that the enemy dirigibles were nearly upon them. "They need my gun, 'Vienne, or none of us will get out of here alive."

Time froze for a moment as the two strong and stubborn women stared at each other. Olivienne spoke so no one could hear. *"Do you think we should use..."* She was afraid to finish the statement for fear of anyone overhearing, even mind to mind.

Castellan gave a small shake of her head. *"Absolutely not unless we have no other option. I swore a Sovereign Oath to not divulge their existance. As did you. Please say you understand. It would mean peril for all if the rebels knew what we had aboard this ship."*

Finally, Olivienne capitulated, knowing that she couldn't sway Castellan from her duty no matter how much she worried for her lover. *"Fine, last resort only."* Instead of following her mental statement with a verbal one listing her own fears, Olivienne leaned forward to give her a kiss. "Be safe, my love."

Suddenly, the ship rocked as the first shell hit. "I have to go!" And with that, Commander Castellan Tosh left the bridge at a dead run after grabbing her rifle that had been carefully secured in the corner near the entryway.

Captain Velten called into her ship com. "Return fire! Knock those shelling stone-suckers from the sky."

The first sounds of shell fire filled the bridge as the ship rocked yet again. Given the way they were outnumbered, Velten assumed the fight would be short and tragic. Luckily for them, the impenetrable bladder was holding up well, but not so much the engines. By the time the five ships had come close enough to do real damage to the *Quaesitum*, they were directly over King's Marsh. It was good because it was a large, uninhabited area and not likely to see casualties from stray shells fired. It was bad because one of the early volleys had once again taken out the long-range coms. They got one message out requesting aid before they lost signal.

"Ser, we just lost a second engine!"

A cheer went around the bridge as one of the slower moving dirigibles took a direct hit to a tether point on the bladder and two lines snapped, pitching rebels over the sides. The cheer quieted again as the next message sounded over the com system.

"Captain, we've got wounded in the med bay but the medican was injured when a shell struck the dextra engine. Orders, ser?"

Captain Velten looked at her pilot, Seben. "Shut down pipes one and four and divert the rest of our stone aether to the other two engines." She turned to the other woman sitting at the far com panel. "Tell Vex to find a backup, anyone with basic medican training will do."

Gemeda glanced at where Olivienne stood staring out the windows with a worried look upon her face. She kept her words silent to prevent Velten from naysaying her plan before she could make it a reality. *"Olivienne, I need to get to that medican room."*

Olivienne glanced at her. *"Are you sure? You're much safer up here with Velten."*

"I may be safer but there are people dying out there and I would be dishonoring my duty if I don't do everything I can to heal those who are wounded. Are you with me, yay or nay?"

"Of course I'm with you. As for how to get off the bridge, leave that to me." She called out to Velten. "Captain, due to the viciousness of this battle, I think it's best if Doctore Shen and I make our way to the center of the ship."

The captain distractedly turned to look over her shoulder at her two high profile guests. "I think that's a good idea, Connate Dracore. Can you make your way there on your own, or do you need an escort?"

"I've got high enough channel ratings that we should be fine."

"Very well then, be safe, Connate. I'll do my best by you up here."

Given the all clear, the two women quickly left the bridge to help.

THE SHIP ROCKED yet again and Castellan used her telekinesis to snatch one of the captain's crew and prevent the man from falling over the rail. She was currently on Madlin's side of the ship, picking off any rebel she could sight on the dirigibles that were rapidly closing on them. The *Quaesitum* had rail guns permanently affixed to all four sides. They were aided by the two portable rail guns that Castellan's team had brought. Another explosion rocked the ship and two screams sounded in tandem as a rail gun was hit.

"Shield down, Shield down!"

"Commander, Lazaro and Meza were hit and we lost a gun."

Castellan ducked below the solid rail so she wouldn't be a target and crawled with her rifle to the side that had been hit. Both Shields were unconscious, Lazaro with a bleeding abdomen and Meza with a long wound on her head. "Sheddech!" She'd sent Holling to the medican bay to help when the captain put the call out. Yazzie was on the other side of the *Quaesitum* with Savon. She looked around from her crouched position until she spotted Madlin firing her pistol. Her rifle lay discarded nearby with signs of damage. Her left arm was cradled against her midsection and Castellan wasn't sure which part of the woman was injured.

"Madlin!" The lieutenant found Castellan's gaze in the fray and Castellan slid her own rifle across the decking to her. "I'm going to take these two down to the med bay. Hold this side."

"Yes, ser."

Staying low to the ground until they could get inside the dirigible, Castellan floated both wounded specialists in front of her. Once inside, she was able to stand but she kept Meza and Lazaro in a horizontal position as she'd learned to do from Yazzie. Her voteo sounded when she was less than half way across the ship to the medican bay.

"Commander Tosh, we've got three of the ship's crew members down on the dextra side, with two Shields injured. Requesting backup." Savon's voice wasn't panicked but she could tell he was close.

She picked up the pace as the ship rocked again. "I'll head there after the med bay."

"Copy that, ser."

Another explosion sounded and Castellan grew concerned that the bladder wasn't going to hold, especially against similarly equipped ships from Soflin. She contacted the captain next. "How goes it on the bridge?"

"We've got one ship down and another hanging by three lines. Unfortunately, we're a little worse for wear with only two engines left. Connate Dracore and Doctore Shen have gone to the mess hall where they'd be safe."

Castellan's intuition channel jangled with the captain's words. She knew both women very well and neither would choose to hide in the center of the ship amidst such action. Her boots rang in the corridor as she took off running, Lazaro and

Meza's unconscious forms in front of her the whole way. When she made it to the medican bay, she found Spc. Holling and Gemeda but no Olivienne. "Where is she?"

Gemeda was busy with her hands on a crew member who had their guts spilling out onto the table while Holling was sewing a head wound near the temple of Spc. Devin. Holling was the one who answered. "She went to assist Savon."

Castellan quickly placed the two wounded Shields on nearby cots and yelled at Gemeda. "Save them!" Then she was through the doorway and headed for the dextra staging deck where Savon was covering with his team. Castellan pushed through the door onto the deck as another dirigible swung around with a line of guns on the rail. The rebels began laying down fire and Olivienne had failed to notice the enemy ship until too late. Seeing his sovereign in mortal danger, Savon dove for Olivienne, protecting her with his larger body. Everyone else had thrown themselves face down on the decking to be protected by the side rail, including Castellan.

Through the smaller shell fire and muffled *whumps* of the larger rail guns, a piercing yell rent the air. "Savon? *Savon!*" Olivienne's voice carried through the air again as she shook Savon's body while the weight of it pulled them to the deck at her feet. "No! No, you cannot die, Savon." She turned wild eyes to meet Castellan's. "Tosh, do something!"

Castellan's heart dropped as she watched Olivienne roll the lieutenant's body from hers. His eyes were open and unseeing and his body a mess of shell wounds, including one to the head. Something in Commander Castellan Tosh broke in that moment. Suddenly, she remembered the stones in her trouser pocket and anger consumed her. She unsealed the pocket and gripped the stones tightly in her left hand then stood from the decking, heedless of shell fire. One shell struck her arm but she didn't even flinch. Instead, Castellan raised her right hand as if she were reaching out to grab the enemy dirigible. Then an instant later, she used her telekinesis and dashed it straight away out of the sky. It was as if an invisible hand, or the biggest gust of wind had simply thrown it down to the swamp below.

Everyone on the deck froze, including Olivienne. The *Quaesitum* spun in place and another ship came into view. At that point, no one knew what to do or what was happening. It was impossible for someone to have as much power as what Tosh had just displayed. The new ship began laying down fire, striking Castellan in the thigh and shoulder, and met the same fate. That left only one enemy ship but it was in fairly good shape as it was a new one with capability to match the *Quaesitum*.

Castellan dropped to the ground abruptly as blood seeped from her various wounds. Olivienne scrambled to her side as another shell rocked the ship. Black filled the remaining fighters' vision when the enemy dirigible rounded and began shooting everything in sight. A spark from one of the shells started a fire in a stack of wood crates and two crewmembers began fighting the blaze before it could get out of control. One of the bladder lines snapped nearby and everyone aboard knew they were still in trouble. "Tosh! By the Makers, don't you die on me too!"

Castellan's breath was labored so she didn't speak aloud. *"'Vienne...take the stones..."*

Still in shock, Olivienne had forgotten about the antorae-stones. "I don't understand." Rather than answer, Castellan moved her hand toward Olivienne's knee and opened the palm. Olivienne immediately recognized the iridescent glassy black stones. "Oh."

Castellan's breath hitched with pain but they were out of options. *"Finish...it."*

At first, the Connate was confused then she realized what Castellan wanted her to do. Another shell hit the bulkhead nearby and she quickly reached out to snatch the stones, holding them tight in her grip. Olivienne momentarily paused at the enormity of what she held before crawling to the solid rail. Then with precise application of her pyrokinesis, the enemy dirigible caught fire. She focused on the bladder next and even that went up in flames, despite being inflammable. Screams split the air between the two ships and she saw more than one flaming body fall from the decking as bladder lines snapped and the gondola tilted precariously. Then the bladder burned through and the entire thing crashed into the swamp below. The silence was abrupt, leaving the various Shields and crew members with heavy hearts and ringing in their ears.

Olivienne couldn't think about what she'd just done or the screams that she knew would blacken her conscience for rotos to come. Instead she called for Gemeda, forgetting about the amplification power of the stones. *"Gem, Tosh is down!"*

"Quit yelling, I can hear you just fine. I can't leave the med bay, can you get her here?"

"Connate Dracore, let's get the bleeding stopped." Yazzie

scrambled to the commander's side and began stripping Tosh's uniform shirt to see the worst of her injuries. Olivienne stood and stared down in shock, then turned her gaze to take in Savon's body.

"Connate Dracore?"

Olivienne looked up into the concerned face of Spc. Soleng. His big presence was a salve to her wounded psyche, but she couldn't rouse herself from the shock that was taking over.

Lt. Madlin called over the com. "Commander Tosh, Lieutenant Savon, what's your status?" A pause, then the voice came again. "Madlin here, all enemies appear to be vanquished and I need a report from dextra."

Seeing that no one else was going to answer, Specialist Gar Soleng pulled the voteo from his own belt. "Soleng here. We've lost Lieutenant Savon, Commander Tosh is down, Calderon and Qent are walking wounded."

Nothing came back and Soleng took the initiative, pointing at anyone who was able to move around. "You, help tie the wounds of the rest. You, assist Yazzie with Commander Tosh. I'm taking Connate Dracore inside."

That snapped Olivienne out of her mental fog. "No, I'm not leaving her!"

"Connate Dracore, it would be best if we get you off this deck."

"Soleng, I've got a litter in my pack. One shell hit near the lung but she's stable for now. I'll put it together and you can help me transport the commander to the med bay."

Duties carried on around Olivienne and she shut her eyes to the destruction. She was startled by a touch to the shoulder. "Connate Dracore, let's get you inside."

She looked to her left and right, taking note that there were two bodies on the ground covered by thin medican blankets, she assumed done by Yazzie. One she knew to be a promising officer named Gentry Savon. The other she assumed was one of the ship's crew. The first tear slipped from her dark lashes as she followed the litter carrying Castellan. The stones remained clenched in her fist and she knew nothing was going to be the same.

Luckily, Gemeda had been conserving her strength by not fully healing the wounded. She assumed there would be many injured and acted accordingly. While the doctore made sure no one was at the edge of death, some remained in serious condition and required treatment at a medican center as soon as possible.

Because of her conservation, she had enough energy to get Castellan up and walking around, if not completely pain free. As soon as she had finished with the commander, Gemeda passed out into an exhausted sleep.

When everyone aboard the *Quaesitum* was accounted for, nearly all crew members but those on the bridge had taken one injury or another. Eleven of the fourteen Shield guardians had injuries serious enough to require stitching or telesana healing, two were in critical condition. And in the end, four people lost their lives in the battle of King's Marsh. Three of Velten's ship mates and Lt. Savon.

The captain ordered First Officer Vex to oversee immediate repairs while their lone engine kept them moving slowly toward Montesilva, the closest town where they could hope to request help. It was near eleven hundred oors and Olivienne and Castellan were standing on the rear deck of the ship. It was surprisingly intact, all things considered. Both women were in shock from the vicious battle and the loss of one of their own. After a few moments of silence, Olivienne reached into her trouser pocket and pulled out the stones. She held out her fist to Castellan.

"Take these. I can't bear to look at them now." Her eyes grew unfocused. "The screams...the sounds of their screams as they burned will weigh on me for the rest of my life. I don't want these accursed stones!" She looked as if she might throw them overboard but Castellan quickly grabbed her wrist and pulled the stones from her hand. Then she sealed them away into a lower trouser pocket.

"I'm sorry. I should have never asked you to do that."

Olivienne turned red-rimmed eyes to look at her future par. "I wonder...was keeping this last sovereign secret worth it?"

Castellan looked away, out toward the horizon. She was riddled with guilt for so many reasons. "Logically, I can see that it was. If the rebels knew, they'd stop at nothing to obtain them. My intuition says they wouldn't have bothered to leave the ship intact, hoping for a valuable hostage. They would have torn us apart for the stones alone. But..."

"But?"

Castellan shook her head, eyes rife with emotion. "Everything has gone so wrong."

"You had this power...this...awful, terrible, power..." Castellan moved her gaze back to Olivienne to see what she had to say. "And you had it all through the battle."

"You know I did."

Olivienne's eyes welled with tears. "Savon is dead! You had them the entire time and yet Savon is dead. Why didn't you do something earlier, Tosh? Why? The Queen's Sovereign Oath wasn't worth it!"

"I was following orders." Castellan's shout was hoarse, a sure sign that she was both emotionally and physically compromised from the morning's battle.

"Makers *take* your orders!" Olivienne grabbed the front of Castellan's bloody and torn uniform and shook her. "He's dead and he'll never come back! Why didn't you save him?"

Castellan immediately wrapped her in a tight embrace while Olivienne broke down sobbing. "You're right...you're right...I should have done something sooner. I should have disregarded our orders of silence as soon as I saw those five ships approaching on the sonica. I erred, 'Vienne. I don't think I fully understood the capability of the antoraestones until that moment on dextra when I held them in my hand and achieved the impossible. I made the wrong choice and Savon paid for it with his life. For that I'll never forgive myself."

Olivienne's voice was muffled against Castellan's shirt. "I was to sponsor him to adventurist training when this was all over."

The embrace tightened when Olivienne began to cry harder. "I know, love. I know. Savon died a hero, I'll be sure he receives the highest honors."

"He gave his life for mine."

Castellan whispered back. "He was a Shield. Our lives all belong to you."

Both went silent after that but their peace was short-lived. Lt. Madlin pushed through the door and limped onto the observation deck. Her left arm was in a makeshift sling. The lieutenant's mood was as somber as all the other Shields with the news of Savon's death. She hated to disturb the Connate and commander but she didn't have a choice. "Sers, Captain Velten has requested a meeting with you in the captain's room."

"Did she say what about?"

Madlin shook her head at Tosh. "No, ser. Just that she wanted it right away."

"'Vienne, we have to go."

Olivienne's breath hitched with her silent tears as she let out a sigh. "I know." She pulled back from the embrace and wiped the tears from her eyes. "Let's get this over with." She looked at Madlin, where the woman had wandered across the deck to gaze out over the rail. "Are you coming?"

"No, Connate Dracore. I was going to make the rounds and check on the rest of the team."

"Lieutenant Auda Madlin..." Tosh's serious voice drew the attention of both other women on the deck. "You're the only officer in the Connate's Shields now. You need to be in this meeting as well. Have Soleng check the rest."

Madlin swallowed at the reminder that her counterpart was gone and pulled the voteo from her belt. "Yes, ser."

It didn't take long for the trio to make their way through the ship to the captain's room. Madlin knocked to indicate their arrival then held the door open for both Olivienne and Tosh. Velten was inside clutching a glass of amber liquid, staring out one of the port windows. It had taken a stray shell and the plexi itself was broken. There was a slight breeze from the slow progress of the ship. Velten turned when they came in and waved toward the round table on the side of the room. "Have a seat."

Once they were all seated, Velten got the social niceties out of the way. "My condolences for your loss, Commander Tosh. Savon was...he was a good soldier and a better psero."

"To you as well, Captain. We value every Psierian that lost their life todae. All we can do is take courage in the fact that it could have been a lot worse."

The captain leaned back and took another slow pull of the scotch. "You know, it's strange you should say that. It could have been a lot worse...*should* have been. But yet it wasn't. By all rights, we should be the ones who are crashed into the swamp. The *Quaesitum* was both outnumbered and outgunned, yet we are here limping along and they are all dead." She moved her gaze to meet Castellan's dead on. "Do you know how that happened?"

Castellan didn't circle the issue, instead she was direct and honest. After all, Velten already knew about the stones, she simply didn't know that any existed outside Antaeus. "I do. *I* happened. We were getting torn to pieces on Madlin's side and two of my Shields had grievous injuries. I took them to the medican bay and discovered that Connate Dracore had gone to help Savon's group. Fearing the worst, I went to the dextra staging deck next and came out in time to see one of those blasted rebel ships come around and begin firing. Olivienne didn't see the danger and Savon threw himself upon her, taking the shots to keep her safe."

"That tells me where you were, but not what happened to our enemy ships. I did gather some intel based on the call letters on two of the dirigibles. One was a ship for hire that was out of Baen, and the other out of Guin. I know because I've worked mountain rescue with one of the captains. She was a good woman. Sadly it wasn't her on the voteo when I tried to contact the more familiar ship. I recognized the man who did respond, which is why I came to the conclusion that they were taken over rather than simply put off after having their ship stolen."

"Civilians?"

"Yes, Commander."

Tosh paled as the horror sunk in. "There were civilians on some of those ships." She recalled the anger that coursed through her as she dashed the first dirigible to the ground with a negligent swipe of her telekinesis. She didn't even wait for an invitation. Instead, Tosh stood and strode over to the area where the liquor was kept and poured herself a generous helping of scotch. "Sheddech. I should be set out to the island for what I've done."

Olivienne looked to her worriedly but asked more of Velten. "What about the black ones out of Soflin?"

The captain shrugged. "All rebel, I'd imagine."

No one knew what to do and the secs ticked by as Castellan stood with head lowered off to the side of the room. Finally, Olivienne stood and walked over to her, placing a gentle hand upon her shoulder. "It's not your fault, Castellan. You had no more control over the rebels' actions than I did."

Castellan turned abruptly and Olivienne stepped back. Castellan's shield had slipped between them and Olivienne was awash with grief, self-hatred, guilt, and more. "*I* am the one who went against the Queen's direct order, and even then I did it too late. Now, I find that my inaction resulted in the death of one of our own, and my actions resulted in the death of civilians! How am I to go forward from here?"

"Oh, come now, Tosh. You're powerful but you're not that—" The captain stopped speaking at the look on Castellan's face. Velten finally caught on to what had happened in the final moments of the battle. "The stones. You brought some back with you and used them on the enemy dirigibles?" Tosh nodded. Velten herself stood. "Had you not used those blasted things, we'd all be marsh bait right now. The sovereign would be dead or worse, as would her protector and future par. The greatest medican this land has seen in generations would also be gone and so would everyone else aboard this ship."

"I failed, Captain. Either way, I failed."

"People were going to die, Tosh. I had no illusions that we'd come out of that battle on the other side unscathed. The odds were completely against us and I'm telling you here and now that I expected to die todae. Lieutenant Savon did his sovereign duty and would have lost his life todae whether you had the stones or not. And the rest would have been killed if you had not made that impossible choice. You're a commander, the Hero of Temple Beach, and you have one of the most prolific records against the Atlanteens. Surely you've lost people before."

Castellan grimaced and took another swig of her scotch. "Never one so close. Since coming to the Shields, this entire team..." She glanced at Olivienne, then over at a mute Auda Madlin. "They're like family. Savon struck me to the bone. And to find that I've also killed civilians...that's a hard one to come back from. I clearly don't deserve this posting."

"Pardon me, ser, but that's just bollux. You are the best officer I've ever served under, and I'd choose to follow you again and again, before and after todae. We lost Savon, and all our hearts hurt for it. But the bottom line is that we performed our duty." She waved a hand toward Olivienne. "Connate Dracore will be returning to Tesseron, whole and hale. I'm sorry, ser, but you can't save everyone. Even *you* with all your channel strength and intelligence. Surely you must see that."

Castellan gave her a wry grin. "Even so, I'm sure there will be consequences of all this when we return. And I assure you that I will take them all upon my shoulders. It's the least I can do."

"Darling, you don't need to do that." Olivienne wanted to reach out and take Castellan into her arms but she knew her lover's moods too well. Weighed down by grief and guilt as she was, Olivienne knew Castellan wouldn't take to coddling. Rather than keep pushing her, Olivienne turned to Captain Velten. "How soon before we can enact repairs?"

"We're currently running on one engine. I elected to continue on to Montesilva as that's the closest town that will have supplies for us. We can also contact the local Defense Corp office and request aid. Perhaps they'll send another ship to take you and your team on to the capital."

"How long to Montesilva then?"

Velten pursed her lips. "I can't say for sure. We're going

slowly but we also have to compensate direction continuously because of the location of the remaining engine. It wants to spin the ship as much as push forward. Even so, we're still managing about fifteen mahls per. At those speeds it will be daes before we reach our destination."

"Coms?"

"Long-range is still out and Vex said we don't have the items we need to repair it. We've got men and women in critical condition in the medican bay, including two of your own. Things are bad but I'd say as long as we don't come across any more rebels, we should be able to make it to Montesilva and hope for the best from there."

Olivienne was about to respond but they were interrupted by a tone sounding in the captain's room. "Bollux, what now?" Velten strode over to the com box. "Velten here."

"Sebben sending, ser. We've got another ship on the horizon. Short-range coms has picked up their signal. The captain says they're out of Tesseron."

Suddenly, Castellan looked up and took two steps to stand near Velten. "May I?" The captain handed the com mic to Castellan. "Sebben, ask the other ship who the ranking officer on board is."

"Yes, ser."

They waited a meen before Sebben's voice came back on the com. "Says it is General Renou."

Castellan thrilled inside that they'd been rescued, but she also despaired to think that her career would soon be over. Either way, they'd know nothing until Renou arrived and the team was debriefed. "That's the head of the Shields, as you probably know. I also trust her above all others not on this ship, save the Queen and the King."

Seema Velten smiled as relief coursed through her. "That's a bit of sweet luck, isn't it?"

"Not luck, Captain. I'd wager my maman had a vision and sent out help straightaway."

Tosh looked from Velten to Olivienne. "Not about you, surely."

"Of course not. But it could have been about anyone she was somewhat familiar with. I'm certainly not going to look at this as anything other than a boon. Are we done here?" She stood to leave but Castellan forestalled her.

"Wait." She looked around the small group and frowned.

"Despite my actions todae, I need to remind you all that all knowledge of the antoraestones are under the highest security. Keep your mouths shut and your shields tight, savvy?"

"Yes, ser."

Captain Velten nodded. "Of course, Tosh."

Olivienne didn't say anything but her feelings were easily read in the furrowed brow and pursed lips. Castellan knew she'd stay silent but angry on the subject.

"Good." She glanced down at her wrecked uniform. "I'm going to change and cleanup before my commanding officer arrives. I'll come to the bridge after."

Madlin stood when the rest looked like they were heading out of the room. "Permission to do the same, ser?"

Castellan limped with purpose toward the door. "Permission granted." Then she was out of the room and heading down the corridor as if she were being chased by creatures from the ocean depths. Olivienne followed slowly in the same direction, deep in thought.

Chapter Twenty-three

THE *GRYPHEM* WAS another one of the imposing black dirigibles. Castellan knew General Renou and General Leniste had both requested more to be shipped to Tesseron while things were still so tenuous concerning the sovereigns' safety. The *Quaesitum* was the first to be pressed into service, with the best equipment the Corps had to offer at the time, but there were more slated for production. Captain Velten was instructed to anchor and winch down so the officers could rendezvous. Due to the extensive damage to the *Quaesitum*, Castellan suggested everyone meet aboard the new ship.

Sevrik Dondin was captain of the *Gryphem*. He was a short and stocky man of middling rotos, with a scar above his right eyebrow and an easy grin. He led everyone to the captain's room and sent for refreshments. The group around the table included Dondin, Renou, Olivienne, Tosh, and Velten. General Renou requested that the meeting include top ranking officials only, which left the rest behind. That excluded Madlin, who didn't mind in the least. And Doctore Shen was still deeply asleep, recovering from taxing her telesana to its limit.

General Renou was straight to the point as always. "What happened?"

Captain Velten grimaced. "Todae, or the dae we left Endara when this all started?"

"Start from the beginning."

Velten looked to Tosh and got a small nod to continue. "We were ambushed during our stop in Nusquam and took minor damage, including coms. The *Quaesitum* was able to outrun the rebel ships but we knew they'd be waiting when we came back. Without long-range, we had no way to contact the Shield or Defense Corp offices to request help. Rather, we continued on with our mission."

Renou's gray eyes were piercing. She took in everything in the room as well as everyone around the table. Olivienne looked preyed upon by grief, an image Renou had never seen before on her heart daughter. Castellan though looked like a dead woman walking and the general wondered what occurred during the wekes they'd been gone. "What happened todae?"

Captain Velten continued. "We plotted a more southerly course from Nusquam on the return, hoping that we'd evade the rebels' area of observation. We grew concerned when three dirigibles showed up on the sonica, coming in from the north. We thought all was lost when two more approached from the south, at speeds indicating their ships were of similar makeup to the *Quaesitum*."

Both General Renou and Captain Dondin looked shocked. "Five dirigibles came at you and this is all the damage you took? By the Makers, you're lucky to be alive!"

Castellan glanced at her commanding officer and addressed the unfamiliar dirigible captain. "No offense, Captain Dondin, but the rest of this debrief is of the highest security. Because of the events that occurred earlier todae, both Connate Dracore and Captain Velten are privy to the info, but I cannot speak it aloud to another outside the Queen or General Renou."

The man peered at her intently. "Sovereign Oath?"

"Yes. Truthfully, the four people that currently know are two too many in the Queen's book."

Captain Dondin abruptly slid back his chair and stood. He wasn't angry at all, rather he looked a bit relieved. "I'm not one to enjoy such political intrigues. I'd much rather sail the skies from one anchor point to the next." Velten found herself unconsciously nodding to his words. She would rather have skipped all the intrigue as well. He straightened his uniform and looked around the table. "I think I'll take my leave and head for the bridge. Call on the coms if you need anything." He gave a crisp salute and they all saluted back.

Once he was gone, that just left the four of them in the captain's room. Renou leaned forward and tapped on the table as she spoke. Despite her diminutive stature, her commanding presence took up a lot of the room. "Tell me what happened." She looked to Tosh. "What did you find on that island?"

"It was full of creatures...the like you've never seen. There were great dirigible towers on the east and west side of the island and in the hundreds of mahls between the two was a vast lake with a research station right on the edge."

"Research station?"

Olivienne answered. "Yes, Maker-made and highly advanced. We brought back samples, documents, and devices. And in the lake itself, you would not believe it but a giant and highly intelligent greater beast resided there. She said she wasn't from Psiere at all, that her race and ours came from the same planet, deposited here by the Makers. Or the Tau Ceti as she calls them."

Camen Renou's eyes widened at Olivienne's descriptions. "Not from Psiere?"

Castellan answered. "No, ser. We are all from beyond the stars. Based on what we've learned from discovered Maker texts and from what Nessie herself said, I'd be hard pressed to say which species were native creatures of Psiere, and which were brought down with the Tau."

"It certainly boggles the mind, Commander."

"To continue the story without making it overly long," Olivienne sighed because the story had already become overly long, "we eventually found our way across the island to the second dirigible station. From there we discovered a tunnel that traveled beneath a river and terminated directly below the Temple of Antaeus. The temple itself was completely shielded on the outside, locked tight. But Nessie gave us a key to unlock the doors and windows. Inside the charging room of the temple we found a chest of archeostones so we elected to put that in the spent illeostone chamber aboard the *Quaesitum* rather than bring stones over for charging."

Renou's mouth gaped open. "But that means...by the Makers! A ship could go on indefinitely with a much smaller supply of stones."

Captain Velten grinned. "It makes my adventurous heart happy. The places my ship could go if I didn't have to stop and offload illeostones." Suddenly, the grin fell from her face. "Not that my ship is going far or fast right now. I fear she's fairly done in."

The general gave her a small smile. "Never fear, Captain. We'll have the *Quaesitum* right as light again soon enough. Now, finish your tale, Commander."

Castellan sighed. "Yes, ser. What nobody knew save myself, Connate Dracore, and Queen Olivara is that she gave us supplemental orders before setting out for Magna."

Renou raised an eyebrow, clearly surprised to hear that she was not privy to part of the mission plan. "Which were?"

"You may remember that the Queen didn't want the antoraestones found." Renou nodded. "She instructed both of us, more me specifically, to either destroy them or lock them away in the event that they were discovered. Her secondary orders were to retrieve a sample before doing so, to bring back for study."

"And you found the antoraestones?"

"Yes. They were in the lowest level of the temple, in an impenetrable chamber. The Queen made us swear a Sovereign Oath to do her bidding but Connate Dracore was opposed. She was going to enter the chamber despite our orders and I couldn't allow it. By locking away the stones when they were within sight..." She trailed off and glanced at Olivienne, not wanting to speak ill of her love.

Olivienne reached over to grip Castellan's hand. "You can say it, darling. Camen has seen my fits of temper often enough." She looked at Renou. "I was livid at both the fact that she locked them away from me and that she did it so abruptly with no discussion before hand."

Renou's look softened. "I can certainly see her reasoning, 'Vienne. Surely you must by now?"

Olivienne gave a broken laugh. "Oh, I didn't really, at least not fully until the battle above the marsh."

"What happened?"

Neither looked ready to answer so Velten picked up the story. "We were outnumbered and outgunned and would have hit the ground but for Commander Tosh's actions. We had two of the older ships down but had lost two engines during the fight. The other three ships were circling like sharcs, picking us apart with their rail guns." Velten paused to take a sip of her drink before continuing. "I had mates down and Doctore Shen was in the medican bay trying to put people back together. Tosh here was on the laeva staging deck with Lieutenant Madlin and apparently Connate Dracore had run to assist dextra side with Lieutenant Savon." She stopped then and glanced furtively at the Connate and commander.

Castellan finished recounting the actions above King's Marsh. "I was transporting two of my Shields who were in dire condition to the medican bay when I found out that the Connate had left the bridge. It was then that I knew she would go help Savon who had called for backup meens before. After I left Lazaro and Meza with Gemeda, I ran to the dextra deck. I arrived in time to see one of the big black dirigibles coming around to bear. They laid down fire and everyone hit the deck except—" She glanced to her left.

Olivienne answered. "I failed to see the danger in time and

Savon threw himself in front of me to shield my body. He...he died instantly."

Renou reached out a hand to comfort her heart daughter. "I'm sorry, 'Vienne. That must have been heart-wrenching." Tears broke free from Olivienne's dark lashes and Renou turned back to Castellan. "How did you defeat the last three ships?"

The commander's hands clenched on top of the table. "When I saw Savon fall and heard Olivienne's scream...something inside me broke. I suddenly remembered the antoraestones and reached into my pocket and removed them. Then I stood within full view of the enemy and...and I...I simply dashed them from the air as a child would throw down a toy. One moment they were there, then the next, the ship was smashed to the swamp below."

"Sheddech!"

Tosh gave her general a pained smile. "Yes, exactly. As you know, my new channel rating for tee-kay is a seven, meaning my top weight manipulation is a little over nine thousand punds. But with two stones in hand at an amplification power of ten times for the first, then ten times again for the second one..." The entire table shuddered to think of such power. "When the next ship came around I did the same but I'd taken too many shells to continue. I dropped to the decking as the next one circled into place. I had Olivienne take the stones and she torched the last black dirigible."

Renou looked shocked. "Torched the impenetrable bladder?"

Olivienne sobbed and turned to bury her face in the fabric of Castellan's shoulder. Castellan gave her commanding officer a grim look. "Yes, ser."

"And the battle was over?"

Castellan nodded. "Yes, but at what cost?"

"Why, the cost of your lives, I'd say."

"General Renou..." Renou turned to look at Captain Velten. "There were civilians on at least two of those ships. I recognized them and from what I could figure, they'd been taken over by rebels."

"This is quite a mess, isn't it?"

"Yes, ser."

The captain's room was silent while General Renou decided their course of action. After a meen, Olivienne stopped crying and wiped her tears, which left the three of them to stare at the small gray-haired woman. Renou leaned forward with her elbows on the table, lips pressed against her clasped hands.

"Ser?"

Finally, Camen Renou sat back. "Who else knows about the antoraestones and where are they now?"

Castellan reached down to her sealed trouser pocket and retrieved them, then set the stones on the table. "Only those of us in this room and Lieutenant Madlin know about them."

Renou picked up one of the stones. "This? All the trouble and heartache for this pretty bauble?"

"What's your lowest rated channel?"

Castellan got a curious look in response but Renou answered. "I've got a two rating in telekinesis."

"So, you can lift about eighteen punds or so?"

"Yes, about that."

Castellan slid her chair back. "I'm around one-seventy. Keep the stone in your hand and lift me."

Renou's right brow went up but she focused on Castellan anyway. When the commander easily rose into the air, Renou exclaimed, "Son of a sint!" She set Castellan down and carefully placed the stone back on the table.

The chair scraped along the flooring as Castellan slid back to the table. "What are your orders, ser?"

"First things first, I want you to put those blasted stones back into your pocket and don't pull them out again until you reach the Queen!"

"Ser? Shouldn't they go to you, the highest ranking officer aboard ship?"

"Commander Tosh, the Queen trusted you with those stones and so too will I. You've debriefed Lieutenant Madlin?"

"Of course."

Renou nodded then took in everyone at the table. "Good. Connate Dracore, her Shield team, and Doctore Shen are to return straightaway to Tesseron with me aboard the *Gryphem*. I've got two dirigibles on their way, they're about six oors behind us. We followed your initial route from Tesseron so our last stop was Montesilva. We won't leave until they get here. One will tow the *Quaesitum* back to Tesseron and the other to provide protection. We'll take the chest of archeostones with us, which should allow Dondin's ship to run straight through to the capital without stopping." She met Velten's eyes. "That's assuming your ship is livable until Tesseron?"

"It is, ser. It won't be the height of comfort but she won't shake apart. And you assure me we'll be rebuilt as before?"

Renou winked. "Given this new intel about the chest of archeostones, I'd wager the *Quaesitum* will be rebuilt better than before. It's safe to say that you'll never need to offload stones again if I get my way."

Velten nodded. "Yes, ser. I do have one last request."

"That is?"

"I've got a few badly injured mates that I'd like taken back to Tesseron as soon as possible. That is, if Doctore Shen is unable to wake and heal them before she leaves. Running straight through as you are, the injured would only be about thirty-three oors from hospital in Tesseron."

"I'd say if she is unable, we can probably find a berth for them here. And if none of you minds, we'll take the dead back with us too. They should be interred as soon as possible. However, ceremonies will wait until Velten and her crew reach the capital."

Both Tosh and Velten replied. "Yes, ser." But Olivienne remained silent.

As much as Castellan wanted the meeting to be over, she had to bring up her wrong doing. "Ser, what is to happen to me upon my return? Not only did I break a Sovereign Oath by using the stones, but I acted too late to save Savon. Not to mention I also killed civilians when I brought down one of those dirigibles with my channel."

Renou sighed and scrubbed her face tiredly. "The first is not for me to say, that's on the Queen. As for the second two, neither was a dereliction of duty, but rather a sad set of circumstances with a less than ideal outcome. There will always be casualties of war, especially when the enemy has no moral compass. You weren't responsible for those civilians on the rebel dirigible. Your sole responsibility was to protect your sovereign. You did your duty, Commander. I'd wager your conscience will punish you enough for the civilian deaths that occurred."

As much as Castellan wanted to look away from those piercing gray eyes, she held her commanding officer's gaze. "Yes, ser. Will you report to the Queen when we get back?"

General Renou gazed at both Olivienne and Castellan. "The three of us will. There is much to discuss and I'd rather all pertinent people are in the room when it comes out. Savvy?"

"Yes, ser."

"Now, gather your gear and your team. We've got six oors until the other dirigibles arrive. Have someone speak with Doctore Shen as soon as she wakes, and let's get everything ready for our return to the capital. I want to get back sooner rather than later. You're dismissed."

Everyone stood from the table and Velten and Tosh saluted before they left the room. One thing all four of them knew, it was going to be a somber trip back.

IT WAS A little after ten hundred oors when the *Gryphem* moored at the Tesseron dirigible station. Luckily for Captain Velten, Gemeda was able to wake in time to heal the rest of the injured shipmates. She even had enough energy to get the two critically injured Shields, Lazaro and Meza, up and walking again. Though nearly all still sported injuries of one type or another, there was not a Shield that wasn't ready to protect Olivienne when they disembarked at the transportation hub.

Because of security concerns, General Renou had at least ten platoons of Shield Corp guardians, and two units of Psi Defense Corp soldiers waiting. She was taking no chances that something unfortunate could occur at the busy station. She led Olivienne, Tosh, and Gemeda to the waiting transports and directed the rest of the Shields to the hauler behind them. "I hope you don't mind but we've been requested to go straight to the Queen's office at the Imperium. Your team will be right behind us."

"What of Savon and the captain's lost mates? What will you do with the bodies?"

"Never fear, Tosh. We'll temporarily inter them until arrangements can be made. I'll personally contact Lieutenant Savon's family and inform them of his death—"

"No!" General Renou looked startled by Castellan's outburst and the commander tried to explain. "Please, allow me. It was just his maman and a sib. His sib was a few rotos older and she's a judex here in Tesseron. I met them both once, not long after I took over the Shield team. I think they will better take it from me."

"Tosh, no one takes the death of a loved one well, no matter who the informant is."

"Maybe not, ser, but I owe them at least that much."

Renou conceded with a short nod. "Very well."

It didn't take long to travel around the bay to the Imperium, which sat upon one of the taller hills on the north side of the river valley. Even with an extra stop. General Renou offered Gemeda

the use of her guesthouse for the time being, at least until the doctore found out if her transfer request would go through. Once the
medican was given over to Camen Renou's par, Pendar, they
were free to continue their trip.

The long walk through the massive halls within the seat of
Psiere's government was not as quickly done as normal. Even the
talented and powerful Doctore Shen had limits and by request of
all the Shields, she focused her healing on the Captain's crew
since they would be a lot later in returning to the capital. The
Shields themselves weren't in terrible shape, though they were
definitely less than one hundred percent. Castellan still sported a
limp from the shell that struck her thigh. Gem told her that if it
had struck little father to the inside, it would have broken the big
leg bone. Even so, Castellan didn't feel very lucky.

Renou pushed through a large door that opened into an ante-
chamber. She instructed the Shield team to wait with a handful of
other Shields in black, one of which was Captain Torrin. He gave
Renou, Olivienne, and Tosh a crisp salute, then nodded toward
the door. "Go right in, General. She's waiting for you three."
They were nearly past him when he called out. "Commander
Tosh..." She paused to look back at Torrin. "I heard about your
lieutenant and I'm sorry. He was a great Shield."

Tosh gave a weary sigh and a small smile. "The best. And
thank you, Captain."

Renou rapped on the door twice then pushed through into
the room. The Queen was already up and in motion around the
desk. She didn't stop until she held Olivienne within her arms.
"Oh my darling..."

Olivienne wrapped her arms around her mother and held her
tight. "Maman!"

"I feared for you. When we found out that Soflin had fallen, I
knew we couldn't take any chances with your safety, so I sent
Camen and a trio of ships after you just in case. I'm so glad I did."

Castellan looked at the Queen curiously. "So it wasn't a premonition then?"

"No, Commander." She waved for them to have a seat at the
long meeting table. "I had instructions for Leniste to be notified
as soon as you arrived at the station so he could come straightaway here for our meeting. I'll explain all when he arrives."

"Where is Papan?"

"Your papan has been stuck in meetings all morning at the
Imperium. Much has happened since you left. Though I'd wager

he'll be along shortly."

Suddenly, the door burst open and General Leniste strode through, slamming it behind him in his wake. "Blast but those Shields are thick as illeostones in a charging room out there." No one laughed at his observation and he quickly sat at the meeting table.

"Good, we're all here." She looked at Olivienne and Castellan. "Camen sent a missive about twenty oors ago informing of all of what you reported about the trip to Magna and the attack on the way home. We need to fill you in on what's occurred here since you've been gone. Leniste, if you will?"

"Nothing I have to say is good, my Queen." He looked at Olivienne and Castellan. "While you were gone, Havington finally made his move. When the rebels first took over Soflin, we assumed that they'd simply overpowered the local Defense Corp garrison and the Psi Security Corp officers there. We later learned that the city was taken with the aid of both groups. We have received official word that Dromea has declared their own sovereignty from the ruling government of Queen Olivara and the Imperium."

Olivienne's mouth dropped open. "What?"

Castellan tried to picture her old Defense compatriots turning against the crown and found it impossible. "There must be some mistake, ser."

"No mistake, Tosh. Not only that, but Praefectus Havington has been promoted to interim leader until a vote can be tallied among the Dromean city representatives."

"What has my contact in Ostium given us? First Lieutenant Cando?"

Leniste shook his head and gave her a somber look. "I'm afraid we lost contact with Cando wekes ago."

Castellan thought of all the men and women she'd served with in the Defense Corp down in Ostium. "Surely not all are backing Havington? Have we seen any come north who are loyal to the Queen?"

"General Tennet of the southern forces is in Pon Havington's pocket. Not only has he taken control of the railer lines on the continent, but he's also pulled all troops and automatons from the section between Gomen and Annexus." He shrugged. "Without coverage where the bridges span the islands across the Solis Sea, there is no protection from leviathans. And with Havington working with the Atlanteens..." He left the consequences unsaid but all around the table knew it would be unsafe for anyone to cross.

Queen Olivara sighed. "Even if the rebels don't control all the major cities, we've halted all railer service south for safety concerns."

"But...we'll be leaving the loyalists unsupported, subject to the whims of that wicked man!"

The Queen looked at the only other sovereign in existence. "And what would you have us do, Daughter? Send hundreds of psi to their deaths? We need time to plan."

The news was beyond shocking and both Castellan and Olivienne reeled with it. But General Leniste wasn't finished. "On top of that bit of shite, my interrogators finally got something from that Camillo Binn character. If you recall, he was one that we were able to detain during the attack on Tesseron. I'll give the psero this, he resisted standard techniques for a long time but he finally let something of value slip. He mentioned that documents were found in an adventurist dig site that were translated to mention something he called the Shards of Antorae. They were fabled stones that could grant great power to the possessor. The rebels were directed to scour various locations around Dromea, including a promising spot on the northeast end of Zha Dromain."

Olivienne sat forward. "The Mea Mountains? Why that would put them nearly directly south of Soflin."

"It gets worse, 'Vienne."

Olivienne looked at her mother. "How much worse can it get? This is...civil war!"

Olivara gazed at the two younger women, her violet eyes dark with worry. "We believe the rebels have found these shards and are using them to subdue any who don't agree with the Havington decree."

"But how? All the antoraestones are at the Temple of Antaeus." Castellan was still reeling from the fact that friends and comrades had been left in such dangerous circumstances.

Olivienne thumped her fist on the table, "Wait!" then turned to Castellan. "Do you remember the one passage that references the stones in the document we translated from the siren cave?"

Castellan frowned. "While I've got a head for numbers and spatial relations, I'm not much one for memory and we only read through it once. Which part?"

"The texts said that they gathered as many of the antoraestones as could be detected. It stands to reason that these 'shards' would have been too small and thus not collected by the Makers. I'd bet my last cred that a large piece struck somewhere in the mountains and splintered. It looks much like obsidae and I wonder if it fractures the same way."

"Wait," The Queen broke in. "You found the stones?"

Castellan met her gaze. "Yes, my Queen. I also did as you asked in both regards. Unfortunately, events over King's Marsh dictated that I had to risk discovery by using the stones to protect our ship." She reached into her sealed trouser pocket and pulled out the two antoraestones, then slid them across the table to Olivara. "Samples, exactly as promised."

Olivara's face lit up with surprise and joy. "Very well done, Tosh."

Castellan glanced to the right where her future par wore a dark look and decided to speak her mind. "And after conversing at length with Olivienne following the worst row we've ever had, I am telling you now I'll never blindly do as you say without deep discussion with my par. Orders or no. If you choose to send me to Aetate for it...so be it."

Rather than look angry at the clear display of insubordination, the Queen appeared quite pleased. "Well then..." She glanced over to Olivienne. "It appears as though you've found your protector and more, in one Castellan Tosh."

Olivienne's fury returned in an instant. "Did you believe that your forcing us to Sovereign Oath would have no consequence? You've been in her head and knew Castellan would follow your orders, despite the rift it would cause between us! Do you think I'd forgive you so easily for pushing this agenda?"

Olivara frowned and her shoulders drooped. It was as if she carried the weight of the world upon them, or at least half their world. "No, darling. My reasons were solid and I stand by them. I know I put Commander Tosh into an impossible position but she performed her duty. As for breaking a Sovereign Oath by using the stones and revealing their existence to some of the people around her, well that can be forgiven as well. Extenuating circumstances, such as saving my daughter's life and the lives of those on your ship certainly qualify."

"Begging your pardon, my Queen, but not everyone came home from King's Marsh."

The Queen's face fell further but rather than sorrow, a fury washed over her much like the one Olivienne sported a meen before. "No, they didn't. And there will be a reckoning when we finally get our hands on Havington and his top lackeys. That I can promise!"

All around the table, the rest of them sucked in a breath. It was as if the Queen had infused her righteous fury into all of them. The quick anger and desire for retribution came out of nowhere and Castellan realized what was happening. "My Queen, I think you should release the stones. They are amplifying your empathy and affecting the rest of us."

Olivara abruptly released the antoraestones and her shocked gaze moved from them to Castellan. "Do you all have your shields up?"

Castellan answered. "I did, my Queen. But if you recall, each stone has a ten times amplification. The power of both together is…" She searched for a word until she finally found one a few secs later. Olivienne had her own opinion of the stones as well and spoke at the same time.

"Formidable."

"Destructive."

Olivara tilted her head, as if to understand her daughter's abrupt change of mind on the subject of the antoraestones. "I see you've altered your opinion on them."

Olivienne's voice was low and rough sounding, filled with pain. "I heard the screams of Psierians as they burned under the power of my amplified channel. It's not something I'll ever forget. I watched entire dirigibles swatted from the sky like they were naught but insects. I have seen the truth of the antoraestones' capability and I'd much rather had the luxury of staying blind."

Olivara reached out to grab her daughter's hand. "I'd rather you not have come to your understanding in such a way either. And for what it's worth, I'm very sorry for the loss of your lieutenant. He served your team loyally for many rotos and will be missed, I'm sure."

The table was silent for a few secs, then Castellan moved them forward from the moment. "Queen Olivara…what is to happen now?"

Olivara gazed around the table, stopping at General Renou. The general nodded and Olivara continued until she met Castellan's pale gaze. "Now…Captain Tosh, we prepare for war." Castellan abruptly leaned back in her seat at hearing the new title but Olivara wasn't finished. "We will show those rebels what loyal citizens of Psiere will do to protect their homes and peace. They will rue the dae they ever thought they could usurp the Dracore line and go against the Maker's wishes. We were made to rule and the truth shall prevail. The real trick will be to win for the side of right with as few civilian casualties as possible."

Castellan looked unsure, not of the Queen's truth but of their chances. "How can we win such a fight if they have the ship yard, the shards, Atlanteens, and half the Psi Defense Corp on their side?"

Olivara smiled and pushed one of the stones across the table back to Tosh. "By having the best people on ours."

Chapter Twenty-four

THE DAE SHONE bright under the light of the two suns and rays fell through the skylights into the gathered crowd below. It was at odds with the somber mood in the Grand Chamber of the Temple of Archeos. The large space was filled with a sea of the infamous black and silver uniforms of Shield Corp guardians. Castellan stood at attention to the right of Olivienne, while Queen Olivara, King Keshien, and Captain Torrin stood to Olivienne's left. Psera Tryven Savon, and Judex Trylgen Savon were seated on the other side of Torrin. Both held each other, crying softly.

Templar Zane Aislyn raised her hands high above to call the chamber to silence and the crowd took their seats. "We are here to honor a psero who gave his life to service. Lieutenant Gentry Savon was a leader, not by brash action but rather by compassionate thought. Though he started as Psi Defense, his talents and temperament were soon recommended to the Shield Corp."

Castellan listened as the lead templar eulogized Savon and her own thoughts turned inward. She knew Olivienne had taken his death extremely hard, they all had. Savon's entire Shield team was seated in the row behind them, desperate to pay their own respects. The newly-promoted Captain wasn't sure what the future would hold with such a dire conflict on the horizon, but she knew there was a possibility that they'd lose even more of the ones they held dear. The sovereigns would surely be the biggest targets and, while the power of the gifted antoraestone was immense, Castellan was still only one person. Not to mention she loathed the thought of using it again with such a purpose as she had done aboard the *Quaesitum*.

She looked to her left where Olivienne gazed intently at Templar Aislyn and knew she'd do it again in a heartbeat if it meant protecting the one she loved. Castellan sorely regretted not being able to save Savon, but she vowed that if the opportunity arose again, she would choose the path of her conscience over that of her career.

The lead templar spoke for another twenty meens before she finally yielded the ceremony. "As Captain Tosh was Lieutenant Gentry Savon's commanding officer, I would like to call her to the dais to say the last few words."

Castellan stood and walked forward carrying a small box. When she reached the dais, she gazed out across all the faces gathered there. This was *her* Corp, these were *her* people. The Shields had to know they were honored, worthy, and essential. What they did was dangerous and necessary, and she wanted them to understand that their sovereign duty and sacrifices were not in vain. "Lieutenant Gentry Savon was the most loyal and dedicated soldier I've ever had the privilege of meeting. He was also Shield Corp through and through. He had potential that I saw early on as his commanding officer and I knew he'd soon go beyond his current rank. Because of his potential *and* his final actions in the battle of King's Marsh, I am presenting his family with the insignia of his official posthumous rank of Lieutenant Commander."

Captain Tosh turned to face Savon's family. "Tryven Savon and Trylgen Savon, please come to the dais."

The two grieving women stood and slowly made their way up the steps until they were directly in front of Castellan. She handed the box to Gentry Savon's mother, Tryven, then carefully stepped back. "Pseras Savon," Castellan looked out over the crowd then back at Savon's family. "The Shields honor you." With those words, every black and silver-clad guardian in the chamber stood and saluted the two surviving family members on the dais, including Castellan. It was the most significant salute of her life.

In that moment, Captain Castellan Tosh was aware of three things: the weight of grief, the wash of love emanating from her future par, and the press of the newly-created necklace between her breasts. The rebels of Psiere would see no mercy from her.

Glossary

Administre [People] – Administrator, assistant, scheduler.

Aeons [Measurement] – Ages, eons, a long time.

Aether [Natural] – Enhanced radiotope gas that is produced by archeostones and illeostones. Archeostone aether reacts with illeostone mineral and charges the illeostones. Illeostone aether is emitted and used to power gadgets and machines. The Archeostone aether changes babies at a genetic level while in utero. The more exposure the more power.

Aetherkinesis [Channel] – The ability to sense and physically manipulate aether, with the mind. (Soft Channel)

Amita [People] – Family. Aunt, female sib of parent.

Animal Empathy [Channel] – The ability to communicate and read emotions mind to mind with animals. (Soft Channel)

Antaeus [Planetary] – Exploded moon, source of the Archeostones and half source of the fused Antoraestones.

Antoraestone [Planetary] – Pieces of powerful fused rock created when the asteroid Torae collided with the moon, Antaeus. The power imbued within provides 10x magnification of illeostones or Psierians.

Apportation [Channel] – The ability to instantly physically move objects within your sight from one point to another, with the mind. (Hard Channel)

Apree [Measurement] – Second lune (month) of the roto (year).

Archeos [Planetary] – Larger yellowish-orange sun, first to rise in the morning. Part of a binary stars set.

Archeostones [Planetary] – Fist size and glow yellowish orange, very rare. These charge illeostones with two days of exposure.

Armicruste [Natural] – Giant aggressive armored crabs sent by the Atlanteens. 3000 lbs.

Arslick [Society] – Expletive, curse. Derogatory term for someone of ill character.

Atlanteens [People] – Race of humanoid fish people who live in the seas and hate the Psierians. Cannot survive on land any more than Psierians could survive under water. They have telepathy and empathy, but no other known channels.

Automaton [Industry] – Robot powered by a single illeostone. Controlled by a specialized soldier programmer.

Avi-amita [People] – Family. Great aunt, sister of grandparent.

Avia [People] – Family. Grandmother, mother of parent.

Avu-patrus [People] – Family. Great uncle, brother of grandparent

Avus [People] – Family. Grandfather, father of parent.

Barde [People] – Writer, poet, storyteller, and more.

Bollux [Society] – Expletive, curse.

Bosair [Society] – Bra, bosom support.

Bovid [Natural] – Large hoofed stock mammal, primarily for eating.

Broadreps [People] – Broadsheet representatives, reporter, news agent.

Calla [Natural] – Beautiful.

Cathedress [People] – Title for the Queen, the ruling sovereign, the current seat of the Divine Cathedra. (throne)

Chemistrae [Natural] – Chemistry.

Chupacabra [Natural] – Roughly the size of a Dromean ursine in stature, both smaller and heavier than a human. Chupacabras feature a row of spines reaching from the neck to the base of the tail. They will kill any prey they can subdue, preferring to suck the blood from their bodies.

Clairvoyance [Channel] – The ability to gain information about an object, person, location, or physical event. (Soft Channel)

Coacas [Natural] – Coconuts.

Connate [People] – Immediate heir.

Consor [Society] – Marry.

Consorage [Society] – Marriage.

Consoral [Society] – Married.

Copere [Natural] – Copper.

Corm [Finance] – Money, currency delineation = 1 corundem.

Corma [Finance] – Money, currency delineation = $1/10^{th}$ of a corm or ten cred.

Cormi [Finance] – Money, currency delineation = $1/10^{th}$ of a corma, segmented to break into halves or quarters.

Corundem [Natural] – Super hard precious stones found in blue, red, and white. Used for mining, communication, jewelry, science, and as a base for the Psierian financial system due to its value in all parts of society.

Coz'n [People] – Family, child of an aunt (amita) or uncle (patruus).

Cred [Finance] – Money, slang general term.

Credit [Finance] – Money, general term.

Cycle [Transportation] – Two-wheeled vehicle 120 mph standard max (prototype 150).

Dae [Measurement] – Day.

Deka [Measurement] – Tenth and last lune (month) of the roto (year).

Dir [Planetary] – Lake.

Dirigible [Transportation] – Air zeppelin filled with heliopus gas, powered by aether driven props. Max speed 40 mph. Max distance at full capacity of illeostones is 1400 miles.

Divine Cathedra [Society] – Royal throne. Set with two Archeostones. The throne has existed for the entirety of written Psierian history. The Divine Cathedra can only be held by female sovereigns of the family and is inherited by the first born woman of each generation. It can be held in regency by a male, if no other female heirs exist, until the next female in the royal line is born.

Divine Mystery, The [Society] – Origin of life on Psiere. Who were the Makers, where did the Makers go, and why is there no history for Psierians beyond a few hundred rotos?

Doctore [People] – Doctor. Psi with advanced training in all healing techniques.

Dolpheens [Natural] – Dolphins.

Dowsing [Channel] – The ability to sense the location of water. (Soft Channel)

Dromea [Planetary] – Southern continent. Population: 11 million. Square Miles: 1.5 million.

Eidetic Memory [Channel] – The ability to perfectly recall the details and image anything that it seen. (Soft Channel)

Empathy [Channel] – The ability to communicate and read emotions mind to mind. (Soft Channel)

Endara [Planetary] – Northern continent. Population: 19 million. Square Miles: 2.5 million.

Enhanced Awareness [Channel] – A superior ability to sense and react to every physical thing around you in faster than normal time. (Soft Channel)

Enhanced Memory [Channel] – A superior ability to store and recall all information you are exposed to. (Soft Channel)

Ferrokinesis [Channel] – The ability to physically manipulate iron, with the mind. (Hard Channel)

Foot [Measurement] – 12 inces.

Git [Society] – Expletive, curse. Derogatory term for someone who is an unpleasant or contemptible person.

Gozen [Natural] – Goose.

Grav [Natural] – Gravity.

Griffin [Natural] – The body and rear of the creature is that of a large feline. The head, front claws and wings are all of a bird of prey, very much like the rocs on Mater. Their diet consists of both land and sea creatures and they are very long lived. Like the rocs, they only lay a few eggs every couple rotos and the population is typically quite low.

Gryphem [Transportation] – The black dirigible captained by

Sevrik Dondin.

Guardian [People] – This is a soldier serving in the Psi Shield Corp, placed in protective duty of a sovereign.

Hand [Measurement] – 6 inces.

Hauler [Transportation] – Six-wheeled vehicle for supplies = Max speed 100 mph

Humore [Society] – Humor.

Hydra [Natural] – Hydras are large water serpents with seven heads and poisonous blood. They live and breed in the pools of water and are extremely aggressive. They have regenerative capabilities similar to that of salamandus and can even regrow lost heads with enough time. Because of advanced cellular meiosis, when they lose one head, two will grow in its place. The average hydra is about three yords tall and they are extremely dangerous. Both territorial and aggressive, with fire recorded as their only weakness.

Illeos [Planetary] – Smaller blueish-white sun, second to rise in the morning. Part of a binary stars set.

Illeostones [Planetary] – Mineral that releases aether in the presence of water. Size can vary from larger down to microscopic elements that can be found within the bodies of all living things on Psiere. The stones glow blueish white when emitting aether and are fairly common. Full Illeostones release aether which powers machinery and other devices.

Imperium [People] – The elected body that rules Psiere in conjunction with the Queen. The Queen has the majority of the power. The King is an automatic member of the Imperium and is responsible for presenting the Queen's agenda as well as breaking voting ties when enacting new laws and governing Psiere in general.

Ince [Measurement] – 1inch.

Instrae [People] – Professor, researcher, teacher.

Interpretists [People] – Citizens whose sole career is translating ciphers, ancient artifact schematics, and other texts of the Divine Mystery.

Intinerist [People] – Scheduler, administrative assistant.

Intuition [Channel] – A superior ability to understand something immediately, without the need for conscious reasoning. (Soft Channel)

Judex [People] – Judge.

Juni [Measurement] – Fourth lune (month) of the roto (year).

Kevlan [Industry] – Woven black material that is impervious to fire, knives, and shells.

Leviathan [Natural] – Giant squid, a beast of the Deep, controlled by the Atlanteens. Has an average weight of 5000 lbs, tentacle length of 140 foot, and a 12" eye. The tentacles are covered in suckers with jagged teeth ringing the inside, and feature claws along the edges of each appendage that can rotate or even retract.

Levitation [Channel] – The ability to physically lift yourself, with your mind. (Hard Channel)

Lune [Measurement] – Month (Marte, Apree, Maia, Juni, Quinta, Sexte, Septa, Octobra, Novea, Deka).

Mahl [Measurement] – Mile, 5000 foot.

Maia [Measurement] – Third lune (month) of the roto (year).

Makers [People] – Race of unknown people responsible for creating the pyramids and all the artifacts and documents.

Maman [People] – Family. Mother, informal like mama.

Mamanar [People] – Family, Mother-in-law.

Marte [Measurement] – First lune (month) of the roto (year).

Medican [People] – Medical professional.

Meen [Measurement] – Minute, 60 meens in an oor.

Mir [Planetary] – River.

Moto [Transportation] – Four-wheeled vehicle for passengers, average max speed of 100 mph.

Mous [Natural] – Mouse.

Nessie [Natural] – A large pre-historic water creature with advanced telepathy. Nessie lives in Dir Lacrimise, the largest lake on Magna. She has a hump back, long neck and tail, and feeds on water plants and piscis. (The Monster of Loch Ness)

Novea [Measurement] – Ninth lune (month) of the roto (year).

Oathing [Society] – Betrothing.

Oath of Consorage [Society] – Betrothal.

Obsidae [Natural] – Glassy, black, natural mineral. (Obsidian)

Octobra [Measurement] – Eighth lune (month) of the roto (year).

Oor [Measurement] – Hour.

Operae [Society] – Opera.

Ova [Natural] – A mature female reproductive cell.

Papan [People] – Family. Father, informal like dad.

Papanar [People] – Family. Father-in-law.

Par [People] – Family. Spouse.

Paren [People] – Family. Parent.

Parsib [People] – Family. Sibling through consorage. Brother-in-law or sister-in-law.

Patruus [People] – Family. Uncle, male sib of parent.

Pelma [Natural] – Palm tree.

Pisci [Natural] – Fish.

Plexi [Industry] – Strong, clear material similar to glass but more flexible and sturdy.

Polycyclon [Society] – Truth serum in gas form, nut derivative.

Portea [Planetary] – Port, distilled wine.

Praefectus [People] – Continental governor.

Prescience [Channel] – The ability to know something before it takes place, foreknowledge. (Soft Channel)

Preservist [People] – Salvo Corp personnel. Search and rescue, fire, life guard, and more.

Psera [People] – Madam, honorific.

Psero [People] – Mister, honorific.

Psi [People] – Citizens of Psiere, Psierian.

Psi Academic Corp [Citizen Corp] – Instructors, and teachers at the academy, and other primary schools around the continents.

Psi Codice Corp [Citizen Corp] – Psi that deal with Psierian law in some capacity. Telepath/ psychometry teams, executioners, security specialists for the islands, judex, and judiciary reviewers, etc.

Psi Defense Corp [Citizen Corp] – Soldiers and officers that are tasked with defending home and country. Military corp.

Psi Divinity Corp [Citizen Corp] – All professions related to solving the divine mystery. Adventurists, interpretists, engineers and other professions assigned to adventurist teams. Funded partially by the government and partially by the schematics, inventions, and artifacts found on their expeditions.

Psi Engineering Corp [Citizen Corp] – Psi whose responsibility lies within public service works, roads, bridges, inventions, schematic adaptions, research, etc.

Psi Medi Corp [Citizen Corp] – All medicans. Doctores, caretaker, therapist, etc.

Psi Politia Corp [Citizen Corp] – Imperium officials, governors, representatives (all elected). Kings have the option to transfer to Politia Corp upon ascendency to King, or they can decline and remain in their original Corp. Elected Politia help define problems in regions and potential solutions. Organize all the other corps.

Psi Resource Corp [Citizen Corp] – Psi that work with all parts of the resource industry such as mining, for stones, gems, minerals, as well as wood and other building materials. Also responsible for illeostone recharging and recirculation throughout Psiere.

Psi Salvo Corp [Citizen Corp] – Preservists. Fire and rescue, cross-over medicans and caretakers for rescue missions.

Psi Security Corp [Citizen Corp] – Law enforcement in the towns and cities across Psiere. First enforcers of Psierian law.

Psi Service Corp [Citizen Corp] – All other customer driven industries, such as art, entertainment, eateries, shoppes, and more.

Psi Shield Corp [Citizen Corp] – All personnel related to sovereign security. The military Corp personnel with the highest and most varied training of all others. Best of the best.

Psi Stock Corp [Citizen Corp] – Responsible for all Psi involved with food harvesting. Farmers, Fishers, hunters and more.

Psiere [Planetary] – Planet and country name.

Psychometry [Channel] – The ability to discover facts about an event or person by touching inanimate objects associated with them. (Soft Channel)

Pund [Measurement] – Weight measurement, pound.

Pyrokinesis [Channel] – The ability to physically create and control fire, with the mind. (Hard Channel)

Pyrs [Measurement] – Degrees, Fahrenheit.

Quaesitum [Transportation] – The new dirigible captained by Seema Velten. 60 mahls per oor top speed, 1400 mahl range.

Queen [People] – Divine Cathedress, Her Royal Highness, Supreme Sovereign. She is the head of Psiere with an overall say in government decisions and direction, but she leaves the day to day running of the nation to the Psi Politia Corp.

Quinta [Measurement] – Fifth lune (month) of the roto (year).

Railer [Transportation] – A Train fueled by aether, with supplemental carts attached to hold illeostones and water. Passenger and goods conveyance on two rails sent on the ground. Max speed 100 mph.

Ringdocus [Natural] – Alternately known as shunka warakin in the texts. They are large canoid hybrids that live in packs somewhere between ten and twenty in size. They require a lot of territory for hunting, and will defend it. They'll attack with little provocation and their territory should be avoided at all costs.

Roto [Measurement] – 1 Year (10 lunes).

Salamandus [Natural] – Salamander.

Sasquatch [Natural] – Very large hairy upright hominids, like a cross between the skunk ape and a Psierian. They range in size anywhere from three to four yords in height. They are non-aggressive, but will protect their tribe and territory if provoked. Their diet consists mainly of flora, but they do supplement with piscis. Nuts and river swimmers are their sole source of protein. Because they are more intelligent and wide ranging, they control the entire territory surrounding the Temple of Antaeus.

Sculptiste [People] – Artist, sculptor. In the Service Corp.

Sec [Measurement] – Time measurement, second. 60 per oor.

Seg [Transportation] – A shortened form of segment, slang.

Segment [Transportation] – A single car of a railer.

Seme [Natural] – Male reproductive fluid.

Septa [Measurement] – Seventh lune (month) of the roto (year).

Ser [People] – Military honorific, Sir.

Sexte [Measurement] – Sixth lune (month) of the roto (year).

Sharc [Natural] – Shark.

Sheddech [Society] – Curse.

Shell [Industry] – Metal bullet fired from a pistol, rifle, or rail gun.

Sint [Society] – Curse. Derogatory term for someone of ill character.

Siren [Natural] – A previously undiscovered greater amphibian-like species that live in a cave on Instrucia. They are pale, with large milky white eyes. Their ears and nose are nothing more than slits but the size was offset by their mouths full of long sharp teeth. Sirens lay their glowing eggs under water like froglets. The species produces a tone that will stun other creatures so they cannot move other than autonomic functions. They also have a mild toxin in their saliva and they typically eat stunned creatures alive. The stunning sound can only be neutralized with a three-note tone comprised of Re, Ga, and Nie.

Skunk Ape [Natural] – A larger, stronger version of the mountain hominids of Dromea. Skunk Apes are roughly one and a half times the size of a Psierian and capable of lifting entire tree trunks. They typically live in high population densities and are a curious species but can turn aggressive quickly.

Sonal Ocilloscope [Industry] – Sonar using sound for depth measurement. Sonal oscillator with scope. Also known as a sonalscope.

Sonica [Industry] – Radar, frequently used in dirigibles to scan around them and below.

Sovereign [People] – Any member of the royal family with a direct line to the Divine Cathedra, including both the Queen and the Connate.

Stele [Industry] – Steel.

Sturgeous [Natural] – Sturgeon, giant fish and common food source.

Sub-Connate [People] – Supplemental or secondary heir, not in line for the Divine Cathedra.

Sub-Instrae [People] – Assistant, lower level. Also an instructor.

Telekinesis [Channel] – The ability to move and manipulate physically objects, with your mind. (Hard Channel)

Teleo [Industry] – Wired communication device, like a telephone.

Telepathy [Channel] – The ability to communicate and read thoughts and words mind to mind. (Soft Channel)

Teleport [Channel] – The ability to physically move yourself from one point to another point that is within sight, instantly. (Hard Channel)

Telesana [Channel] – The ability to physically heal the body, with the mind (subtle vibrations that speed bone repair, blood flow, disease eradication). (Hard Channel)

Telesthesia [Channel] – The ability to see a distant and unseen target using extrasensory perception. Far sight. (Soft Channel)

Temple Charging Rooms [Society] – All expended Illeostones from around Psiere are returned to the nearest temple and sealed into a room with the Archeostone to charge. Five days in room with max capacity, about 3000 stones. (Small room 500 stones is 2 days) Charged stones get shipped out to the entire continent as discharged ones are brought back in. Each temple has 4 stones in the charging chamber.

Temple of Antaeus [Society] – Lost pyramid of unknown origin on the island of Magna.

Temple of Archeos [Society] – Great pyramid of unknown origin near Tesseron, the capital city of Endara.

Temple of Illeos [Society] – Great pyramid of unknown origin near Ostium, the capital city of Dromea.

Tempyrature[Measurement] – Temperature.

Tinkerist [People] – Hobby inventor.

Tracker [Transportation] – Treaded and armored military vehicle that can go nearly anywhere.

Tun [Measurement] – Weight measurement, ton (2000 punds).

Unicorn [Natural] – Herd beasts similar to an equine but slightly smaller. They have a single spiral horn protruding from their forehead. History texts mention that the horn was rumored to have healing or mystical properties but detailed examination of expired individuals debunked that theory.

Vectis [Society] – Tax on wages to pay for medican services and academy training.

Vectura [Transportation] – Transportation or vehicle.

Vineo [Natural] – Wine.

Vinier [People] – A vintner, or person that makes portea and other vineos.

Voteo [Industry] – Wireless communication device, like a walkie-talkie but longer range.

Weke [Measurement] – Week (6 day).
Whal [Natural] – Whale.
Yord [Measurement] – Distance measurement, yard (3 foot).

About the Author

Award winning author and Michigan native, K. Aten brings heroines to life in a variety of blended LGBTQ fiction genres. She's not afraid of pain or adversity, but loves a happy ending. Kelly's goal with each new novel is to make people #Think, #Feel, and #Discuss.

Motto: "Some words end the silence, others begin it."

2019 GCLS Goldie winner
Waking the Dreamer - Science Fiction/Fantasy

2019 Lesfic Bard Award winner
Burn It Down - Drama

Other K. Aten titles to look for:

The Fletcher

Kyri is a fletcher, following in the footsteps of her father, and his father before him. However, fate is a fickle mistress, and six years after the death of her mother, she's faced with the fact that her father is dying as well. Forced to leave her sheltered little homestead in the woods, Kyri discovers that there is more to life than just hunting and making master quality arrows. During her journey to find a new home and happiness, she struggles with the path that seems to take her away from the quiet life of a fletcher. She learns that sometimes the hardest part of growing up is reconciling who we were, with who we will become.

ISBN: 978-1-61929-356-4
eISBN: 978-1-61929-357-1

The Archer

Kyri was raised a fletcher but after finding a new home and family with the Telequire Amazons, she discovers a desire to take on more responsibility within the tribe. She has skills they desperately need and she is called to action to protect those around her. But Kyri's path is ever-changing even as she finds herself altered by love, loyalty, and grief. Far away from home, the new Amazon is forced to decide what to sacrifice and who to become in order to get back to all that she has left behind. And she wonders what is worse, losing everyone she's ever loved or having those people lose her?

ISBN: 978-1-61929-370-0
eISBN: 978-1-61929-371-7

The Sagittarius

Kyri has known her share of loss in the two decades that she has been alive. She never expected to find herself a slave in roman lands, nor did she think she had the heart to become a gladiatrix. But with her soul shattered she must fight to see her way back home again. Will she win her freedom and return to all that she has known, or will she become another kind of slave to the killer that has taken over her mind? The only thing that is certain through it all is her love and devotion to Queen Orianna.

ISBN: 978-1-61929-386-1
eISBN: 978-1-61929-387-8

Rules of the Road

Jamie is an engineer who keeps humor close to her heart and people at arm's length. Kelsey is a dental assistant who deals with everything from the hilarious to the disgusting on a daily basis. What happens when a driving app brings them together as friends? The nerd car and the rainbow car both know a thing or two about hazard avoidance. When a flat tire brings them together in person, Jamie immediately realizes that Kelsey isn't just another woman on her radar. Both of them have struggled to break free from stereotypes while they navigate the road of life. As their friendship deepens they realize that some-times you have to break the rules to get where you need to go.

ISBN: 978-1-61929-366-3
eISBN: 978-1-61929-367-0

Waking the Dreamer

By the end of the 21st century, the world had become a harsh place. After decades of natural and man-made catastrophes, nations fell, populations shifted, and seventy percent of the continents became uninhabitable without protective suits. Technological advancement strode forward faster than ever and it was the only thing that kept human society steady through it all. No one could have predicted the discovery of the Dream Walkers. They were people born with the ability to leave their bodies at will, unseen by the waking world. Having the potential to become ultimate spies meant the remaining government regimes wanted to study and control them. The North American government, under the leadership of General Rennet, demanded that all Dream Walkers join the military program. For any that refused to comply, they were hunted down and either brainwashed or killed.

The very first Dream Walker discovered was a five year old girl named Julia. And when the soldiers came for her at the age of twenty, she was already hidden away. A decade later found Julia living a new life under the government's radar. As a secure tech courier in the capital city of Chicago, she does her job and the rest of her time avoids other people as much as she is able. The moment she agrees to help another fugitive Walker is when everything changes. Now the government wants them both and they'll stop at nothing to get what they want.

ISBN: 978-1-61929-382-3
eISBN: 978-1-61929-383-0

Running From Forever

Sarah Colby has always run from commitment. But after more than a year on the road following her musical dreams, even she yearns for a little stability. Her sister Annie is only too happy to welcome her back home. When she meets Annie's boss, Nobel Keller, she's immediately drawn to the woman's youthful good looks and dangerous charisma. The first night together leaves Sarah aching for more, but the second shows her the true price of passion.

ISBN: 978-1-61929-398-4
eISBN: 978-1-61929-399-1

Embracing Forever

Sarah Colby is a musician, teacher, lover, sister, and so much more. In the past year, she learned that sometimes life takes you places you never even knew existed. For Sarah and her sister Annie, they found out that not only were the monsters real but sometimes you loved them. Now the Colby sisters and their friends are being targeted by someone with a grudge. They must discover who is attacking the people of Columbus or risk losing all that they hold dear. Nobel Keller is with them every step of the way but will she bring salvation or merely the end of their lives in Columbus?

ISBN: 978-1-61929-424-0
eISBN: 978-1-61929-425-7

Burn It Down

Ash Hayes was failed by the system at the tender age of sixteen and suffered an addiction. As a result she lives her life weighed down by the guilt of her past. To atone for childhood misdeeds, Ash trained as a paramedic after high school and eventually became a firefighter with the Detroit fire department, along with her childhood best friend Derek. Friend, confidant, brother, he has been her light in an otherwise dark life. When tragedy strikes on the job, injury and forced leave from the department are the least of her concerns. Suffering from even more guilt and depression after the loss of her two closest friends Ash is set adrift in a sea of pain.

When Mia Thomas buys the house next door, Ash finds friendship in the most unlikely of places. It's Mia's nature to help and to heal. Many would say she has a knack for finding the broken ones and leading them into the light. But Ash's secret still lives deep inside her. Before the firefighter can even think of a future, she has to amend her past. Like the phoenix of legend, Ash has to burn her fears to the ground before she can be reborn.

ISBN: 978-1-61929-418-9
eISBN: 978-1-61929-419-6

Children of the Stars

The world was forever changed when a government genetic experiment created the Chromodecs from a dead alien in 1952. Decades later, when it became apparent that society needed a way to deal with a hybrid humans with unheard of powers, the CORP was created. The Chromodec Office of Restraint and Protection was a special government police agency formed to keep track of the Chromodecs.

This particular tale involves two refugees, young babies who were sent down to Earth to escape being used as pawns in an interplanetary war, despite the fact that Earth itself wasn't so safe. Destined to be Q'sirrahna, or soul mates as the humans called it, Amari Losira Del Rey and Zendara Inyri Baen-Tor would grow to be more powerful than any other beings on the planet, if they could find each other first.

After being forced to hide from the CORP when it's realized their powers could level entire cities, Amari and Zen will have to answer one question. Who will save the world when it all falls apart?

ISBN: 978-1-61929-432-5
eISBN: 978-1-61929-433-2

Remember Me, Synthetica

What happens when a woman loses her memory but gains a conscience?

Dr. Alexandra Turing is a roboticist whose intellect is unrivaled in the field of artificial intelligence. While science has always come easy, Alexandra struggles to understand emotional cues and responses. Driven by the legacy of her late great-uncle, she dedicates her life to the Synthetica project at her father's company, Organic Advancement Solutions (OAS).

Her life is rebooted when she wakes from a coma, six months after being struck by a car. Traumatic brain injury altered Alex's senses, her memory, and her personality. Despite the changes, she feels reborn as she navigates her way back into her old life. Part of her new journey includes dating the alluring Doctor of Veterinary Medicine, Emily St. John.

Emily is enamored with the hyper-intelligent scientist, but there are things about Alex and OAS that don't add up. With Emily's prompting, Alex undergoes testing that leaves her with more questions than answers. What she discovers changes more than her life, it will change the world around her.

ISBN: 978-1-61929-442-4
eISBN: 978-1-61929-443-1

MORE REGAL CREST PUBLICATIONS

Anna Furtado	The Heart's Longing	978-1-935053-83-5
Anna Furtado	Tremble and Burn	978-1-61929-354-0
Melissa Good	Eye of the Storm	1-932300-13-9
Melissa Good	Hurricane Watch	978-1-935053-00-2
Melissa Good	Moving Target	978-1-61929-150-8
Melissa Good	Red Sky At Morning	978-1-932300-80-2
Melissa Good	Storm Surge: Book One	978-1-935053-28-6
Melissa Good	Storm Surge: Book Two	978-1-935053-39-2
Melissa Good	Stormy Waters	978-1-61929-082-2
Melissa Good	Thicker Than Water	1-932300-24-4
Melissa Good	Terrors of the High Seas	1-932300-45-7
Melissa Good	Tropical Storm	978-1-932300-60-4
Melissa Good	Tropical Convergence	978-1-935053-18-7
Melissa Good	Winds of Change Book One	978-1-61929-194-2
Melissa Good	Winds of Change Book Two	978-1-61929-232-1
Melissa Good	Southern Stars	978-1-61929-348-9
K. E. Lane	And, Playing the Role of Herself	978-1-932300-72-7
Kate McLachlan	Christmas Crush	978-1-61929-195-9
Kate McLachlan	Hearts, Dead and Alive	978-1-61929-017-4
Kate McLachlan	Murder and the Hurdy Gurdy Girl	978-1-61929-125-6
Kate McLachlan	Rescue At Inspiration Point	978-1-61929-005-1
Kate McLachlan	Return Of An Impetuous Pilot	978-1-61929-152-2
Kate McLachlan	Rip Van Dyke	978-1-935053-29-3
Kate McLachlan	Ten Little Lesbians	978-1-61929-236-9
Kate McLachlan	Alias Mrs. Jones	978-1-61929-282-6
Lynne Norris	One Promise	978-1-932300-92-5
Lynne Norris	Sanctuary	978-1-61929-248-2
Lynne Norris	The Light of Day	978-1-61929-338-0
Schramm and Dunne	Love Is In the Air	978-1-61929-362-8
Rae Theodore	Leaving Normal: Adventures in Gender	
		978-1-61929-320-5
Rae Theodore	My Mother Says Drums Are for Boys: True	
	Stories for Gender Rebels	978-1-61929-378-6
Barbara Valletto	Pulse Points	978-1-61929-254-3
Barbara Valletto	Everlong	978-1-61929-266-6
Barbara Valletto	Limbo	978-1-61929-358-8
Barbara Valletto	Diver Blues	978-1-61929-384-7
Lisa Young	Out and Proud	978-1-61929-392-2

Be sure to check out our other imprints,
Blue Beacon Books, Mystic Books, Quest Books,
Troubadour Books, Yellow Rose Books,
and Young Adult Books.

VISIT US ONLINE AT
www.regalcrest.biz

At the Regal Crest Website You'll Find

~   The latest news about forthcoming titles and new releases

~   Our complete backlist of titles

~   Information about your favorite authors

www.ingramcontent.com/pod-product-compliance
Lightning Source LLC
Chambersburg PA
CBHW072348030726
47505CB00014B/1250